Defining Deandra

Louise Spencer-Strachan, Dr. Ph.

Noble House
Baltimore, Maryland

Defining Deandra

Copyright © 1996 Louise Spencer-Strachan, Dr. Ph.

All rights reserved under International and Pan-American copyright conventions. No part of this book may be reproduced, stored in a retrieval system, or transmitted in any form, electronic, mechanical, or other means, now known or hereafter invented, without written permission of the publisher. Address all inquiries to the publisher.

This is a work of fiction. All names and characters are either invented or used fictitiously. Any resemblance to persons living or dead is entirely unintentional.

Library of Congress
Cataloging in Publication Data
ISBN 1-56167-245-9

Library of Congress Card Catalog Number:
96-67919

Published by

8019 Belair Road, Suite 10
Baltimore, Maryland 21236

Manufactured in the United States of America

I wish to thank Maureen Rowe who read the manuscript and made some helpful suggestions.

CHAPTER ONE

Deandra had been sprawled out on the beige carpet of her upper West side apartment in Manhattan. She'd been trying to sort out some of the things she'd take on her assignment to the Caribbean. She shifted herself, forgetting about the mug of black coffee that was next to her until she felt something warm underneath her buttock and saw a dark brown circle forming on the carpet.

"Damn it," she snapped. "Look at the mess I've created. I'm just about finished paying off this rug, and look what I've done to it."

She hastily pulled herself up to clean up the mess. The phone started to ring. She ignored it and continued to clean the carpet.

"I'm going to remove that damn receiver from the phone if folks don't stop calling me," she murmured as the machine recorded the message.

"Deandra, I know you're home. Why don't you stop being so stubborn and face up to reality? Get real, baby. Even with love, patience can run out too. I'd like to talk to you. Please call me. Paul."

As she tried removing the stain, she swore at Paul under her breath.

"Who the hell does he think he is, to believe that he is the only man for me? He might have been the first, but who says he'll have to be the last?"

This was the second message Paul had left on her answering machine. He'd been trying desperately for weeks to have a good heart-to-heart talk with Deandra about their future. He had no doubt that Deandra was the woman of his dreams, and although being lovers was wonderful, it was important at this stage of their lives for them to make some commitment towards their future. He had difficulty comprehending her resistance or, more correctly, her fear of marriage. Had he not known her small family of just her mother and her, he might have thought that she had grown up with an abusive father or stepfather. But she had a loving and secure home, and that's why he had difficulty understanding her evasiveness to his proposal for settling down. There wasn't anything that he would not do to make her happy, yet she continued to be stubborn.

When she had finally cleared up the clutter in the apartment, she pulled out the contract for her assignment, held it to her chest and muttered, "This assignment could not have come at a better time. I'd hoped for something like this for a long time, and finally, here I am with a contract and an airline ticket to Nufuma."

She finished getting her things in order and anxiously waited for her departure date to Nufuma.

* * *

When the plane touched down at the airport, it was high noon. Deandra joined the group of American tourists at the visitor's line. The customs officer stamped her passport then welcomed her to the island. She quickly cleared her luggage through customs, followed the porter and stepped out into the glare of the midday Nufuman sun.

Just as she was about to slip on a pair of sun glasses, a voice behind her spoke. "Taxi, miss?"

She had been filled with so much excitement that she hadn't seen him approach her. He was a slim and handsome black man with mischievous eyes and a wholesome smile.

"Taxi, miss?" he repeated.

Deandra nodded. He beckoned to the porter with her luggage, then walked over to a blue motorcar. He opened the front door and waited for Deandra to enter. She was not accustomed to sitting in the front seat of a taxi and hesitated. Pablo knew that American visitors often reacted this way. He explained that the suitcases would be placed on the back seat, then remarked, "Don't worry. Miss, leave it up to me. I'll take care of everything. In Nufuma we have our own style. We do things a little differently, but we aim to please I'll show you."

As soon as the porter had put the bags into the car, Pablo tipped him. Deandra was amazed and asked indignantly, "Why did you do that?"

"Because they'll charge U.S. dollars and you'll end up paying too much. I gave him fifty Nufuman dollars. I'll include that in your bill. By the way, my name is Pablo."

"Well Pablo, let's talk business," said Deandra. "I'm going to the Vine Guest House, but I would like to be taken on a mini tour before going there."

Pablo scratched his head before answering. "Well, that can be easily arranged. A tour can be quite expensive though, but I'm sure we can work out something special for you."

They discussed the tour and agreed on a reasonable price.

"I'll show you some interesting places," said Pablo, "and you will also get a chance to meet some fine Nufumans."

Pablo was one of the popular taxi drivers who knew the right people. He was an excellent tour guide and a good ambassador for his island of less than three million people. As he drove, Deandra quietly observed the beautiful landscape. The place seemed to have a unique character of its own, with motor vehicles winding their way through the narrow curving streets, occasionally shared by donkey-drawn carts, and bicycle riders. The people appeared unhurried, moving to the rhythm of this small place.

Pablo drove through some of the newly-developed areas. He drove through the center of the developments called New City, pointing out the unique buildings. She saw a city of tall, large buildings, not quite skyscrapers but tall on the scale of an island.

The New City was full of activities, with plenty of motor cars driven by equal numbers of women and men. She couldn't remember many women driving cars when she left the island twenty years ago. This New City looked more like a developed country than a small island.

As they drove, Deandra noticed that the buildings were giving way to large vacant tracts of land. Pablo explained that they were now heading into a rural area. Farther along the winding roads, the terrain took on a different appearance. On one side of the road were high rugged mountains, and on the other side were valleys of lush green plantations and pastures.

They drove by rivers and ponds and came to an area where the road widened significantly. Pablo remarked, "I'm going to stop here for a few minutes to show you some of the old customs. Maybe you might want to take some pictures of the activities on the river bank, miss."

"That's a good idea," answered Deandra. "As a matter of fact, I'll videotape, if there's no objection."

"Everybody knows me round here. I'll arrange things for you," answered Pablo.

The river before them was one of the few that still harbored fish. Standing on the rocks that surrounded the river, were some young men. They were shirtless and the sun shone on their bare backs and muscular arms as they threw out and pulled their fishing rods. There was a woman frying fish as soon as the men caught them and people waiting to buy the fried fish as fast as the woman cooked them.

"Would you like to try some fried fish, miss?" asked Pablo. "You probably won't find too many places like this."

"I wouldn't miss this chance for anything Pablo; and by the way, my name is Deandra."

Pablo smiled, then remarked, "Now I can address you properly, Miss D. But I notice that many visitors coming to the island kind of take time to reveal their names."

"I'm not a total stranger, Pablo. I was born here."

With a broad smile on his face, Pablo replied, "I want you to feel at home, Miss D," and led her along the narrow stone path to the river bank.

He shouted to the woman cooking the fish, "Hello there Junie. Can we get some fish?"

"Sure man, you can get as much as you want. You know you are number one," she replied.

He selected a fish and recommended it to Deandra. She bought it, sat on a stone, removed the bones with her fingers, and ate her first meal in the island.

There's no better way of getting into a true island mood than to eat fried fish sitting by the river where it was caught, Deandra mused. She chatted with Junie and discovered that this friendly woman had been frying fish at the river for the last six years.

Further down the river bank were women washing clothes. As they washed they sang. Deandra recalled her mother's description of washer women. There was a time when rural women met weekly at the river to wash. And even when there was hardly any washing to be done, they would go just the same, because that was a place where they socialized and had time-off for themselves. The women at this river were middle-aged. Deandra was fascinated to see one of them pull up her dress and tie it with a string. She put aside the wooden scrubbing board and, instead, scrubbed the clothes on one of the smooth rocks. She paused in her scrubbing, spun a piece of the wash and slapped it against the stone, singing as she worked. "Make me clean, make me neat. Make me whole, an' make me strong . . ."

Pablo suggested they continue the tour. Deandra was excited about the range of activities and the pace of life. She felt then that Nufuma was an ideal place for her work. As they drove on, Pablo advised her to keep her eyes wide open so she could enjoy the small community with houses built on the hills. The houses were large. Most of them were painted white and to Deandra they seemed precariously perched on the hillsides, many of them almost hidden by tall trees.

"So, tell me Pablo, who are the people who own and live in these gorgeous homes?"

"They are owned by our own people, Miss D."

Things had really changed, thought Deandra. She remembered her mother's description of the people who lived on the hills, but it didn't fit the people Pablo was talking about. Those were powerful people and some rich foreigners.

"Explain what you mean by 'our own people.'"

"It's like this, miss. Some of the people look like me, some brown like you, and some white. Some of the people like me start out wid two rooms, then later add two more, an' two more. An' before you know it, the house just grow."

Deandra realized she was back on the island where color coding fell into different shades—from black, dark brown, chocolate brown, light skin, yellow, fair, copper, to red. It didn't matter whether you had tightly curled hair or straight hair, wide eyes or narrow eyes, for in Nufuma, many people were mixed with two or more races. She reflected on Pablo's description quietly and mused to herself,

"Come to think of it, the different shades are universal. The problem is, too many people separate themselves, causing confusion."

She turned to Pablo and said, "Are you saying that all these beautiful homes took years to be built?"

Pablo laughed haughtily. "No Miss, not everybody. For some it did take a long time, as I said, but lots of people out here have money. Some mek money right here, some went to foreign to mek extra money to build their homes. If you notice, some of them are colonial Georgian style, some have French windows and doors. Most of the roofs are built in a special way to prevent them from being blown off during a hurricane."

"That's interesting. Thanks for the explanation. Things have really changed."

Not far from the exclusive hillside community, they went to a shanty town. It buzzed with a different kind of vitality. There were sidewalk vendors peddling their goods. Some people were dressed in sparkling silk blouses and dresses, some in jeans and sneakers, and some in worn-out working clothes.

"I'm going to stop here so you can meet some ordinary Nufumans, miss," explained Pablo as he brought the taxi to a stop.

The people were full of life, uninhibited, and engaged in friendly bantering. They shouted and waved as Pablo opened the taxi door for Deandra. Pablo waved back to his friends and turned to Deandra.

"Follow me, miss. I want you to meet a friend of mine. They went into a small refreshment store where Deandra was introduced to the store owner. In the background, reggae music played.

She moved her shoulders to the beat of the music and the store owner inquired, "Do you like reggae, miss?"

"I more than like it. I love it. As a matter of fact, I collect records, including reggae."

"Nice lady. I like the way you sound, miss. Enjoy your stay."

He turned to Pablo saying, "Dis lady is okay, Pablo. You want me to make her a special juice?"

"Yes man, but do your thing fast; we got to leave soon."

The juice was made from soursop. "It's delicious and the taste reminds me of the small community of Cedar Grove where I spent my early childhood. Thanks again for the delicious juice," she said and left with Pablo.

It had been her intention to visit Cedar Grove after she had settled down, but the soursop juice spurred her to ask Pablo a question. "Would it be possible to drive by Cedar Grove before taking me to the Vines?"

"No problem, miss. The only thing—it will cost you a few more dollars since it will take at least half hour more."

"That's okay. I trust you. I can't wait until tomorrow to see what has happened to the place where I was born."

They drove for about fifteen or twenty minutes then suddenly there was a sign "Welcome to our new Cedar Grove where you and your family can have a day of fun." The place had changed so drastically that there were hardly any familiar landmarks. Pablo explained that the supermarket was built where the school once stood. There was an amusement park with all sorts of rides and activities. Deandra decided to return another day to walk through the modern Cedar Grove.

When she arrived at the guest house, she was exhausted, but pleased about what she had seen and experienced. She thanked Pablo for having been an excellent tour guide and paid him.

Pablo handed her his business card, saying, "I'm available to take you any place, any time. If I'm not in, just leave a message where I can reach you."

Deandra checked in at the reception desk of the Vine Guest House. Two receptionists were manning the desk, one a young male, the other a young woman They welcomed her warmly inquiring about her flight over.

The young man took her bags and accompanied her to a room on the top floor, which was the second floor. The room had a large French window and a balcony overlooking a courtyard with spreading grape arbor. As soon as the young man had left, Deandra showered and slipped into a cool kaftan. With the window open, she slept until late that afternoon.

When she awoke, she recalled the lighthearted conversation she and her friends had had at a surprise going away party they had held for her. "Now Deandra," they had teased, "from all the stories we've heard, you might not return to us."

Deandra had laughed and said, "Come on you all, I'm a devoted career woman."

"But girl friend," blurted Nancy, "they say there are lots of wealthy eligible men down there, and although there is Paul, they say it's difficult to resist romance in the tropics."

Deandra laughed, pulled herself back to the present, and reflected on the reason for her visit to the island. She then wrote in her diary her day's activities that would become a part of the book she would write.

That afternoon, dressed in a flaming orange, off-the-shoulder dress complemented by large black earrings and black patent leather sandals, she went downstairs. It was early for dinner, so she collected some travel brochures and sat at a corner table in the small lounge. She flipped through the brochures while the waiter went to get the drink she had ordered.

She had not seen the man sitting in an armchair not far from her table until she looked up. He smiled at her. She smiled back. In a few seconds he was standing in front of her table.

"Hello there. I hope you won't consider me rude, but you make such an unusual picture sitting here, I just had to come over and say hello."

Deandra was looking at the stranger as he spoke. He was a decent looking man with some grey hair at his temples. She smiled as the stranger continued to speak.

"Do you mind if I share the table with you?"

"Not at all . . . be my guest," replied Deandra.

The man sat at the table and ordered a Tom Collins while he tried to make small talk. "Is this your first time visiting our island?"

"Not really. As a matter of fact, I'm a product of the island."

"I should have known that only Nufuma could produce such beauty." The stranger openly admired her and looked down at the table. Deandra did strike a pretty picture with her unblemished skin and big dark brown eyes.

She had just swallowed the last of her drink when the waiter returned with the man's Tom Collins. Before tasting the drink, he turned to Deandra and introduced himself. "By the way, I'm Cliff Riggs."

"Hi Cliff, I'm Deandra."

"I notice your glass is empty, Deandra. What would you like to drink?"

Deandra hesitated, not wanting to reveal that she was as unsophisticated about drinks as a vegetarian was about meat. "Well, let's see . . . I don't like to switch my drink, especially on an empty stomach."

"So, what were you drinking?" asked Cliff.

"Ginger beer."

"May I order a drink for you? I promise you'll like it," he said before Deandra could object.

"Bring the lady a drink of our premier dark rum, mixed with ginger beer or lemon soda, and another Tom Collins for me. Have some fun, Deandra."

Deandra accepted the drink, requesting extra ice to dilute it, just in case it was too strong.

She invited Cliff to join her for dinner and as they ate he told her about himself. He was a farmer and owned acres of land in the southern part of the island. He usually stayed at the Vine Guest House during his business trips. She got the idea that he was a take-charge type of man.

He wanted to know her plans for getting around the city and she explained. "I'll take one day at a time. There are taxis around so that shouldn't be difficult."

The following morning, Deandra had breakfast alone and decided to see the shopping centers that the travel brochures had recommended. Just as she was calling Pablo to take her around, Cliff appeared on the veranda of the guest house and interrupted her call.

"Hello Deandra, it looks as though you're all set for seeing some of our beautiful sights."

"So it is, Cliff. I was just calling a taxi. But, how did you arrive here so suddenly?"

"I just had a hunch I might find you here. Anyway, why don't you let me take you around?"

"Are you sure that wouldn't interfere with your schedule?"

"On the contrary, taking you around would please me very much."

"Okay, Cliff, we have a deal. I accept your gracious offer."

Cliff drove an expensive BMW. He took her to a couple of new plazas and shopping centers, explaining that there were several such centers in the newly developed areas, some of which Pablo had shown her briefly.

As they walked through the malls and plazas she could hardly believe that she wasn't in New York or London. The stores had all the latest fashions; boutiques were stocked with high fashion clothes, specialized items from jewelry to cosmetics.

They finished their tour and had lunch at a cozy little creole restaurant.

During lunch Cliff asked, "Well, have the centers met your expectations?"

"As a matter of fact, I've seen more than I expected. This is a very sophisticated place."

"I suppose we must be doing something right. That's quite a compliment coming from a New Yorker, but I must tell you, Deandra, I still like some of the old customs. They sort of help to give me a sense of belonging and of who I am."

"That's an interesting way to balance the changing culture," responded Deandra.

"So, would you like to see a little of the Nufuma I remember as part of my youth?"

"I would love that."

After lunch, they drove a few blocks away from the sophisticated malls. There they saw small, old-fashioned shops that sold everything from hairpins to hammer and nails, pots and pans to groceries. There were men selling sugar cane and pineapples in push carts.

Cliff pointed out the wooden structures dating from the eighteen hundreds and remarked, "Can you find this in any other place—where the old and the new stand side by side, just like the people?"

Deandra could sense the pride in Cliff's voice for his island and agreed that Nufuma was special. He told her then that he also farmed and exported pineapples.

From there they departed to the Vine Guest House.

* * *

When they arrived, it was late afternoon. Cliff said he would see her later. Deandra thanked him for escorting her around and went to her room. She finished reading the newspaper, having enjoyed both the local and foreign news, then rested for a while.

It was about eight o'clock when she went downstairs. Cliff was absent from the dining room, which caused her to ponder his whereabouts. She couldn't recall any indication that he was planning to leave. "I musn't forget," she mused, "the guy was probably just passing the time to help him through a long week."

The following morning Cliff was back in the dining room. He joined her at the table, ordered juice and coffee, then picked up the conversation from where they had left off the day before while they toured the city.

"So, tell me Deandra, have you had time to think about what you've seen so far, compared to when you left us for the U.S.A.?" he inquired.

"Interesting that you should ask that question. As a matter of fact, I've been doing a lot of thinking since I set foot on Nufuman soil."

"I'm glad you're doing that—I mean reflecting about the island—which seems to indicate that you still have some attachment to the small place. I hope I'm not reading too much into your answer.

Deandra smiled then answered, "It would be better not to read anything into the untold."

Cliff looked at her, realizing that she was a complex and sophisticated woman.

"You know something, Deandra? Two days ago when I saw you sitting in the lounge you seemed exceptionally beautiful and familiar. You are like the twin of my late wife, except much younger, of course."

"I'm very sorry to hear that you've lost your wife."

"Thank you, but I've accepted it since no one can escape it. What is amazing is that the day I saw you it was exactly eighteen months since Ruby died, and there you were, almost a younger version of her. That was one of the reasons I couldn't keep my eyes off you."

Deandra leaned on the table and touched Cliff, then remarked, "Your story is moving. Imagine seeing a younger version of your wife eighteen months to the date of her death. Do I really look that much like her?"

"Yes. There's something uncommon about you, something that radiates warmth and beauty, things that were very much a part of Ruby."

Deandra was beginning to feel uncomfortable and hoped that Cliff would stop comparing her to his late wife, Ruby, even though she realized it must be difficult to lose someone so close and dear to him. It could also be a well-rehearsed story to impress her, Deandra thought.

He leaned on the table and looked at her. "I'll be leaving for my home in Lilly Valley today and hope that you will accept my invitation to visit my place. It's not that great, but my family and I are proud of it. The property has been passed down from my great grandfather and we sort of try to keep the family tradition of farming alive."

They walked to the lounge and just before they said good-bye, Cliff held her firmly by the shoulder and kissed her on the cheek. He told her, "I'll be in touch. We'll meet again."

This took Deandra by surprise. She had heard about island romances, but hoped that Cliff hadn't conjured any fantasy about her, for although he seemed to be a nice guy, he wasn't the man she wanted for her future.

The following day, Cliff telephoned her. She agreed to visit Lilly Valley the following weekend.

* * *

When Cliff Riggs drove up to the steps of Vine Guest House on the appointed Friday morning, Deandra did not recognize him until he got out of the Jeep. He had not mentioned a Jeep to her and she was expecting the BMW. On their way to the manor, Cliff drove slowly.

The house was gorgeous. It was built on a slope, surrounded by open grassland where a few horses grazed. He showed her to her room. It was large with a high ceiling, situated at the southwest end of the house, with a view of the sea.

She freshened herself, then joined Cliff for lunch on the back veranda. Lunch was served by Miss Chin, the housekeeper who Cliff described as half Chinese. Miss Chin's skin was beautifully smooth and shiny black. Her hair was chemically straightened. The only thing that looked Chinese about her were her eyes.

After lunch Cliff showed Deandra the outside of the house and his prized orchid garden. She was impressed by the garden and sat on a low stool watching him tend his precious plants.

"So, what do you think of the place, Deandra?"

"I'm quite impressed, Cliff. All this beauty around you makes me jealous."

"Come to think of it, jealousy can be a good thing sometimes, especially if there is a chance of changing the situation. I remember a man who was jealous of his neighbor for owning a prized stallion. The man finally bought himself a mare and paid the stallion's owner to have his mare mate with the stallion. The mare conceived and soon the man had his own prized stallion, replacing jealousy with ownership." Cliff chuckled, "A typical farmer's story, my dear."

"I've never had anyone explain jealousy to me like that before," replied Deandra. "It's worth thinking about. But going back to the orchids, are you a commercial grower?"

"Not at all, my dear. Although we are surrounded by an abundance of flora in this part of the island, the orchids help me to see that beauty and survival are very closely linked."

"That's a new and interesting theory. Would you explain that a little more, Cliff?"

"You're not trying to put me into a classroom I hope?"

"Not in the least. If anything, I'm exposing my ignorance of the observation you've made."

"Well, in my humble approach to life, the orchid is a plant that manages to borrow a small space and blooms on another plant without disturbing that plant. Some people call it a parasite, but it isn't. It only uses a part of the tree or plant as a support. Another interesting thing about the orchid is that it adds a unique beauty to its host. Come, let me show you the point I'm trying to make."

Cliff held Deandra's hand and helped her up from the low stool on which she sat, then smiled before saying, "I hope you don't think that I see you as a helpless female."

"On the contrary, I like to be assisted when there is a need for it." Truth is, it hadn't been so long ago that she was opposed to such assistance, but this was Nufuma and she wanted to know about the male-female dynamics of the island. She had heard a lot about the island's macho men.

Cliff took her to one of the hanging orchids. It was one of the most beautiful purple orchids in the garden and it was growing in a dried coconut husk. It was called Vanda Rothschildiana.

"You've made your point, Cliff, the contrast is outstanding. I have always loved orchids, and now I can appreciate them more. Thanks for your explanation."

Cliff held her hand as they walked out from the orchid garden onto the sloping green that surrounded the house. A girl of about ten years was skipping rope.

Cliff waved and called, "Hi Shana, you're home early from school."

"Who is your pretty friend?" asked Deandra.

"Oh that's Shana. She's my housekeeper's niece. She's been living here for the last six months since both of her parents died in a dreadful accident."

"Poor child. What a shock that must have been for her. But you are a very generous man to let her live here."

"Thank you, Deandra, but let me tell you something my dear, with all the social problems and violence that we are experiencing, there is still another side of Nufuma that people outside need to know. Believe me, a lot of us are still trying to help in whatever way we can. Look straight ahead of you and you will see a man limping. He is Dan, my gardener. It takes him longer to do the job, but he does his best and that's all I ask of anyone. Let me take you back inside and not over tire you."

"You're not making me tired. You are teaching me something new. You are a very good teacher."

"Good, I like to hear that coming from an intelligent and beautiful woman."

They went into the huge family room where Cliff had a stock of farming magazines all over the place. He asked Miss Chin to bring them some cold drinks. He had asked her to make a special fruit punch for the occasion.

Deandra drank some then remarked, "Oh, this is different and delicious. How did you know I would like this drink?"

Cliff smiled then replied, "I try hard not to forget certain things. Remember what you were drinking when I saw you sitting across from me?"

She laughed, revealing her white teeth, and retorted, "Don't you rub it in now, ginger beer it was, if my memory serves me right."

By this time they were both laughing and enjoying each other's company, but Cliff had difficulty containing the feelings Deandra was rekindling in him. He got up, walked around the room, then stood and looked at Deandra and asked, "Have you ever considered living in a farm house on a small island?"

Deandra was more than surprised. She uncrossed her legs

deliberately, blinked her eyes and said teasingly. "Are you trying to entrap me by any chance, Cliff?"

"Not in the least my dear. I believe in democracy, but at the same time, I'd like to hear how you feel about living in a place like this especially seeing that you're not a total stranger."

She passed her fingers through her hair and toyed with her private thoughts. How unfair, she thought, that this seemingly fine man was hoping for a serious relationship with her and all she wanted was simple platonic friendship.

"This is a beautiful place and if I had plans to live permanently in Nufuma, perhaps I would welcome this opportunity."

"Since you arrived this morning, you've brought sunshine into the house. You've made me feel, at fifty, like I did at twenty. I have only myself to answer to; my two sons have finished college and are on their own, and my only daughter is away in law school. There are all sorts of possibilities we can consider," explained Cliff.

"Your approach and view to future possibilities are quite logical and interesting, but in a broader context, things are a little more complicated than that, Cliff. Remember I'm only here on a special assignment."

"I know all that, but things can be arranged. People travel all over the world these days. They live in one country and work in another. I possess what I consider to be a great asset, I am patient. Furthermore, you'll be here until Sunday."

There was a brief silence as both Cliff and Deandra pondered silently about relationships. While Deandra felt that she had too much to give up at that stage of her life, Cliff felt that he had a lot to offer.

The silence was broken when Cliff spoke. "By the way, Deandra, I just showed you the room and left you alone to find your way around, forgive me. Do you like it?"

"Yes Cliff, it's absolutely charming and the view is truly breathtaking."

"Glad you like it. Let me show you the rest of the house."

The house was large. It had four bedrooms—all very large—four bathrooms, a huge living room, dining room, family room and an extended one-bedroom unit at the west end, where Miss Chin and Shana lived. There were front and back verandas and a kind of basement that served more as a storage area. There was a large water tank that kept the Riggs' well supplied during periods of drought.

After the tour Cliff remarked, "I've kept you busy since you arrived. I imagine you need some time to unpack and get some rest before dinner."

"I've been having such a great time that l m not at all tired, but it's a good idea that I unpack as you suggested. When do you want me down for dinner?"

"My dear Deandra, I would love to have you beside me for ever, but that's too selfish. We are very informal. Miss Chin usually serves dinner around seven, but you are free to come down whenever you want."

"See you later, Cliff," said Deandra as she left him standing looking at her pensively.

She unpacked the pair of shorts and couple of summer dresses and her toiletry and left the rest of her things in the suitcase. She soaked herself in a tub of bubble bath and relaxed with a magazine as she lay on the double bed in the large room and thought aloud, "It's not that I'm naive, but maybe the old adage is right, when you're not looking for a man, it's more likely you will attract them. There's no doubt now that Cliff is interested in more than simple, uncomplicated friendship."

Later that evening, Deandra got dressed for dinner. She wore a simple, loose-fitting, narrow-strapped, dusty pink dress, a pair of hanging coral earrings, and her favorite natural colored thongs. She twisted her hair and pinned it on top of her head, then dabbed some toilet water around her neck and arms.

She went down about fifteen minutes before dinner and decided to enjoy the beauty of the sloping surroundings from the veranda. Her thoughts drifted as she studied the landscape.

She suddenly felt a warm hand on her bare shoulder. Turning, she saw Cliff's smiling face.

"You seemed so engrossed that had it not been for your compelling beauty, I would not have interrupted, but it's all your fault." He kissed her on her forehead and put his arm around her shoulder as they both enjoyed the view.

A few minutes later, they went to the dining room. Before sitting down to dinner, Cliff fixed himself a rum mixture, telling Deandra it was his special recipe which he dubbed "Cliff's hi-ball." He poured her a glass of wine.

After cocktails they sat down for dinner. Miss Chin had used their best china, lead crystal, and a beautiful hand-embroidered table cloth. It was an elegant setting. The table was large enough to accommodate between eight and twelve people.

Miss Chin had surprised Cliff with the dinner. All she had told him was that his lady friend would like it and indeed she was right. The curried goat was delicious. She also served a dish that was new to Deandra, but very good.

When Deandra told Miss Chin that she had never had that dish before, she smiled and remarked, "That's good, miss, because this is a Lilly Valley special and the only way you can have some is to visit the manor."

"So I take it that you won't give away any of your secret recipes?"

Before Miss Chin could answer, Cliff spoke. "I must tell you, Deandra, she is a magician when it comes to surprising us with new dishes. Anyway, I'm sure you'll tell us how you've made this delicious dish, Miss Chin."

"Okay Mr. Riggs, if you insist . . . It's really quite simple. It's made of boiled yam, lima beans, spices, and milk, baked in a greased casserole dish."

"Thank you for sharing your secret with us," said Cliff.

"That's all right, sir."

After dinner, they strolled out into the garden for a while, before Cliff led the way to the living room. By then Miss Chin had finished her work and was in her apartment with Shana. The place was very quiet. Except for the high-pitched sounds of crickets, there wasn't a stir.

As soon as they were seated on the antique sofa in the large living room, Cliff asked Deandra if she had a preference for any type of music, then remarked, "Tell you what, why don't you select something from my collection that you'd like to hear tonight?"

"I'd love to."

As she selected the albums, she remembered the jazz festivals she enjoyed in New York, then commented, "What a collection you have, Cliff. I could get lost listening to some of these vintage pieces."

"Glad you like my musical taste. So we can agree that at least we have one thing in common."

She helped him to select a mixture of jazz and ballads, then stacked the record player while Cliff prepared drinks. They returned to the living room with Cliff carrying the drinks.

Deandra was scanning the living room that was almost as large as the apartment she had in Manhattan when Cliff spoke. "I want you to be comfortable. We're very informal in this neck of the woods."

"I'm very comfortable, as you can see. This is a very homey and cozy place. What is it really like living on a farm? I mean the average farm, also Lilly Valley Manor?"

"Well now, any farm, large or small, requires dedication and hard work. Lilly Valley is considered a large farm because we have a few hundred acres. It is also expensive to run, but under good management it can be very lucrative. Do you know much about farming?"

"Not really, except what I can remember as a child in the small community where I was born, where people rented land. I suppose those could be considered mini farms with no more than five acres."

"You're correct. Those would be mini farms. But, my dear, let's talk about you. It's not often that I have the pleasure of sitting next to someone I admire as much as I do you." Cliff put his arm around her shoulder as they talked. "I'm very serious. How would you feel about living in Nufuma at Lilly Manor, even on a part-time basis? I realize that this is quite sudden for you to think through, but if you allow yourself to see things from a broader perspective, it might help you to realize that falling in love doesn't always mean waiting for years. It could be minutes and just as lasting."

Deandra listened carefully to what Cliff was saying and asked, "Are you saying that you could fall in love sitting in a small lounge?"

"That's exactly what has happened. Furthermore, I've known you two weeks now, maybe better than some fellow who has been courting you for years."

Deandra blushed when Cliff said that. She thought of Paul, her friend for many years, and her heart began to race.

Cliff turned her around to face him, held her hands between his palms, and said, "My dear, you're blushing like a girl."

They both sat silently for a few minutes, then Deandra spoke. "Cliff, I've read about these things—I mean love at first sight—but had not imagined that I would be in the center of one. It's too fast for me, I need time."

"Of course you need time," said Cliff. "And I want you to take your time. But whether I tell you now or some other time, I want you to know how I feel about you. But as I told you, I'm a very patient man." He gently kissed her on her lips.

They listened to music and talked well past midnight. By then Deandra's hair had become loose and hung on her shoulder. Cliff was delighted with this development and ran his fingers through it.

After a while he whispered, "I think your hair is telling us it's time for us to retire for the night."

She waited while Cliff closed the windows. They left the living room holding hands and walking slowly. They paused at Deandra's door to say good night, when Cliff took her face in his hands, kissed her gently at first, and then more passionately. He began to explore the contours of her body, and Deandra realized that this was more than friendly. She stiffened her body as Cliff held her in his trembling arms. He moved away awkwardly.

"I was overwhelmed and carried away," he said to her. "Forgive my aggressive behavior . . . sleep well and good night, Deandra."

Cliff went to his room and showered to suppress the passion that Deandra had awakened in him. After that, he told himself, "I would never make love to her or any other woman under force. I don't believe in rape, but it's been a long time since Ruby's death that I've been so aroused by any woman. I hope I've not turned her off and killed any chances I might have had."

That night each thought about the other. Cliff convinced himself that there were possibilities for developing a relationship beyond mere friendship with Deandra. He envisioned her living at Lilly Valley. Deandra felt uneasy and wanted to get away. Even though there was some attraction for Cliff, all she wanted was friendship without any strings attached. She couldn't imagine herself acquiring a ready-made family, with the likelihood of becoming a step-grandmother before mothering her own child.

By Saturday morning they were ready for another day. Shana was invited to have breakfast with both of them on the veranda. She was friendly and quite articulate for a ten year old.

Shana shared with Deandra her excitement about her selection for the Spelling Bee contest. She was really a cute child and looked more Chinese than her aunt, Miss Chin.

After breakfast they strolled out onto the lawn. The atmosphere seemed somewhat strained as they talked. Cliff was quick to detect that something was wrong.

"By the way, Deandra," he said, "I hope I've not made you uncomfortable—I mean about last night. But to be on the right side, I apologize for that outburst . . . yet, I do hope you understand . . ."

Deandra laughed, then replied, "I'm not angry Cliff; we're still friends."

A few minutes later, they were on their way to the Lilly Valley shopping center. It was a miniature of the larger centers. Nufuma was an interesting place; there were pockets of shanty towns interspersed among the lavish homes.

This was also true of the Lilly Valley area. She saw acres of pineapples and bananas on Cliff's farm. He had a stable of horses which he described as thoroughbreds. He was very proud of his horses as he talked about their pedigree and racing abilities.

When they returned home, it was late afternoon. They had a light lunch, dinner would be later at a restaurant with live music. The restaurant was warm and friendly. There was a family-like atmosphere without ostentation.

As they entered, Cliff's presence was noticed. Most of the patrons greeted him with smiles and nods of recognition. It was obvious that he was a well-respected citizen.

As they ate, the conversation drifted to various topics, then Cliff said, "I hope you are feeling the way I am—and it has nothing to do with our talk yesterday—but having you here this minute gives me a lot of pleasure and a new outlook on life. Regardless of how I come out of this situation, I would hope that we can be in touch as good friends."

Deandra felt like answering, but restrained herself. Maybe she would get a chance to explain her feelings in a more private place. She remembered what her friends had said about romance in the tropics and smiled.

It was nine o'clock that evening when they got back to the manor.

Cliff poured himself some Scotch and brought Deandra some wine. They were in the family room, and this gave a feeling of informality.

"Cliff, the day was educational and interesting, and this evening was the icing on the cake."

"I'm glad to hear that because I really wanted you to have fun and to remember the manor as the first family house you've been in on your visit to your birth place."

"How could I ever forget, especially with a host like you . . . the most interesting man I've ever met. You know so many things and explain them so well—better than some professors I've had," she said while remembering how he had stepped beyond the boundary of friendship the night before.

"So that's all you can think of, interesting and good teacher?"

"Not really, I'm not doing a very good job of explaining. You are expecting an answer to the question you asked yesterday. I've given it a great deal of thought because I realize that you are very serious about it. I believe you could make me love you in many ways, even if I'm not in love with you now. Don't get me wrong, Cliff, being around you makes me feel at ease and safe, but at this stage of my life I don't want to make promises that I can't or may not keep. Furthermore, I would not dream of hurting someone like you."

Okay Deandra, you seem to be the winner. But at least you've admitted that you're feeling something even though you're fighting it. You must stop running away from love, my dear."

They watched the late news on television and went to bed.

Before she left Lilly Valley Manor that Sunday afternoon she thanked Miss Chin for her graciousness and gave her a pair of earrings and a box of sweets for Shana. It wasn't a very long ride from the manor to the guest house. Cliff and Deandra talked about current affairs as they drove.

When they got to the guest house, he helped her from the car and kissed her on her lips. She'd already decided not to see him again and, with that in mind, she decided to find herself an apartment.

CHAPTER TWO

Apartment hunting took Deandra to quite a few interesting semi-urban communities. Within three weeks of her arrival on the island, she had found herself a suitable, furnished, one-bedroom apartment in a small and intimate suburban area called Lucky Pond. She fell in love with the area because of its close proximity to the city, yet with its lush green surroundings and unpaved road leading from the main streets, it gave her the feeling of living in a more rural area. The other good features were a supermarket with a delicatessen and a couple of small restaurants. The apartment was part of a new complex of modern buildings. It was equipped with a television, a small combination record player, a telephone, and a small but well-equipped kitchen. The community was quiet with modest homes surrounded by vegetables and flowering plants.

As soon as Deandra had settled into the apartment, she set out to look around and learn more about her new surroundings. She took the road that was only a block from her apartment. The lane ran west of the main road, leading to a narrow dirt track which took her past small farms of mixed crops. The narrow road reminded her of a rural area in northern Carolina. She walked for about twenty minutes down the track and discovered along the way another world unlike the plazas.

The morning following her exploration Deandra set out for a walk, retracing her steps. Something unusual caught her eye. As she approached a clump of bushes, she could see the form of a woman moving toward a large tree. The woman appeared to be talking to herself and sprinkled something from a bottle. Deandra stood still, using the shrubbery to conceal her presence. She stood just close enough to get a good view of the woman. The woman was old and toothless; she seated herself on a stump under the tree. Her face showed sagging wrinkled muscles, and her hands were coarse. She wore a pair of shoes that seemed to be two sizes too small for her feet. She had made them into slippers by breaking down the backs and freeing her heel to hang out of the shoes. Deandra studied the woman's face, which revealed the world of her experience. The old woman rubbed her forehead, sprinkled more liquid from the bottle onto the ground, and stared into the distance. It was as though she was trying to recapture something from the past, or waiting for something to happen.

Just when Deandra was about to leave, the breeze began to blow. The branches of the tree under which the woman sat started to sway and the woman swayed to the movement of the branches. The ripe fruits began to fall to the ground as Deandra watched and listened to the woman talking loudly and animatedly to herself saying, "I know you wouldn't let me down ole fren . . . you always come true, especially when I praise you."

To Deandra it seemed as though the woman had some special power to release the fruits from the tree. The woman smiled revealing toothless brown gums. Her eyes lit up as she attempted to pull herself upright, but she suddenly sat down with a pained look on her face. She pulled up her dress, partly uncovering her knees. Nestling her hands around her knees, she rocked back and forth until, finally, she slowly eased herself upright. Gathering the hem of her dress together, she formed an apron-like carrier into which she put the fallen mangoes. Deandra watched quietly as the woman returned and sat down. Settling herself into a comfortable position, she reached for a mango and bit into it with her hardened gums as though she had all thirty-two of her teeth.

The longer Deandra observed the wrinkled face, the more fascinated she became. She felt a kind of magnetic pull toward the old woman. She was so immersed in her observation of the woman that she lost track of time.

As the woman swallowed the last piece of mango, Deandra suddenly remembered the expected visit from a friend whom she had not seen for twenty years. As she left, she made a pledge to herself to return to the tree to find out more about the intriguing woman and to record what she had seen in her diary.

Deandra walked slowly back to the apartment, for she wanted to get the feel of the red earth beneath her feet and to observe the beauty of nature that she had too long forgotten. Yellow and brown butterflies were everywhere, soaring up and down like miniature diving airplanes while chirping birds flew from branch to branch in the flowering trees.

A feeling of nostalgia and happiness took her back to her childhood. She recalled the simple and uncomplicated days, days when she romped in the bushes running barefooted while her mother made her dolls of different sizes from the plants growing wild around them.

After a while she realized that she had to quicken her pace to prepare for the visit of her friend Lucreta Clarke and, as she walked faster on the dirt road her childhood memories of Lucreta returned. They had both lived in the same neighborhood, had attended the same church, but never became friends until she started to attend Lucreta's school. She was seven years old and Lucreta was nine, but people often said, "Child you're more seventeen than seven, you behave like an old lady." She hadn't been sure what they meant by that.

The two girls visited each other's homes and Deandra had felt that Lucreta's home was grander than her own. She remembered Lucreta as being pretty with reddish hair that matched her copper color, as Deandra's mother, Marion Boggs, had described her. Lucreta's mother, Mrs. Green, had been a teacher at the school they attended, but she never knew what work Mr. Green did. She had always felt jealous when Lucreta bragged about her father, maybe that was one reason she had not tried to know very much about him.

Deandra smiled as she recalled Lucreta's going away gift to her. It had been a large doll with a porcelain face and the body stuffed with sawdust. The doll had an English face, in those days there were no black dolls. She remembered unpacking her suitcase when she and her mother arrived at the strange house in New York; the doll fell and its head shattered into small pieces. "Chile, her mother had said, that is not a good sign. I hope you and Lucreta won't part friendship."

Deandra smiled as she recalled those days. Her mother had been wrong. The broken-doll omen meant nothing. She and Lucreta had remained good friends, exchanging letters and photographs over the years.

As soon as she entered the apartment, Deandra started to prepare for Lucreta's visit. Despite the letters she did not know what to expect. She worried that they might have grown apart, so much had happened over twenty years.

As she prepared the meal the memory of the toothless old woman kept returning to her mind. She tried to refocus and turned on the radio.

She had just finished her preparations and was relaxing with a cool drink when the sound of a car in the driveway attracted her attention. She uncrossed her shapely legs, smoothed the wrinkles from her skirt and went to the kitchen window which gave her a clear view of the driveway. She opened the blinds and saw a sherry red sports car parked outside A woman got out and headed towards her door. She was tall, attractive and expensively dressed.

Deandra was overcome with excitement and, in a flash, she was at the door. She opened it and there was Lucreta. The two women faced each other, stared in amazement for a while until suddenly Lucreta hugged her friend exclaiming excitedly, "Let me catch my breath! I can't believe it! Is this a dream, or am I really looking at my old friend Deandra?"

"Yes! Yes! It's real, my friend. After twenty years you are finally looking at Deandra Boggs. But Lucreta, do you know what it's like to be home, talking to and looking at the face of my best friend?"

The two friends embraced, talking excitedly and at once. They lingered at the door as though they were locked out of the apartment. The sight of the middle-aged couple in the next apartment peering through their window to see what was causing the excitement prompted Deandra to remark, "Lucreta, we have so much catching-up to do that we could stand here talking all afternoon. Let's go inside before the neighbors think we are losing our minds. It doesn't take much to get a story going. You won't believe this; there's a story going around that one of the apartments is haunted. A young wife is supposed to have jumped through a window, committing suicide after her husband caught her in bed with another man. The true story, I'm told, was that the woman fell in her bath tub and suffered a fatal head injury."

They both laughed as Lucreta said, "Welcome to small town excitement."

They entered the apartment and closed the door behind them. Lucreta was a little plumper than she had appeared in the last photograph Deandra had received, but she retained her copper color and long reddish hair.

Deandra had prepared what she considered a Nufuman meal, cooked in the Creole tradition, consisting of soup, a salad, and a main course of broiled snapper, breadfruit stuffed with onions, tomato and green peppers, and steamed calalloo. She served her favorite local white wine and ended with a dessert of glazed bananas garnished with nuts.

Lucreta was impressed by Deandra's cooking, commenting, "Girl, I didn't think you'd remember breadfruit, let alone surprising me with this special way of preparing it . . . I'd not had it prepared like this before."

"Glad you like my cooking, Lucreta, but I can't get over how beautiful and young you look, my friend."

Lucreta chuckled then answered mischievously, "The formula is not that difficult, Deandra."

"I wouldn't mind finding out your secret, my dear," replied Deandra.

"Well, first take care of yourself, then find a good husband who is also a good lover, and have a couple of kids. She sighed, then continued, "But seriously speaking, Deandra, the key to my well-being is just being me. I don't worry about what people may say about me, as long as I'm satisfied with me."

"You've put it nicely, Lucreta, even though my philosophy might be somewhat different. But taking care of one's self is definitely crucial."

They talked continuously, trying to catch up on twenty years of events. Just listening to Lucreta gave Deandra the feeling that her friend was financially and professionally secure. She had earned a Masters Degree in Business Administration, married a successful surgeon and, to top it all, was the mother of two beautiful and gifted children named Jennifer and Raymond. Her life sounded exciting and full. She seemed to be successfully balancing mothering with holding a position as an executive for a large international corporation. She lived in the exclusive neighborhood of Embers Glade in a large house surrounded by a manicured lawn edged with mixed vegetables and flowers. By any standards, Lucreta was a woman of beauty, sophistication, and good fortune.

But with all this apparent success Deandra couldn't shake the feeling that there was another side to her friend's life. It sounded too perfect, leaving her to comment, "From our childhood days you had always generated so much energy that I wondered where you were storing it all, Lucreta."

Lucreta laughed and threw her head back. Her hair swirled around her shoulders. "Deandra, there you go giving me all that credit. If I remember correctly, you were not a slow boat to China either."

I'm really serious, Lucreta. How do you manage to juggle your time so well, being a devoted wife and mother and also a professional with a lot of responsibilities?"

"I understand what you are saying, Deandra, but a small island provides some support systems such as the extended family and a good housekeeper. But going back to the wife and mother part, you must not forget that we were raised to be good mothers and wives. Furthermore, Daniel would not have agreed with my leaving the children until they had reached four years of age."

"Don't rub it in now, Lucreta," remarked Deandra jokingly. "Another question, how have you managed to retain such a great figure after having two kids?"

Lucreta laughed as she replied, "Don't tell me you're afraid of carrying around a big belly for nine months for fear of losing your shape, Deandra. Exercise and muscle toning help. I make it a rule to go to the gym once a week and walk in the backyard whenever I get a chance. And, of course, with Raymond and Jennifer around, they provide me with a lot of exercise, just by trying to keep up with them."

There was so much to catch up with that time passed without their noticing until the clock chimed twelve at midnight. Lucreta finished her cup of coffee, pulled herself from the chair and said a reluctant good night to Deandra.

After seeing her friend off, Deandra locked the door, kicked off her shoes and lay on the sofa. She was aware of the fact that her friend had done most of the talking, but she had enjoyed listening. It had been an interesting and instructive reunion, and since there would be more friendly visits, she would have her chance to tell her story.

She was awakened at two o'clock in the morning by croaking frogs in a nearby pond, only to discover that she had slept fully dressed for two hours.

She went to the bedroom to ready herself for bed. As she got undressed, the crisp lilac lace curtains were floating like streamers, lifted by the cool breeze that was blowing into the room. The full-length mirror on the back of the door revealed Deandra's well-proportioned body of smooth satin-like skin, glowing with a natural radiant beauty, and her hair pulled back, accentuating her high cheek bones, large almond eyes and full, dark lips.

She glanced at her image for a moment and acknowledged her beauty. It had been told to her so many times in her life and repeated by Cliff Riggs only a few weeks ago.

The twirling streamers of lilac lace, gently brushed against her breasts, taking her by surprise. She shivered for a moment then wrapped her arms around her full bosom and climbed into bed. The cool cotton sheets felt good against her warm skin.

She hugged her pillow and thought of the opportunities for marriage that had come her way. She recalled her college days in the southern United States and smiled as she remembered the circumstances under which she had met and fallen in love with Paul.

He was a Canadian, working for a large car manufacturing company in the United States. It was the end of the spring semester and Deandra had just finished teaching a course at her alma mater. She had been planning to invite a few friends from the college to her place to celebrate the spring break. She decided on the well-liked, inexpensive, and easy to prepare American chili con carne as the main dish.

In the supermarket, she had already selected the chopped beef, sausages, canned red kidney beans, herbs and spices, when she double checked her shopping list and discovered that she had left out the tomato paste and tomato sauce. She pushed the shopping cart to the other end of the aisle and as she reached for the tomato sauce, several bottles came tumbling down.

"Oh my God!" said Deandra as she jumped back and found herself surrounded by broken bottles of tomato sauce.

Standing there was a man who had been splattered from his waist down. He was looking at his soiled clothes when Deandra spoke, "I'm so sorry to have caused such a mess."

The man looked at her. He just looked without speaking. Deandra sensed his disgust and stood silently waiting.

"I would recommend that you watch your step to avoid falling and creating another accident," he said.

Deandra suddenly felt irritated and tense, but had no intention of allowing herself to be intimidated by this patronizing stranger. She calmed herself and replied, "Thank you for your concern for my safety, but I can take care of myself. What I am concerned about is resolving the problem of your soiled clothes."

"Your concern is a little late, wouldn't you agree? It would have been better had you not included me in your clumsiness."

Deandra bit her lip, stuttering, she replied, "I . . . I said I was sorry, didn't I? Furthermore, how did you manage to typecast me so fast?"

The man looked down at the pool of sauce, then answered, "Some things don't require an Einstein to figure out, you know."

By then they had moved away from the red, sticky sauce. Deandra shifted her position and made a funny face, screwing up her nose.

"Beats me to see how Einstein got into the middle of a tomato sauce problem. I didn't know he was also a food chemist."

"If you are that keen about who is who, I'll suggest George Washington Carver; he was a food chemist. But let's return to the problem please. You knocked the bottles off the shelf, but others had been there before you and taken stuff from the same shelf without creating a mess. So, in my book, you're clumsy," he ended with a smirk.

"I still fail to see how you can make such an assumption, as you're seeing me for the first time in my life. Are you a chemist and a mind-reader wrapped up in one?"

Now it was his turn to tease. He replied, "Can you swear by the good book that this is the first time I'm seeing you?"

"I'm not about to swear by any book; all I know is that you are wrong to label me clumsy . . . I feel so silly standing here, and doubly so for apologizing to someone who is so quick to form an opinion about me—and a totally wrong one at that."

Paul detected some defensiveness in her voice and even though he was upset, he turned and stared at her coldly before speaking. "Let me give you some free advice: don't make food chemistry a part of shopping in supermarkets. You might just splash the wrong guy. Play it safe with gravity."

Deandra realized then that having a fight in the supermarket would get her nowhere in resolving a sticky problem, so she calmed herself and replied, "I said I was sorry. What more do you want from me? Tell you what, I will pay the bill for cleaning your suit since I caused the accident. Furthermore, the cleaning might not only help to redeem your clothes, but it might also help your attitude."

With a serious look on his face, Paul replied, "So now you're trying to blame the victim; you're trying to attack my personality. Are you from another time zone? How did attitude get into the middle of this mess anyway?"

"Although it hadn't been my intention to insult or blame you for my error, I still think you have an A.T."

"A.T.? What the hell is that?" retorted Paul.

"So you're going to tell me you don't know the sisters talk?"

"Damn right," answered Paul teasingly.

"I mean attitude . . . you have an attitude. Why else would you form an opinion about me so fast?" asked Deandra.

By then the store manager had appeared on the scene to check the damage and to have the mess cleaned up. He talked briefly with Deandra and instructed her to pay at the checkout counter for the damage she had caused.

As she pushed the shopping cart away, she paused before saying to Paul, "I wish it hadn't happened. Anyway, it's no good crying over spilled milk. I've always lived up to a commitment and I would really like to know whether or not I'll have to replace your suit with a new one, or pay the cleaner's bill. Here is my card. Please let me know what to do."

It was then that Deandra had time to focus her full attention on Paul's physical appearance. He had to be at least six feet three inches tall, muscular, but not fat. His skin was almost ebony black. He had a pointed nose, brown eyes, and square jaw that gave him a distinguished look. His tightly curled hair was cut short. The guy was a hunk.

Paul took the card from Deandra and pushed it into his pocket, thinking to himself, "She must be one of those from the college up the hill. They say sometimes those bookworms lose their marbles and go crazy. Anyway, I kind of like her fiery spirit and the way she defended herself."

* * *

Two weeks after the incident, while she was in the middle of packing to leave for New York, Deandra's phone rang. She picked up the receiver.

"Hello, may I help you?"

"Yes, you can help me. I want to speak to Deandra Boggs."

"This is she," answered Deandra.

"Miss Boggs, this is Paul. I am the guy you bathed in tomato sauce at the supermarket. Remember me?"

"Yes, of course, I remember you very well. I'm glad you've called now, otherwise I might have missed you. So tell me about your grey suit."

"Well," said Paul, "since I am in the neighborhood, I'd like to drop off a cleaner's bill."

His voice was deep and resonant. It reminded her of the melodious notes coming from the throat of a baritone singer.

There was a brief moment of silence as she thought how best to handle the situation, and then replied, "Well, let's see. Right now I'm in the middle of packing, but I can interrupt that."

Truth was, she had been taken by surprise. She had not really thought about him since the incident. Suddenly she remembered him standing in the middle of the tomato sauce and giggled like a girl. "But what if this guy should really present me with a bill?" she mumbled. The money she had was just enough to pay the cab from the college to the airport; she would have no more until she got paid. She finally brushed aside her thoughts.

The door bell rang and when she answered it Paul was standing on her door step, all six feet three inches with the shiniest biceps bulging through his white linen sport shirt. From where he stood, he could see the pile of books sitting in the middle of the room.

"So when do you think you'll be through packing those books and have time to handle this bill I have for you, Miss Boggs?" asked Paul with a tease in his voice.

Paul was creating an excitement in Deandra she had not experienced before. "Oh, I'm sure handling that bill won't take too much of my time, unless you had something else in mind."

"As a matter of fact, there is something else on my mind," answered Paul as he winked an eye at her.

"Well, are you going to tell me, or keep me in suspense?"

Paul smiled deliberately, causing more excitement in her and answered, "How about dinner this evening?"

"I'd love that, if you don't mind sitting among boxes and suit cases. Please, come in."

They entered the room. Paul waited in the small living room admiring a Bearden's painting on the wall while Deandra got dressed.

That evening Paul took her to a cozy restaurant which served Caribbean food. At dinner they talked about their reasons for being in the South.

"Tell me Deandra, why were you teaching in this part of the world?"

"The university is my Alma Mater. That's where I got my first degree, prior to going to London where I did my Masters in Journalism. Teaching a summer course down here is my way of sharing some of my experiences with young students. So what about you, Paul?"

"Well, my experience is a little different than yours. I'm an engineer from Canada who wanted to explore another world outside of that country. A buddy of mine told me about a position in the car manufacturing business. I applied and got the job, and that's how I landed in the South."

* * *

Deandra roused herself from her reverie and prepared for bed. Thoughts of Paul filled her mind and made her restless. She finally fell asleep in the wee hours of the morning.

When she awoke, the room was flooded with sunlight which, by then, was shining on the full-length mirror. She stretched, then pulled herself out of bed, still stimulated from the visit with her friend Lucreta. She plugged in the electric peculator and, while the coffee perked, she planned her day's activities. She then poured herself a steaming cup of coffee, savoring the aroma and taste that came from the island's famous High Mountain coffee. As she drank, she recalled a childhood taboo.

Children in Nufuma were not allowed to drink coffee because

the older folk believed it was too strong a stimulant for them and would stunt their growth. Curiously, she thought, those older folk did many things that were correct for good health, even though they didn't give any scientific reasons.

Over breakfast, Deandra found herself in a restless mood which she tried to attribute to the events of the previous evening with her friend's visit.

She wrote in her diary, "Seeing Lucreta last night is only one of the reasons causing me to feel the way I do. Something else came alive last night. It kept me thinking of Paul Wisdom's warm body against mine, his special way of making love to me, the way no other man can. There's space in my life for a meaningful relationship. Hormones seem to be influencing my feelings. After all, I'm only thirty-two years old, in the prime of my life. Furthermore, this is exactly the same age Mom was when she gave birth to me." She remembered how Paul had caused bells to ring in her ears when he had made love to her.

She pulled herself back to the present, focusing on her assignment. As a journalist and respected writer, she had been commissioned by Dawn Publishing House to write a book discussing the customs and life-styles of the people of Nufuma. This was an exciting project, and one she had dreamed of doing for years. She hoped to present a more honest and objective picture of the citizens of the small island than did the tourist brochures which only presented the people as exotic and fun-loving. This assignment would give her the opportunity to learn more about the culture and people of the country she had left as a young girl. She had also hoped to try to get Paul out of her system.

Her mind drifted again to the old woman under the tree and she decided then that the scene would be a good beginning for her book.

Getting around Nufuma required having a car, and for several days Deandra toyed with the idea of renting one. She finally decided on a small Volkswagen, which suited her purpose.

She found that she had to go to the village post office to collect her mail. In Nufuma, despite the rapid development of new cities, many of the quaint customs still prevailed. Cliff Riggs had pointed this out to her. A good example was the nonexistence of home delivery for mail in a small community such as Lucky Pond, and from the appearance of things, this custom would remain for some time yet.

When she arrived at the post office there was a long line of people waiting. Most of them were senior citizens, mainly women. She was interested and pleased to see the seniors since the people she had seen in the shopping malls, plazas, and streets were mostly young, leaving her to wonder if the older people ever left their homes.

She introduced herself to three old ladies who appeared to be friendly. "Good morning, ladies."

"Good morning to you, miss," they replied in chorus.

"My name is Deandra."

The women looked at her, then one remarked, "Can't remember seeing you in this area before."

"You are correct, ladies. I'm new in this area. I'm living in that village over there," said Deandra, pointing in the direction of her home.

"Oh, we know where you mean, that's Lucky Pond," said one of the women. "As a matter of fact my daughter, the pharmacist, lives over there. It's a nice place and very modern, like a town, but bwoy, it's expensive!"

"I hope you won't consider me rude, but I'm so pleased to see you seniors today, that I just had to come over and talk with you."

One of the women whispered to her friend, "I wonder what she wants from us now?"

"Why are you so glad to see us, miss?" asked the women.

"Well ladies, since I arrived a few weeks ago, I've seen mostly young people in the streets."

"You're right, miss," said the women, talking all at once. "This is a country of restless young people. Most of them don't want the quiet life anymore. They leave the small villages like ours to go to the new towns. You only see them driving through in fast cars. So you will find that most seniors, especially retirees, seldom venture out. Where are you from?"

"I'm from America, but I'll be living here for a while."

"Welcome to our island, and we hope you enjoy yourself," they chimed.

Deandra was impressed by the seniors' politeness and patience as they waited in line to collect their monthly checks.

One of the women turned to her and whispered, "I'm going to let you into a secret. Don't come for your mail on the first of the month, unless you don't mind waiting until we get our little money."

She thanked the woman for the advice and decided to collect her mail on a different date. It was one o'clock in the afternoon when Deandra finally got her mail. She had waited two hours.

She got home just before the rain began falling heavily. The rain was mixed with the loud pealing of thunder and blazing streaks of lightening almost touching the ground. The rain did not last long and as it ended, the thick dark clouds floated away, revealing a clear blue sky.

Deandra's thoughts returned to the old woman. She hoped that she had not been caught under the tree in the rain storm.

Pulling herself back to the present, she scanned the pile of mail, sorting the pieces out in order of priority. The letter from her mother, Marion Boggs, was the first one read. The news from the United States was uneventful. Things were about the same as when she had left for Nufuma. The second letter was from her publisher, it was one of these polite psychological letters that was meant to motivate her and remind her about the work she was being paid to perform. The rest of the mail was letters from friends and magazines.

The day had passed quickly and as the short tropical evening approached, she decided to spend a relaxing evening looking through the magazines.

CHAPTER THREE

    Rising early the day after her trip to the post office, Deandra dressed for the day in an old pair of blue jeans, loose-fitting cotton shirt, comfortable canvas shoes and a wide-rimmed straw hat. In her carryall bag she packed the usual paper, pencil, wet wipes, a soft wash cloth, a sandwich, and an orange. Being compulsive for details and order, she double-checked her bag and discovered that she had left out her container of water, a most important item in a tropical climate.
    As she walked through the narrow dirt path to that special tree, she felt strangely happy, peaceful and somewhat connected to the surroundings. The area was one of unspoiled beauty, a virgin to high technological changes. The regal palms and sturdy lignum vitae trees were truly magnificent.
    As she walked, she hoped desperately to find the old woman; the closer she got to the tree, the more excited she became. She occupied herself by trying to figure out how best to approach the woman without causing alarm.
    When she reached the spot, Deandra could see the woman in the distance, walking toward the tree. When the woman got to the tree, she stood under it surveying the hanging fruits with great interest and a look of anticipation. Then she sat down on the flattened tree stump under the tree. Deandra waited for the woman to use her powers to make the fruit fall to the ground, but instead, she poured some liquid from a small bottle into her hand, then rubbed it on her face, arms, and legs.
    At that point Deandra decided that perhaps the woman was going

to let nature do the work for her, so she made her appearance. She removed her straw hat and stepped out in full view of the woman. She could see the old woman shielding her eyes from the glare of the sun with her hands and trying to see who was intruding on her special spot. Deandra walked steadily forward.

The old woman watched for a while then suddenly called out, "Hoo dat?"

"A friend to see you, ma'am," replied Deandra.

"A fren? Dats strange cause me don't have much fren to come visit me under dis here tree."

Deandra stepped closer, slowing her pace to allow the woman time to get a better look at the stranger who was approaching. "Good morning ma'am," she said.

The woman was now looking directly at her face. "Morning miss," she replied. "So what bring yu up here, let alone to call yuself my fren?"

"Well ma'am, I'm just taking a walk to know the community and to meet nice people like you." Deandra kept her distance and waited.

The woman looked at her, thinking how peculiar that this stranger should call her nice. She had a feeling that she had been spied on by this young woman and wasn't thrilled about it. "Yu know miss, these days people got to be careful of those who sey dem a fren. The newspaper full wid story 'bout robbery and all manner of crime me never imagine could happen. Anyway, I'll take a chance wid yu. From de way yu sound and look yu can come closer."

Deandra began to move closer to the woman when a mango fell. She picked it up and handed it to the woman.

"Tank yu miss, me was waiting on dis same mango to drop. Dats the one me was looking at and trying to mek fall, before me sit down. But sometimes yu got to be patient."

She sniffed the mango as she talked. "I tink this fruit will need another day to get nice an juicy."

Deandra smiled as she listened to the musical lilt of the woman's voice. She was beginning to feel uncomfortable with the stare of the old woman.

She stood for a while and asked, "How do you manage to make the mangoes fall, ma'am?"

The woman knitted her brow and replied, "Well miss, yu

wouldn't understan'. It's a special gift I have and I have to concentrate real hard to make this gift work. Anyway, sometimes de mangoes will fall by themselves."

"You must be a very special person to possess such a gift, ma'am. Do you mind if I sit next to you?"

The old woman cleared her throat before replying, "Well, yu soun' like a decent person, and since yu claim to be my fren, I'll take a chance and see. You can sit down."

Deandra found a nice soft spot, cushioned by fallen mango leaves and sat down. She placed her bag and hat next to her, putting a rock on the rim of the hat to prevent if from blowing away. At that moment, she felt a sense of relief and acceptance as she made herself comfortable next to the old woman.

From the corner of her eye she could see the woman carefully putting the mango she had handed her into a small brown paper bag, then tucking her dress between her knees.

The time was right to formally introduce herself and get to know the woman's name. "Well, ma'am, my name is Deandra."

"De . . . handy, yu seh?"

"Deandra, ma'am."

"Oh, DeHandra. Dats a nice name, but very hard to pronounce."

"Please to meet yu. My name is Clementine Thomas, but dem call me Aunt Clem."

Aunt Clem had added an "H" to her name, but this did not disturb Deandra. Nufumans liked to accentuate H's, so from then on she would be DeHandra for Aunt Clem.

"Would you mind if I call you Aunt Clem?" Deandra asked.

The old woman hesitated, rubbed her forehead, and answered, "It's like dis, miss. Calling people Aunty is a sign of respect, especially for young people. So, is that de reason why yu want to call me Aunt?"

Deandra realized then that the woman was not to be taken for granted. "I'm glad you said that, ma'am. It is also my way of showing you respect. I would be honored to be added to your list of respectful young people."

"I like the way yu explain yourself. It will be nice if yu call me Aunt Clem," said the woman, smiling and showing her bare gums.

"Well Aunt Clem, my mother left Nufuma a long time ago when I was a small girl and this is my first time coming back home."

The old woman nodded and listened while Deandra talked, before responding, "Me glad fe true dat a nice lady like yu decide to come back home. Plenty people lef' de country and never tink of coming back, but me always say, there's no place like home. Yu must know though that lots of changes going on. To tell the trute, sometimes I can hardly recognize de place where me was born."

By the end of the day, not only had Deandra shared her lunch with Aunt Clem, but she had also gotten a lot of important information about the small community. Aunt Clem told Deandra that Happy Grove used to be a very closely knit community. Most of the people were small farmers who produced enough food to feed themselves and to sell at the local market. But the younger people refused to farm and left the village. The old woman's story sounded very much the same as that of the women at the post office.

The day spent with Aunt Clem was very enjoyable, but the most important achievement was the friendship that developed between them. Deandra vowed to return to that special tree by the next week to talk with her new friend.

When Deandra got home that evening, she ran the bath and soaked herself to get rid of the red dust that clung to her body and the smell of the mouldy mango leaves that she had sat on. She finished her bath, put on a cotton robe, and fixed herself dinner.

The place was peaceful; it was almost too quiet. Not even the telephone rang. She remembered how she had ignored the ringing of the phone as she sprawled out in her New York apartment, and refused to answer Paul's message.

"Damn," she said. "To hell with Paul. Why does he keep popping up in my mind?"

She sighed, closed her eyes and tried to shift her focus to the witty old woman.

* * *

By the end of the second week it had become a routine for Deandra to pack a lunch basket for two in readiness for her daily rendezvous with Aunt Clem. She felt more at ease getting the information she needed from the woman.

That morning when they were both comfortably seated, she asked, "How different would you say things are now, compared to when you were growing up, Aunt Clem?"

The old woman placed her hands on her thighs and rocked gently backward and forward. She spoke as she rocked. "Miss, that's a whole heap of story I will try and see if I can remember way back. To begin, as yu can see for yourself, de young people don't listen to older folks anymore. In my days, your parents had de last word. Today's children don't have no childhood; they all want to have boyfriends and girlfriends before dem understand anyting. Dem grow up too fast. My madda an' fadda had six children—four girls and two boys. I was de last one, dem call me wash-belly. Me only remember a little 'bout my fadda, cause him was struck dead by lightening at his farm, when I was only four. Me madda always cry when she talk about pappa and tell us how him work hard and buil' de house we grow up in."

Deandra listened intently as the woman talked about her childhood then turned and said, "It sounds as though you had a nice and close family, even though you lost your father. I am writing a book about the people of Nufuma and if you don't mind, I would love to include your story in it."

"Where is this book going to be?" asked Aunt Clem.

"It will be printed in America, but copies will be sold here."

"I wouldn't mind then, as long as yu let me know bout de things yu write down. Sometimes people have a way of changing what yu said. But tell me Miss D, do plenty people write about someone like me? All the stories I remember talk about high-class people, rich people, pretty people, an young people, and yu poor Aunt Clem don't have none of those."

Deandra thought about Aunt Clem's remark carefully before replying. "Aunt Clem, to a certain extent you're right. But the world is changing and more people are realizing that a woman like you has a story to tell. You have experiences that people like me will never know until you share them with us. Writing your story is the best way to tell it. You're a historian and folklorist. Furthermore, you're a fine-looking woman. I can imagine you as a pretty girl in your young days."

"You know something, Miss D, I like talking to you. Yu give respect and demand respect. You're a sensible young woman."

* * *

The mango season was almost over, leaving only a few mangoes on the tree. When two of them fell from the tree, Aunt Clem stopped talking, looked down at the fruits and said, "Yu know what, we have to get them mangoes before the bees get to them to suck up the juice."

The woman picked up the mangoes and handed one to Deandra. Deandra thanked her. The incident reminded her of being stung by a bee on the sole of her foot as a child, when she had stepped on a busted mango. Her mother had carried her to an old bench made by her late father, Frederick Boggs.

She recalled the story her mother had told her about her father. He was a carpenter by trade, but like most working-class Nufuman men, he was also a small farmer. He had built the house in which she and her mother lived until they left the island for New York. He had died when Deandra was an infant. Her mother always spoke affectionately about him, as a good and hardworking man. She would say, "Your father was a generous and decent person first of all, not to mention that he looked every inch like you. In my book, he was the greatest man around and I must tell you, there were a lot of women running after him and a lot of them were jealous when he marry me . . . Yes indeed, I can still remember that strong man dying from pneumonia because they didn't have the magic medicine yet." Marion Boggs always had some sadness in her voice whenever she talked about Frederick.

Bringing herself back to the present, Deandra decided to allow the old woman to tell her story at her own pace. The woman was obviously tired now, so she decided they would break for lunch. After lunch Aunt Clem was refreshed and ready to continue her story.

"Well now, Miss D, as I was saying, my madda talk a lot 'bout me fadda. It seems like it was hard for her to get him outta her system. A man can do dat to a woman. Anyway, being the las' one, when my madda got sick, I stop school to tek care of her, cause de older ones was working in de city. But don't get me wrong, me never regret caring for her cause children mus' tek care of dem parents."

The more the old woman talked, the more philosophical she became. There was something special about her; she had a lot of common sense and insight into life. She also had a zest for living.

As a matter of fact, she was one of the few people Deandra had met who said that she was happy and showed it in her behavior. She was in harmony with her surroundings and seemingly at peace with herself.

She continued her story, "When I was seventeen, I went to stay wid me sista in town. Those days town wasn't like what we have now. It wasn't as develop. My first job was working in a big white house, own by rich people. Me didn't stay there too long, though, cause the mistress of the house was sort of over proud, if yu know what I'm saying. She was what yu might call peculiar an hard to please. It was always girl do this, girl do that.

"Her husban' wasn't too bad though. But come to tink of him now, him had ideas. One evening as me was cleaning up de dinner table, him said, 'Clem, do you like working for us?' To tell yu de trute, him take me by surprise since none of them ever talk to me before, except when dem give me orders. In the meantime he start to feel up me bosom. Dat same night, it musta been past midnight, when I suddenly wake and see de man standing over me bed pulling down his pants. I started to scream. Him put him hand pon me mouth and sey, 'One sound from yu and I throw yu in de street,' and left the room. It wasn't long after that when my church sista got me a job at de railroad station to clean the offices, waiting room, an' lavatories. I was glad to leave that job an' de sourpuss proud lady an' her sneaky husband. Dats most of what I can remember to tell yu now."

"But with all the changes taking place, how do you feel about home helpers today?" inquired Deandra.

"It's like I told yu, tings change a lot; matter of fact, from what I hear, a lot of women mostly do days work now and employers understan' life much better and give dem plenty respect."

At that point the old woman stopped talking, turned her back to Deandra and pulled up her dress. She then readjusted the piece of red cloth that was wrapped around her knees and gently rubbed them with some of the mixture that she carried around. The medicine was aromatic, giving off a pleasant scent.

Deandra felt like saying something to the woman when she saw her deformed knees, but restrained herself, realizing that she wanted privacy when she turned her back to her. Finally she remarked, "Aunt Clem, your medicine reminds me of the mixture of white rum and pimento seed that my mother makes."

"Yu have good nose chile, that's what it is."

Deandra concealed her astonishment when she saw the woman's knees. She had never seen anything like them before and wondered what could have caused anyone's knees to be so grotesque. The knees were protruding several inches from the leg, resembling some type of animal snout. She imagined the deformed knees as causing the old woman pain even though she didn't complain. She decided to stop working for the day. She helped the old woman to stand as they prepared to leave for their homes.

That night Deandra did not sleep well. She had a recurring dream in which an old woman resembling Aunt Clem was trying to escape the scene of a fight between a snake and a mongoose. She knew that the mongoose was a snake killer, but could not make the connection between the dream and Aunt Clem, except that she was upset by the sight of Aunt Clem's knees.

The following day she told Aunt Clem about the dream, leaving out the part with the old woman. Aunt Clem advised her friend to be on the lookout for enemies because dreaming about snakes was a definite warning about such people.

After discussing the dream, Aunt Clem turned and said, "Yu know, Miss D, I can remember dreaming 'bout me madda when I was working in town. I dream dat she was sitting on the doorstep crying. I ask her what was de matter. 'Well Clem,' she said, 'I'm feeling weak and tired all de time.' When me wake up, I tink bout the dream and feel dat something was wrong. Me hurry up and went to visit her. Sure enough, she was having de flu. Anyway, I tek her to de docta an' him sey she had some sugar in her blood. De dream was a warning 'bout me madda.

Deandra poured herself a drink of iced water from the thermos. The day was unusually hot and humid; she felt as though gallons of warm water were being poured down on her. She soaked the wash cloth in cold water, unbuttoned her shirt a few inches down, and wrapped the cold cloth around her neck. She sighed with pleasure.

"Is something the matter, Miss D?" asked Aunt Clem. "No ma'am," answered Deandra. "I'm just trying to cool off before we begin to work."

"I'm glad to hear yu are fine, cause I'm not able to help wid sickness dese days. I can remember how I would get de right kind of herbs to make strong medicine, and hot baths. Even when I was working in town, I would buy them in de market from de country folks. Those were de days when we use to help one another when people got sick and couldn't pay doctor's bill. People still help out, but yu have a harder time finding them. But tell me something, how come when people live in foreign fe long, dem can't tek de heat out here?"

"Well Aunt Clem, in foreign it gets hot only for a couple of months during the year and most people work and live in air-conditioned buildings."

"Oh, a so it go. Me always tink and wander 'bout dat, cause we who don't come from foreign don't seem to feel the heat like yu all. Now I know why all de foreigners walk around half-naked and some a de young people out here going naked too."

Deandra looked up into the tree and saw a lizard with its head held high and the red dewlap protruding underneath and thought maybe the lizard was cooling off too. Farther out on another branch she saw another scene, two more lizards so tightly wrapped around each other that she wondered how they managed not to fall. Looking at the old woman Deandra detected that she was ready to begin her conversation.

"I don't know if yu want to hear bout what me was tinking after we went our ways last night?"

"Sure, Aunt Clem."

Aunt Clem shifted herself on the smooth flattened stump, patted her knees, and started to talk. "Las' night when me got home, I look out and see a dry-up coconut tree and feel so sad when me remember days when me was a girl and how we grew up wid coconut. Me madda use to mek the sweetest peas soup, rice and peas and sweet potato pudding with coconut milk. She put coconut milk into bush tea, chocolate tea, and coffee tea and believe me, it was nicer dan milk. She put de oil in our hair and rub us down wid it so we always look nice and shiny. She would put some garlic in de oil and give us for cold. At school, a lady use to sell us grater cake and coconut drops made from coconut. De coconut was every ting to us. Yu couldn't wait to get the fresh coconut oil with some fresh bammy; de run down wid broad bean an mackerel always mek me lick my finger. An bwoy, we use to mek de floor so shine wid de coconut brush dat if yu didn't walk good yu would slip and slide and even fall down. Even the dry-up part dat fell on de groun' we use as broom to sweep de yard. Me tell yu, me miss de coconut a lot."

"So what is happening to coconuts these days?"

"Well miss, some kine of disease kill off all de trees in some a de islands, an' people start to use other kine of oil and say coconut oil is not good for yu health. But me can't understand dat, cause all of me family was raise pon coconut and live to be real old, except me fadda and it was a bolt a lightening dat kill him and not the coconut. Me hear that dem find out dat it's not so bad as dem once believe. They even say coconut water is good for high blood pressure and plenty people round here got pressure."

The old woman clasped her head with both hands and continued, "Even though I'm no science—I mean scientist—but I still believe that someting peculiar happen to de coconuts. All dese years we never had trouble wid them, then suddenly, every plant was dead and it was a time when a lot of people mek them living from coconut. May God help us!"

Aunt Clem's account of the local dish of coconut run-down reminded Deandra of her friend's description of hominy-grits, pig's feet, and black eyed peas in the southern United States. She was truly fascinated by Aunt Clem's keen observation and description of the uses of the coconut. To be honest, she had not given much thought to the coconut as an important commodity for small island people, but now the old woman was educating her.

During the lunch period Deandra recalled the many breakup and makeup scenarios between herself and Paul. The only good reason for their on-going tug-of-war, she admitted, was her resistance to settling down. Paul loved her and felt that it was time for them to settle down and start a family, even though he was hoping to have his own business. Deandra on the other hand, wanted to further her profession before starting a family. That was the core of their on-going, so-called problem.

In the meantime back in New York, Paul was beginning to seriously wonder if things would ever work out for them. He'd dated other women in-between their relationship, but his need for Deandra had always lingered and he'd told himself that it would be only a matter of time. Deandra would come to terms with the real world and see things differently.

* * *

After lunch, the two women returned to the conversation. Aunt Clem was in an exceptionally good mood. She was humming an old folk song—"Jane and Louisa will soon come home . . ."

Not only did the old woman have excellent recollections of the past, she also had a great sense of humor. Every once in a while she would surprise Deandra with an Anancy or ghost story.

Once she had asked, "Suppose yu find yourself in a tight spot, Miss D, who would yu call to help yu out?"

I haven't given much thought to that. Maybe I'd call you, Aunt Clem."

"No, no, chile, you really forget a lot 'bout our custom. Yu should call on Anancy. He can get yu out of all sort of problem. One day Anancy bet a fren that he could drink hot cornmeal porridge. Well, de fren cook a pot of porridge, pour it into a clay bowl, and give it to Anancy. Anancy run his finger roun' de edge of de bowl and say, "It's not hot enough. Put it in de sun till the hedge get hot and bring it back to me.' Anancy knew well what would happen. When the friend brought him the bowl of porridge, later, Anancy never stop drinking straight from de bowl till it was finish and won de bet!"

They both laughed while Deandra remarked, "That's a great story, Aunt Clem."

By then dark clouds were gathering, signalling rain. Deandra noticed that the old woman was getting restless as she looked at the darkening sky. "It looks like rain any minute now."

"Me was tinking de same. Maybe we should leave now. I don't like to stay under tree when it's raining, for sometimes lightening can strike de tree and I never forget what killed me fadda."

The two women had started out for home when it began to drizzle. Deandra offered to walk home with her friend, but Aunt Clem hesitated before accepting the offer. Instead she began to describe her humble home. The explanation, although it made Deandra uncomfortable, also made her more aware of Aunt Clem's pride. Anyway she had no intention of intruding on the woman's home. She had planned to jog home before the heavy rain came.

As Aunt Clem opened the door to her one-room cottage, Deandra said good-bye and started to leave. The old woman spoke. "Yu couldn't come to me house an' leave in de rain, but I should know that rich people who live in dem big house wouldn't want to visit a house like mine."

Deandra was genuinely upset to hear the old woman speak like that. She had hoped that with all the changes that were occurring in Nufuma, people would by then have gotten rid of such social barriers. But obviously some of the issues were very much alive, surfacing even though some Nufumans would prefer to push them aside.

"I would love to spend some time with you, but I was waiting until you invited me. I will stay until the rain stops before leaving for my place," answered Deandra.

* * *

It was a large clean room, though somewhat cluttered. There were two windows, and on each window sill were the usual bric-a-brac. On one sill was an old photograph of a tall, stately looking woman holding the hand of a small girl. She watched as the old woman busied herself stuffing some of the newspaper she saved for several uses, under the window panes to keep the water out as it started raining heavily.

Aunt Clem offered Deandra a seat on the only chair in the room, while she sat on the edge of the bed. To break the silence that followed their entrance into the room, Deandra asked about the photograph on the window sill. She was informed that the woman was Aunt Clem's maternal grandmother, named Miss Hilda and the little girl was Aunt Clem.

The downpour of rain suddenly stopped and the clouds gave way to the brilliance of the afternoon sun which, by then, had filled the room with light. Deandra could now get a good view of one wall of the room which was completely covered with recycled picture postcards and faces from the pages of magazines.

Deandra went outside and stood on the concrete slab in front of the small house that rested on an incline. Below, in the valley, was a breathtaking view. The scene was the kind usually romanticized in novels. Looking down, she could see orange trees filled with perfumed white blossoms and in between, a few red plum trees. Some distance away was a patch of papaya trees with bunches of yellow fruit hanging from their trunks. As her eyes travelled, she saw some old tools which seemed to have been left in the open for some time. Deandra was totally absorbed by the view and could have remained there looking at the valley for hours.

"Yu seems to like de view, Miss D," said Aunt Clem.

"As a matter of fact, yes, I like it so much that I could sit here for hours. I was also thinking how clever you are to have selected one of the most beautiful spots on the island for your home."

"Yu not de only one who thinks so. Everybody likes this spot cause when de oranges are ripe, de yellow papaya and de red plums are hanging on de trees an' de sunshine on dem. It's like a golden garden, and dats why they call it Golden Valley. Matter of fact, one time some rich people from foreign come to buy me out. Dem offer me a lot of money, but I could never leave dis place dats so pretty an' clean."

"It is indeed beautiful. Are there other Golden Valleys in Nufuma, Aunt Clem?"

"I believe so me dear, but this is de prettiest one I'm sure. This is where I talk wid God in de late afternoon, cause in de morning de sunshine on the other side. But later in de afternoons it gets to de valley. I must tell yu how I come to own dis place. I don't know if yu ever heard 'bout partner. It's when people pool money together every week and every week one person get a draw. That mean dat yu get plenty money one week and pay back by putting back your portion every week. Well, me dear, when I was still youngish an' working, de people who own dis property was moving. It was me lucky day, cause it was my turn to get de big draw. I didn't blink an eye. I just went and got me dis pretty place. I might sound selfish, but I'm glad dat too many people don't know 'bout dis lookout spot. We who lives here feel dat we are special cause no big building could bring us so much pleasure.

Deandra listened to the poetic description of the valley by the old woman and agreed that the name was most appropriate for such a place of beauty. She inquired about the old discarded tools.

"Well miss, those tools been sitting there for sometime now. They was going to dig up some land nearby. Scientist say dem have to dig up tings for de museum."

"Did they actually start digging?" inquired Deandra.

"Yes miss. Me hear dat dem fine pieces of ole Spaniard jar, but me doubt very much dat it was any Spaniard jar."

"So what is so mysterious about the Spaniard jar?"

"Yu too young an' been in foreign country too long to know 'bout dat, so I will tell yu 'bout it."

"I'd like that very much, Aunt Clem."

The two women seated themselves on the concrete slab step and looked down at Golden Valley as Aunt Clem continued to talk. "Yu remember de photo of me grandmadda, Miss Hilda? Well, she was a very smart woman an' taught me plenty of tings. I remember how she tell us about the Spaniard jar. Dem say hundred of years ago, the Spaniard hide gold an' tings dem took away from de Indians an' put dem in big jars then bury them in de ground. Them also kill a slave at the site and bury him wid de gold so his duppy would guard de gold. What de Spaniard didn't know was that de Indian duppy would never let anybody bring up that gold. Every time people start to dig, de closer they get to de jar, de further down it went. They could hear a loud rumbling sound an' see de dirt going round in a circle as de jar disappear. Now den, dere's no way anybody is going to get those jars cause duppy never sleep."

Deandra was spellbound by the fascinating details given by Aunt Clem about the Spanish jar and her interpretation of the Indian duppy. "Well Aunt Clem, what do you think about the pieces of jars that the scientists are finding?"

"To tell yu de trute, me don't believe dat what dem fine is de Spaniard jar. It could be some other jar and me just want to set de record straight. De Indian won't give up de jar."

The story of the jar struck a cord in Deandra, taking her back to what she had read about the Carib and Arawak people who had first inhabited the island and who saw themselves as caretakers and not destroyers of the land.

"Yu know what I believe, Miss D? I believe dat de jar is like de mixing of the African and de ole time Indians when dem was hiding from de slave owners. They just let dem run up and down dem big mountains, while they was hiding. And the dirt dats moving in a circle is like de wind when it blows and knocks everyting down and yet nobody can hold it. De wind is magic."

Deandra turned and looked at the old woman who, by this time, was smiling, showing her gums, and decided that she was a very deep person.

"You know something Aunt Clem, you've been holding out on me, keeping all this beauty to yourself. But I must tell you, this story that you've told me about the jar has taken me back to some of the history I read about Nufuma and the original people who lived here."

The old woman smiled and said, "Me glad dat I can teach a educated woman like yu someting new."

CHAPTER FOUR

Deandra was about to get up from the concrete slab when, to her amazement, she saw what appeared to be a large clay jar lying among the fruit trees in the valley. Then, suddenly, it disappeared. When she finally stood up to leave, the tiny rustic one-room cottage had taken on a whole new dimension. It had become a unique place where history and tradition converged in a golden haze while the sun was disappearing in the west, behind the peaks of the mountains that were once the fortresses for runaway Africans. Those Africans had refused to be slaves and had escaped from their bondage.

As she walked home through the wooded dirt path, she could hear the high-pitched sounds of tree frogs and watched the shimmering leaves with water dangling from their tips, like the prominent nipples of nubile girls.

She had no need to be fearful of stumbling in the dark since the fireflies, large and small, were out in their shining glory, directing her path like the gleam from the light of a distant lamp. She slowly absorbed the sounds of crickets, tree frogs, and the occasional sound of birds seeking out their nests while comparing such sounds with those of the great concerts she loved and enjoyed. She was in the mood for some music to complete a wonderful and enlightening day. Maybe she would play one of her favorite jazz records when she got home; maybe it would be from the jam session of the Duke, the Count, and Mr. Gillespie, or a Miles Davis.

At home that evening, Deandra had a leisurely bath then brushed her teeth. As she examined them closely she realized why she always got compliments for her teeth. The even, white teeth did indeed add a beautiful contrast to her dark brown gums and full, heart-shaped lips.

She put on the dressing gown Paul had given her for the big three plus zero birthday. Her chocolate-brown bare feet complemented the red satin gown.

She put Miles' long playing record on the player and prepared to relax and enjoy the music. She nestled herself into the contours of the convertible sofa which half-filled the living room, and went back in time as she listened to the music. Miles could reach deep down inside her the way he played that horn. His music was almost like an aphrodisiac. Paul always played Miles to help create a mood when they were together.

Just then the telephone rang. She was in no mood for interruption and hoped that whoever was on the other end of the phone would hang up. The caller was persistent and the ringing continued until she finally reached for the receiver and, with her musical voice, answered. "Hello!"

"Is this Deandra Boggs?"

She recognized Paul's voice and paused for a moment.

"Hello, hello . . . are you still there?"

Deandra leaned against the door and played with the telephone cord then answered. "Of course I'm here, trying to listen to some music that you've interrupted."

Paul could hear the music in the background and replied, "I have always liked your taste for good music, my dear . . . Why are you giving me such a hard time? It took me six months to track you down. I must talk to you."

Throughout their on-and-off relationship for four and a half years that they had been friends, she had tried on several occasions to break up the relationship, but Paul's persuasion always prevailed, and she would change her mind. But this time she was determined to be strong and not allow him to influence her. It wasn't just their strong personalities that clashed at times, but she was not about to give up her freedom and profession to become a housewife.

When she finally answered there was an edge of anger in her voice. "How the hell did you get my phone number?"

"It really doesn't matter how I got it, I have it now. Listen, I'm having a serious problem that only you can solve. I need to see you . . . I must see you."

Deandra stroked the red satin gown and held on to the receiver, remembering Paul's ability to change her mind. She recalled how sensitive and considerate he was to her on that special birthday two years ago, when she was depressed about leaving the youthful twenties behind.

"You never give up . . . you seem to believe that you can eat your cake and have it too!"

"Stop that crap. You're twisting it. You're the one who wants to eat the cake, yet have it at the same time. You're caught up in that feminist thing. Don't get me wrong, I'm all for women's rights, but not when it's ruining the relationship between us."

"I said good-bye to you forever when we parted eight months ago. Why don't you find yourself another woman who's not caught up in anything?"

"You irritate me. I don't understand you at times. What do you really want? Stop wasting time and let's call a truce. I'll say it again, I love you dearly and no other woman can take your place, neither do I intend to lose you again."

Deandra could detect the intensity in Paul's voice. She couldn't remember him being so emotional. As she listened to him, she realized that he still had a hold on her. She was fooling herself. Paul was the only man who could love her so intensely and yet was her best friend.

"Grow up before time runs out, Deandra, stop running away from love. You're bright enough to realize that the older you get the less chances you have for having normal children."

"What the hell are you saying, Paul Wisdom? You're sounding more like an obstetrician than an engineer."

"Damn right, baby. I'm the guy who will be your man, lover, and father of your children. Everybody knows that after thirty-five a woman has to subject herself to all kinds of tests to make sure that the baby is normal. I don't want you to go through that with our first child."

Deandra swallowed and remained silent. She couldn't help remembering that Cliff Riggs had also warned her about running away from love.

"Are you still there?"

"Yes, Paul. I'm still here."

Paul was right, she admitted silently. She wasn't so far away from thirty-five, and she was hoping to have normal children. Her palms became sweaty, and silently, without another word, she replaced the receiver.

The music had stopped playing. She tried to calm herself by sipping a glass of cool fruit juice. Her thoughts drifted back to the unorthodox situation that had brought them together. She smiled at the memory of Paul surrounded by tomato sauce and marvelled at the ease with which Paul had persuaded her to return to the South and spend the summer with him. The memory of their meeting caused a sudden rush of blood to pass through Deandra's body.

Paul had rented a car to take them to the best beaches and summer resorts that were open to them. He was witty and used the right words to describe her. He was the first person, aside from her mother, to place her on a pinnacle and make her feel so very special and beautiful. He had awakened the passion that she had suppressed during her years of study and work. The chemistry between them was so special she had no qualms about surrendering to him, and that's why she always got goose pimples whenever she thought about that day.

On that special day, they had a picnic in a quiet wooded area. Paul had felt certain that the place had been carved out only for them. She had carefully packed a lunch basket with some crisp, golden, southern fried chicken, potato salad, French bread, and strawberries. She then packed two long-stemmed glasses for the wine that Paul would bring and a dusty pink table cloth. She wore a wide yellow cotton frock, a pair of red sandals, and no makeup.

Paul spread the picnic blanket for them to sit on, while she put down the lunch basket and brushed the bangs from her forehead. She then reached into her bag for a pair of purple sunglasses that she had bought in London while studying at the University School of Journalism, and was about to sit down and put them on when Paul caught her by surprise. He held her so tightly that she thought they would dissolve into one.

As she was about to speak, he placed his fingers on her lips and said softly, "Shhh . . . shhh my angel, stand still and let me touch you and look at the most beautiful princess I've ever seen."

He caressed her face exploring the contours of her high cheek bones, the shape of her lips. Then he cupped her face in the palm of his strong hands. It was like an artist examining the human body to carve a near perfect piece of sculpture.

"Baby, with your perfumed beauty and big brown eyes, you are driving me crazy," said Paul.

He held her face in his hands, pulled her to him and kissed her with the passion he was feeling. No one had ever made her feel like that before, and she wanted it to last forever. She felt certain that it was more than infatuation and passion; it was passion tempered with love, beauty, tenderness, and respect.

Unexpectedly, Paul lifted her in is arms, danced around then lay her on her back. He kissed her ears and eyes and whispered, "Close your eyes my pretty and lay still for a moment."

Deandra felt as though it was a dream, but as the wind blew the skirt of her dress over her face, she pulled herself back and realized that it was real.

A few minutes later, she opened her eyes to see Paul standing with his legs straddling her body. He was holding a bunch of wild red flowers he had picked from hanging branches. She lay still, waiting for him to speak. He touched her lips with one of the red flowers and pulled her up into a sitting position. On her head, he placed a wreath made from the wild flowers, telling her that the color red was instrumental in their love and she was his queen.

The summer's day seemed to have ended too quickly as they talked and revelled in love, sometimes behaving like adolescents. Deandra was experiencing something she'd not felt before; her body shook as Paul held her tightly. They entered the car and drove to his apartment.

When Paul discovered that he was Deandra's first love, he was overwhelmed and treated her with extra patience and tenderness. He kissed her eyes, her ears, and her breasts to make her initiation into love-making a joyful experience. He kissed her and whispered, "My dearest you are special, you've waited for me all these years."

From then on he knew that he wanted her to be his wife. On that day, Paul talked about his childhood and family. His paternal grandfather was born in Jamaica and had migrated to Canada where he met and married an American woman from Texas. He and his two younger sisters were raised in a single-family home by their divorced mother, who was a self-made business woman. She had used their home as collateral for a bank loan, which she had used to start a small three-stool luncheonette.

Paul could remember the first day the small luncheonette was opened. The menu consisted of two dishes, roasted chicken and cured salt fish, which she called bacalau, mixed with red sweet peppers, white onion, and Jamaican spices. Mrs. Wisdom served rice and some salad with her two dishes. Paul and his two sisters were up most of that Thursday night helping their mother to get everything ready by 10:00 a.m. the next day.

At this point, Paul paused. "Have you ever cried because onions got into your eyes, Deandra?" he asked as he pulled her down on top of him and kissed every corner of her mouth, leaving her no room to answer.

"Anyway, I remember tears running down my cheeks that Thursday night as I chopped onions for my mother. We put up a big sign in front of the store, WISDOM'S LUNCHEONETTE: WE CATER TO ALL YOUR NEEDS AND SERVE WITH A SMILE. The opening went well, and we were especially glad when Dad dropped in to wish my mother good luck."

"It sounds like your parents remained friends even though they were divorced," remarked Deandra.

"Sure. Why shouldn't they be friends? They both made three kids including a knockout like me."

Paul made a funny face and continued talking. "My mother then added fried chicken wings, pushing back some of the flesh from the bones. Soon they were called buffalo wings. Next she added deep-fried codfish cakes, which were the same old Jamaican salt-fish fritters, fried golden brown plantain, and jerk fish. She also provided for takeout orders. My mother worked very hard to please her customers. Everyone who tasted her creole cuisine returned for more and brought their friends. Her customers were her best advertisers.

"It wasn't long before the business had grown to be a four star restaurant with a staff of ten people. The rest is history. Violet Wisdom's restaurant is a well-known Toronto eating place."

Deandra was fascinated by the story of Violet Wisdom. "Your mother is a great woman, remarked Deandra. As a matter of fact, she's a trailblazer for younger women."

"I'll agree to that," answered Paul. "She's influenced a lot of women and men in venturing into business."

During the course of the day, Paul told Deandra how his mother had hoped for him to go into the restaurant business after finishing high school, but with the urging of his father and the offer of a full scholarship, he had opted for further study and went to the university where he earned a degree in engineering.

He felt that Deandra had been somewhat protected from the hard knocks of life. But that was one aspect that made her so lovable and unspoiled. His college experience was unlike hers, he attended an almost all-white university. He felt that she had the best of three worlds, having gone to an all-black elementary school in a small island, a predominantly black college in the United States, and then receiving her Masters in Journalism at an integrated university in London.

He spoke passionately about working hard and setting realistic goals, with the hope of climbing the corporate ladder in a large engineering firm, only to discover that there was an invisible ceiling for a man like him, despite his talent and merit. His story, though not exactly similar, reminded her of stories she'd heard of fathers doing menial jobs and mothers working along to earn the money that would help send their children to college. Such discussions made a lasting impression on Deandra.

* * *

There was an odd sound repeating itself at intervals which gradually brought Deandra back to the present. She had forgotten to switch off the player. The scratching sound of the needle was the sound she'd been hearing but not absorbing for some time. She switched off the player and returned the record to its sleeve.

Her thoughts strayed to Aunt Clem. Deandra had become very fond of the old woman and looked forward to their meetings. She wondered whether or not Aunt Clem would continue to visit the tree since it was then bare of fruit.

She realized that her fears were unwarranted when they met the following day. The old woman informed her that she always visited the shady mango tree; not only was it a safe and quiet place, but it was one of the coolest spots around, with its hanging branches encircling her like a mammoth parasol, protecting her from the sun.

She had bought a pair of loafers as a gift for her old friend and wondered how she would react. Before Deandra presented her with the shoes, they chatted briefly about an eight-year-old boy who had fallen into a river and died.

The old woman prayed loudly, asking God to bless everyone and save the children, then turned to Deandra and asked, "How did yu manage going home last night in de dark, Miss D?"

"I managed very well, Aunt Clem. It was a beautiful and lazy walk through the bushes, with the fire flies guiding my feet."

"De what yu say, Miss D?"

"Fire flies, Aunt Clem."

"I think yu must mean peeny-wally an' blinkey-blinkey; de big ones are peeny-wally, an' de little ones are blinkey-blinkey."

"Yes, ma'am, that's it. Thanks for reminding me of the correct names."

In Nufuma there were exotic names for plants and animals, giving the island a distinct and unique character of its own. After acknowledging the old woman's correction for the fire flies, she recalled the stories about duppies turning themselves into fire flies, then misleading people to the grave yard where they sang "skin and bone come together" and disappeared into smoke. And when those stories were told at night, as they usually were, children would cling to adults so that the duppy or ghost couldn't get them.

"I have a present for you, Aunt Clem, and I hope you will like it."

"I will like anything dat yu give me, miss. It's not often dat an old woman like me get present from a pretty young woman, yu know."

Deandra stood in front of the old woman and handed her the pair of shoes.

She took them and held them close to her chest. "De Lawd above will bless yu. I tank yu from the bottom of my heart. Me was worrying 'bout where me was going to get a pair of shoes from, cause this here have only uppers and no soles."

She examined the shoes carefully, stroking them gently with her rough hands.

For a long while they were both silent. Finally, Aunt Clem said, "Bwoy, dese shoes feel soft like gloves."

Deandra was pleased that her gift was appreciated and suggested that Aunt Clem try them on. As Aunt Clem tried to lift her leg to put on one shoe, she squirmed and said loudly, "Oh, me knee!"

Deandra asked, "Would you like me to help you?"

"Yes, miss. Dese ole knees is a big problem in me old age."

Deandra knelt in front of the old woman and slipped on the shoes. They fitted perfectly. Aunt Clem thanked Deandra again telling her how pleased she was that they were not laced shoes requiring bending to tie them.

This was an opportune time to find out about those deformed knees, which had haunted Deandra ever since she had seen them.

"What's the matter with your knees, Aunt Clem?"

The old woman gave a loud sigh, then answered, "Dats a long story chile. In de old days when yu didn't have floor cleaning machine in de island, people had to kneel to scrub and shine wooden floors wid coconut brush. After I got de govament job at de railroad, it was my duty to clean de wooden floor waiting rooms. It was hard work, but me never mine, cause once yu did your work good nobody bother yu, and furthermore de pay wasn't too bad for that time. I could tek care of meself and me madda. Dem days, I was young and strong, and never know dat kneeling daily scrubbing floor could spoil me knee cap. Me know dat yu hands would get big an rough, but nothing bout de knee. I did dat kine of work close to forty years. Me knees started to get big an' long before them start to hurt. One day me started to get real bad pain and had to go to de docta. By that time de knees grow bigger an' bigger. Docta send me on sick leave. Dem allow me then to use a mop to clean de waiting room an' lavatory, but I was hurting too bad an' had to stop working at sixty-one. Dem call it early retirement."

"So, how do you manage to support yourself?" asked Deandra.

"Well, Miss D, for the three years since I stop working, de govament gives me a little money every month. It is very small, but I manage wid what I have. I never mine doing that kine of work as I say, but I give up a lot. I always love to bathe in de river an' mineral springs, but people use to stare an' point at me knees so much dat I had to stop going to de river."

At that point she pulled up her dress, straightened her legs, looked at her feet, her knees, and then her hands and continued to talk. "Bwoy, look pon me pretty soft shoes pon me old feet, me deformed knees, and me rough hands; but they are all a part of me. Dem serve me well and me neither complaining or ashamed a dem, cause plenty people wid money an' big house, can't walk nor use dem hands. So, dear Lawd, me tank yu for good times an' hard times, and tank yu for sending me a good fren name DeHandra."

Listening to Aunt Clem as she talked made Deandra realize that her instinct and intuition had served her well by leading her to this unusual woman. The old woman went back in time and space as she revealed her most intimate life story.

She recalled how at twenty-seven years old, she had met a man who got off the train at the railway station where she worked. She described him as dashing, a man you couldn't help noticing. He was good-looking, wore a crisp white suit every day, and walked with his head held high. According to her, whoever washed and ironed those white suits must have taken special care and time since washing machines weren't known on the island then and people had to bleach white clothes for days in the sun.

She revealed how they had met one evening after she had finished her work and put on a pretty dress she had made for a special occasion. She described the dress in detail. It was a beautiful Chinese blue dress, worn with a black sash around the middle, accentuating her small waist and the firm rounded hips that physical work had rewarded her with. As she descended the steps leading from the waiting room of the railway station, she heard a man's voice saying, "Good evening young lady, may I offer you a ride to where you are going?"

"'Good evening,' I answered the man. I was so surprised dat I missed me step, stumbled, an' almost fall down, but de man hold me shoulder as I stood dere shaking. He help me down de stairs. Before I knew it, I was sitting in a taxi next to this gentleman, when him say, 'How nice you look. Are you a secretary?'

"I smiled but never told him what kine of work I did. From dat time we would see one another every week. It was really nice. But something tek me by surprise an' I didn't know how Mr. G would handle it. One night when we was in de room settling down, he hol' me roun me waist an' turn me roun' to face him. Him look me all over an' said, 'Clem, I think you are pregnant.' I didn't answer cause I wanted to find out how him was so sure an' how him would react. Well, him sit in de chair an' pull me up to him. He look an' look at me till I was feeling embarrass, den him said again, 'You're pregnant, Clem.' Den I said, 'I tink so.' Yes chile, it was something when him kiss my belly and say, 'You've made me happy, Clem. I hope you will have a girl.'"

The old woman continued to tell her story. "Well, yu know

what almost sen' me crazy, Miss D? When de man said everyting would be fine, but I had to give up my pickney to his wife who couldn't have no more babies cause of sickness. I couldn't believe what I was hearing. All de time we was keeping company, him pretended dat him was single. I never know he was a married man.

"Dat was de time when I really grieve 'bout me madda who couldn't help me to care for her granchile. Me madda got blind cause of de sugar in her blood, bad diabetes, de docta said.

"It wasn't all bad though, Miss D. I think dat I would feel sick when I was carrying de baby, but I feel good. Everybody said I was prettier than ever. My skin was smooth and shiny brown, just like when I was a chile, an' me madda use coconut oil to rub me down. As I remember now, it was one of de best times I had."

There was a smile on the old woman's face as she talked.

"Mr. G jus' fuss bout me eating an wearing de right tings. He did take good care of me when I was carrying dat little girl. Him said I had de perfect nipples to nurse de baby. I wasn't sure about that cause some women say dat breast-feeding will cause yu breast to hang. But de nurse convince me to breast-feed my baby an' as I think back, it was a very nice experience to hold my baby close to me an' let her get de milk straight from me body."

The old woman gave a detailed and graphic account of the long and difficult labor she endured before delivering her nine-pound baby girl. She remembered how, back in the maternity ward, she had felt lonely after giving up what was apart of her for nine months and six days. But her loneliness would soon disappear when the nurse brought in her beautiful baby, wrapped in a green blanket, with her fingers stuck into her mouth. She could hardly wait to inspect the baby. She unwrapped the blanket to kiss the soft pink fingers and toes.

There was some sadness in the woman's eyes as she described the following day when Mr. G visited her, smiling from ear to ear when he was told that she had a girl. She continued to talk but suddenly her voice was barely audible and tears welled up in her eyes. Deandra was touched by the story as she talked.

"Well, I could only tink dat he was grinning to tek away my baby to his wife who couldn't have no more pickneys. Anyway, for de first few weeks, he was good to me an' de baby, till one day him said, 'Clem, it's time now to give me de baby. My wife is waiting to receive her.' I could hardly hold back me temper. I really try my best to keep my baby, but after tree months, tings was getting hard. Mr. G was threatenin' to stop supporting me an' de baby an' de people at my job was pressuring me 'cause I was absent too much from work. I didn't know where to turn an' I had to give up my baby.

"I use to visit me daughter till she was tree years. One day I went to de house, but they had gone without telling me where to find them. An' dat was de last time I saw my beautiful Lukie. I don't have any hate for him though . . ."

Deandra handed her some tissues to blow her nose.

"I thank you very much, Aunt Clem, for sharing with me something so dear and close to your heart. I shall try my best to write your story just the way you've told it."

They sat together, side by side, two women, one young, one old, both reflecting on the old woman's story of love, deception, and loss.

Deandra stirred herself, reached for her notebook and wrote:

Should sagging muscles and wrinkled skin,
Become a tomb concealing many accounts
From where no love stories are told?
Or should they be unearthed and explored
To tell the stories so real and true,
That was
That is
And shall always be.

Another day had come to an end, and it was time for them to leave the shady mango tree.

CHAPTER FIVE

That evening, Deandra thought about the old woman's story. Come to think of it, she mused, age, money, or geographical location don't seem to make much of a difference when you narrow them down to relationships.

She remembered dating Stanley for a short time during one of her breakups with Paul. She'd been at a track meet at Madison Square Garden and had been so involved with the race that she didn't realize that she'd been standing and shouting from the moment the starting signal for the race went off. She had felt certain that the North Carolina team would win the race, but just before the runners had finished the last two meters, the Jamaican sprinter suddenly appeared and passed the finishing line. She'd won the race by a mere ten seconds.

Deandra slumped in her seat, talking to herself. "That was some upset. The Jamaican girl was good though."

The man sitting next to her spoke, "You seem to be a sports enthusiast."

"You might say that. What about you?"

"I too have the bug. I love sports, as a matter of fact, I'm here not as a mere fan, but also to pick up some new techniques for my group."

"Are you a track instructor?"

"Only as a volunteer. By the way, I'm Stanley Black."

Deandra smiled and said, "I'm Deandra."

"Just Deandra?"

"Just Deandra, Stanley."

People had started to leave the Garden.

Stanley stood and said, "How about joining me for a drink?"

"Thought you'd be meeting your wife or girlfriend for dinner," answered Deandra.

"If I had any such plans I wouldn't have asked you," replied Stanley with a smile on his face. "So does that answer your question?"

"That will do for having a drink with you Stanley."

The bar was buzzing with excited customers. It was a regular stopover deli-bar for sports writers and enthusiasts. Stanley led the way to a corner table for two. He looked at the menu hanging on the wall and asked, "So Deandra, what do you want from the menu?"

"I'll pass the sandwich and settle for a drink."

"Okay then, shall I get you a beer?"

"That will be fine."

Stanley called the waiter and ordered a roast beef sandwich and two beers.

"So tell me Deandra, how come you're so interested in sports?"

"Well, in high school I was quite good at running. When I went to college, I tried doing a couple of courses in physical education but discovered that to be a good athlete required commitment, and since I also wanted to be a writer, I realized that I couldn't handle both. But there's always a part of me out there running whenever I see those athletes giving everything they've got on the field. So what about you?"

"I'm a physical education teacher at a high school. About four years ago I started an after-school gym class for boys and girls. They really surprised me. Three of them have won prizes in the local city events. I'm hoping that by next year we'll be able to have at least two in the national track meet."

"That's admirable, Stanley. I respect athletes. It's one of the few activities that defies barriers and boundaries. The true athlete relies on talent and determination."

They had finished eating. Deandra looked at her watch and remarked, "I thank you for the drink, but I must go now."

"Suppose you have a story to write. But how about my seeing you again for a drink or dinner?"

"My schedule is tight, I only make tentative plans."

"That's okay with me. Here's my card."

Deandra took the card, looked at it, and said, "I'll think about it."

"Don't tell me you're not going to give me your card. How will I be able to call you?"

Deandra decided against giving him her card, and instead wrote her phone number on a piece of paper.

Stanley took the piece of paper, looked at it questioningly, then said, "Thought you'd have given me your card?"

"I've just discovered that I haven't a card with me," said Deandra and stood to leave.

"Okay Deandra, I'll call you even though I don't know your last name."

The next time Stanley took her out, they went to a restaurant on the lower East side of Manhattan, which served the best spareribs. She had arrived a few minutes ahead of him and was about to order some mineral water when Stanley walked in. He was handsome, in a way, medium built and seemed in good shape.

"I wanted to get here before you, but something came up suddenly with one of my girls. Hope you haven't been here too long."

"Only ten minutes," answered Deandra.

"I'm sorry, but I'll make it up to you."

The waiter had arrived and took their order then returned with the wine Stanley had ordered. Deandra went to the dressing room, washed her hands, and returned to the table. They sipped the wine slowly and waited for the food.

Stanley looked at her deliberately and said, "You don't seem to carry around your profession with you."

"I don't understand what you mean by that."

"Well, you impress me as being a regular . . . I mean you talk about sports instead of journalism."

"I'm sorry to disappoint you. You weren't expecting me to talk in a foreign language? You're okay too. You don't talk about crossbars and double axles either."

They both laughed and continued talking.

When the waiter brought the food, Deandra asked, "Could you bring us some hot sauce please?"

"Sure," answered the waiter, and brought them a full bottle of sauce.

Deandra separated the large ribs, tasted it, and added some extra sauce. Using both hands she held the ribs between her thumbs and first fingers and ate from one end of the rib to the other as though she were playing the harmonica.

Stanley had been alternating with his fingers and the fork. He finally put the fork away and used only his fingers.

"Who taught you the technique for eating ribs, Deandra?"

"I grew up in New York and went to college in North Carolina. That should answer your question."

"I would have liked to be at one of those barbecue parties you alluded to . . . Anyway, you're fun to be with."

When they had finished dinner, Deandra said she'd get a cab to take her home.

"Don't play me cheap," remarked Stanley. "I'd never take a lady to dinner and not see her home, even though I was late in getting here. I'll drive you home if you don't mind riding in an old Ford."

"When I take a taxi I don't notice the make of the car, so I'll let you take me home in your Ford."

As they were about to leave the restaurant, an attractive white woman with flaming red hair stepped into their path. "So Stanley, am I going to dine alone tonight?" asked the young woman.

"Take it easy baby . . . simmer down, it's early yet," he answered.

"Stanley, I'll catch a cab," said Deandra and walked away to hail one.

"You wouldn't do that to me Deandra, I'm a man. I'll see you home."

She ignored him and waved for a cab, but the driver looked at her and drove away. She realized that it was tedious at times for a person like her to get a cab, especially at night, outside of their neighborhood.

"Well, are you going to let me take you home?"

"I don't seem to have much of a choice, do I?"

Stanley opened the car door and Deandra went in.

"I really enjoyed having dinner with you. That girl you saw, she's one of those who won't take no for an answer. So if that's what's making you so unfriendly, you can forget about her."

When they got to the brownstone building where Deandra lived, she quickly got out of the car and headed to her apartment on the first floor. As she turned the key to unlock the door, Stanley's hand was over hers.

"Let me do this for you please."

Before she knew it, the door had been flung open. He stood in her path and continued to talk. "Aren't you going to ask me in for a night cap. I really want to know you."

She looked at him quizzically and replied, "Come in."

Deandra felt uncomfortable with Stanley in her apartment. She went and got two glasses of wine and returned to the living room. She handed one glass to him.

"Thank you, beautiful woman. What shall we drink to?"

"To good-bye."

"You sure don't mean that baby. I could make this night one you'll never forget."

"I think it's time you went."

"Don't be a kill joy, Deandra. I could love you all night and make you scream at the top of your voice. You must know that the ultimate end to an evening out is making love, baby. It's a natural thing."

Deandra was shaking with anger. She stood and held the door wide open. "Go before I scream."

"Okay, all right, you don't have to be so nasty. I wouldn't be surprised if you're still a virgin," said Stanley and left.

When he'd gone, Deandra was still angrily talking to herself, "That bastard! One meal and he wanted to go to bed with me. I'm so glad I didn't give him my full name. Just as well I had waited for Paul. He's a gentleman."

* * *

She finally refocused her attention and planned her schedule. Deandra was filled with excitement and anticipation as she planned her visit to the small historical museum. She'd decided to drive her rented car even though it would take her at least two hours to reach the museum.

It was exactly 8:00 a.m. that Wednesday morning when she left Lucky Pond in the black Volkswagen. The traffic was light on the road and even though she had to look out for the bicycle riders and occasional donkey-drawn carts in some areas, she made good time and was at the museum by half past ten that morning.

It was an old restored three-storied building situated in one of the old sections of the island. The museum had very few people at that time of day, just what she'd hoped for. She looked around at some of the ethnic clothing and wall-hangings, then went to the pottery section. There she found a rich collection of artifacts dating back to the time when only the indigenous people lived on the island. She examined the pottery displayed in the glass case, but there was none similar to the Spanish type pottery that was described to her by her old friend. She looked for the wooden mortar and pestle that the old woman had also described, but there was none.

Finally she sought the help of the young man at the desk. It turned out that the few Spanish jars were kept in a locked room to which only his supervisor had access and who, unfortunately, would be arriving late that particular day. He had not known about the large wooden mortar she described; he had only seen those used by chemists before there were prepackaged medicines.

She couldn't help remembering her mother saying that many young locals were replacing old wooden items with plastic. Deandra realized what an important historian Aunt Clem was, for even if she hadn't the chance to see the Spanish jars and the wooden mortar and pestle, the old woman's description was so vivid that she had a very good mental image of what they had looked like.

Deandra struck up a conversation with the young man at the desk. "Tell me," she said, "are many people writing about the old customs of Nufuma?"

"Yes, miss. They are writing our own history, but there's still plenty of work to be done. As a matter of fact, they are discovering a lot of artifacts at the port that was once destroyed by earthquake. But tell me, how did you, an American, know so much about the big mortar?"

"Well, to begin, never judge anything by its appearance only. I have roots here too. But regarding the mortar and pestle, an old woman, old enough to be your grandmother, told me about it. "

"That's interesting, we really have more work to do, but we also need funds."

She finally said good-bye to the young man. As she turned to leave the museum, she caught sight of a special display and followed her eyes. That special sight brought sadness when she saw the iron rings that were worn by humans around their legs, chained to one another. She wiped a tear from her eye and left the building.

Feeling a little low after leaving the museum, Deandra walked aimlessly around First Town. People were milling around on sidewalks and suddenly she found herself observing them. It was hard to believe that they faced daily problems as Deandra herself had left in New York. What was the difference between the two lifestyles that made these people appear to be stress free, she wondered as she walked.

The street was not overcrowded and she glanced from left to right without obstruction as she walked. Most of the people walking down the street were young. The young women were slim in a healthy way, with rounded hips and small waists. They walked gracefully in their high-heeled shoes with the ease of people wearing sneakers. Deandra wondered how they managed to look so cool and crisply dressed without a wrinkle; more amazingly, there was not a drop of perspiration on these young people, while she was having difficulty keeping her sunglasses from sliding down her nose because of her profuse sweating.

She caught up with one of the young women, smiled at her then spoke. "Hi, how are you today?"

The young woman looked at her, sizing her up then replied, "I'm fine, thank you."

"Is it always as hot in First Town as it is today?"

"It's no hotter than usual. But you mustn't forget, you're in the tropics."

"You are right. People, including me, tend to forget that the temperature doesn't change to suit our liking."

They walked on for a couple of blocks before Deandra spoke. "I would like to get your secret for appearing so cool and calm, despite the heat and everything else."

"What do you mean by everything else?"

"I mean, looking at you and everybody walking down this street gives me the impression that you have no problems at all . . . and, by the way, my name is Deandra."

"Well Deandra, it's like this; we Nufumans have our own problems, plus new ones that are creeping in. But being angry and constantly rushing isn't going to resolve them, so while we have problems like other people, we try dealing with them the way that suits us best. Many people might say that we are too leisurely and laid-back, but that's only one approach to our lives. We are much more complex than many want to believe."

Before they parted, Deandra paused while saying, "I want you to know that I enjoyed talking with you, miss."

"Likewise, miss. Next time you're in First Town, stop by our main library. I'm one of the librarians there. See you soon."

Deandra wondered why the librarian had not volunteered her name but had continued on her way.

She continued to observe the people as she walked. They were neatly dressed. Young men were in shirt sleeves and ties; some were more casually dressed in jeans and sport shirts or T-shirts, while a few wore jackets.

The few middle-aged women were plumper, with thicker waistlines. There was a clear distinction in their posture, hair style, and dress code. Their hair was severely drawn back from the front of their heads; their dresses looked more like uniforms and made them appear to be older than they were.

She remembered her mother saying how she had rebelled against the rigid dress code and when she had made herself stylish and youthful looking clothes at age forty-one, the village people had called her "madda young gal" behind her back.

Deandra saw Main Street as a fascinating place which reflected some of the old and new customs. But she doubted that the middle-aged women who lived in the new cities of Nufuma would ever conform to the old time dress code that some of the women in their old city of First Town held onto.

Deandra waited for Lucreta at the fashionable Water Front Restaurant where they were to have lunch. The restaurant was built on the harbor. It was busy with activity by the time Lucreta arrived. She observed the flow of people and judging from the clientele, she could see that the Water Front was frequented by the well-to-do. Many of the customers were greeted as regulars by the waiters. She was surprised to see the place crowded within an hour, while people waited for available tables.

The table that Lucreta had reserved, faced the sea in full view of the boats that docked in the port. When they were seated, Deandra turned to Lucreta and asked, "Have you always lunched here?"

"Most of the time, but whenever I'm in a rush, I usually go to a more local type place. Anyway, Deandra, before my time, many of the locals didn't have access to a place like the Water Front

Restaurant, but since Independence, many changes came about; some good, some not so good."

The food was excellent but overpriced, Deandra thought. Sitting there enjoying the grilled seafood, she could understand why so many visitors opted to spend part of their lives on the island.

During the lunch, Lucreta felt more comfortable with her friend and remarked, "You know Deandra, I would prefer less material things and more of Daniel's company. His work has kept him away most of the time, leaving me to wonder if he has lost sexual interest in me."

Deandra listened and, without any comment, patted her friend on the shoulder and suggested that Lucreta and Daniel go away to one of those all-inclusive resorts for a week, to try and recapture what she perceived they were losing.

At this point they ended the luncheon because Lucreta had a staff meeting to attend. Before they parted, Lucreta gave her an invitation to what was considered the gala of the year, to be attended by the Who's Who in Nufuma.

On her way back to where she had parked her car, Deandra decided to explore another street. She came upon a scene she had not witnessed since her arrival in the island. The once-paved street looked more like a pile of broken concrete with uncollected garbage piled on both sides, reminding her of a street she had once seen in Manhattan.

Next to the garbage was a young woman talking to herself as she deposited things she had picked from the garbage into a plastic bag that she carried. The woman couldn't have been more than thirty; her eyes were large and round with the longest eyelashes Deandra could remember having seen.

Standing idly at a corner, were several young people; some had been asking people for money, some were talking, and two were crouched on the sidewalk in tattered clothes, seemingly too weak to stand. The two young men crouching had blank looks on their faces.

Further down the street were some young women involved in one of the oldest street professions.

As Deandra walked on, she came upon a young man who seemed to be no more than twenty. He was lying in the fetal position, with bent knees almost touching his chin, as though trying to return to the safe womb of his mother. A few people stopped to look at the young man lying on the heated concrete sidewalk. She soon learned that he was one of those considered to be a little crazy.

As a matter of fact, there were several people who had flooded the city, many looking for work, and many lured by the dazzle of the city. A man went to get the police to take the young man to the hospital, who in the meanwhile had started to have a convulsion.

The scene affected Deandra very much and reminded her of her reaction to *Crime and Punishment* which she had read as an undergraduate in college. She couldn't help thinking that maybe each city was little more than the backyard of the world, where exclusivity and affluence were separated only by a street or a lane from the ugly and seamy side of society. She found her car and drove back home rather depressed from what she had seen.

When Deandra arrived home, she read the invitation again and thought about the required formal dress. She had attended several galas in New York and had found some of them to be rather stuffy. It seemed to her then that such events were more like show places where people were jockeying for social visibility and prestige. Anyway, she found herself quite curious about the invitation and was rather anxious to experience her first gala affair in the place where she was born. Such an event would also be an added dimension to her book.

Although the invitation stressed formal dress for the occasion, she had no intention of exceeding her budget to buy any elaborate evening gown. Furthermore, she would be unescorted, going as a guest of Lucreta and Daniel.

She decided to wear the old dress she had bought in Senegal during her vacation a year ago. It was a simple white sleeveless crepe dress, made in the traditional wide robe African style with a neckline that revealed her right shoulder. It was trimmed with gold braid and hung loosely from her shoulders. Each time she moved, the dress encircled her body, revealing the fullness of her bosom and the curve of her beautiful rounded hips, slightly exposing the gold slippers that encased her feet. She completed her outfit with a pair of gold earrings and her paternal grandmother's large gold bangle.

Whenever she wore the bangle she felt transformed. It was large and heavy with a bird carved into it. Marion always reminded her that the bangle came all the way from Ghana, the home of the gold and once called the "gold coast."

She was picked up by Lucreta and Daniel. Lucreta wore a beautiful black dress that had a low back and a split in the back of the straight skirt, revealing just enough of her legs. She wore silver accessories that highlighted her complexion. She looked elegant.

Daniel looked distinguished in his horn-rimmed glasses and formal dress suit worn with a black satin cummerbund.

When they arrived at the gala, the three of them were escorted by an usher to their table. There was hardly a table where Daniel and Lucreta didn't stop to greet friends, and those they had missed waved to them. The brief conversations were sufficient for Deandra to realize that she was mingling with the rich and powerful people of Nufuma.

That night she was introduced to a wide range of people including lawyers, doctors, college professors, business tycoons, foreign ambassadors, nurses, artists, and secretaries of large corporations. What impressed her most though, were the large numbers of women in responsible and powerful positions. She was introduced to two women who really impressed her; one of whom was a manufacturer of unique beauty cosmetics and one whom was a top dress designer with an export business to North America and Europe.

It was a dazzling affair. Deandra couldn't remember being in a place where everyone wore the most expensive designer's clothes. Daniel and Lucreta knew all of Nufuma's high society. But then she realized that, as one of the island's leading surgeons and consultants, Daniel would be well-known. There was also the fact that his wife had a powerful position in the corporate world, which gave her the exposure to a wide circle of professional and business people.

Nufuman's were not only smart dressers, they were good dancers and with two bands playing at intervals, people could have danced all night, nonstop had they wanted to. Daniel was a good dancer and alternated dancing with Lucreta and Deandra.

Once when he was dancing with Deandra, a man came close to Daniel saying teasingly, "Caught you, Dan. I'm going to tell Lucreta that you're a two-timer."

The man was Doctor Lee, a Chinese and one of Daniel's best friends, Deandra discovered following her introduction to him and his African wife.

During an intermission, a very distinguished looking man walked up to their table. He bowed to her, said hello to Lucreta, then clapped Daniel teasingly on the back. "Old boy, you've been holding out on me, hiding this beautiful lady all night without introducing us."

Daniel seemed genuinely surprised then responded, "Don't place all the blame on me, Jeff. You weren't at your table when we made our rounds."

"That sounds more like you. The onus is off you then," said Jeff with a broad smile on his face.

When Deandra saw Jeffrey Boles she was quite impressed. She could describe him as extremely handsome. He was about an inch under six feet tall, with freckles on his nose and a full head of wavy black hair. He reminded her of the late Adam Clayton Powell, who she had seen for the first time one Sunday when her mother took her to hear him preach at his church in Harlem.

As she sat and listened to the conversation at the table where Jeff had now joined them, Deandra realized that Jeff belonged to the upper crust of Nufuma society. They talked about yachting and golfing with more casualness and ease than she and her friends did when they talked about riding the subway in New York City.

There was something mysterious and mischievous about Jeff which caught Deandra's interest. He seemed to have a good sense of humor and she liked the way he laughed, way down from his belly bottom, as Nufumans would say.

The gala was more than she had anticipated. It was a beautiful affair and she was having the time of her life. Before the end of the gala, Jeff led Deandra onto the dance floor. As they danced to a waltz, he paused, pulled her to him, and began to dance very slowly. Deandra could feel how hard and muscular his body was, as they moved almost imperceptibly to the music.

Finally he remarked, "I suppose you've been told this before Deandra, but you are an extremely beautiful women with a kind of . . . compelling grace and charm. I must tell you, what you've done to this dress, no other woman could. Your elegance and carriage have set you apart tonight."

Deandra blinked her eyes and gave him an impish smile as she replied, "Thank you for the compliment Jeffrey."

Before she knew it, the music had changed from a waltz to a quick step. He spun her around and, as she faced him, he pulled her closer to him, then pressed his face against her forehead. Deandra's entire body tingled. She felt as though she was experiencing a small part of a fantasy world.

On their way back to the table, Jeff held onto her hand tightly. A soon as they were seated he gave her his business card asking teasingly of Lucreta and Daniel whether they objected.

They all laughed while Daniel and Lucreta simultaneously answered, "No, but what if we did?"

The food was superb. Everything was perfect and plentiful. There was ackee pate, escovitched fish on sticks, curried crab quiche and codfish cakes to select from the carts that the waiters brought around. The five-course dinner included roast duck, roast beef, jerked pork, and fish. They even had a special vegetarian dish.

Deandra thought they must have emptied a large liquor and wine cellar to supply Nufuma's celebrated gala that night. There were different kinds of wine ranging from champagne to several of the local wines. The local wine was moderately dry but not too sweet, with sparkling bubbles similar to that of champagne. There was one thing that struck her most as she heard a waiter briefly say while taking orders, "Nufuman man prefers his rum to any other drink we have."

The dinner conversation was lively and general and allowed Deandra to participate equally. After dinner, Jeff stood, held out his hand to Deandra and asked, "How about joining me for a stroll to the other end of the terrace, Deandra?"

Deandra excused herself and left with Jeffrey Boles, holding hands as lovers. He took her to the far end of the terrace. He snuggled up to her as they leaned against the bannister in full view of a huge ice sculpture.

"This is a superb piece of art work," remarked Deandra, "and what better place to display an ice sculpture than in the tropics."

"Thought you'd like it. That's one of the reasons I took you away from the crowd, so we could enjoy it together."

"It's beautiful, Jeff."

"Come, let's walk over to the art work, D."

As they were just about to move, a voice close to Jeff called out, "Jeff! I've been looking for you all evening, and here you are."

Jeff stood, holding Deandra's hand with a strong grasp, while the woman moved into their path and with a sarcastic tone said, "Well, are you going to introduce me to the lady, Jeff?"

Jeffrey smiled at the pretty woman who looked like a high fashion model, brushed her cheek with his fingertips then answered, "We'll get together before the end of the night," then walked away with Deandra as the woman watched with a disturbed look on her face.

Deandra sensed that the pretty woman had a special liking for Jeff and she could understand. Jeff was a handsome man. They strolled around the sculpture as the ice slowly melted.

"Describe the form for me, Jeff?"

"If you look carefully you can still see the form of what was a huge sea lion, perched on a huge piece of ice . . . and notice how cleverly the artist has blended our flora and fauna to complete the scene."

"Yes. The hibiscus and bird of paradise flowers are truly beautiful and the white sea gulls bring about a certain harmony to the scenery."

"The artist would like to hear what you've just said D . . . By the way, the work was done by a local man who had gone to Europe to learn the skill. He's doing very well for himself."

As soon as Jeff had finished telling Deandra about the ice sculptor, a man called out to him. He turned and said, "It's great to see you Cliff. For a while I was beginning to wonder if you were in permanent hibernation."

"Not exactly Jeff. I'm just taking my time."

To Deandra's surprise, the man was Cliff Riggs from Lilly Valley manor.

"Hello, Miss Boggs. It's great seeing you again," said Cliff.

Deandra smiled and replied, "It's very nice to see you too."

"Do you two know each other?" inquired Jeff.

"It just happened that I was at the guest house the first day Miss Boggs arrived in the island and it was a pleasure meeting the lady."

"Well Cliff old boy, now that you're back in circulation, we'll get together soon," said Jeff as he and Deandra said good-bye and walked on.

They talked as they strolled slowly around the terrace. Deandra had seen and mingled with the other side of Nufuma in their splendid and lavish life-style. Silently, she reflected that there were indeed many rich and powerful citizens on the island.

Before returning to the table, Jeff said to her, "I would like very much to see you again D. How about lunch or something?"

Deandra hesitated. Her mind had drifted to the pretty girl who had approached Jeff and she felt that there may be others with whom he was associated. Furthermore, the women she had met that night were extremely beautiful and intelligent. Would she be competing with them, she wondered.

"Are you seeing someone in Nufuma?"

"Not really Jeff. The person I'd been seeing is far away."

"So then, you don't object to my seeing you, just as a friend?" he asked, with mischief oozing from his eyes.

"Okay Jeff, I accept your invitation."

It was about four a.m. when Daniel and Lucreta drove Deandra home. The three of them chatted. Deandra thanked them for taking her to the gala, which had given her tremendous pleasure.

There was a telephone call from Jeffrey Boles a couple days following their meeting. The conversation was lighthearted but sophisticated, focusing mainly on current events and the history of the gala affair.

Deandra received several phone calls after that, resulting in luncheon invitations. Luncheons were very popular in Nufuma for many practical reasons. Many of the restaurants catered to business people and after business hours, the flow of customers was low and customarily dinner hours ranged from six to nine in the evenings, which was really too short and did not allow diners much time to linger and talk.

For their first luncheon date, Jeff had selected a small and intimate continental restaurant that was managed by a friendly and efficient Haitian woman who made certain that her customers were satisfied and would continue to patronize her. He picked her up in his convertible Saab sports car. It was a sunny day and he had the top of the car down. If a car could be an extension of the owner's personality, then Jeffrey's car was. It suited his well-proportioned body and outgoing personality.

As they drove, the wind ruffled Deandra's hair; he pulled out his handkerchief from his pocket and handed it to Deandra. "D, want to cover your hair with this?"

"That's an excellent idea. Why not?"

As she elegantly tied back her hair, she thought, this guy knows how to win friends and influence people. She was having fun.

"By the way, D, I hope you'll like this little place we are going to for lunch. I find it relaxing and pleasant."

The food was good, but very rich with heavy cream sauces as expected with French cuisine.

Over lunch that day they talked about Deandra's work and local events. He told her he was going through his second divorce, from a seven-year marriage he referred to as the "seven-year hitch."

Even if she didn't want to make eye contact with Jeff, there was no way out; each time she looked away, he would say, "Why don't you look at me, am I growing horns or something?"

"I'm not scared of horns . . . maybe I drank too much wine and that's making my eyes droopy."

"Your eyes droopy? Get off that lady. If you ask me, your eyes are part of your uniqueness and I'd like to have them looking at me for a long time."

"But wouldn't you get bored looking at them for a long time?" Deandra answered teasingly.

"Not in the least, as a matter of fact, I'd like to know how you see me through those big beautiful eyes," said Jeff as he reached across the table and held her hands in his.

They had almost finished the main course when the waiter came and asked about their choice of desserts. Both decided that they could do without the extra calories.

"I'll be away for two days on a business trip. As soon as I return, I'll call you and we'll take it from there. Be good while I'm gone, don't get into any mischief," remarked Jeff teasingly.

Deandra reflected on the fact that Jeff was not only urbane, but he was interesting and fun to be with. He was definitely the type to get what he set out for. Anyway, since they were only casual acquaintances, she pushed such ideas to the back of her mind.

When Jeff pulled up in front of Deandra's place, it was two-thirty p.m. He kissed her hand and helped her out of the car. "Got to rush D. I have a meeting at three o'clock. Take care. I'll call you," said Jeff and sped away in the open-topped car.

Deandra felt very vulnerable, even though she was hoping not to become involved. Furthermore, if the rumors floating around were true, Nufuman men were adept at philandering and she could not deal with that. She was strictly a one-man woman who believed in monogamous relationships.

The following day, a beautiful bunch of flowers arrived from Jeff with a brief note. "To D with the big brown eyes. Keep as sweet as the flowers. We'll talk . . . Jeff."

As she put the flowers in a vase, she felt excited and strangely happy. There was no doubt that she had been receiving more attention from the men in Nufuma than she was used to. Could she have been giving off signals she wasn't aware of, she wondered.

As she stood in front of the mirror combing her hair, her eyes seemed larger and reminded her of the first time Paul had made love to her and after, he had sung, "Your eyes, are the eyes of a woman in love."

She had intended to resume work, but had been having so much fun that she decided there and then to take off a couple of weeks. That same night Jeff called. As one of the island's rich men, he was at the other side of the island, involved in some of his business ventures, including a coffee conference with some Japanese people.

"Hello D," Jeff greeted her over the phone. "How are you? I miss you. I'll be back tomorrow from the coast. I hope you have tomorrow evening free. By the way, did you receive some flowers?"

"Yes, Jeff, I received the flowers. They are beautiful. Thanks a lot. About tomorrow, I'll check my calendar."

He was in a hurry. There was a long-distance call waiting. "Okay sweetheart. I have to go now, sleep well."

There was no doubt Jeff had stirred something inside her very soul. Something she'd tried desperately to suppress since breaking up with Paul.

CHAPTER SIX

Although Deandra had been trying to resist any deep emotional involvement with Jeffrey Boles, she was gradually and cleverly pulled in that direction. Jeff was self-assured and knew how to court women. He wooed her in the traditional way. He sent her flowers specially arranged with subtle messages intertwined, boxes of chocolates. They had candle-lit dinners at his place and he took her sailing on the Caribbean Sea.

The first time he had taken her sailing on his yacht was a Sunday afternoon. Deandra was designated co-captain and, as she steered the boat, Jeff was impressed. She stood at the helm in deep concentration.

"Tell me D, how often have you steered a boat?" Jeff asked.

"You've thrown me a curve with that question, Jeff."

"Why is it a curve?"

"Because my sailing expeditions are zero. Don't forget that I'm a working woman whose only sailing experience involves taking a boat ride around the island of Manhattan, or the ferry to Staten Island. As a matter of fact, this is my first time steering a boat. And that's the main reason for my being so extremely careful, especially when a special person's safety has been entrusted to my care," she explained, ending with an impish smile.

"You could have fooled me. From the way you are handling the steering wheel, I'd say that you're used to being on the water a lot."

"Don't downplay one very important thing. There's a very experienced sailor directing me."

"Ha-ha. So this is how you use psychology to throw me back a curve eh? You seem to have a great sense of concentration though."

"Well Jeff, it's as I said, your instructions are key. I'm concentrating on whatever you're telling me."

"I like hearing that. I hope you'll retain that skill, and not just for steering a boat."

Deandra was enjoying herself. The Nufuman sun shone on her bare shoulders as she steered the boat, giving her a rich tan. She was much darker than when she had arrived.

Jeff watched as she steered. As they got close to the dock, he reached for the steering wheel saying, "Let me help you to take Lady Bell in, D."

Deandra stood by his side as he steered the boat to an almost isolated dock at the island's yacht club. The area had a beautiful beach surrounded by sea grapes, small hills of sharp-pointed rocks, with wild bluebells and red berries growing among them.

They went ashore and strolled barefooted on the white sand of the beach before returning to the boat. It was a quiet afternoon.

The sea was equally calm and quiet and, except for the sea gulls that flew around and the pelicans that dived for fish, they were alone and loving it.

"This is an ideal place for relaxation as well as concentration. Wouldn't you agree, D?"

"Yes, Jeff, it's a perfect setting for the good life and I'm enjoying it immensely."

"Tell me about New York life. I've visited there quite often, but mostly on business which doesn't allow me sufficient time to get around to visiting the historical landmarks."

"Well, New York is a large state, but I take it you are asking me about the city, since that's where I've lived most of my life. New York City life can be hectic, exciting, intimidating, lonely, and full of possibilities. I like to call it the crossroad of the world, where you can find almost anything you'll need within a ten block radius. There's glamour, glitter, sadness, poverty, and great wealth, plus the international flavor of course."

"Talking about international flavor, I was impressed by the United Nations. I once attended a special session there, followed by a luncheon by the invitation of a friend. The multi-cultural setting was quite enlightening. It reminded me at the same time of the Herculean tasks that members are expected to perform."

"Yes, I agree. The U.N. is an important body. Its role is another subject. But getting back to New York City, lots of opportunities are there. But it requires determination, hard work, and a sense of purpose. It's like Jimmy Cliff, the Jamaican, sings, 'You can get it if you really try.'"

"So, you seem to know a lot about Caribbean culture in general, spreading all the way to Jamaica."

"I try hard not to lose touch with my roots, while appreciating other cultures such as Jamaica. I even speak their type of patois."

"But, going back to New York City, D, how did you manage to be so focused having been brought up in the heart of the city?"

"Well, it all depends on what you mean by being focused," questioned Deandra.

"Don't be over modest. You're an accomplished journalist, and obviously enjoying life on your own terms as a single woman in a big city."

"Jeff, with a mother like Marion Boggs, I didn't have a chance to be otherwise. But I must tell you, there are several American women from various ethnic backgrounds who are not very much unlike Nufumans. All my American friends are very focused. Some could be described as overachievers. I was surprised when I went to college in the South to have found several African American women, in particular, whose backgrounds and values were similar to mine. There is also a mistake many of us make by using New York as the model for America. America has many faces."

"Now that you've been so erudite, tell me what you mean by similar values?"

"Well, my friends and I seem to strive for similar goals."

"If you and your friends are so very similar in goals and values, am I to believe that they are as single as you are," he said, winking at her.

"There you go again, Jeff," answered Deandra. "You have a way of catching me off guard. Being single has nothing to do with values. The way I see it, marital status is not a yardstick by which to measure values. Many people from both sides of the fence have what I consider to be correct values."

"That may be so," answered Jeff, "but 'correct values' is a loaded term."

Deandra thought about Jeff's remark before commenting. "As

you've pointed out, they are indeed loaded words. A better description might be, ordinary hardworking folks," she said realizing that he was a man of few words, but very probing and analytic.

The afternoon was almost gone when Jeff, with Deandra at his side, sailed for the port. They headed for Deandra's apartment where they were to have dinner.

Jeff seemed more relaxed and reflective as he shared some of his experiences with Deandra. He told her about his greatest loss. His first wife had been his high school sweetheart. They had gotten married when they were both only twenty-three years old. They had planned when to start a family and had their son four years later. They had decided for this wife to stay home and care for their child for the first three years of his life.

One week before Jeff Junior's birthday, he had received an urgent call from a neighbor telling him about an accident at his home. The neighbor said that his wife, Gwen, was hysterical and had asked her to call him.

He looked at Deandra and continued talking. "I must tell you D, when the neighbor said accident, I conjured all sorts of things in my mind, but I was not prepared to find people around our swimming pool. When I saw the crowd I realized that something dreadful had happened. I pushed through the crowd and there I saw Gwen kneeling by the doctor who had been trying to pump life back into our son. But it was too late, our son had drowned in the damn pool. It was pointless blaming anyone for the accident, but our lives were never the same again. Gwen and I couldn't connect after that. We finally divorced."

Deandra was very moved by the story, reacting sympathetically. "I'm so very sorry. That must have been a horrible experience for both you and Gwen."

As they dined and talked that evening, they both got to know each other much better. Before leaving for his home, Jeff turned to Deandra and remarked, "You know something D, you're an interesting woman, with many talents. I like the way you don't allow your academic qualifications to get in the way of being good at things some people frown at, such as cooking and, not to mention, you are also an excellent sailor."

"I'll let you into my secret; gourmet cooking is one of my hobbies.

* * *

When Jeff left Deandra that night, she sat up making notes in her diary. During her absence from the old woman she often thought about her, as she carefully kept notes of all the things she'd done and the places she'd visited. She wrote of the contrast between the rich and the poor; the circumstances of Aunt Clem as opposed to Jeff's. Nufuma truly was an island of contrasts.

The following Wednesday, Jeff called her from the North coast. He talked briefly about his business, then told her that they were invited to a dinner party by one of his friends.

On hearing that, Deandra replied, "Sounds interesting, but don't you think it might be a little too much, your taking me along?"

"That's a strange way to look at things D, especially by someone as cosmopolitan as you are.

"I'm really a country girl at heart Jeff."

"That may be so and I like that part of you too, but please, don't force me to indulge in unnecessary explanations. I'll talk with you when I return Friday. See you then," and he hung up.

So, what the hell do I have to lose, if he is happy taking me around that's okay," mused Deandra to herself.

The following Saturday evening, Jeff picked her up for the dinner party at the Nwanga's home. They were both casually dressed, she in a pale-blue dress and Jeff in brown slacks and yellow sport shirt.

That small party would turn out to be one of her most interesting experiences. Emanuel Nwango was a West African with an export business in Nufuma. Esme Nwango was a Nufuman woman who worked as a chemist in one of the colleges. The Nwangas were young, about Deandra's age, with a two-year-old boy. They lived in a modest apartment and, except for help by the baby sitter, Esme took care of their home. Deandra was very pleased to interact with a more real world, one more similar to hers.

The other two couples were young professionals. During dinner, the conversation shifted to creative writing. "By the way, Deandra is a writer, she's here to write about us, so we might read about ourselves in her book," explained Jeff.

"How interesting," said Esme Nwango. "I've toyed with the idea of writing, but I don't think I have such a talent."

"Nonsense Esme. My wife is one of the most talented women in

Nufuma, but she is too modest," remarked Emanuel.

"We would love to hear a little about your book, if you don't mind Deandra," interjected Esme Nwango.

"It's really not totally creative. Its focus is on the history and culture of Nufuma, but with a twist. I'm putting everything together to form a novel. I hope it will encourage great readership. In my opinion, I believe it's important for people to know more about other people's customs—what gives them joy. Take Nufumans for example, they are stereotyped as being exotic and oversexed. People need to realize that all people make love in almost, if not exactly, the same way."

By then they had just about finished dinner when Esme stood and announced, "Let's move to the living room where we'll be more comfortable." Deandra helped to clear the table and Esme thanked her.

The evening ended, and everyone agreed that it had been a delightful occasion. Deandra was glad that she had had the chance to see Jeff in another setting, unlike the high-powered and very affluent surroundings in which she was used to seeing him. Not that she was complaining about the good life; truth was, she was thoroughly enjoying the change, because soon she'd be back in New York where her life-style would be more like that of the Nwango's.

It was about ten o'clock that evening when they said good night to Esme and Emanuel Nwango. On their way home, Jeff remarked that it was a long holiday weekend; his business was closed down until the following Tuesday. This took Deandra by surprise. She hadn't known about this special holiday. This was one of the changes that came about in the island since she and her mother had migrated to America.

"Well D, did you enjoy yourself?"

"Most definitely, Jeff. The group was warm, earthy, and friendly. Esme and Emanuel were such excellent hosts that I felt very much at home."

"I'm glad you like them. They think you are a very special woman and so do I."

"Thanks for taking me with you."

"I should thank you for going with me, lady. Anyway, I hope you'll have more trust in me now. I'll be busy tomorrow, but I hope you'll be free for Sunday."

Jeff knew darn well that she was free. What good would it be to pretend? "I'll be free on Sunday, but I'd like to know what you have up your sleeve this time."

"Thought you said you trusted me? But if you insist, sailing, dinner, and looking at you."

"Okay Jeff Boles. I'm free and at your command for Sunday."

That would be their first holiday weekend together and Jeff wanted her to remember it. Deandra had once said that falling in love was not a priority on her agenda, he hadn't been convinced. Furthermore, she knew he was a good catch. Women of all persuasions were constantly seeking his attention. He enjoyed the freedom to choose and he had chosen her. She had no reason to resist.

They started the Sunday with breakfast at her place. She made omelets stuffed with mushrooms, tomatoes, onions, and cheese, served with toasted bammy instead of bread, fresh juice and coffee. They both enjoyed breakfast and left to go sailing on Jeff's yacht.

Jeff had a picture of himself and his dad in the forecastle of his boat. His father was tall, with blue eyes and reddish hair.

Deandra looked at the photo then turned to Jeff remarking, "You make a handsome pair. Is your dad as good a sailor as you are?"

"Dad, the Englishman, taught me to sail. He's the best." He then pulled out a picture of his late mother from his wallet. She had died two years ago. His mother had been a beautiful Nufuman woman.

"Now I know a little more about you," remarked Deandra.

"Now that you know a little more about me does it make a difference?" asked Jeff.

"Why should it? You're not so different from many of us Nufumans who have mixed ancestors. All that matters is for people to be comfortable with who and what they are. But now I realize where your freckles come from."

"Where are they from, D?"

"Your mother of course," Deandra answered with a smile.

"So now I'm finding out that you are also a geneticist," said Jeff as he pulled her to him and kissed her long and hard.

When they finished sailing, Jeff took her home to pick her up later for dinner at the celebrated Blue Hole Restaurant where he had made reservations. He arrived at her house a good thirty minutes before it was time for them to leave. He waited in the living room, flipping through the pages of the latest National Geographic magazine.

As Deandra dressed she felt carefree and happy, her heart started racing with excitement. She entered the living room wearing a pink silk dress with lavender accessories. When Jeff saw her, he gave a long low whistle.

"You look lovely, darling, but you could make even a burlap dress look like silk," he said pulling her gently toward him. "I have one request, and hope you'll grant it," he whispered in her ear.

"Try me and see darling," she replied, snuggling up to him.

"Could you wear the white dress you wore at the gala?"

"I thought you liked this outfit, Jeff."

"Of course I like it, but tonight is special. I want to recreate and celebrate our first meeting at a quiet little place in the hill."

When Deandra changed into the white crepe dress and returned, Jeff stood and took a deep breath. Stand still killer, damn it, woman, you are more than you'll every know. What's the scent you're wearing?"

"Oh, it's Blue Grass. It's guaranteed to knock you dead."

He kissed her on the back of her neck, saying softly, "You smell delicious. I won't mind being knocked out by you," as they walked to the car.

The ride to the Blue Hole Restaurant was steep and winding. It required expert driving skills, but Nufumans drove up those hills as though they were in the plains. Jeff had reserved their table in the Look Out dining room. It was a cozy and intimate room with plenty of space between tables where diners could talk without their conversation being heard by others. Their table faced Look Out Valley, from where they saw the lights of the city below. They both decided to block everything from their minds that night and to enjoy themselves.

Jeff looked more intriguing than ever and created more excitement in Deandra, excitement that she found difficult to conceal. "Tonight is a very special night for me. I'm alone with a beautiful and fascinating woman who I may not have met had it not been for the annual gala."

"That's interesting to hear coming from someone like you who, I imagine, has no problem meeting people," Deandra retorted with a smile, "We aren't going to debate tonight. All I know is, I'm having a hell of a time, and I want to hear how you feel, D."

Deandra hesitated before answering. "Truth is, Jeff, I'm having so much fun that it's almost scary. Everything seems to be affecting me tonight. The air, the moon, the scenery and . . . you."

Jeff wanted to kiss her on her exposed shoulder, but the table separated them. He reached for her fingers and kissed each one slowly. They were having such a great time, that neither one realized how late it had become until the waiter brought Jeff the dinner bill. Jeff paid the bill and they left.

Deandra surprised Jeff as she took off her shoes and walked barefooted to the car.

"You're full of surprises. I didn't know that you are a peasant girl. Barefoot becomes you, especially up in the hills. How about helping me to do some farming up here?"

Jeff headed straight for his place, while Deandra sat barefooted next to him in the car. They were both silent, as the car travelled down the hilly, winding road.

Jeff was analyzing Deandra silently. She was refreshing to be with. She was not a prude by a long stretch of the imagination. She was not afraid of admitting that she had had a good time and, most interestingly, she could switch from being a princess to being a peasant girl with the same elegance and grace. Come to think of it, none of the women he'd known would ever consider walking barefooted, especially at the exclusive Blue Hole Restaurant.

As they drove on, Deandra rested her hand against his thigh without speaking. His thigh muscles were as hard as rock. Jeff reached down and held her hand.

No sooner had Jeff entered his house when the phone started to ring. He ignored it as the machine recorded the call, then took the receiver off the phone. He had left the champagne on ice and stocked the player with his favorite CD's, the ones Deandra had said she liked when they chatted about music before.

That night as they made love, Deandra revelled in the pleasure Jeff got from her body. He hugged and kissed her from her head to her feet, nibbling at her toes. He had opened a warm bottle of champagne which he kept pouring in the hollow of her navel, licking it clean on each occasion until the bottle was half empty.

Deandra gave as good as she got. She'd kept herself free of involvement since her break with Paul and that night she gave into the passion that Jeff aroused in her.

The following afternoon when Jeff took her home, he lingered at her door, raking his fingers through her hair before planting a long and languishing kiss on her full lips. She had a broad smile on her face as she recalled how Jeff had removed the receiver from the phone to ensure that they had an undisturbed night.

Later that day, she read a letter from her mother that had arrived two days before. In the letter her mother had continued to remind her of Paul's love and good intentions for her. She had come to accept the fact that her mother was almost obsessed with having Paul as a part of her family. The letter brought back memories of her mother's lecture to her before she had left for college in North Carolina.

"Now Deandra," her mother had said, "as you leave for college I want you to listen to me real good. Remember that you have only a mother to call on and I can't say what your father would say if he was alive, but remember one thing, carry yourself like a lady. Your father and me got married before you was born. He was the only man I ever knew and I would like you to remember that. Don't listen to anybody who may try to change your mind and lead you astray."

"But Mother, you should know that I'm smarter than that, after all you've set me a good example," she had replied.

From the time her father died, her mother had dedicated herself to raising their only child. Deandra always wondered why her mother had not married again. She was a good-looking and attractive woman, slightly taller than her daughter. Deandra guessed that she had not wanted a stepfather for her daughter.

In college Deandra had dated, but had never met a guy she wanted to settle down with. Furthermore she, like her friends, was bent on putting a career before settling down as a wife and mother. The only man who she really liked had turned out to be a playboy. Marion never failed to call her attention to the teenagers who were having babies, but were themselves children.

She finished reading the letter and decided that she had reached the stage of her life to make decisions about who to love or who to marry even though she would always welcome her mother's advice.

* * *

The following day, Deandra was determined to put more time into her work. She wanted to finish writing her book as quickly as possible. As she sat reviewing her notes, she was reminded of the last job she had before switching to freelancing. She remembered the details of that job as though it had happened only yesterday. She had answered an ad in the Sunday newspaper for a journalist with a large newspaper firm. The morning of the interview she wore her pink and grey suit and a pair of ethnic earrings. She had always felt extra good in that suit, and always came out on top whenever she wore it. For that reason she had labeled it a good-luck charm.

Mr. Gray was a slim man of medium height with a bronze complexion, resembling an artificial tan. He had deep-set blue eyes, greyish blond hair, and a rather long pointed nose. His office was large with a high ceiling, and there was a display of original paintings hanging on the walls. The heavy Persian rug was another sign of wealth.

He was a distinguished looking man of sixty-two; he was sitting behind a huge mahogany desk when Deandra entered his office. On the desk was a silver stand with at least a dozen carved wooden pipes of different sizes and shapes. Deandra wondered whether or not he was using them or whether they were just collector's items for decoration.

Mr. Gray came from behind the desk and greeted her politely. He was soft spoken and erudite as Deandra had expected. He was frank and proud in telling her that he considered himself many cuts above the average employer because he was not a sexist nor a prejudiced man. He was fair-minded and looked only for the best people to work in his establishment. As a matter of fact, he could boast of having the only large newspaper firm in the city to have equal representation of males and females on the staff.

Deandra was the last of twelve people he had interviewed and, after passing his psychological test, as she called it, he told her that he was impressed by her credentials, especially the kind of infectious energy that she had generated during the interview. He felt that she was the best person for the job and made her an excellent offer. She accepted the job.

It was just what she had hoped for. The working atmosphere was good for any up-and-coming young journalist who didn't mind working hard, for to be an Associate Editor for the oldest newspaper in the country was an enviable position. Her co-workers were as diverse as the city's population, reflecting a mixture of ethnic groups, which made Gray's newspaper more appealing to the larger community. She had no problem fitting into the new work place.

As the weeks went by, Mr. Gary was quite impressed by her overall performance. He was especially struck by her analytic and probing journalistic style which she used to get to the root of a story. She wasn't afraid of the competitive and sometimes dog-eat-dog world. Her jealous, but admiring, colleagues liked the way she carried herself, and even when getting important sources for certain stories was difficult, she avoided compromising herself.

The cloakroom gossips couldn't find anything juicy to say about Deandra, for she was determined not to mix her social life with her work. When they would teasingly call her "Saint D," in return she would only laugh and tell them that it was better that way than to be a drunken fool. They resented that side of her and laughingly told her, up front, that she was a damn prude. Sometimes she felt as though her job was too good to be true, even though she worked very hard for what she was rewarded.

She admired Mr. Gray for his diplomacy; he was, to her, the perfect boss who respected his employees and treated them fairly, though demanding no less than one hundred percent in return. He was a no-nonsense man, yet liked by most, if not all the staff. And that's why Deandra almost fell out of her chair when she was propositioned by Mr. Gray during an office party.

She had been sitting quietly enjoying a glass of wine when she felt as though she was being watched. Not that she was paranoid or anything like that, but she had that peculiar feeling. She turned around and sure enough, someone had been staring at her. Mr. Gray had been staring at her from where he sat. Their eyes met. He winked and smiled at her, quite unlike an employer-employee interaction, she felt.

Before she realized what was happening, Mr. Gray was sitting next to her. With a martini in his hand, he had turned to her with searching eyes and commented, "You're looking unusually pretty today, Deandra."

Deandra had not wanted to give the impression that she was naive, but she was so taken back by the sudden and obvious flirtation by her boss that she shifted in her chair and clasped the glass of wine with both hands.

Mr. Gray must have picked up that she was uncomfortable as he remarked, "You don't have to be so edgy dear. I won't bite you. But I'll repeat, you are unusually pretty tonight. Maybe it's the black dress you're wearing."

In the meantime he beckoned the waiter to bring him another martini and to refill Deandra's glass.

Deandra finally worked up some courage, looked straight at Mr. Gray, whose tanned face was quite red from the many martinis he had drunk, and replied, "Thank you for your compliment, Mr. Gray."

"You're welcome, Deandra," he said, winking his eyes at her. "Where do you shop, Sak's Fifth Avenue or Bloomingdales?"

"Neither one, they're too expensive. Deandra was lying; the truth was, the long-sleeved high neck black dress she was wearing came from Sak's Fifth Avenue. It was a basic dress that she could play around with and she wore it from the newsroom to a cocktail party.

"Well," said Mr. Gray, "that can be taken care of. I'll personally speak with the managers at both stores and have them send you two personal charge cards, accounted to Gray's newspaper."

"Mr. Gray, that's a magnanimous offer, but it is not necessary. I just couldn't accept those cards."

"It's nothing but a perk that goes with the job, Deandra."

She knew that Mr. Gray's offer had nothing to do with perks. She felt that he was behaving more like a man who wanted to be intimate with her through the job. That night, she tried to soften the shock he had given her, and finally convinced herself that it was nothing more than the bad effect of too much booze on an aging brain.

When Deandra went to work the following day, nothing much had changed. The staff was busy getting stories for the newspaper. As was her usual habit, she worked in her office until late that evening.

Mr. Gray was always working late too, and so she had no reason to believe that there was any other motive for him working late that evening. But, as she was getting ready to leave the office, she noticed that his door was open and he was still at his desk.

He called out, "Deandra, would you spare me a minute please?"

Why not, after all she was paid well to work late; she thought that he had recovered from the effect of the booze.

Mr. Gray got up from his chair just as he had done on the day he greeted her at her interview and as she closed the door, he said, "Hi Deandra, please sit down."

He returned to his sitting position. He was in shirt sleeves. He loosened his tie and played around with it for a while, then leaned back in his huge leather chair, spun around, then inquired, "Have you been able to crack that story yet?"

"Sure, it's all ready." The story involved a prostitution ring that was run by four housewives in one of the affluent suburban neighborhoods in New York. They catered to the rich and the famous. A neighbor blew the whistle on the women, fearing that soon everyone who lived in the neighborhood would be a suspected prostitute. As usual, Deandra was on target. The story was ready to make the headlines in Gray's newspaper the next morning.

He complemented her for always meeting deadlines, then changed the subject. He told her that he had a personal interest in her and that he wanted her to know that she was special and greatly admired by him. This feeling, he said, was from his heart, whether she believed him or not. He assured her that he was neither a wolf nor a womanizer, but she had brought something special to the place, that far outweighed her professional skill, and it had affected him.

She had listened carefully to what this powerful, mild-mannered man had been saying and felt confused. Mr. Gray must have picked up on her body language as she sat, stiff as a mannequin, in the chair. He spun around in the chair while he continued to talk.

"As a matter of fact," he said, "you must not allow my marriage to get in the way. As things are, my marriage has been more like an arrangement since my wife was confined to a wheelchair from the effects of polio."

Deandra remained silent while she shifted her position in the chair trying to deal with her boss's declaration of love for her. Mr. Gray went to his private bar and asked her what she preferred. Her mouth was a little dry, a sign of nervousness, she realized.

"Do you have wine?" she asked.

"Yes," replied Mr. Gray as he pulled the cork from a bottle of New York wine, poured some, and handed it to Deandra. He then poured himself a scotch from the crystal decanter. "Tell me, Deandra, have you ever tried scotch?"

"As a matter of fact, I've tried scotch, but have not developed a taste for it."

"So what else besides wine is your favorite drink?"

"I suppose I'm unsophisticated when it concerns drinks, but I usually stick to wine."

"Most newspaper people enjoy a strong drink at times. I'm sure, with time, you'll change from wine to something a little stronger."

Deandra smiled and finished her drink. She looked at her watch then remarked. "It's later than I thought."

Mr. Gray also looked at his watch, then said in a serious voice, "Yes, of course. It's been a long day and we are both tired, I'm sure. And by the way, about my proposal, take your time. Sleep on it, but be sure to make the right decision . . . bear in mind that you will be treated with the greatest respect and discretion, and there will be no limitations to how far up the ladder you may reach in Gray's newspaper firm."

Mr. Gray called a taxi to take Deandra home. That night, Deandra had a problem falling asleep. She knew that as a young black woman, she was already holding a position that was the envy of many black and white professionals in her field. She thought seriously about the proposition. Mr. Gray was handsome, in a way, he was certainly a man of the world and one of the power brokers in that art. He could be the ideal mentor to her. She would have liked and even welcomed that without the sexual favors. She wondered if there was something she could discuss with him. His proposition certainly went against everything she had been taught and stood for.

Deandra kept turning the proposition over in her mind as the night crept slowly into dawn. She finally fell asleep in the morning. She decided to seek advice from Sara, her African-American co-worker at Gray's newspaper.

She had developed a very good working relationship with her, and occasionally they lunched together. Deandra was impressed with Sara because of her strong self-esteem and unaffected manner. As a matter of fact, Sara could have easily passed for white if she had wanted to, with her green eyes and straight hair, yet she was one of the most culturally aware persons Deandra had met. She specialized in writing feature articles concerning the different ethnic groups and their contributions to the city.

Over lunch that day, Deandra tried picking Sara's brain by

inquiring about Mr. Gray. "You've been here for sometime, Sara, and may be a good person to describe Mr. Gray," remarked Deandra.

"What do you mean by, describe, Deandra?"

"I mean, the type of man he is, regarding personal and romantic connections between himself and his staff."

"Well, as far as I know, he is a very respectable man who commands the respect of his staff."

"So, as far as you know, he's not a womanizer or a dirty old man?"

"Not in the least. I think he's a great guy to have stuck with a wife in a wheelchair for years. But I get the feeling that there is something very personal between you and Mr. Gray."

"Yes and no," answered Deandra. "There's the possibility for such a development, but that's as far from my mind as night is to day."

"Well, Deandra, you should consider yourself as being a very special person. For the twelve years I've worked here, I've seen women actually throwing themselves at him, but he has not shown any interest. The only woman that was once rumored to be dating him was a young black fashion writer who didn't stay on for long. She left and went into full-time modeling, for more glamour and travel, she said."

"Well, Sara, listening to you describe Mr. Gray gives me the impression that he likes dark-skinned women."

"So, does that bother you, Deandra?"

"You make it sound so easy, Sara, but it's more complicated than that. I'll have to think long and hard to make a decision."

"I agree. I think you need to think carefully, with an open mind, of the realities of a hard, cold world, girlfriend, and the possibilities involved."

Their coffee had gotten cold by then; they pushed the two cups aside and left the dining room.

Deandra decided to walk the thirty blocks from Gray's newspaper to her apartment that evening. The walk helped her to carefully examine Mr. Gray's proposition. It wasn't that she was a prude as some of her co-workers had once teasingly called her, but rather, the principles that she believed in. Sleeping with Mr. Gray could possibly ensure her a place at Gray's, but on the other hand, it could also diminish her true merit that she had worked so hard for. She felt that accepting Mr. Gray's proposition would only prolong the power play between the sexes in which women had to surrender their dignity for position, money, and power regardless of their qualifications.

Needless to say, the working atmosphere had become somewhat strained between Deandra and her boss, whom she had once admired. There were times when she had felt like bringing a sexual harassment charge against him, but it was only her word against one of the most powerful men of the city. Realistically speaking, she could end up being dragged in the mud as a vixen and gold-digger, with her picture plastered on the front pages of tabloids. She finally handed Mr. Gray her resignation and turned her attention to freelancing.

CHAPTER SEVEN

Deandra walked excitedly down the now familiar dirt road. She was looking forward to seeing her old friend again and wondered what other stories awaited her. She was about halfway to their meeting place when she heard the moan of a woman. She tiptoed forward, hiding herself among the bushes where she could get a glimpse of the moaning woman. She saw a couple.

The man was of a medium build and appeared to be about ten years older than the woman who was much taller than he. Deandra guessed the woman to be no more than thirty years old, at best.

The man spoke angrily. "It look like you want me to lick you, eh Corrine? Is a long time since I don't drop two licks pon you. You feel say thru I love you, you can tek me for a fool. Is so you feel eh Corrine, is so you feel?"

"No Jewel. Is not so I feel. I know that you love me. That's why you take care of me and Keisha. Keisha don't know any other father but you, so I know that you love us and that's why you don't hit us around."

"You better not provoke me more wid that uptown fancy talk, Corrine. Me don't hit you, me lick you, an' I think you want some good licking now."

Corrine stood in front of the man with her arms folded in front of her. He grabbed one of her braids and pulled it so hard, she screamed. "Jewel, I beg you, don't lick me! I love yu."

"I want to put some sense in you head," Jewel snapped. "If you love me, den why you mek your frens have you out in de road, making a fool out of me, going to the bar wid a strange man, eh

Corrine? I also want you to fine out if dem friends you have got a man who care fe dem, like I do fe you."

"I don't need no fren to tell me what I know, Jewel."

"Corrine, you say one ting and do anada."

Corrine didn't answer, she was digging a hole in the ground with the toe of her red sandal.

"So is dum, you dumb now, Corrine? What happen, you lose you tongue or is because you can't talk them fancy uptown language?"

"Me listening to you Jewel."

"Why de hell you didn't listen to me before," retorted Jewel, while pulling Corrine to him with his belt in his hand.

"Don't hi . . . lick me Jewel!" screamed Corrine as Jewel started hitting her.

Whap! Whap!

The woman whimpered quietly, like a puppy.

Jewel stopped hitting her and shouted, "You don't feel de lick. Pull up you frock so I can see you backside dat you shaking roun' wid bad company . . ."

Whap! Whap! Whap!

"Lawd me God, whoi! Stop Jewel!" screamed Corrine.

Jewel stopped hitting the woman, dropped the belt in front of him and stood silently watching Corrine as she sobbed. He then walked over to her and touched her face while saying, "You see how yu made me have to lick you, an' yu know I don't like to do it."

"I know that I get outta han' sometimes an' yu might have to give me a few little licks, but I don't like when yu lick me so hard. Sometimes yu handle me too rough," replied Corrine.

"But is de roughness yu want; yu tink me don't know. Never mind, come let me see . . ."

By then Corrine's convulsive sobs had stopped. Jewel held her around her waist and stroked her gently, whispering softly in her ear. Soon they were hugging and kissing and proceeded to make love.

Deandra withdrew, hardly believing what she had just witnessed. In one sense it could be considered domestic violence, and it was. But on the other hand, the woman went along with it, without any resistance or an attempt to stop it. She walked away confused, talking to herself.

"Well, I suppose de Sade's sado-masochistic, behavior is found all over the world, from the palace to the peasant farm. It is frightening to know that some women actually believe that beatings and love go together. There's no doubt this is a form of control.

Later that day Deandra would learn more about Corrine and Jewel from Aunt Clem. As the story went, Corrine once worked as a secretary for the same company that employed Jewel as a truck driver. Jewel always liked Corinne and tried to date her, but she had that uptown suburban class thing and wanted more than Jewel could offer her. She became pregnant by the boss when she was twenty-four, and was forced to leave her job when the pregnancy became too obvious. In Nufuma, women were still subjected to such unfair treatment in the workplace.

Her family didn't want her around with a big belly and no one to support her. She then turned to Jewel who had persisted in his pursuit of her. She poured out her heart and her regrets to him. At first, Jewel was sympathetic and their relationship had been more of a friendship than love. But after Keisha was born, Jewel became very attached to the baby. Finally Corrine and Keisha moved in with Jewel and the three of them lived as a family. Jewel adopted the baby and three years later, Corrine miscarried at six months the baby she was carrying for Jewel.

Jewel had been very upset about the miscarriage, but had promised to take care of Corrine and Keisha. He had grown to love them both and, from all appearances, he had no intention of losing his middle class, uptown woman and hoped to marry her some day.

People had always gossiped that Corrine was lazy and didn't want to work, for Keisha was already four and was in nursery school. Aunt Clem seemed to feel that Jewel didn't really want Corrine outside of the house. Aunt Clem explained that they lived outside of her village, but Jewel did small farming on that plot of land on weekends. People always said that Jewel was jealous of his beautiful uptown girl.

* * *

The news in the letter from New York to Deandra gave detailed accounts of current events. There were the usual political demonstrations by various interest groups. Some were against drug abuse, some for conserving the environment, and others for animal rights. Women in furs were special targets for animal lovers. There were two counter demonstrations on one of the fashionable avenues on a cold day. Women wearing furs were sprayed with red paint.

Her mother made sure to give her the general news before mentioning the overworked subject. This was an issue on which Marion Boggs couldn't see eye to eye with her daughter. She had been quite outspoken and opinionated about women marrying early and raising a family, while Deandra had different views about settling down. Deandra was convinced that one of the main objectives of many mothers was to get their daughters married to the "right" man. Women from the old school, like her mother, were actually traumatized by the new-found independence and freedom of their daughters.

In Nufuma, these mothers put a lot of effort into socializing their daughters. They were raised to be good mothers and good wives. Marion Boggs had raised her only child to be a good catch for a nice guy, and with her college education she was really expecting no less than a professional man for Deandra. Paul was such a man.

Marion's letter was without a doubt pleading Paul's case. She had written a lot of information about Paul and his new engineering firm that he'd started in New York City. To Marion, Paul was a shining star for any woman, especially now that he would be his own boss. Behind all the news, she was trying to convince her daughter to make up with Paul.

Deandra finished reading the letter and directed her attention elsewhere. She thought about Lucreta. The two friends had grown very close to each other since Deandra's arrival. They visited each other regularly and unceremoniously, many times debating social issues, which Lucreta called redundant at times. Deandra, on the other hand, was determined to sensitize Lucreta about the other Nufuma that she seemed to know very little about.

Once when she had tried to describe the scene she had witnessed following their lunch at the Water Front Restaurant, Lucreta had abruptly remarked. "Deandra, you sound like one of those ultra do-gooders who believe that they can cure all of society's ills."

They had ended that discussion as Deandra said, "Don't get me wrong, Lucreta, I understand fully well that no one individual can change the world, but each one can put a little effort into making a difference."

Both women ended the conversation laughing as Lucreta reminded Deandra about their special dinner date.

The weather was perfect on the evening of the dinner. It was one of those glorious January evenings, almost without a cloud in the sky, with the cool, gentle, tradewinds blowing. It was the type of day when there was no need for any intrusive electric fans or air conditioners.

Nufuma had an interesting climate; it could be hot and humid, there could be hurricane and flooding, thunder and lightening, then perfect cool dry air, sometimes making a light jacket necessary and a blanket at night.

That they had had good fortune, which allowed them to acquire the best of the material world, was evident in the Clarke's home. The dinner table was elegantly set with sparkling crystals, exquisite bone China, and sterling silverware. Their home reflected the life style of Embers Glade's rich folks.

They started off with Lucreta's special dip served with uncooked vegetables, other canapes, and cocktails. The two women were having fun. Deandra even gave in and had a martini.

At the end of the cocktail, Deandra noticed a sudden change in Lucreta; she had become nervous and edgy, wringing her hands and going in and out of the kitchen as the dinner hour drew closer.

The phone rang and at the other end was Daniel's secretary saying, "Mrs. Clarke, Dr. Clarke has just been summoned into surgery for an emergency, he asked me to let you know that he will be late for dinner, but you should go ahead without him."

Lucreta thanked the secretary and announced that they would have dinner without Daniel. One could understand the loneliness and broken dates Lucreta talked about, but on the other hand, she knew where her husband was. The unasked question could have been, what would life be like had the situation been reversed and Daniel had to deal with last-minute cancellations from his wife?

The dinner was superb and exquisitely served. The cook had marinated the duck in the special Nufuman spices and had glazed it with fresh pineapple juice, mixed with nutmeg and ginger. She had made a rich brown sauce that was served with the duck. The dessert was a semisoft sweet potato pudding, garnished with crushed nuts and shredded coconut.

Deandra was genuinely impressed with the meal, especially the duck. It was her first time having it since her return to Nufuma. Even when she had eaten Peking duck in China Town in New York City, she couldn't remember tasting anything like this.

She raved about Aunt May who was the family cook. Lucreta explained that Aunt May was accepted and treated as a member of the family. She had been with them ever since they were married. She'd helped to raise their two children. Aunt May was one of the best cooks in the island and had won many prizes for her special sweet potato puddings at the annual culinary festivals. The pudding served for dessert that evening was considered one of her specialities.

After dinner, the two women moved to the family room where they were served coffee while Lucreta poured some brandy. Everything seemed so perfect, but the house was empty of Lucreta's version of love and the place seemed even more so since the two children were away on vacation.

But as Deandra thought about the word love, it evoked other things in her head and she reflected that an important aspect of love was maturity. Yet, she could understand Lucreta's side of the story; it didn't matter how rich and famous you were, you still needed your man or woman around. With all her intellectual rationalization about self-denial and understanding, she wasn't sure that, was she in Lucreta's position, she would have reacted much differently.

She suddenly thought about Jeff and tried to imagine what life would be like living with such a high-powered man. While Deandra had not yet finished her glass of after-dinner wine, Lucreta was literally gulping down a lot of brandy. She wondered whether her friend was used to drinking as heavily as she was.

Lucreta soon broke down in tears mumbling to herself. "It doesn't have to be this way. I've put up with this too God damn long."

It seemed to Deandra that Lucreta had suddenly slipped into another world, forgetting that she was in the room as she rambled on and continued in her monologue.

"Oh Daddy, your Lukie needs you now. I miss you so much, and wish you were here. You always had the answers to my problems."

Deandra felt like moving closer to her friend, but on second thought decided to let the woman give vent to her frustration. Lucreta continued talking while tears rolled down her cheeks. "There must be another surgeon who can cover for you sometimes, Daniel."

When Lucreta had finally stopped talking to herself, Deandra moved closer to her on the beige sofa which blended in with the blue room and, without speaking, placed her hand on Lucreta's shoulder.

In the meantime, something triggered in her brain. Where had she heard the unusual name of Lukie before? Yes, she remembered now! Could she have been wrong all these years, believing that her friend's natural mother was Mrs. Green?

The silence was broken when Lucreta spoke. Sorry to be such a cry baby, but after a while, things get to a point where you feel like screaming and, since I can't scream, I cry."

"No apology is necessary, there comes a time when we all need a third ear to listen, or a shoulder to lean on. As a matter of fact, it might be very helpful if more of us, including me, would just loosen up sometimes, let our hair down and cry."

Lucreta tried to compose herself while replying, "You know something, Deandra, you always seem to come up with the right answers. I remember as girls how you were always willing to help out a friend."

"Lucreta, I too remember you as caring and loving. Remember that time when I was climbing up the orange tree and fell and cut my leg, how you went and picked green bush to dress the cut?"

They both laughed as Lucreta wiped the tears from her eyes and continued to talk. "Don't get me wrong. Daniel is really a good guy, who loves me and takes care of his family. It's just that living this life as a surgeon's wife is not as glamorous as many think it is. There are constant broken engagements from dinner parties to vacations, all because of his work. I understand that his patients need him, but should they always he given the priority in his life? Sometimes I get angry when I remember giving birth to our two children alone, while he was in the operating room, and the first man to see my babies was my dad. I'm so glad that he was around to cuddle his grandchildren."

"While I empathize with you, Lucreta, let's try and be realistic. Would you be willing to exchange Daniel for a charming philanderer? What I'm trying to find out is, what did you expect from your marriage?"

"Well, to be honest with you Deandra, I always thought and hoped that my marriage would be like that of my parents."

"In what particular way?"

"My dad seldom ever disappointed the family, except on occasions when he had to attend business meetings. My mother could make plans without fear of breaking them because of Dad's lateness. He was a nine-to-five man and planned yearly vacations with the family, which took priority in his life."

If her hunch about her friend was right, it wasn't that Lucreta's father was the perfect husband she believed him to be, but rather that his wife, Mrs. Green, had long adjusted to his shortcomings.

"Lucreta, if a surgeon should hang out his shingles with a nine-to-five only schedule, maybe soon he or she would be out of business and, of course, spending more time at home. By the way, who delivered your children?"

"My children were delivered by a wonderful midwife who just retired. She was a terrific lady."

"From what I've heard, many women are now using midwives, they feel that they are more able to be with them. Would you agree with their reason?"

Well, it's hard for me to agree or disagree with other women's choices, but based on my experience, I love my midwife. She was comforting, patient, and understanding. She stayed with me from the beginning to the end, leaving her warm bed in the wee hours of the morning, staying with me for the ten or twelve hours while I was in labor. As I think about it now, she was a special person and if I should have another child, a midwife would be my choice. It's a pity dear Mrs. B has retired."

Lucreta appeared happy as she reminisced about her birthing experiences, so Deandra continued the dialogue. "You know something, you are educating me about midwives. Now I understand how the saying came about, 'once a midwife, always a midwife.' I must keep that in mind just in case I should find myself pregnant one of these days."

Both women laughed and continued the conversation.

"You've described how caring and gentle your midwife was and how you always went into labor in the wee hours of the morning, keeping her for hours for you alone. Maybe, if you try to see Daniel's role and commitment to his patients in the same way the midwife was to you, it might help you to feel less lonely and neglected. From your description of your midwife's devotion, it sounded as though she gave up a lot of her family time in caring for you in the delivery of your two children. Furthermore, midwives don't make a hell of a lot of money. So, in a nutshell, she was a dedicated professional whose patients were her major priority when she was needed and called upon."

Lucreta's expression had changed. She stood and looked away from Deandra, then sat on the floor in a yogi position as though she was about to do some exercises. She then cupped her face in the palm of her hands, and replied, "While what you've said is something I hadn't thought about before, I do believe that when you are giving birth and feeling pain that's indescribable, the man who is part of the process should plan things so that at least you could cuss him instead of digging your toes into the sheets and hollering at the poor midwife."

"Lucreta, you've got me cold. I can only imagine what you're talking about since I've never given birth, but sometimes someone like me may be able to weigh situations differently."

Lucreta looked at Deandra and remarked, "Don't misunderstand me, you're making sense. It's as though you're helping me to come out of a trance. Just imagine, all these years I've been wallowing in needless self-pity and loneliness because of sheer selfishness. Now when I look back at the situation of my midwife, you are right. Thanks to you, I am beginning to understand Daniel's position, but even more importantly, his professional responsibility is to his patients and students who rely on him so much. You have sent me back into time and space. You are helping me to grow up and not to be so self-centered."

Deandra smiled at her friend and felt genuinely pleased that she was getting through to her, realizing that both of them were living in two different worlds. "Well Lukie, as I said before, that's what friends are for. I'm glad that I can help. By the way, how come all these years I didn't know your nickname?"

"Well, Deandra, it's a special name that was only used by my dad, and then only sometimes. My brothers and my mom never called me by that name. What about you, do you have one?"

"Sort of. You know how Nufumans like nicknames. Mine is Deedee, but used only by my mother. But listening to your story, you and your dad must have been very close."

"Truth is, Deandra, I didn't realize how close we were until his death. So much has happened since he died, some of which I would like to forget, but as you have reminded me, that's part of life."

It must be difficult to lose a parent, especially one you were so close to. I always had a fantasy about having a father around and wondered whether or not he would be a doting parent."

"Come to think of it, your father died when you were a baby, right Deedee?"

"Yes, you are right. My mother raised me all by herself and, God knows, if I mess up my life it's not her fault."

"Mrs. Boggs was a sweet, kind lady. I remember her always making me feel comfortable and welcomed whenever I stopped by your house and I'm sure she is still the same. She has imparted to you some of her fine qualities and that is why you are able to help me see the world beyond my narrow, rose-colored glasses."

"How kind of you, Lucreta, to say such nice things about my mother, but without any modesty, I think Marion is a great woman."

Lucreta sighed and continued talking. "All along I believed that I was the daughter of Mr. and Mrs. Green, only to discover when my father was dying that it wasn't so. When my dad became ill, my mother Carol started to act up, showing another side of her I'd not known before. She wanted Dad to change his will so that I would inherit less of the estate than my brothers. At the time, it struck me as peculiar, but I attributed it to the gender thing in Nufuma, where they still believe that men should have and own more than women.

"Dad would not allow her to browbeat him into changing the will, saying that there was enough for all of us. From that time, I started to notice a change in my mother's attitude toward me, but the big jolt came the day before Dad died.

"I suppose people know when they are close to death, especially when they have suffered like he did from that dreadful cancer. I can remember so clearly, sitting at his bedside, holding his thin hand. He was so weak that when he tried to kiss my hand, he hadn't the strength to lift it. As I stroked his hair, he whispered softly, 'Lukie, you are my special child, take care of yourself. Carol is your stepmother, but she loves you like a daughter.'

"I was shocked and confused, hardly comprehending what I was hearing from my dying father. I calmed myself and asked him who was my real mother. He told me that her name was Clementine Thomas, but they had not kept in touch for several years, since I was a toddler. It then clicked in my brain why all the fuss about the will."

Deandra allowed a brief period of silence to pass before saying, "That revelation must have been quite a shock, especially at a time when your father was dying. I can understand the void you must be experiencing, but then again you have a lot going for you, a very special asset is being the proud mother of two beautiful children."

"That's true. Life goes on, and it could be worse. I suppose I ought to be thankful for all the good things in my life, including my stepmother, Carol."

"So, tell me, how is the relationship between you and the family?"

"My brothers are terrific, they have remained the same and I'm still their baby sister. My mother, or correctly my stepmother, has been a little distant and this has bothered me a lot since she has been the only mother I've known and loved, only to be suddenly shut out like an outsider. It makes me feel like a person who is split into two halves, but doesn't quite know who the other half belongs to. And to make it even more devastating, I don't know if my real mother abandoned me at their doorstep or at the church door or what. Since then, whenever I read the papers and see notices where people are searching for their biological mothers, I get a pain in my abdomen because I believe it is important that you should know something about the woman who carried you in her body for nine months."

Deandra didn't want to take on the role of a therapist, even though friends do play that role more often than they realize. She had said and heard enough about her friend's problems so she changed the conversation, feeling that it was time for her to be going.

In her private contemplation, Deandra couldn't help thinking that life was indeed filled with irony as well as drama played out in different or similar circumstances and it didn't really matter who you were. As a child, she knew only her loving, caring mother who spoke with respect and love for her late father. At an early age she had to deal with having a one-parent family and felt good about it. And now, here she was sitting in her friend's home, listening to a story that was sounding more like fiction that was causing Lucreta to feel confused and traumatized about the discovery of who she really was. She felt more fortunate to have grown up with Marion alone who taught her how to face reality in her formative years, than to have lived in an almost perfect world, only to have that reality or 'unreality' shattered by the last gasp of a dying parent.

But now she had to be careful in trying to put the pieces of

Lucreta's life story together. It was just like an important jigsaw puzzle that required thinking through, especially if indeed there was a connection between Lucreta and Aunt Clem.

CHAPTER EIGHT

Deandra's interest in the uptown/downtown syndrome was intensified by Jewel and Corrine, the couple she had accidentally come upon that day on her way to meet with Aunt Clem.

As luck would have it, that Friday when she stopped at the takeout counter of the small restaurant in Lucky Pond, she bumped into Claire, the friendly young girl who usually waited on her.

Claire wished her a happy New Year, then turned to her saying, "I thought you'd left us, Miss Boggs."

"I'd never do that without saying good-bye," answered Deandra.

"I'm glad to see you. So, what did you do for the holiday? Have you been to any jam-down dance hall sessions as yet?"

"I'm glad you've asked. I've not yet been to a dance hall show or session. I'm anxious to go to one or the other, but would like to go along with someone who can explain some of the dances and groups. That way, I'd be better able to appreciate the art, while enjoying myself."

"Are you serious about going with someone?" asked Claire.

"Sure, man," answered Deandra.

"There's going to be a big show tonight. Me and another girl will be going. We will take you with us."

"Are you sure your friend wouldn't mind if I went with you, Claire?"

"No, she won't mind. Furthermore, you're even beginning to sound like us, man," answered Claire as they both laughed.

At about nine o'clock that evening, Deandra, with Claire and her friend in the back of the Volkswagen, were on their way to the show. There would be some of the top D.J.s such as Jagajaga, Red Robin Breast, Tiger Mane, and the sultry Lady Know It All.

The event was held at one of the largest stadiums in that region. Luckily Deandra and her two friends had arrived early enough to select good seats. The huge stage was decorated with silver, orange, gold, green, and black. The stage managers and engineers double checked the sound systems while people settled down to enjoy the show.

Deandra carefully scanned the crowd, trying to differentiate between the up-towners and the down-towners, but realized that she needed the assistance of her friend Claire.

"Well Deandra," explained Claire, "you must first look at the clothes." She pointed to the right of her. "Most of the up-towners tend to dress more conservatively, they wear less jewelry and stick to traditional hair styles. I want you to look straight ahead, you'll notice some men sitting scattered among the crowd. Some of them are wearing dark glasses. Notice how close to the stage they are sitting. They are the rich men from the corporate world. They are without their wives. I wouldn't mind sitting up front myself, that way I wouldn't miss anything."

Claire then turned to Deandra and asked, "Do you think you can identify some of the down-towners by their dress?"

"I'll try, but there must be more to the two groups than what they wear."

"You're right, but for now the dress thing will help you."

Claire was right. As a matter of fact the other people who were classified as down-towners were expensively dressed. Both men and women wore colorful clothes. They displayed a lot of jewelry. The hair styles of both sexes were interesting, but the men were outdone by the women who had their hair dyed to match the color of their outfits.

The Kellarians in the audience and on stage were easily identified because of their long braids. They were more conservative in their dress and avoided garish jewelry. They reminded her of the Rastafarians in Jamaica.

The show was opened after the singing of the National Anthem. The audience and entertainers had an international flavor. There was a Japanese D.J. and a Dutch D.J. who did their acts in Nufuman Patois. The first artist was a young D.J. who sang about peace and unity. The crowd greeted him politely, but they screamed for Jagajaga. As Jagajaga sang and the music played, the youthful crowd was putting on its own floor show. They danced in the aisle showing off their spectacular clothing and did the different kinds of dances. The dancers moved their hips, bending low while opening and closing their legs as they did the "butterfly."

Deandra tried doing the "butterfly," but the closest she got to doing it was moving from side to side while clapping her hands.

When the dance hall queen came on stage all the men and some women stood and shouted, "Give it to we tonight, Queenie!"

Queenie wore a fishnet costume of gold and silver. She concealed her face with a green mask, removing it only when she was about to finish her act. Queenie really had a beautiful figure and when she did the special "butterfly big-dip," the crowd roared.

In the meantime, Queenie's backup dancers were doing the new "doctor bird dance." Deandra liked the doctor bird dance and before the end of the evening, she was dancing with her palms turned upward and her hands flapping behind her as though they were wings.

When they left the stadium, it was 3 a.m. Deandra drove the two young women home and, before she went to bed, wrote in her diary. "The dance hall is a culture within a culture. It reflects some of the past and more of the present, but most of all, it displays much creativity and energy, far exceeding what I'd experienced elsewhere. The dance hall is like a community of spontaneous artistic happenings. There are fashion shows on stage and off stage. New dances are developed by the audience as each dancer tries to outdo the other.

"Regarding the uptown/downtown barrier, as far as I understand, the difference cannot be defined just by the way people dress. It seems to be more of a class thing, based on money, education, and family status. Many conservative people live downtown, behaving much like up-towners. The only difference between the conservative down-towners and the up-towners is money. The way I see it, the term down-towner is nothing more than a euphemism used to describe people from the poorer and less affluent neighborhoods. Nufuma is indeed an interesting microcosm of the world. In a way it can be compared to the eastside and westside barrier in New York City, where it takes more than money to cross the invisible line.

"New York's two most famous and prestigious avenues always fascinate me. You could be very rich and yet not able to live on certain sections of those avenues. But on the other hand, anyone can walk down the avenues undisturbed. You can also sit on the benches on the avenues and watch the world go by. On any given day you can rub shoulders with the greatest power brokers and the factory workers, walking side by side down the avenues."

It was about four-thirty in the morning when Deandra finally flopped into bed and she slept until late that Saturday. The dance hall scene had truly made an impression on her, one she wanted to share with her mother, so in a letter to Marion, she described the dance hall which would also be new to her mother.

She also raved about the rum fruit cake and sorrel drink she had during the Christmas season. Christmas in Nufuma was almost a week of celebration. She had attended concerts, a Pantomime, and private parties. She had met and made new friends.

She closed her letter by saying, "So my dear Mom, you can see that your daughter is not the chronic workaholic you thought. Anyway, I miss not spending Christmas with you."

When next Deandra met with Aunt Clem, she also shared some of her dance hall experiences with the old woman. She was especially fascinated by the names of the artists as she asked her friend, "Tell me Aunt Clem, when you were growing up as a young girl, what were the popular names that people gave to their children?"

"Well, let me think. As far as me can remember, some people go way back to de Bible, some to de church, and some tek names from movie stars or big people in de country that dem admire. Some use family names."

Deandra tried to connect the old woman's name to history, recalling an old folk song that spoke about, "My darling Clementine." She remembered also that the name Clement went back to the Roman Catholic Popes, from Clement the First to Clement the Fourteenth.

"How did you manage to come up with such a pretty and unusual name as 'Lukie' for your baby?"

"Dats a long story. To tell de trute, it was her fadda who name her Lucreta after some dead family. One ting him never know was dat I did want to have a son an' name him Luke after the disciple in de Bible. Anyway, me love me daughter so much that I call her Lukie as a pet name, and dats how I came up wid de name."

"You are an amazing woman, Aunt Clem. The more I talk with you, the more I find out how smart you are. I've never heard of another girl called Lukie. The name Lukie must have added something special to your daughter."

"I tink so and I hope that all's well wid her."

"Is there anything else that you consider as very special about your Lukie?"

"Oh yes, I can remember very well de one big dimple on her right cheek. It was so deep and pretty dat you could almost fit a big button into it. Everybody used to say, 'what a pretty chile,' and it made me feel very proud. And one other ting, she had a reddish brown mark on her arm . . . let me tink now . . . yes, it's on de inside of her left arm. She got dat mark cause when I was carrying her me had de craving for apples an' couldn't get any. When I touch me arm, I give her de apple mark; de mark is round like an apple. She was really de apple of me eye."

"It seems as though people are now giving their children some strange sounding names compared to the names used in your childhood."

"Yes miss, dats right. Dem say dat they are trying to include some African names wid de English, Irish, Scottish, and German names. Some of de new names are hard to pronounce, but after a while yu get use to dem."

Later that day, Deandra noted the discussion on names in her diary. She wrote a postscript at the very end explaining that, "In Nufuma people believe that if pregnant women can't satisfy their cravings for certain foods and touch their bodies, the babies will be born with marks resembling the foods that the mother crave."

Before retiring, she reflected on Aunt Clem's relationship with Lucreta. The pieces of the puzzle were beginning to form a perfect picture. Deandra had always admired Lucreta's big dimple. As a matter of fact, she had been downright jealous, especially when her friend got all the compliments and attention because of her big dimple. Deandra smiled as she recalled how she used to puff out her cheeks and push her fingers down to try to create her own dimple.

She couldn't remember which of Lucreta's arms had the dark brown birth mark, but the next time she saw her she was wearing a white short-sleeved dress and the birth mark was visible, still dark brown, on her left arm.

Deandra realized that soon her meetings with Aunt Clem under the tree would come to an end. And, for that reason, she welcomed Jeff's absence, which allowed her more space and time to be with Aunt Clem and to finalize her assignment.

The cool air that lingered on the island seemed to have affected Aunt Clem physically. Her knees were causing her great pain. She was even beginning to have difficulty walking. When Deandra tried suggesting getting some special help for her friend, the old woman responded saying, "Miss D, me know yu is a good fren, but me don't like to burden people. Anyway I know a young girl who can help out if me need anything."

As time went by, Aunt Clem's visits to the tree had become less frequent, until finally she stopped leaving her cottage.

That cool February morning when Deandra visited her old friend, she found out that the young girl who once assisted her had gotten a job and had moved away from Golden Grove. This prompted Deandra to seek out community assistance for her. Her intervention resulted in some assistance—daily visits by a health worker and daily hot meals.

Deandra's visits to her old friend's cottage had become quite regular and during one such visit, she tactfully tried to get the old woman's reaction to having another visitor. She asked, as casually as she could, "Do you think you'd be able to cope with having a visitor, Aunt Clem?"

"Hoo would ever want to visit a sickroom like dis? Yu are de only stranger an' foreigner to visit my humble home, but if de stranger is as nice as yu, me wouldn't mine."

"Okay Aunt Clem, the situation is like this, maybe my friend may want to visit you, and if she does, I'll bring her."

Even in her illness, the old woman was a fighter.

Deandra's next move would be to pick Lucreta's brain about visiting Aunt Clem. Even though Lucreta had come a long way since their heart-to-heart discussion about Daniel, she wasn't sure how she would react to such an invitation. There were obvious changes in her. She even seemed younger, more relaxed, and more understanding of her husband's situation—to the point of recalling that Daniel always supported her in her desire to pursue a career and was instrumental in her getting her present job.

That evening, following her talk with Aunt Clem, Deandra had a long telephone conversation with Lucreta. As they talked, Deandra remarked, "By the way, do you remember me telling you about a fascinating old woman I met since I've been here?"

"Sure. How could I forget the way you described her—as witty and intelligent. Not many older folks get the chance to meet and talk with someone like you, who will acknowledge that they are intelligent, even if not educated book-wise. Is something the matter with the old woman?"

"As a matter of fact, something is the matter as you put it. The old woman has been confined to her home for the past few weeks and I just thought a new face might help to cheer her up."

"It sounds like a good idea to me. I see no reason why I cannot go with you to visit your good friend. Just let me know when you plan your next visit."

"I felt all along that you wouldn't refuse me, you are a good trooper. I'll certainly let you know in plenty of time, Lucreta."

They visited Aunt Clem one sunny afternoon. Aunt Clem, though appearing to be weaker, was still a woman of wit and warmth. She chatted with the two young women and thanked them for the visit. Because of the short time spent, Deandra felt certain that the old woman had no time to notice the dimple on Lucreta's cheek, which had become less pronounced with the years, and the spot on her arm was well-concealed by her long sleeve silk blouse. Knowing Aunt Clem as she did, if indeed she had the slightest inkling about who Mrs. Clarke might be, she would certainly let it be known.

On their way home, Deandra again thanked Lucreta for visiting the old woman.

"Everyday I learn something more about you, Deandra. I think you are in the wrong profession. Imagine, you have just returned here, almost a stranger and a foreigner, yet you know so much more about the issues than I do. You really should be a social worker to rescue and counsel people in need."

Deandra sensed a little envy and jealousy in her friend's voice, knowing very well how Nufumans liked to refer to those who left the island as foreigners. The word, "foreigner" seemed to say, " go back to where you came from," without acknowledging how much those artificially created foreigners contributed to the small island.

Deandra and her mother had previously discussed this sensitive issue concerning the so-called new Nufumans who had left the island— many in search of their fortune, some in pursuit of education. Although Nufuma had an open door policy to foreigners, there was a silent antagonism between Nufumans returning home and the locals.

Marion Boggs explained it best when she had told her daughter,

"Well Deandra, some of us when we travel and go back home, we kind of flaunt it and show off sometimes and the locals resent that. On the other hand, sometimes we also feel jealous of the locals because of the air of freedom and importance that they throw around, and the God's truth is that sometimes it's just selfishness and envy. Some locals still believe that everything in foreign is sweet perfume. There's one thing that bothers me from what people are saying and that is that some Nufumans give rich, powerful people a warmer welcome than Nufumans returning home, instead of treating everyone alike. I hope it's not so. People do sometimes over react."

"Do I hear a tone of sarcasm in your voice, Lucreta?"

"Oh no Deandra, sarcasm for you, never. What I'm trying to say is, how unusual a person you are. Watching the interaction between you and the old woman in that little one-room place was revealing and something I will always remember. There I was, almost suffocating, while you were so relaxed and at home, it was almost as though you were standing on holy ground, or in a mansion."

"That's interesting. How did you manage to come up with 'holy ground'?"

"Well, to me it seemed like something unique was happening between you and the old woman, the way her eyes lit up when you sort of gently floated to the chair and touched her. To me, your interaction in that room was like entering a cathedral and finding peace by just being there. Without a doubt, there was a definite kind of chemistry going on between you two."

"That's quite an observation, Lucreta. Come to think of it, the one room is Aunt Clem's castle and is really the true mirror of life. The physical body cannot occupy more than one space at a given time and the old lady is in a space which provides her peace and tranquility."

"Okay my philosopher friend, but I must admit that you're exposing me to some new places and situations. I'd not been to this neighborhood before."

As they discussed the visit with Aunt Clem, Deandra felt certain that there was a connection between Lucreta and the old woman. There was a definite sharp resemblance between the two; their eyes and especially their heart-shaped lips looked almost identical. She would wait for the right time to tell Lucreta about her discovery.

The day following Deandra and Lucreta's visit to Aunt Clem, Deandra decided to take her old friend some homemade vegetable soup. It was an exceptionally cool afternoon, forcing even Deandra to wear a light jacket. When she arrived at Aunt Clem's house, there was another elderly woman visiting her friend.

"Good afternoon, Aunt Clem."

"Good day, Miss D. It's good to see yu so early in de day. Meet my fren, Miss Helen."

Deandra chatted with Aunt Clem and her friend, then left the container of soup, promising to return another day. As she walked slowly home, she pondered on the prospect of growing old, then smiled realizing that aging was a daily process and hoped that she would be around long enough to reach Aunt Clem's age.

As she reached the gate to her apartment complex, there was Jeffrey Boles leaning against his car. At first she thought her eyes were playing tricks on her, or maybe she had missed Jeff more than she wanted to admit and it was nothing more than a mirage. But then she heard Jeff's voice.

"I didn't know you had a secret hide-a-way too, D."

"Jeff!" exclaimed Deandra, "You really know how to surprise someone. I thought you were still down at the south coast."

Jeff walked towards her, then held her closely and kissed her.

"Well," continued Deandra, "what happened?"

"The conference was a long and tedious one. The Japanese wanted a new coffee contract. I was tired, but because I missed you so much, I couldn't afford to waste another minute by talking on the phone. So now you know, D."

By then they were in front of Deandra's apartment. She reached for the key in the wicker lunch basket she carried, and opened the door. Along with the acid bleached jacket, she had worn her faded blue jeans that were threadbare at the knees, and loafers that were covered with red dirt. Jeff sat on the sofa and his eyes followed her every move as she put away the lunch basket, then removed her jacket and shoes.

Deandra poured two glasses of blended fruit juice then joined Jeff on the sofa. They both drank some juice, then sat quietly looking at each other in private contemplation.

"You know what?" Jeff began, then smiled. He was discovering something new about the woman whom he was sitting next to.

"What Jeff?" she asked.

"I've been sitting here thinking how little I really know about you," answered Jeff as he reached for Deandra's hand.

Deandra faced him with a serious look, then remarked, "My life is really a very simple and open one, totally free of secrets. Anyway, it's a very pleasant surprise to have you sitting beside me at four o'clock in the afternoon."

"That's good to hear. But Nufuman men don't think they need permission for when and how to visit a lady. We are really easy going, although we don't beat around the bush when there's something we really want."

Deandra noticed that Jeff's glass was empty and asked, "How about some more fruit juice?"

"Thank you," he replied, "but I'd much prefer you to remain sitting beside me, so I can find out more about you. I watched you walk along that dirt road before you got to your gate. I saw a different Deandra than the one I thought I knew."

Deandra uncrossed her legs, then inquired, "What do you mean by different, Jeff?"

"Well D, as I watched you walking through the bush with your wicker lunch basket, you looked like a real Nufuman woman, without pretensions . . . you belong here. It seemed to me as though you had been visiting someone down the road."

"Yes, I've been visiting a very good friend by the name of Aunt Clem. It's not a secret, but I thought it unnecessary to involve someone as busy as you in such mundane activities."

"It sounds like missionary work. Anyway, whatever you're involved with in the village, I hope you'll be successful."

They were both relaxed by then, as Deandra revealed to him her involvement with the old woman.

Jeff looked at his watch, then remarked, "I knew all along that you were an unusual and modest woman. This afternoon has proved me right. I must leave you now to stop by the office and sign some documents that my secretary has left on my desk."

She look languishingly at Jeff as he left.

That afternoon had proved to be an instructive one. They both discovered something new about each other. Jeffrey Boles wasn't just a hardworking and wealthy man, he was keenly aware of the social problems and poverty that coexisted with his privileged world.

As a matter of fact, his company had adopted a school in one of the less affluent communities, which he visited once a year to talk to and mingle with the young people. Two boys were currently attending college on full scholarships awarded by Boles Export Company.

On his way to his office, Jeff thought about some of the characteristics that made Deandra so irresistible. They weren't just intelligence, education, and looks. After all, Nufuman women were second to none in terms of those attributes. There was something very humble, yet exceptional about her. She was genuinely unaffected. She enjoyed what he shared with her and she admitted being fond of him, yet she was self-assured and not overwhelmed by his wealth.

Before leaving for home that evening, Jeff called Deandra. "How about coming over to Embers Glade this evening, D?"

"Thought you'd never ask," answered Deandra. "I could drive over and save you those extra few miles of driving, if you don't mind."

They were both equally excited and there was an undercurrent of longing in both their voices.

"No sweetheart, I won't mind you driving over at all," said Jeff.

Deandra said, "I'm leaving now, see you in a few minutes," and hung up the phone.

That night in their passionate love-making, Jeff treated her with all the tenderness that he had in his heart for her, and the following morning before she left his place for Lucky Pond, she wrote:

"A man a woman
a woman a man
Probing, searching, probing
Narrow passage, secret corners
Nostrils flare as scents escape
Lungs contract, scents inhaled
Nostrils flare as pulse beat races"

* * *

A week later, Deandra had just finished packing some fruit and canned food to take for her friend on the next visit when Lucreta telephoned requesting to revisit the old woman whenever she was going. Lucreta informed her that she was becoming involved in voluntary work in the poor and depressed areas of the community and felt that Easter should be a good time to visit the sick and needy.

The sickroom was clean and airy and the old woman, while sitting in the chair, leaned against the table to support her body. She seemed thinner and sicker since Deandra's last visit.

She told them that Miss McKenzie, the health worker, had just left and remarked, "I'm so glad fe see yu Miss D and it's nice that yu bring your fren again."

"We thought two more people would help to liven up your party," joked Deandra.

The three women chuckled as the old woman answered smiling, "We will dance de quadrille and mento at the party. But Miss D, yu fren have a pretty dimple, but not half as big as de one me baby got."

On their way home, Lucreta asked, "Have you ever been to a place, or seen someone and felt as though you had been there before, or seen that person before?"

"My answer to the second part of your question is yes," replied Deandra, "but no to the first part."

"When I went with you to see your friend the first time, it gave me a funny feeling that was difficult for me to describe, and seeing her again today, even though she seemed sicker and a little different, still gave me that feeling that I must have met this woman before. I've racked my brain and cannot place her."

Deandra wondered if the blood tie could be so strong that after more than thirty years of separation her friend could be experiencing the interrupted biological bonding.

"I supposed that's annoying when you want to recall and the brain won't connect, especially when the problem seems to be an easy one to solve."

"Aunt Clem seems to be getting good care though, she was clean and so was the room, and all of that is because of your friendship with her."

"No doubt my intervention helped to untangle some of the red tape to get some community service, but I still believe what Marion Boggs taught me—'do good and it will return to you.' Aunt Clem is a good woman and I believe that if I wasn't around, there would be someone else to help, and that person could have been you."

"I understand and like your humility, but you make things much easier for her. Furthermore, I was so far removed from the real world—which is right under my nose—until you came along, that I know I wouldn't have been the one to do what you did."

Deandra looked at Lucreta's face as she talked and decided that she was genuinely concerned about the old woman. She turned and asked, "What would you do if you found out that the old woman, Aunt Clem, was a relative of yours who you saw once a long time ago. How would you handle that?"

"That's a tough situation you are setting up and it's difficult to give you a quick answer. But if I had seen this person only once, it would be difficult for me to have any close attachment—I would think."

"That's a reasonable answer, Lucreta. Don't forget, very few of us have the correct answers to the situations we face daily."

As soon as they arrived in Deandra's yard, Lucreta got into her car and, as she drove off, Deandra called out, "How about the two of us getting together next week, Saturday?"

"That shouldn't be difficult. We have a date," answered Lucreta as she drove off in the open-top car.

After seeing her children off to their Saturday activities, and Daniel to his surgery, Lucreta carefully selected some white gardenias and red roses from her garden to take for Deandra.

When she arrived, Deandra was prepared to spend the entire afternoon leisurely with her friend. They talked about the popular debate surrounding land reform and the subject which haunted Deandra most.

The two women had settled down to a leisurely lunch of ice-cold lemonade and the baked chicken and salad Deandra had bought at the restaurant, when Lucreta remarked, "You know Deandra, the talk we had the last time we visited Aunt Clem really left me thinking. What if indeed she was a relative of mine, how would I feel and react?"

"I know what you are saying. Who knows? Just be yourself. How else could you react?" Deandra tried to find the appropriate words that would help to soften the delicate and sensitive subject. She was aware that in spite of the depth of their friendship, to broach the topic of the old woman's possible relationship to Lucreta required the utmost care and tact.

They finished lunch and moved to the living room. Deandra sat directly across from her friend and rested her feet on the coffee table in front of the sofa on which she sat.

"Are you okay, Deandra?" asked Lucreta. "You look a little pale with dark lines under your eyes."

"The dark circles may be the result of my staying up late at night trying to finish my writing."

"Well, only you can do something about that, don't work to hard . . . Can we continue with the conversation where we left off?"

"Sure," answered Deandra.

The truth about Deandra's dark circles was that the very thing she'd fought against, had happened. She had fallen in love with Jeffrey Boles, who was still a married man. Of late she'd been struggling with what she privately called her predicament, sometimes losing sleep.

"You were saying you felt intuitively that you had met Aunt Clem before."

There was a long pause. The two women sat silently contemplating their private thoughts.

Deandra suddenly removed her feet from the coffee table, sat up straight on the sofa, and told Lucreta that she was about to tell her a story that required her complete attention and understanding. She explained the details of her meeting Aunt Clem, the development of their relationship, and the necessary levels of trust which made Aunt Clem the key resource person who provided her with information for her book.

As Deandra related some of the stories told to her by the old woman, Lucreta remarked, "This is quite a story and she is really an important woman who, if given the opportunity, could have been an instrumental leader in her community."

"That's precisely the way I felt about her from the very first time I saw her," answered Deandra. "There is also another side to Aunt Clem that has captured my respect and admiration."

"More surprises?" asked Lucreta.

"Yes . . . that's one of the main reasons we are having this chat today."

"I'm anxious to hear your story."

Deandra explained to Lucreta some of the disappointments and low points in the old woman's life, and how in such times she was able to maintain her self-respect, sense of humor, and the capacity to forgive.

"Would you believe this, Deandra? It was the self-esteem and sense of humor that struck me most of all on my first visit to her house," remarked Lucreta.

The sun had shifted and the room was flooded with brilliant sunlight that shone brightly on the vase of gardenias and roses on the table which Lucreta had brought with her. Deandra excused herself, moved the flowers away from the sun, and lowered the window shades.

She returned with two glasses of cold lemonade, offered one to her friend, then resumed her seat and continued the conversation where they had left off. She told Lucreta how as a child she had admired her big dimple and was even jealous at times when she got so many compliments for it. She then asked if she still had that special birthmark on her arm, pretending not to have noticed it before. Lucreta obligingly rolled up the sleeve of her fuschia blouse, revealing the mark on her left arm.

She drank some of the lemonade, placing the half-full glass on the table, and continued the story. Lucreta was listening raptly, the only sound in the room was Deandra's voice. Deandra was being careful not to leave out any part of the story told to her by Aunt Clem concerning Lucreta. This was very important to complete the picture.

She repeated the story, starting with the meeting of Mr. G in the white suit, leading to the conception of her only child. She discussed the special identifications on the baby's arm and on one cheek, the coining of the name Lukie, and how she lost contact with her pretty Lukie.

By this time Lucreta's body was convulsing with emotion. She stood and started to pace the floor of Deandra's living room, then went into the bathroom and slammed the door.

Although Deandra realized that it was a very sensitive and delicate matter that she had just revealed to Lucreta, she was a bit surprised about her friend's immediate reaction. She hoped she had not said too much to her, thereby opening a Pandora's box. She remembered reading about some adopted children who didn't want to know their biological parents. She comforted herself with the recollection that Lucreta had earlier expressed a desire to know who her mother was.

She walked to the French door and looked outside, then went back and sat down.

When Lucreta returned to the living room, her eyes were red, she was still crying. Deandra wasn't so sure anymore how to start a conversation with Lucreta, and felt that it would be better for her to be quiet and let Lucreta handle the situation her way.

Lucreta sat on the sofa, turned to Deandra, and said softly, "Deandra, I could do with something stronger than lemonade."

The only thing she had stronger than lemonade was wine. She went to the kitchen and returned with two glasses of local wine for herself and Lucreta. Lucreta almost emptied the glass in one long swallow. Deandra wondered silently if her friend was an alcoholic, but pushed the idea out of her mind feeling that she would have wanted something strong herself had she been in Lucreta's place.

She went and got the wine bottle and left it on the table. Lucreta refilled her glass and started to talk. "You know something, Deandra? Sometimes we search for the truth and when we find it we are not ready to deal with it. What I am trying to say is, truth can result in shock, for although I wanted to know about my natural mother, not in my wildest dream did I expect to meet her this way! As you talked, I felt shocked and numb."

"I'm sorry I started this thing, Lucreta, maybe it's a coincidence and not the truth you are seeking."

"No, Deandra, I think this revelation is true. What shocked me was finding my mother in this condition. It is true, blood is thicker than water. Aunt Clem is my mother and that was the special tie that gave me a feeling of attachment to her. I thank God for sending you to me Deandra, now I can reconcile my mixed and split feeling of being abandoned by a woman who did not want me. Thank you for helping me to find my natural mother."

She was trying to be logical and understanding as Deandra had suggested, and as the afternoon progressed she was able to understand that she was the product of love, even though it was one-sided and her father was selfish. In her logic and rationalization, she felt that had her father not given her love, education, and an excellent home, her life and present situation would have been much different.

She tried to think back to the story in the *Bible* where two people claimed one child. The matter could only be resolved when it was suggested that the child be cut in two halves. The mother gave up her claim, similar to Aunt Clem's giving her up to avoid problems that she alone couldn't handle.

Lucreta asked for Deandra's support and advice as to whether or not she should reveal her true identity to Aunt Clem. The two friends examined and reexamined the situation as Deandra told her that such a decision could only be made by her. They later decided to delay any revelation until their next visit to the old woman.

CHAPTER NINE

In the days following Lucreta's discovery of her mother's identity, she found herself more involved with social issues. She had joined the Poverty Alleviation drive and had organized a program to collect and distribute clothes to the needy. She was so involved in outside activities that Daniel and the children began to be jealous of the organizations that were keeping her away from them. On the other hand, Daniel was proud to see his wife taking more of an interest in the depressed areas of the community, and told her so.

One Saturday morning when Lucreta had grabbed a slice of bread, leaving the ackee and saltfish untouched, Aunt May, her housekeeper, began to scold her. "Mrs. C, yu will get bad stomach if yu continue to hurry an' don't eat a good breakfast. Yu never use to rush so much. Furthermore, yu losing weight, soon yu will lose your nice shape."

"Stop fussing, Aunt May. I'm just trying to help out some people. I'll be okay, don't worry about the shape, too much hips is as bad as having none, mine is a little nuf," answered Lucreta, smiling.

"Okay ma'am, if you say so," said Aunt May.

In Nufuma, a woman without a nice rounded behind was viewed as lacking an important aspect of beauty. Lucreta was well-rounded and felt that missing an occasional meal wouldn't affect her hips.

* * *

It had only been two weeks since they had last visited the old woman. When they returned to the one-room cottage, the change in her condition was dramatic. Although still coherent, she was now confined to her bed, requiring assistance even to feed herself.

The health worker was at the house when they arrived and explained that Aunt Clem's health was rapidly deteriorating. Her mood, however, was still stable and she was an easy patient to care for. There was only one thing that was almost an obsession with her and that was the wish to see her pretty Lukie.

Lucreta touched Deandra on her shoulder and suggested that they go outside for a moment. There Lucreta decided that this was the right time for her to reveal herself to her biological mother.

Mrs. McKenzie was asked to leave the two friends alone with the old woman in the sickroom for a while. Aunt Clem was lying on her back with her sunken eyes closed. Her face was pale and drawn. Deandra touched her forehead and called her name.

The old woman opened her eyes and smiled before speaking. "De Lawd sen' me fren again, so glad to see yu my child. Me only other wish is to lay me eyes pon my Lukie."

Deandra drew the chair close to the bed and sat down to talk with the old woman.

"Aunt Clem, I have a nice surprise for you."

"Me don't need much surprise now, all me need is me Lukie."

"Do you remember my friend who visited you a few times?"

"Yes, dat nice lady, how could I forget her? There's something special 'bout her."

"Well Aunt Clem, I think that nice lady is your Lukie."

The old woman's eyes widened as she tried to raise herself from the pillow but fell back.

Deandra stroked her hand and tried to calm her as she moved away, making room for Lucreta.

Lucreta sat in the chair. She placed Aunt Clem's wrinkled hand into her palm and spoke softly. "Aunt Clem, I'm Lukie, your baby . . . you are my real mother. I'm so glad I found you," said Lucreta in a choking voice as she tried to hold back the tears.

The old woman held her hand tenderly, stuttering from excitement, and softly spoke, "Don't play games wid me cause me too weak now for anybody to fool. Show me a sign, let me feel de dimple."

Lucreta told her about her late father, Mr. Green, then showed her the birthmark on her left arm. She then directed the old woman's fingers to her dimpled cheek. Aunt Clem tried to encircle her daughter's face, but needed some help. Lucreta had to bend forward to allow her mother to caress her face. She was satisfied then that the woman sitting at her bedside was her baby and said, with tears trickling down her face, "Tank yu Jesus, yu answer me prayers. I am ready to go whenever yu ready for me."

Deandra left the room so that mother and daughter could be alone, and stood with Miss McKenzie on the concrete slab in front of the one-room house, overlooking Golden Valley. She thought about the unpredictability of life and the unfolding of an almost unbelievable drama that she had just witnessed.

The reaction of the old woman on seeing her lost daughter made a lasting impression on Deandra. She recalled hearing of people who were dying, but would somehow hold on to life until that last important wish was granted. She had also read that it was called bargaining. She wondered if Aunt Clem had bargained with God and was now ready to give up her fight for life, or if she, Deandra, was exhibiting the fear of death and dying.

She was not the only one who had a strange feeling or premonition following the meeting of mother and daughter. Lucreta, having had the experience of her father's demise, could not help thinking about the possibility of facing another crisis in her life. After all, everyone in Nufuma knew the signs and signals of death. She dreamed of her father, dressed in his black suit and white bow tie, and that kind of dream was a sure sign that tragedy was on its way. Surely, seeing her real mother lying on her back in that bed typified death knocking at her door.

Lucreta's visits to Aunt Clem became very regular. Those visits were like a soothing salve on an aching wound to both the old woman and her daughter. One afternoon, Aunt Clem asked Lucreta to bring Deandra with her when next she visited. Lucreta relayed the message and arranged with Deandra to visit on the following day.

When Deandra and Lucreta arrived at the small cottage, the look on Miss McKenzie's face gave them the feeling that something had happened.

As they reached the door of the little house, Miss McKenzie whispered, "She is no longer with us."

Deandra and Lucreta went into the room where the old woman looked as though she was sleeping. As Miss McKenzie pulled the white sheet down from Aunt Clem's face, the two women bowed their heads in silence for a moment, then left the room.

Aunt Clem had finally gotten her wish, she had always said that she wanted to breathe her last breath in that small rustic room that she had helped to build with her own calloused hands.

When Deandra stepped on the concrete slab and looked down Golden Valley, the sun had just shifted and was shining in the valley. The view reminded her of the conversations she had had with Aunt Clem at that very spot.

"Look down the valley," said Deandra softly to Lucreta. "These are some of the special but simple things that Aunt Clem enjoyed."

"What a beautiful place, Deandra. My visits with Aunt Clem were early afternoons, before the sun got to the valley, and I never really caught this view. It's breathtaking."

"Aunt Clem had told me," explained Deandra, "that when the sun was in the valley, that was the time of day she talked with God. I wonder if she died talking with God."

"Did she really say that, Deandra?"

"She sure did, Lucreta. She was a very special woman."

Both of them left in Lucreta's red car. Lucreta drove slowly through the narrow dirt lane that led from the one-room house to the main road, then dropped off Deandra at her house.

Deandra was very upset, something important had gone out of her life. She finally calmed herself and accepted the fact that life was nothing more, nothing less, than borrowed time.

With all the development that had overtaken Nufuma, some old traditions remained. For it didn't matter whether you were young or old, rich or poor, when a Nufuman died, the news got around and people came from far and near to perform certain rituals.

All the seniors in Happy Grove had gotten together to help organize a wake for Aunt Clem. Men and women from other communities came and erected a tent, using green bush to cover the top. Everybody volunteered food; some brought fried fish, some curried goat and boiled green bananas, some fried bammy and bread, and some white rum.

Deandra had not experienced a wake in Nufuma before and this was indeed an eye-opener and an education for her. The night of the wake, there was a man who automatically became the leader of the wake. He had a bottle of white rum, a candle, a drinking glass, and a hymnal placed on a table. The man's name was Brother Moses, he was well-known as a great singer and an organizer of wakes. Before he started, he called out to the crowd of people who were in the tent.

"We are gathered here to pay respect to Aunt Clem by keeping dis wake, or set up, which ever yu prefer. Before we begin to sing, we mus' bless the earth an' feed de spirit."

He poured some of the white rum into the glass, then poured some to the east, some to the west, some to the north, and some to the south. When Brother Moses had finished pouring the rum on the ground, he drank some.

The wake was officially opened for singing. All the men and some women got themselves paper cups to get their rum. Brother Moses started to sing and, as he sang, he read verses from the hymnal for the crowd to follow. The singing was beautiful and whenever anyone went off-key, Brother Moses put his hands to his ears and took the lead so that the singing would be harmonized.

People sang, ate, and drank from 10 p.m. to 6 a.m., for three consecutive nights. There was a man who came every night with his guitar which he played sometimes. Deandra learned that the man was a Mr. Proudfoot, a professional wake follower; he would travel miles to sing at anyone's wake.

Lucreta never attended the wake, but she sent plenty of food and drinks to feed the people. The funeral expenses were handled by her, as a volunteer worker for deprived and underprivileged people. Deandra wondered whether or not Daniel knew the relationship between his wife and the old woman, but as far as she was concerned, that was strictly Lucreta's life and she had no intention of intruding on it.

During the planning of the funeral, the community of mostly senior citizens made certain that Aunt Clem would be buried in the right direction, facing paradise, because if she was buried the wrong way, her spirit or duppy would haunt the village. Aunt Clem was buried in front of the one-room cottage, overlooking Golden Valley on a sunny afternoon in March.

For Deandra, the two weeks following the funeral passed slowly. The days were dull and uneventful with Aunt Clem no longer around. But before she finished that chapter in her book, she felt she needed to make one last visit to the mango tree.

As she turned the key to lock the door of her apartment, Lucreta drove up unexpectedly.

"Hi, Deandra, I'm so glad I got here before you left," said Lucreta who was standing in the driveway.

"Your timing was perfect, another five minutes and I would have been gone."

"I really should have telephoned, but it was difficult getting through, so I took the chance and came unannounced. I hope I won't get in your way?"

"It's no big deal. If you don't mind walking through the bush and on a dirt road, you are welcome to join me."

The two friends talked as they walked through the short cut to the special spot.

"If you remember, I told you how Aunt Clem provided me with information for my book, but I never mentioned where we met on those occasions. Well I'm going to that place to say farewell and to close that chapter in my life."

"Truth is stranger than fiction," said Lucreta. "After all I've missed out on with Aunt Clem, I'm now getting the chance to tread upon the path where she shared so much of her private life with you."

They were both silent as they went under the tree that was then laden with young fruits and blossoms. Deandra pointed out the stump that the old woman had used as a stool. It was smooth and shiny as a result of regular use by the old woman. She watched as Lucreta touched the stump then sat on it. Deandra walked some distance away from the tree and her friend. She again felt lucky for having arrived in Nufuma at the time that she did, everything seemed to have meshed so well.

As they walked back on the narrow dirt road, Lucreta told her how sitting under the tree reminded her of some of her happy childhood days. She also had a sensation that Aunt Clem had been sitting there smiling with pleasure to see her daughter.

When they reached Deandra's place, Lucreta did not linger. She headed immediately for Embers Glade. Deandra went directly to her desk and wrote:

". . . Life is more than a drama
It's a happening that constantly changes
It grasps you where you least expect it
And lands you in places you never imagined;

Two halves meet to make a whole one
But then it comes to an end
With only one half, and no one can prevent it.

The next letter from Marion Boggs grated on her daughter's nerves. Deandra felt her mother had started to sound like a broken record, constantly gnawing at her about how great Paul was. She stopped reading the letter, recalling how on one special occasion when her mother wanted to emphasize her point she had lectured her.

"You must never forget how things were rough when we came to New York, Deandra. We didn't have an apartment of our own; we stayed with family. The first winter was wicked, chile. Remember how I used to tie up your head, then pull down the knitted cap over your ear lobes so they wouldn't freeze? You would take off the tie-head as soon as you saw the kids from your school because they'd tease you. I never bothered you about it though. I did all kinds of work before I landed that very good and well-paying job in Fashion Centre in Manhattan. I looked after other people's pickney, old people and worked in a factory packing pencils.

"One day a rich woman by the name of Mrs. Grimes saw me in a woolen suit that I made, without any of those paper patterns. She didn't believe that I had made the suit, so she gave me a dress to make for her. The dress was a hit. Her friends liked it and she took me to see the manager of a designing place on Seventh Avenue. And that's how I got where I am today. So don't make a fool of yourself, walk good and look straight ahead. Never forget this, chile. Do the right thing."

Deandra finally disengaged herself from the past and resumed reading the letter in which her mother had concluded with profuse apology, "Well Deandra, I hope you understand that I'm not in the least trying to run your life nor to tell you who to choose for a mate, but just the same, I think I know a good man when I see one, and I see one in Paul. Please forgive me if I've overstepped my boundary, but you must know that you're all I have. Your loving mother."

Deandra finally folded the letter, returned it to the envelope, then turned her attention to her writing.

She had not realized that she'd been writing for so long until the telephone rang. When she looked as her watch it was indicating five p.m. The connection was bad, and when Deandra picked up the receiver she could hear only static. "I can't hear you, Jeff. The connection is bad."

"Hang up and I'll dial again."

Deandra did as Jeff suggested and they were reconnected.

"So, what's been happening over at Lucky Pond since I left?" inquired Jeff.

"Catching up with my writing and thinking of you of course."

Sounds as though you're very busy accomplishing a lot, especially the thinking about Jeff."

"So, how about you? What's happening over there Jeff?"

"Things have gone the way I had hoped. I'm quite pleased. I'll be home in another day or so. Oh, by the way, I picked up a paperback at the airport on my way out. It talked about polygamous relationships. Thought you might be interested in that topic."

"I'd love to read it if you haven't thrown it out," commented Deandra laughingly.

"Without a doubt, you'll have that paperback."

They chatted for a while and then Jeff remarked, "It's eleven p.m. where I am, so I'll say good night and sweet dreams until I get back."

As Jeff walked down the ladder of the South American plane that Friday evening at Nufuma's airport, it was raining heavily. His regular taxi driver greeted him and took his luggage to the car. Despite the heavy rain, they had made good time driving.

Jeff was in his house by ten p.m. There were four messages indicated on his answering machine, but he had decided not to listen to any until the following day, after he had gotten a good night's sleep.

He had just stepped out of the shower when the phone rang. He ignored answering it and listened to the message that was being recorded.

"Hi Jeff, this is Sandra. Been trying to reach you all week, but I suspect you're away or with the lady from foreign. I heard you've been seen all over the place with her. You musn't forget, new broom sweeps clean, but the old one knows the corners. Call me darling, I have something nice planned for both of us on Sunday."

Jeff turned off the light, went to bed, and slept soundly. When he got out of bed it was six o'clock Saturday morning. He switched on the machine and listened to the messages. Three of them were from Sandra.

Sandra was a charming and attractive woman, lots of fun to be with. Jeff had taken her out occasionally and had enjoyed himself. However, he kept her at a distance. Her interests, where he was concerned, were far too obvious and they did not fit with his plans for the future. He cleared his head and called Deandra.

"Must I assume that you're home, or still in South America," Deandra teasingly remarked as she talked with Jeff over the phone.

"I'm relying on your strong sense of telepathy, my dear."

"How great it would be to be telepathic. That way, I wouldn't have to guess what some people are up to."

"And do I know any of those people you are referring to?"

"That shall remain my secret. Anyway, did you manage to get some sleep after your arrival?"

"Most definitely. I'm well-rested, ready to challenge even you. By the way, have I taken you to my private hide-a-way on the south coast?"

"I can't recall your taking me to the south coast Jeff."

"Tell you what D, how about us driving down tonight and returning tomorrow evening? By doing that we will be together while I unwind."

Before Deandra could get a word in, Jeff had said so long and was on his way to the office to check on what had transpired during his absence.

Deandra had two choices. She could either refuse to go to the coast or prepare herself for the short trip. She finally voiced her opinion in a monologue by describing Jeff as outrageously unpredictable, but charming.

She wondered what life would be like living with him, which brought her back to the reality of his marital status. She quickly pushed the thought aside and set out to surprise him with a Spanish dish known as Rella.

The meal consisted of rice, mixed seafood, green peas, onions, scallions, Nufuman herbs, and some Jamaican jerk seasoning, all cooked in one exotic dish and served with a tossed salad.

Jeff arrived about four o'clock in the afternoon at Deandra's just when she was almost through cooking. He had intended for them to dine out before leaving for the coast, but as soon as he entered the apartment, the aroma of the exotic meal entered his nostrils, causing him to remark, "Someone is being super creative again."

They greeted each other with a kiss. Jeff took a couple of steps backward and surveyed Deandra from head to toe, then asked as he moved closer and held her tightly, "Have you been dieting? You look thinner since last I saw you D."

Deandra tingled with excitement and tried to loosen his grip around her waist. He kissed her again and said, "I'll be a good boy, but may I see what you're creating in the kitchen that's stimulating my taste buds?"

He followed her to the kitchen and she showed him the food that was now ready to be served.

Deandra had outdone herself with that meal. It was an excellent dinner. As Jeff sat across the dining table from her he couldn't help mentioning, "You know something, I was a dinner guest at one of my South American friend's last week. They served a similar dish, except that this is nicer. Anyhow, his wife explained that it was a traditional Spanish dish. I didn't expect to be fed this dish by a lady in Nufuma. I'll remember this dinner when I'm retired to a rocking chair." He laughed raucously.

Deandra smiled, thanked him for his compliments, and inquired, "Have I told you what that laugh of yours does to me?"

"I'm afraid not, Miss Boggs. Do tell."

"Your kind of laugh is what I call a belly-bottom laugh. It stirs up something inside of me, a sort of warm and relaxed feeling."

As Jeff looked at her, he couldn't resist the urge to touch her. He pushed back his chair, went over to Deandra, and gently bit her on the back of her neck, saying, "This completes the most delicious meal I've ever had."

After dinner, they relaxed with a cup of demitasse each, made from the imported Jamaican Blue Mountain coffee. Jeff had become so comfortable around Deandra that he had no compunction in taking off his shoes and lying down on the overstuffed sofa in her living room. While he did just that, Deandra got ready for the trip.

They left Lucky Pond about seven-thirty that evening and arrived at Jeff's villa around nine-thirty. The villa was located in a rural area, far removed from the hustle and bustle of the town. The road to the hide-a-way was unpaved, surrounded by tall trees on either side.

As they drove, Jeff explained that the area was preserved to protect birds, but once a year bird shooting was allowed. The only requirement was a valid license.

The villa was built almost on the beach, with a lovely sun porch, large enough to accommodate four people. The villa housekeeper had made certain that everything was in place for Mr. Boles when he arrived. There was a variety of drinks, ranging from bottled water to Nufuman rum.

The place was equipped with color televisions, a large audio component system with CD changer in the living room, and a remote TV and VCR in the bedroom. It was sparsely furnished, but very comfortable with colorful lounging chairs and a sofa in the living room.

Jeff checked to make sure that everything was right before they sat down to enjoy their evening in Hide Away. He fixed himself a rum drink, poured Deandra a glass of wine, then joined her on the balcony.

Except for the white foam that lay on top of the calm sea, it was a flat surface of darkness. They sipped their drinks in silence, sitting next to each other, holding hands.

The silence was broken when Jeff spoke softly. "Look darling, there's a ship passing by."

He went and found binoculars for her.

"How enchanting," remarked Deandra, "and romantic for lovers on board."

"But not to be compared with us, my darling," Jeff interjected.

"Yes," she sighed and snuggled up to him.

A few minutes later they had moved into the living room.

They sat on the sofa with Jeff's head in Deandra's lap as they enjoyed the music. The touch of Deandra's fingers passing through Jeff's hair was rather soothing and helped him to unwind.

They finally went to bed around one o'clock that morning.

When they awoke, the air was fresh, the sunlight was dimmed by floating clouds. Jeff yawned, then wrapped his arms around Deandra and whispered with a mischievous smile, "How was your night at Hide Away, Miss Boggs?"

Deandra snuggled closer to him murmuring, "More than anticipated. This place is indeed what the name infers. And how was your night, Jeff?"

"Do you really need an answer to that? You're a deep one, but I'll paraphrase you . . . beyond my expectations."

He kissed her and, before she knew it, their bodies were wrapped around one another.

Jeff showered and in a few minutes he was standing beside the bed handing Deandra a glass of orange juice.

"Thank you darling," she said.

Jeff resumed his morning toilet while Deandra climbed out of bed and plugged in the coffee percolator. She went into the bathroom and slapped him on his behind saying, "This is the greatest body I've ever seen."

They showered together, completed their morning toilet, and settled down to read the newspaper while they had coffee.

"Would you mind if we went for a swim before having brunch, D?" asked Jeff.

"That sounds perfect to me," she replied.

They both continued to read. The paper had been carrying a series on ethical conduct in business. Deandra directed Jeff's attention to the article.

"So, what's your idea about the discussion on ethics these days, Jeff?"

Jeff ran his fingers through his thick black hair, faced Deandra, and replied, "Well, the way I view ethics is strictly within certain limits."

"And what are those limits, may I ask, sir?

"Everyone abides by some kind of ethical code. Sometimes it can be twisted, depending on the situation."

"Situation, like what?

"For example, as a lawyer and business man I'm supposed to function under two codes, and sometimes one might even run counter to the other."

"That sounds like a catch twenty-two, Jeff, which brings to mind the situation of a man who has a wife and a lover at the same time."

"Leave it to you to think about that too."

"I think it's important. When a man or a woman cheats in a relationship it shouldn't be seen any differently than the merchant who cheats his customers."

Jeff knitted his brow and continued, "In a business there's an option, either you accept the offer or refuse it. In your scenario on relationships, when no one is hurt I don't think ethics is involved."

"Why is it not, Jeff?"

"Because, my dear, both women may be equally in love with the man, as much as he is in love with them."

"That sounds like a power-play situation to me."

"In what way, D?"

"The way I see it, the one who wins is usually the one with the most power. Like the consumer who may not have a choice of not purchasing a special product, both women may be circumstantially unable to get out of the situation."

"I won't accept that view. The women have options too, but it could be that thing called love, my dear," said Jeff winking at her.

"That woman issue is a very complex one, Jeff, especially if the woman is dependent."

"And what if it was the other way around, D?"

"I'd think the same. After all, Jeff, women are not angels."

"You've made a strong argument, but tell me how you avoid violating your journalistic trust or ethics when you're given certain information that may very well include heinous crimes, but because of the confidentiality code you are not supposed to divulge it. Is it very different than the man with a wife and a lover?"

Deandra sighed before retorting, "Well Jeff, you've proven your point and I admit that there's a gray area that journalists tread and that's why we have smart lawyers like you."

She looked at her watch and exclaimed, "I didn't realize we've been talking so long!"

Jeff put aside the paper, pulled Deandra to him, kissed her, and whispered, "Yes Miss Boggs, we've redefined the ethical codes in two hours. Seeing it is so late, why don't we go over to the restaurant for brunch and swim later?"

"I'm all for that, Mr. Boles."

The small dining room was almost empty when they entered. As they walked toward a corner table for two, a couple who had been sitting by the window waved to Jeff and he responded.

The waitress told them the brunch menu from memory. They ordered their meal and when they had finished eating, they walked down to the beach.

The sky had suddenly become dark as they walked along before going into the water. It wasn't long before Jeff waded into the water and swam away from Deandra, who stood watching him.

It had started to drizzle when Deandra finally ventured in and before she knew what had happened, Jeff suddenly reappeared in front of her and pulled her further into the water. He lifted her and dipped her into the salt water.

They swam for about twenty minutes then returned to shore as the drizzle became heavier. They walked slowly in the light rain back to the villa.

When they had showered and changed into comfortable clothes, Jeff rested for sometime while Deandra read the paperback he had brought her.

It was still early in the afternoon when Jeff proclaimed that he felt like a youthful athlete ready to run a mile. Deandra had finished reading the paperback and quietly mused about the author's attitude toward man-woman relationships.

"How did you find the book?" Jeff asked her teasingly.

"I find it not only patronizing, but biased and sexist."

"Well, well! It really got to you, D," Jeff remarked with a look of mischief in his eyes. "On the contrary I found the book to be charming and outrageously intimate."

"Don't tell me, Jeff Boles, that some folks are a little more equal than others, especially where men consider it right to have a harem of women, yet at the same time each woman is expected to be faithful to the lord of the harem."

Deandra was really reacting strongly to the book. Jeff was enjoying his harmless teasing. Her eyes seemed larger, he thought, as she protested the author's treatment of women.

"Well Jeff, how about making things a little more equal? If memory serves me right, I think I once read about a society of polyandry where women were allowed to have more than one husband or lover and there was nothing immoral about that."

Now then that's quite extreme. Personally, I'd never share you with another man, but seriously speaking, people usually accept their cultural beliefs and practices."

"That may be so, Jeff, but our culture preaches one thing and does another. Men can philander without remorse, but women must not, even though many are breaking the barrier despite male resistance."

Jeff had slightly changed the topic and asked, "How about the age difference that the writer briefly touched on?"

Deandra decided to turn the table around and be the teaser.

"I'd say he approached it quite logically. Why shouldn't an older woman be in love with a younger man?"

"I won't argue about that," said he whimsically. "I would want you even if you were seventy, although sometimes you sound like a hundred."

"I'm going to strangle you, Jeffrey Boles," laughed Deandra as she moved over to the lounge chair he occupied.

Jeff turned and pulled her down in his lap. He looked at her intensely. The look in her eyes made him conclude that he had penetrated and demolished her resistance to falling in love with him.

There was a broad smile on his face that came from his sense of accomplishment. Deandra stirred in his lap and attempted to get away. Jeff held her face between his hands and kissed her longer than he'd ever done before. Their hearts pulsated. He lifted her in his arms and carried her inside the apartment.

At dinner that evening, as they dined courtesy of room service, they both ate heartily. The clean, country air mingled with salt water had stimulated their appetites. They ate in silence, interrupted only by the cutlery rubbing against the dinner plates. They were both savoring the last couple of hours left in the tranquil surroundings before leaving for home.

When they had finished eating and pushed the plates away, Jeff spoke. "Well, what's your honest opinion about this little place?"

"It's the ultimate for getting away from a hectic schedule. It has recharged my battery. I think it is eminently suitable for someone like you who is constantly on the go. I just love it, Jeff."

"I thought you'd like it, and I'm glad you do. I must tell you what a fantastic job you've done to help me unwind."

"How fantastic was it, my dear?"

"It was a lost weekend, and sweet. Never had sex so good!"

"Although it's hard to believe that, I'm pleased to hear it."

"Darling, our love making was outrageously delicious. You really set me on fire," said Jeff blowing her a kiss.

"You were terrific too, Jeff. I enjoyed it a lot."

By the time they had packed their bags and Jeff had locked up the villa, it was eight o'clock in the evening. By half past eight they had driven away from the Hide Away Villa. There was hardly any traffic on the road. They listened to reggae and jazz as Jeff drove.

He must have driven sixty miles an hour, for they arrived at Deandra's place by nine forty-five p.m. Jeff arrived at Embers Glade within half an hour after dropping off Deandra. This allowed him sufficient time to pack his brief case for Monday morning before retiring for the night.

CHAPTER TEN

With the friendship of Claire at the village restaurant, Lucky Pond had taken on a new dimension; the place seemed to have grown larger. Claire knew the local places where Deandra could meet people who still held onto some old customs they brought from Africa.

She invited Deandra to an outdoor church and instructed her to dress comfortably and to be sure to wear flat shoes as they would have to climb a steep hill to reach the church.

When Deandra drove up to Claire's house that Sunday afternoon, there were two other women waiting to be taken to the church. One was Claire's mother and the other was her aunt. The two older women informed Deandra that such churches were dying out due to competition with new religions. They lamented the fact as well as the attitude of their husbands who didn't embrace the old time church any longer.

The church was indeed outdoors. As they walked up the hill, they could hear the beating of drums and the harmonious singing. The church was a large thatched roof tent. There were benches on both sides of the church, a simple table covered with a white cloth, and a jar of water in the center covered with a piece of red and black cloth.

Most of the congregation were women. The lead preacher was a relatively young man named Brother Solomon, whose head was intricately wrapped in layers of red cloth. Sister Katinga, a handsome middle-aged woman, was his assistant.

Deandra followed the three women into the church as Claire pointed to the seventh row on the right side. There was just enough space to accommodate the four of them. Some of the women were dressed in white, with their heads wrapped in black, red, and white.

By the time they had settled in their seats the drumming and singing had stopped. Brother Solomon stood and read a passage from the *Bible*, then sprinkled some of the consecrated water from the clay pot around the table as a libation to honor the ancestors.

As Brother Solomon poured the libation, one of the women sitting in the front row suddenly stood up and shouted, "Praise de Lord and peace to our ancestors."

The congregation swayed from side to side and shouted "Peace!"

Finally the congregation became quiet and Brother Solomon resumed his preaching. "Today we praise your name Lord, for all the blessings big an' small. We give praise for our meeting together. We worship you because we know that it's easier for a camel to go through the eye of a needle Lord, than for a rich man without compassion to get into heaven. Hallelujah! God is good to us. Prepare yourself and walk away from wickedness and evil doers, for as there's a tomorrow, the wicked will not go unpunished. Praise the Lord!"

The congregation shouted in a chorus. "Praise the Lord! Hallelujah."

Brother Solomon preached for a while, then shifted his attention to where Deandra was sitting and said, "Bless our visitor today, Lord."

Some of the women looked at Deandra and responded with a soft "Amen."

As Brother Solomon preached about repentance, his voice became an intonation. Members began to participate more by swaying to the sound of his voice. One woman stood, raised her arms, and started to speak in tongues, while Brother Solomon invoked the Holy Spirit to come into the hearts and souls of everyone present.

Brother Solomon then ended the preaching and walked over to the sister who, by then, was in a trance and making utterances in tongues or an unknown language. The women whose heads were wrapped made a circle around the woman who was in the trance. Brother Solomon then sprinkled her with some consecrated water. Drums roared; the women with wrapped heads moved in circular motion as their wide dresses swirled around them. They jumped, sang, and shouted to the beat of the drums.

Finally the woman in the trance, opened her eyes and shouted, "Thank you, Father. Hallelujah!"

Sister Katinga held the woman's hands.

As Deandra absorbed the rituals and drumming, she felt as though she was drifting into another world. She resisted and gradually pulled herself back to her surroundings. She listened to the melodious voices of the congregation as they sang and danced in praise of God, asking eternal rest for their ancestors.

At the end of the service, Deandra was introduced to Sister Katinga and Brother Solomon. Sister Katinga was a soft-spoken woman. She greeted Claire, Claire's mother and aunt as mutual friends.

Deandra was invited to have lunch with the congregation. The lunch was very much like a banquet. Members had brought their own special dishes.

On their way home, Mrs. Cones, Claire's aunt, explained that Sister Katinga was an esteemed spiritualist. She had been an excellent healer as well.

As Mrs. Cones described Sister Katinga, Deandra inquired, "Tell me Mrs. Cones, how does one go about getting spiritual advice from Sister Katinga?"

"She usually sees people through recommendations. You sound as though you'd like her advice, Miss Boggs."

"As a matter of fact," answered Deandra, "I'd like that very much."

As she ruminated privately, Deandra recalled hearing about obeah men, now she wanted to find out if a woman could do as well with her special gift as the men reportedly did.

Before she had dropped off her three passengers, she thanked Claire for taking her to the Outdoor Church and planned to follow up with a possible visit to Sister Katinga.

As she drove home alone, Deandra couldn't help thinking about the similarity between the ritual she'd experienced at the church, and some of the African dances she'd seen in her travels.

It had been over a week since Deandra and Jeff had been together at his villa and they were equally eager to see each other. No sooner had she entered the apartment when the telephone rang. Jeff was on the line.

"I've been trying to reach you since twelve today. Have you

covered the entire island by this?"

"Not totally," answered Deandra, "but I must admit that my education is expanding."

"That sounds interesting. May I ask what area of your education is being enhanced, D?"

"The cultural aspect, but more specifically old time religious rituals."

"Don't tell me you're being converted to wrap-head church," replied Jeff teasingly.

"I don't think it's a matter of conversion, but rather my exposure to rituals that were practiced by my great-great-grandparents. Furthermore, if I'm going to do a good job, Nufuman old religious practices are intrinsically a part of the culture."

"All right, inquiring D, no one shall ever accuse you of being shallow."

"Thank you, Jeff, but the same goes for you. You're an amazing man."

"Oh! Tell me more."

"You are amazing in many ways. To begin with, your charming personality, your socioeconomic status, and your ability to attract beautiful women."

"I won't argue with that," laughed Jeff as he said good-bye.

Later that Sunday afternoon, Jeff picked her up in his brand new Saab. They dined at a Chinese restaurant and proceeded to see a show that was based on a rich uptown man having an affair with a young down-towner. The play was hilarious, and on their way to Embers Glade, Deandra teasingly asked, "Do you know anyone who could identify with the play, Jeff?"

Jeff looked at her quizzically then remarked, "Why would you want to know that? You know the saying, 'what you don't know, won't hurt you,' my darling."

During the course of the evening, they listened to music in Jeff's living room and talked about the performing artists they most admired.

"By the way D, I was intrigued by your reaction to McBanes' paperback. I've been thinking about the polyandrous system you mentioned. Do you believe it would make a difference?"

"Well, Jeff, you know as well as I do that in our society such a practice would not be allowed. But, for argument's sake, it could very well reduce the number of children who are cared for mostly by one parent."

"I'm afraid you've lost me. How could that be when it would be impossible to prove paternity?"

"That's just the point. The system would be based on everybody caring for the offspring to a certain extent. In that way, there would be, possibly, no fatherless children."

Jeff pulled her to him, kissed her, and said, "You're a hard nut to crack."

"Since we're on the topic of men-women boundaries, Jeff, how is your divorce coming along?"

"I was hoping you wouldn't ask this question just yet."

"Why?"

"Because I'd have liked to give you a more definite answer."

"It sounds as though you've been caught off-guard, Jeff."

"It's not that I'm caught off-guard, but I was hoping for a civilized and peaceful parting of the ways with Angelica. Obviously that's not her intention. My wife is protesting the divorce. This has left me only one recourse. According to Nufuman law, you can get your divorce after three years of separation."

"So, what time frame does that involve?" asked Deandra.

"Fifteen months to be exact, my dear . . . but that shouldn't have any bearing on us."

"Well I suppose not. By then I should be long gone out of your life."

"Will you stop saying such nonsense, D. Where do you think you can go where I can't find you? You told me I was the only man in Nufuma with whom you are involved. And, as for that guy you left in New York, he can just resign himself to his loss and back off, or challenge me," said Jeff as he squeezed her hand.

"I thought the days of gallantry had long gone."

Jeff was about to respond, but instead kept silent. He didn't want to give the impression that she was his number one woman and that he had fallen in love with her. He turned and asked, "Are you telling me that you're uncomfortable with our relationship?"

"All I'll say, Jeff, is that I wish it wasn't so."

"You're not making much sense, D. So why don't we drop this silly subject."

Jeff had to be at a board meeting by eight o'clock the following morning, so he decided to drive Deandra home soon after their discussion. Before he left her that night, he held her closely in his arms and whispered, "I love you, but you must be open-minded."

She locked the door and proceeded to write in her journal, "Love is great, but family is greater. I want to have children and a home of my own. Jeff is terrific, but there's a wife standing in the way."

The unique experience of the Outdoor Church was still fresh in Deandra's mind. This stimulated her interest in seeking out an audience with Sister Katinga. Claire was able to set up an appointment for her the following week at her house very near to the Outdoor Church.

As Deandra set out the following Tuesday morning to visit Sister Katinga, she had mixed emotions ranging from anxiety to ambivalence to intimidation. When she reached her destination, she felt a sense of relief.

The entrance to the house had white-washed rocks on both sides, with a mixture of colorful crotons behind them. The house was flat with a small porch in front. Honeysuckle flowering vines ran around it. As soon as the small volkswagen entered the driveway, a dog started to bark. A woman met Deandra, greeted her, and lead the way to Sister Katinga.

As soon as she entered the room, Sister Katinga stood and greeted her warmly. The room was large and airy, situated at the back of the house. There were two large cushions on the floor, on which Deandra and Sister Katinga sat. In the center of the semicircle was a Bible on which stood a glass of crystal clear water.

As soon as both women were seated, Sister Katinga was moved by the spirit. Her entire body shook. She spoke briefly in tongues, then leaned over to Deandra, pressed the back of her head and forehead with her hands, then sprinkled her face with water and spoke.

"Praise be to the Lord, my sister. I'm glad that you've been moved by the spirit to visit me today. Welcome to Hopewell."

Deandra smiled and replied with a soft. "Thank you, ma'am."

"Well, is there anything special that you'd like to ask or tell me, Miss Boggs?"

Deandra hadn't really thought of anything special and answered, "Not really, Sister Katinga, it may be good if you did an analysis of my life and from that you could base your advice."

Sister Katinga closed her eyes and her body moved with a jerking motion. She stood and walked around Deandra, then pulled her to a standing position. She moved around Deandra and passed her hands over her head, her arms, then the upper part of her body.

Both of them returned to sitting on the cushions, then Sister Katinga held Deandra's hands and started to talk. "You're an interesting young woman. You've been to many places and done quite a bit. But I see big, big things in store for you."

She patted Deandra's head and continued speaking. "You have something on your mind that's causing you confusion. You're not sure about what you really want to do. The spirit tells me your health is good now, but you must be careful. There's a woman in your life. I don't know if she's your mother or friend, but whoever she is, she loves you so much that it's hard to describe.

"You're a decent and quiet woman, but stubborn in your own way," Sister Katinga paused and smiled.

"I see children . . . your children. They'll be lovely children too."

She closed her eyes, stood, walked around Deandra, then resumed her sitting position.

"Men. Yes, men. I see men around you, but especially a white or near-white one, and interestingly one who is very black, and there's one who seems to be standing outside, looking in."

Sister Katinga spoke in tongues as her body moved to the spirit.

She returned to her monologue. "These men have power and plenty of love for you, miss. The choice is up to you. But they love you, out of this world. Be careful though, don't let anyone pressure you into doing things only to please them.

"I'm getting a signal that you are someone like an artist; sometimes you can do quite well and sometimes things are slow. It looks to me that the kind of work you do requires a lot of travel. Be careful how you travel."

During the reading, Deandra had experienced different levels of reaction. At times Sister Katinga sounded as though she was reading a part of her personal history. At times she was vague, leaving openings for wide conjectures while always advising safety.

Sister Katinga had finished talking when she turned and asked Deandra. "Are you wearing a plain gold ring, miss?"

"No, Sister. My ring has my birthstone."

"I'll use my plain ring then. I want you to pull a long strand of your hair and pass it through the ring, and hold it steadily in this glass of water," she said as she removed the glass of water from the *Bible*. "I will call out some letters of the alphabet and take it from there."

Deandra felt slightly anxious and intimidated.

Sister Katinga explained, "It's nothing to be nervous about. Just calm yourself, steady your hand as you hold on to the strand of hair."

Deandra held the strand of hair that passed through the plain gold ring. It sparkled in the crystal water. Sister Katinga passed her hand over the glass as she spoke in tongues. Deandra held steadily to the strand of hair on which the ring hung motionless.

Sister Katinga started her incantation. "Z, F, K, L."

At the mention of "L" the ring swung from side to side hitting the tumbler.

She then continued, "A, C, T, P, B."

She had scarcely ended saying "B" when the ring went into motion, even though Deandra's hand was steady.

Sister Katinga began again. "N, R, M."

With the mention of "M" the ring moved, but this time it didn't hit the glass.

Sister Katinga then said a brief prayer and terminated the procedure.

Deandra was genuinely shaken. Had she not been holding the ring, she would have sworn that there was deception involved. How, and why did the ring move? She wondered.

Sister Katinga seemed spent. She unwrapped her head, revealing her thick, graying black braids. "Well, Miss Boggs," she began, "how do you feel now?"

"To tell you the truth, I'm mystified about the gold ring phenomenon. Although my hand didn't move, the ring had its own momentum that was totally out of my control. I'm rather anxious to hear your explanations and the ramifications for me."

"Miss Boggs, the spirit is a powerful force. The water is life force. The spirit was able to pull from both of us and detect things we're not even aware of. The letters are only symbols for some of those things. Sometimes they are one hundred percent correct, depending on the individual I'm reading, and sometimes seventy percent right."

Deandra listened with her eyes bulging, then asked, "Sister Katinga, can you explain why the letters L, B, and M caused those reactions?"

"I want you to listen to me carefully. The first letter, L, without a doubt means plenty of love in your life . . . could be from a lover, lovers, or a parent. The letter, B, could mean more than one thing. It could be bigger and better things in store for you, as well as a baby. The last letter, M, is tricky. It could be something to do with your mother. I'm assuming you have one, or the future mother you'll be, or quite possibly, marriage. There are lots of exciting things in store for you, miss."

Deandra handed Sister Katinga the fee for her work, without any regrets, regardless of how prophetic her words really were.

When they stood, Sister Katinga asked, "Would you like to see my garden at the back of the house?"

"I'd love that."

They walked outside and moved among the fruit trees. Golden ripe tangerines hung on low branches. Sister Katinga picked some and gave them to Deandra to take home.

They talked about the Outdoor Church and its connection with the immediate community. The church played an important role for many families, ranging from counselling to helping to bury the dead of poor families.

Finally, the two women said good-bye. Deandra drove back home more relaxed yet amazed.

When she arrived home, she decided to take a nap which was quite unusual for her. Late that evening, after supper, she settled down and wrote her mother a revealing letter about her most recent exploits, before writing in her diary, "There's no time for boredom, and even if I was once unsure, today Sister Katinga gave me a lot of food for thought. Enough to keep me thinking, working and planning. Thoughts to increase my curiosity. And even though the predictions are vague, they will help me to be constantly searching, analyzing and open for new ideas and opportunities."

CHAPTER ELEVEN

The months that followed placed tremendous pressures on Jeffrey Boles and the business community in general. With the growing demand for coffee and cocoa beans, he had been spending more time away from Nufuma. He had also become involved in banking. He was indeed a powerful force to be reckoned with.

It was no secret by then that Deandra was the woman of his choice, even though other women were not to be discouraged. Sandra was one of those who wasn't about to give up easily. And why should she? After all, Jeff was a good catch and among the richest. She was jealous of Deandra and had no qualms about making her feelings known to Jeff, even though he had been distancing himself from her.

On one occasion she put aside diplomacy, and with sarcasm confronted Jeff directly. "Tell me darling," she asked, "what is it that your new friend has got that I haven't?"

Jeff evaded Sandra's question and replied, "You've got a lot going for you, Sandra. You're beautiful and intelligent. Just calm down and believe in yourself."

"Stop evading me, Jeff. You know damn well what I'm talking about. This woman has got you wrapped around her little finger. It's as though you were married to her."

Jeff had remained silent. Sandra finally calmed down and left, remembering the good times that she and Jeff once shared—and now this stranger had suddenly appeared to ruin it all.

Despite Deandra's self-assurance, her growing attachment to Jeff continued to gnaw at her independence, creating ambivalent feelings about her future. She worried about the existing possibilities in Nufuma for a young writer like herself, not to mention Jeff's marital status.

She shifted her thoughts and prepared for the fishing trip she had been planning with Claire and her friends. They went fishing in one of the old Arawak-type canoes. She felt like a child celebrating a birthday when she caught her first striped parrot fish.

As she helped to paddle the canoe, her thoughts returned to Sister Katinga. She remembered her explaining the water as a life-force, and there she was literally paddling against a force that was stronger than she.

That afternoon she went home with fish caught with her own hands.

She had just finished writing the day's events in the diary when the doorbell rang. She felt spent from the day's activities and was not really looking forward to any visit.

When she opened the door, Jeff was standing there. But before entering he remarked, "It might be better if I had a key to apartment 6A, wouldn't you say, D?"

"I hadn't given much thought to that," responded Deandra.

Not that he hadn't hinted about the key before, but Deandra felt that giving her apartment key to Jeff would deny her some of her private space. She had not yet reached the stage in her life where she would be willing to give up privacy.

When Jeff stepped into the apartment, the sun had begun to disappear behind the clouds. He stood by the French doors and remarked, "You know something, darling, I'll be missing this picturesque view for about a month and I'm savoring every moment of it in your apartment."

"It sounds as though you'll be heading for a long trip very soon."

"Yes. That's one of the reasons I'm here. I need to talk with you, but if it's not asking too much of you, could you throw a few things in your overnight bag and spend a couple of days at Embers Glade?"

"This is quite sudden, Jeff. It sounds serious too. It would have been better though, had you given me longer notice . . . Don't forget, I'm busy too."

"I know, but be a sport. This intended trip only came about after this morning's three-way, trans-Atlantic telephone conference.

This is something I've been working at for a long time and, finally, I've succeeded. I'm supposed to fly to Canada to attend some business discussions, then later I'll go to Tokyo to finalize the discussions with the Japanese group of business people. So I didn't have much of a chance to plan in advance."

"I'm happy for you, Jeff. Give me an hour or so to put a few things in order."

Deandra carefully put her notes in a locked drawer, packed her bag, and locked the windows while Jeff waited quietly on the sofa.

On their way to Embers Glade, she talked about her fishing expedition with Claire, extolling the healthy appearance and naturalness of the fishermen and their women.

Her exuberance was almost infectious, causing Jeff to say, "I feel cheated and left out. But seriously, I'm so glad that you are having a wonderful time. I'll see to it that you continue to have fun."

The two days at Jeff's place provided Deandra with greater insight as to the other side of him. She also made sure not to interfere in the housekeeper's role.

The first morning, before leaving for work, Jeff introduced her to Mrs. Cato, his housekeeper. "Mrs. C, I want you to meet my friend, Miss Boggs. Find out if there's any special food that she prefers and make sure she gets it."

With a questioning look on her face, Mrs. Cato replied, "All right Mr. Boles, I'll do as I'm told," then shifted her position and smiled at Deandra.

Jeff had asked Deandra to help him with some of his packing. At first she'd turned it over in her mind then asked, "What's your motive for asking me to help you pack, Jeff?"

"Don't tell me what I suspect you're thinking is true."

"What am I supposed to be thinking, Jeff?"

"That I don't value your time. I'm asking you because I feel comfortable with you. Furthermore, everything is in order, waiting to be put in the case."

"Okay Jeff, I accept the challenge."

The packing turned out to be easier than Deandra had expected. Jeff's clothes were compartmentalized and neatly arranged according to color scheme, causing Deandra to remark, "This guy is so organized that even his clothing arrangements are like a department store."

That evening when Jeff arrived home, as soon as he opened the door he called out, "D, I'm home!"

Mrs. Cato whispered to Malcolm the gardener. "Seems like Mr. B got it real bad for this lady. He never allowed any other woman to spend longer than a night in this house. She's a foreigner though." Mrs. Cato twisted the corners of her mouth, a sign of caution.

Deandra had just finished packing the last two pairs of socks and replied, "I'm in here, completing the packing you've psyched me into."

Jeff headed straight for the room, threw his jacket on the back of the lounging chair, held Deandra tightly around the waist and kissed her. He looked at the packed suitcase and gave his nod of approval.

"So, have I passed the packing test, Mr. Boles?" inquired Deandra.

"Most definitely my dear."

"Oh, I almost forgot. Here's a list of all the things I've packed for you, Jeff. Don't know where you may like to put it. Here's something that you might also find useful on your trip."

Jeff had been sitting beside her on the edge of the bed and waited silently for Deandra's surprise gift.

"It was by sheer accident that I found this Berlitz book on conversational Japanese. I hope it will help to make speaking the language a little easier for you."

Jeff reached for her hands and clasped them gently as he looked intensely at her. "You know the honest truth? This is the most beautiful and thoughtful gift I've ever received. You're a mind-reader. I've been trying to speak Japanese, but the progress has been slow. It's crucial that I communicate in Japanese over there as effectively as they do in English when in Nufumá. Thank you, my dearest . . . And about that list, you've got one on me. I've never before had a list made up for me. Where would you suggest I put it?"

"What about the bottom of the suitcase?"

"That sounds perfect, but wouldn't it require unpacking and repacking?"

"Guess what! Maybe I'm a mind-reader as you said. There's

already a list at the bottom of the suitcase; this is a copy for your briefcase," said Deandra, giggling like a girl.

"You've left me speechless, D," said Jeff before he went to take a shower.

Jeff had been suddenly transformed into an easygoing and uncomplicated man. He changed into a pair of yellow linen shorts and a red alligator shirt that matched Deandra's halter-top, bold print dress. He had Mrs. Cato serve them dinner on the veranda.

During dinner, he looked at Deandra seriously and asked, "Tell me, what's your theory on falling in and out of love?"

"That's a tall order, Jeff. I don't have an answer to your question."

"Let me rephrase the question. Why is it easier getting into than getting out of a situation, especially when it concerns love?"

"Odd that you should ask such a question."

"Why is it odd?"

"Because I always thought that Nufuman men played the major role in the ins and outs of love."

"In what way, and why only in Nufuma?"

"Well in America too, but even with all the changes that are occurring it would seem that it is still the man who makes the first approach or initial move in an intimate relationship. And, although I'm only guessing, I'd imagine that more men get out of the relationship."

"In a way you're correct, but there must be an element which makes it so difficult for some people to break the relationship."

"Could it be that the two people involved might be expecting too much of each other, sometimes far exceeding what each one is capable of doing for him or herself."

"That sounds logical enough, but why resist parting when there's no other way?"

"I'm not a psychologist, but I strongly believe that separating from what you've had causes a great deal of fear. It creates all sorts of emotions and even though it might be the best thing for both, one of the individuals might resist moving on."

"You've put your finger on it, D. It makes me think of the poet's line, 'Parting is such sweet sorrow.' Move on and cherish the memories, I'll add."

"So Jeff, what's your theory on love?" asked Deandra, laughing.

"How about love, romance, and sex."

"Not bad, not bad," repeated Deandra, "but couldn't we improve on that and make in love, romance, respect, and safe sex."

"Knew you wouldn't let me forget those nuisance condoms. My darling, I want you to have our baby. Can't you understand?"

"But that requires monogamous love, dear Jeff."

"Yes, Lady D, I've got the message. But you're warm, romantic, sexy, and monogamous and I love you logically," said Jeff, winking at her.

"All those accolades for poor little me who's competing with some of the most gorgeous Nufuman women."

"No more of that nonsense talk, D," answered Jeff as he kissed her on the forehead and gave her his devastating and mischievous look.

The evening had almost turned to night when they finally went inside. Jeff had completed his preparation for leaving the island in two days' time.

They were facing each other. Jeff whispered, "Shall we retire early tonight, dear?" The clock indicated that it was nine p.m. when they turned off the light.

They had not spent so much time before in caressing and exploring before love-making. They were both excited and Jeff's love-making could have kept her enthralled for hours. Jeff was extremely creative that night and Deandra responded in kind. They both revealed their fantasies without guilt and acted them out. They were spent but happy as their bodies coiled around one another.

Jeff whispered, "I'll dream about this night every night for one month, my dear."

Deandra kissed him on his neck and said, "This will remind you, my darling."

She stretched, then opened her eyes to see Jeff buttoning his shirt the following morning.

"Good morning. How did you manage to sneak out of bed without my knowing?" scolded Deandra.

"Because you were drugged, my dear. But how are you this morning, Miss D?"

"Fantastically good. So, tomorrow you'll be on your way to Canada."

"Yes, my dear."

The phone rang. Jeff ignored it and the answering machine recorded the message. "Darling this is Sandra. Please call me before the end of the day. Bye now."

Leave it to Sandra to call at this time, thought Jeff as he fixed his tie. This will only help to reinforce Deandra's suspicions about other female companions.

The sound of Sandra's voice not only created some suspicion in Deandra's mind, it brought on some jealousy. By the look on her face, Jeff sensed that she was upset. He bent down and kissed her. She quietly moved to the bathroom and began brushing her teeth.

"May I come in?" asked Jeff.

"Sure."

"Sorry about that phone call, sweetheart."

"That's okay."

"I'm glad you feel that way, but it's not okay. Anyway, it's impossible to stop people from calling me."

By then she'd finished brushing her teeth. She wiped her mouth with one end of the bath towel. "You're the most, darling," said Jeff. "I'll be home early." He kissed her and left.

An hour later, Deandra took her breakfast of fresh juice, coffee, and toast on the veranda. While she ate, she examined her reaction to Sandra's message for Jeff and told herself, "I suppose competing is as difficult as parting. Why should I be so upset, knowing well that Jeff is a sophisticated man of the world? Furthermore, in a matter of weeks I'll be in New York. Whether I return or not is another matter, but the fact is we'll be physically apart. Maybe, Deandra girl, you fit into yesterday's discussion about the complexities involved in moving out of a love relationship."

She then browsed through the newspaper. When she had finished eating, she took the breakfast tray into the kitchen where Mrs. Cato was busy preparing Jeff's going away dinner.

"Hi Mrs. Cato."

"Hello Miss Boggs," she replied, smiling broadly.

"Thank you for the breakfast."

"You're welcome miss, but that wasn't much of a breakfast. Young people nowadays are always watching their figures. My granddaughter is one of those who eats like a bird too."

Deandra smiled in acknowledgment, then remarked. "You look terribly young to be a grandmother, Mrs. C."

Mrs. Cato smiled, showing her almost untarnished white teeth, and replied, "Thank you, Miss Boggs. I had my children quite young. People used to tink that my first daughter was my sister."

"It's great to see a grandmother as young and attractive as you. See you later," replied Deandra as she left the kitchen.

As Mrs. Cato and Malcolm lunched they discussed Mr. Boles' lady friend briefly.

"Yu know something, Malcolm, this foreign lady is not bad at all. She's not stuck up. She even brought the breakfast tray to the kitchen and we had a nice little chat."

"I'm sure glad to heat dat she's okay because poor Mr. B did have a rough time with his wife before they separated."

"You're right, Malcolm. We must say a prayer for him, especially when he's taking dese long plane trips, that God will keep him safe and make him happy."

Deandra had time to write in her diary as she recalled the happenings of the last forty-eight hours.

"Yesterday's activities,
Gone, but not forgotten
Yesterday's relationship comes to an end,
Leaving some anguish and some pain,
But today brings a new approach . . .
Temperate speech softens the pain,
For today's opportunities can mend the aches."

When Jeff walked through the door, Deandra had just written the last line of her reflections.

"Hello there, my working friend."

Deandra looked up. "Hello to you. You're a man of your word. You were able to get away from the office as you'd planned."

"Remember? We believe in order and logic . . . But seriously, I need to unwind for this trip."

"That's realistic and intelligent planning, Jeff " retorted Deandra teasingly.

"Hope I've not interrupted your writing. I noticed you were involved when I came."

"You've not interrupted anything. I was just about finished. Would you be interested in hearing my written thoughts?"

"Most certainly, my dear. Would you read them to me?"

Jeff sat in the leather recliner in his study while Deandra read to him. When she had finished, he said, "Your thoughts and interpretations of life are truly amazing. That's poetry to my soul, D. Thank you."

The following day, Deandra volunteered to drive Jeff to the airport. He was more than pleased with the offer. It wasn't much more than an hour's wait in the airport before Jeff was boarding the plane bound for North America.

On her way back home after seeing Jeff off, Deandra felt somewhat sad. Jeff Boles was flying thousands of miles away from Nufuma and she hoped that things would go well for him.

Not having had time to do her shopping because of the days she had spent with Jeff, her food cabinet was almost empty. She decided to go to the supermarket, then have a late lunch at the Healthy Eating Restaurant where Claire worked.

The restaurant was rather quiet when Deandra entered. Claire took her order. She had some free time and sat chatting with her friend after serving her.

"Well Miss D, how goes the world with you?" asked Claire.

"Very good, Claire."

"I'm glad to hear that. Too few people see the glass as half-empty, let alone full."

"That's an interesting observation, Claire. So what about you?"

"Can't complain, miss. My glass is half-full. By the way, how was your conference with Sister Katinga?"

"Oh, that conference. It was interesting and intriguing, to say the least. She's told me a lot of things to think about, Claire."

"Believe me, miss . . ." began Claire.

Deandra interrupted. "Drop the 'miss' and call me by my first name."

"Okay then, Deandra. I was about to tell you that nine out of ten times Sister Katinga is right. It might not happen right away, but you watch my word—her prediction will come true. If anyone told me two years ago that Jerry and I wouldn't be together, I'd have called them a liar. But Sister Katinga did a reading for me and warned me about deception. Well Deandra, little did I know that Jerry was having an affair with my very best friend. I almost had a heart attack when I found out. I had left work early one evening as I wasn't feeling well. I had a touch of the flu. When I opened the door and went into the apartment Jerry and my then best friend were in bed. To this day I don't know if it was the flu or the sight of that slut in my bed, but I just vomited all over the two of them. This happened exactly one year after Sister Katinga had warned me about deceit."

By then a couple was seated, waiting to be served. Claire turned and said, "We'll talk some more another time."

"Sure Claire. Anytime."

After leaving the restaurant, Deandra stopped by the village post office to pick up her mail before going home. It wasn't unusual for the mail to be delayed, so she wasn't surprised when she noticed that one letter was postmarked in New York City the previous month. The envelope was typed without a return address.

After she'd packed the groceries away, she sat down and went through the mail. She was curious to see who was writing to her without a return address and opened the letter. It began:

My dearest Deandra,

So much has happened since our brief telephone conversation, that it would require a few legal sheets to write them down. Of greatest relevance though is what has happened in the year since we split up. To begin, my life has not been the same. There's a vacuum, without you. But I know that soon this will be remedied.

Let me fill you in with some of my business activities and ventures which include you equally. My engineering firm has taken off on the right track. There's a fair amount of business in this country despite the competition with the big fellows. There are two signed contracts with African countries, one for Latin America, and I'm hoping to break into the Japanese market, which offers great business possibilities. But most importantly, my dear, I' m my own boss with the chance to be in charge of my own destiny, without answering to anyone but God, you—my dearest—and me.

You, like no other, can understand how long and hard I've worked, against all odds and the invisible glass ceiling. But as the saying goes, anything that's important in your life is worth working for. And, Deandra, there's nothing in the world that's worth working for and waiting for like you, my dearest.

By the way, a surprise response to this note would be more than treasured.

I love you very much.

Yours always,
Paul

When she finished reading the letter, she folded it and returned it to its envelope, then locked it away with her notes and returned to the living room. She lay on the large sofa and thought about the letter. She felt strangely exhilarated and happy for him. The tone of the letter was very upbeat and self-assured, but not pig-headed in the least.

Yes, she said to herself, Paul was a fighter and never allowed anyone to manipulate him. The darn glass ceiling was, and is, nothing more than to prevent people from striving to achieve top positions, regardless of their abilities and drive. In a way she could empathize with Paul and that terrible barrier. Come to think of it, her glass ceiling was the proposition for sexual favors. She had purposely stopped herself from going back to her romance with Paul. She was happy for him as a friend, and that was all, she told herself.

She finally pulled herself together and went to the kitchen and made herself a cup of tea with the fresh peppermint she'd bought at the supermarket. She opened her mother's letter.

Marion was delighted to hear that her daughter had been taking time from her work to enjoy some of Nufuma's old religious customs. She was also glad that she had enjoyed Christmas, for Christmas on the island was unlike any other. It didn't matter how poor you were, there was spicy rum cake that could get you drunk if you were greedy enough to eat too much on a empty stomach. In Marion's day, one had to eat at every aunty and cousin's place. It took clever planning not to overindulge or to offend anyone. Her mother said that her letter was nostalgic in its true sense and evoked many pleasant memories for her.

CHAPTER TWELVE

It had not rained as heavily since Deandra's arrival in Nufuma as it did that night. The rain, accompanied by heavy winds, did not stop at all during the night. By dawn, everything had quieted; the rain had stopped and there was hardly any wind. Were it not for a few bent trees and puddles of water, no one would have known that the island had experienced a minor hurricane. The news on the radio said that some parts of the island had been mildly affected, causing some disruptions in the telephone service.

By mid-afternoon, Lucreta had phoned to check on Deandra.

"Hello Deandra. I tried calling earlier, but the lines were down," she explained.

"I too was thinking about the Clarke family. Didn't it rain!"

"We've been lucky so far. Except for the short inconvenience of electrical and telephone cuts, we've been spared. So, were you affected by the rain, Deandra?"

"Actually, according to the news, my area has been spared. We've had no power cuts so far."

"The roads are back to normal, they say. We were wondering if you'd like to come over for dinner this evening."

"That sounds great, Lucreta. But what about making a tentative date? I'll confirm as soon as I can."

"That's fine with me," answered Lucreta giggling. "It sounds as though you have a real heavy date lined up, friend."

"I know you're the greatest teaser, Lucreta, but you know as well as I do that I'm free, single, and disengaged," said Deandra with a laugh.

"Anyway, Daniel did mention that Jeff was supposed to be going on an extensive business trip. Has he left?"

"Actually, he left a few days ago. He should be in Canada by this. I suppose he'll be calling me as soon as he is settled."

"The way I heard the news, there's no suppose about Jeff calling. A little bird told me that you are driving the guy crazy."

"Lucreta, will you stop that silly talk!" The mere mention of Jeff's name made her tingle. "But on a more serious note—life is rather complicated, isn't it?"

"How well do I know that, Deandra. But seriously speaking, Jeffrey Boles is in love with you. As long as we've known Jeff it was the other way around with love."

"What do you mean by other way around, Lucreta?"

"Jeff is accustomed to being chased by women. Even when he was with his wife he had difficulty shaking them off. Now I hear that he's dropping some of those ladies like mangoes falling from a tree."

"But Lucreta, he's still a married man. I must confess that it wasn't my intention to become so involved, but the guy is a magnet. So now you know where my head is at."

"I thought by this he would have been divorced, Deandra. That was a stormy marriage if ever there was one."

"That's interesting to know. Yet, according to Jeff, the lady is resisting the divorce and he'll have to wait another fifteen months. Not that it matters so much, because right now my plans are to return to New York."

"There's a cliche that goes, 'never say never,' Deandra. And although I don't like playing the role of cupid, especially when both of you are my friends, you'd make a marvelous couple. And what intelligent and beautiful children you both would produce!"

"Lucreta, maybe it's better if Jeff and I just remain good friends."

"I'm not going to say anymore, but Jeff is not only a romantic guy, he's also very rich."

"Maybe I need to have my head examined, but I'm not the avaricious type."

"Deandra, what's avarice got to do with it. Believe me, dear friend, sufficient money helps to keep love alive. Furthermore, as practical and sensitive as you are, you'd be ideal for Jeff."

"Lucreta am I being set up?"

"Set up by me? Not at all. If my sixth sense is correct, I think there's still some attachment to that person in New York."

"I refuse to answer to that. All I want is a life that's not so complicated as to stop or destroy sound relationship, and this is not capricious by any means."

Before the two women had ended their conversation and said good-bye, Deandra asked Lucreta to extend the dinner invitation for another time. She felt as though she was coming down with a cold. Lucreta advised her to drink hot tea with plenty of white rum and go to bed.

That evening Deandra took Lucreta's advice and retired early for the night. The rum tea really worked. The following day, her cold had gone and she returned to her writing as usual.

Just after dinner that evening Jeff called from Canada.

"Tell me what's happening over there. There was a news brief about a hurricane that passed through Nufuma. Is that correct?"

"Yes, we did experience a mild hurricane, but everything is quiet now."

"So you were not affected?"

"Not at all, Jeff."

"I'm relieved to hear you say that. By the way, there was a full moon that night. Were you aware of it?"

"Now that you've mentioned it, but I hadn't given much thought to it."

"They say that the full moon influences quite a few phenomena."

"Come to think of it, you're right about the moon's influence. But I must confess that my knowledge of astrology and astronomy is rather limited. Tell me about your conferences or meetings."

"Well, so far everything is as planned. The most difficult negotiation is almost completed and, by all indications, within the next week the deal should be closed. By the way, are you still risking your life in that dug out canoe? I realize you're really an adventurer, but in bad weather those dinghies aren't very safe."

"Thanks for your concern, but I'm aware of such risks. I like to think that many of the things we do involve a certain amount of risk."

"You're correct, D. And although I'm quite aware of your good judgement, this time of year the tide changes rapidly. My advice is based on experience. Now my dear, tell me about you. Have you heard from anyone I know?"

"Strange that you should ask. Lucreta inquired about you."

"Oh yes. How are they and those beautiful children of theirs? I love them so much. I must bring them something from Japan. Give them my regards and tell Daniel we'll talk when I get back. I'll try and talk with you again before I leave for Japan, and—by the way—I managed to get a few minutes each day to practice my Japanese with the help of that handy gift that you gave me. Thanks again," he said before ringing off.

Jeff's declaration of his affection for the Clarke family triggered curiosity in her brain. She recalled Lucreta's comments about the beautiful children she and Jeff could produce. Knowing Jeff's talent for brevity and metaphors with hidden messages, she wondered whether it was sheer coincidence or she was being cleverly pressured into committing herself to him. She couldn't help remembering Sister Katinga's warning about being pressured into making decisions.

Time was moving too fast, Deandra felt. She'd hoped to return to New York as soon as her assignment was accomplished, but with her new found friends through Claire's local connections she wanted time to herself just to explore and experience more of the undiluted old Nufuman customs. And with Jeff not being around most of the time there was no one to get in her way. She decided then to rearrange her calendar and prolong her stay for a few more weeks.

A few days later, Deandra was invited to an unusual wedding. Sister Katinga would perform the ceremony. When she and Claire arrived, there were at least a hundred guests in the church. Everybody waited for the arrival of the couple. Claire and Deandra got themselves end seats so that their view would not be blocked.

The bride and groom arrived in the usual style. They came in separate cars. After all the guests were seated, the drums began to play. The groom came in and took his place. He was a fine-looking young man and was dressed in an off-white tunic suit. Next to arrive were the bride's two attendants who took their places.

The drums suddenly changed their beat as the bride entered the church. She was beautiful and looked to be the same age as the groom. All heads turned to look as she walked slowly down the aisle, escorted by her beaming father. She wore a long, wide, white calico dress that touched her ankles.

Deandra had to look carefully to discover that she was barefooted.

This took her totally by surprise and her eyes trailed to the path of the groom to discover that he too was barefooted. Deandra shifted her attention and refocused on the beautiful face of the bride, whose head dress was a crown made of pink and white flowers.

By this time all the guests were standing while the drums roared in the background. Sister Katinga gestured with her hands and everyone returned to their seats. She then started the ceremony.

"Once again we are gathered here to celebrate a solemn and happy occasion, an occasion of commitment, of love, trust, patience and forgiveness. It is one of the most crucial stages in the lives of human kind. It is a sacred, yet risky, phase of our lives. It is the stage where couples expose their true selves without guilt or shame. Your bare feet are a symbol of your nakedness—the way you entered the world. In the tradition of the ancestors, you love each other the way you are, without reservation.

"Now repeat after me: I Elandro shall love, honor, respect, and care for this woman. She will be my beautiful bride, come what may."

After the groom had repeated the words, Sister Katinga turned to Imane who repeated the same vows. Then they exchanged wedding rings. Sister Katinga took a small clay pot they called a yaba, which contained consecrated water. She sprinkled the couple with some of the water, then said, "Now that you are man and wife, show your claim."

Elandro walked around Imane, held her around her waist, lifted her, and gently spun her around. The guests stood and applauded.

Claire whispered to Deandra, "There are more surprises yet to come."

"I feel as though I'm literally floating and trying to reach back into the past. What a wonderful and intimate marriage ceremony," declared Deandra.

Everyone turned to greet the newlyweds as they strolled to the door, then the guests exited after them. The couple proceeded to walk. The guests followed. They walked for about twenty minutes to reach the reception tent. The tent was professionally covered with heavy, waterproof canvas. There were long tables, beautifully decorated with wild flowers that abounded on the island.

To begin the ceremony the couple's parents toasted them and did a libation of wine to the ancestors, after which the bride threw out corn and orange seeds. Deandra picked up a few seeds and tucked them away in her handbag.

The voice of Imane spoke clearly and softly. "Elandro and I hope that you will plant these seeds in fertile soil and nurture their growth, for as the seeds grow and flourish so shall our lives."

The guests rose to their feet and applauded. People toasted loquaciously with words Deandra had not heard before, neither would she find them in the standard English dictionary. Such words and phrases were strictly Nufuman for such occasions.

The women started to bring in the food that had been prepared behind the tent on an open fire, the old-fashioned way. The men were busy handling the huge pots and pans on the open fire. The feasting and toasting continued until late evening. Deandra and Claire left before the sun had started to set and the celebration was still in progress.

As the two friends walked back to the car, Deandra initiated the conversation and commented, "When you told me that there were surprises awaiting me, Claire, I couldn't envision that it would have been anything near to what I experienced today. This unique wedding is truly a magazine story."

"It sounds as though you really enjoyed it, Deandra," answered Claire.

"Excuse my verbosity, Claire, but I'm fascinated, charmed, and captivated. And you know something? If I were getting married in the tropics, I'd surprise all the guests by doing it the old-fashioned way that I saw today."

"I can fully understand your reaction to the wedding celebration, Deandra. This is my second time seeing this type of wedding, and it still excites me. But you mustn't forget, to have such a wedding both the bride and the groom will have to want it. And I must tell you that you're very lucky to have witnessed this one. The typical young couple today wants everything that's in *Vogue*. The limousine, the live music, the whole package."

"Thanks for reminding me that it takes two to tie the knot, Claire," laughed Deandra. "But it's such a beautiful and earthy way that I'm enthralled."

"You know something, Deandra? I thought that all foreigners, especially folks from New York City would want those fabulous weddings that you see on TV and in the *Bride's* magazine."

"Don't forget Claire, foreigners also have old traditions. Maybe there are places in America where similar wedding ceremonies are performed. It's worth investigating."

They had almost reached the car when Deandra slipped and almost fell.

"Are you okay, Deandra?" asked Claire.

"I think so. It was just a slight twist of my right ankle. I'll apply a cold pack when I get home."

"I hope you didn't hurt yourself badly."

"Stop being a worrying mother, Claire. I'll be okay."

They had reached the car. Deandra opened the door and both of them got in. She dropped off Claire at her house, then drove slowly home that Saturday afternoon, taking with her a new experience.

Waking up to Nufuma's sunlight and unpolluted air was always exhilarating for Deandra. But that Sunday following the wedding it was more so than she had felt before. She pulled the curtains back from the window and lay quietly on top of the covers, staring at the ceiling and trying to relive some of the wedding celebration.

She finally pulled herself out of bed and made breakfast. During breakfast, she felt some mild discomfort in the ankle she'd twisted. She took a warm shower which seemed to lessen the pain.

Later in the day the pain became severe as she tried to get on with her usual activities. She gathered the newspaper and her diary, then went out to the patio. She elevated her leg on a chair and hoped that the elevation would put an end to the silly pain.

But later when the phone rang, it took her a long time to get to it, for her ankle was really hurting. Deandra swore under her breath. "Damn it. This is all I need . . . to be immobilized!"

She finally reached the phone and answered.

"Hello."

"I'm glad I held on. Are you all right, Deandra?" Paul was saying softly.

"Who am I talking to?" inquired Deandra.

"Sorry about that . . . thought you'd have caught the voice. It's Paul."

"You shouldn't forget that long distance may affect the voice quality. Furthermore, there may be other people with similar voices. So, what prompted you to call me?"

"Now that you've asked the question, it's simply this. I had a premonition that you wouldn't call me, neither would you answer my letter—which I hope you got. And I can't afford to sit and wait for what may not happen except initiated by me. This should answer your question, my dear," replied Paul in his usual teasing voice.

"Aren't you jumping to conclusions too quickly, Paul?"

"I'd love to believe that, even by the slightest indication, but unfortunately for me, I've not received any . . . Anyway, tell me about your plans for coming home and what are some of the current events over there," said Paul.

Deandra silently swore at her ankle and said to Paul, "Can you hold for a minute please?"

"I can hold all day for you, my dearest."

She repositioned herself on the sofa, stretched out her legs, and put a pillow behind her head before resuming the conversation.

"You were asking, Paul?"

"About you."

"Well, my latest and most impressive experience occurred only yesterday," said Deandra. She then recounted in detail the wedding ceremony and celebration in the old Nufuman custom. There was complete silence at the other end of the receiver as Deandra talked.

When she had finished describing the wedding ceremony she asked, "Are you there, Paul?"

"I'm glued to my seat, digesting every detail you've mentioned. It's a great piece of history and cultural preservation, that falls into your area of work."

"I see you've not lost your great listening ability, Paul."

"Haven't I, babe?"

"You've just reconfirmed it."

"How I would have given anything to experience that with you, Deandra. You've got my imagination racing," he said with endearment in his voice.

Deandra couldn't help recalling Paul's strong interest in cultural relevance and natural, simple things. "I can quite understand your reaction to my description of the wedding. I was so affected by it that I've been on a high since then, and just had to share it with someone."

Paul welcomed this conversation. He didn't want to rehash the past, for he was determined to renew their friendship. He realized that she wouldn't respond to his first question about returning home.

"So Deandra, did you receive my letter?"

"Yes Paul. But only a few days ago, and without a return address. It could have been put into the dead-letter pile, but back to the letter—I'm very happy for you."

"Are you serious, Deandra?"

"Why shouldn't I be? I know how hard you've worked and think that you've more than earned your right to be your own boss."

"You have no idea how much what you just said means to me, my dear. So are you okay otherwise?"

"Everything is fine. I've learned a lot since arriving here and am enjoying my life," she replied.

Deandra clenched her teeth when a severe pain shot up her leg as she tried to flex her foot.

Paul was still holding and spoke. "Deandra, I'm equally happy to hear that all is well with you. It would be my greatest pleasure if you'd just use your fingers to dial my number, and even more so if you were to call collect."

Before they ended the conversation, Paul again declared his love for her.

When Deandra hung up the phone her right ankle was swollen and very painful. She applied a hot compress and waited a few minutes for relief, but the pain persisted. She finally broke down and called Lucreta.

After they had talked, Lucreta told her that she would call her back and hung up. Luckily it was a Sunday afternoon and Daniel was at home. Lucreta packed some dinner to take for her friend while Daniel replenished his first-aid kit. When she called back, Lucreta casually remarked, "We'll be over there within an hour, Deandra."

"We means who, Lucreta?"

"Daniel and I, silly."

It seemed a long wait as the pain grew more severe. Her ankle was twice its normal size by the time the doorbell rang. Deandra hobbled to the door to let her friends in.

When they entered the apartment, Daniel examined her ankle and confirmed that it was only a sprain. He applied a bandage and instructed Deandra as to what to do. In the meantime, Lucreta had fixed a tray and she served Deandra dinner on the sofa.

Daniel's medical intervention was very effective. The leg was less painful by the next day, but she would have to wear the bandage for probably a couple of weeks.

The next time Deandra heard from Jeff he was in Japan.

"I'm calling from Tokyo, D."

"The connection is extraordinarily good. You sound as though you are next-door."

"Well, technology keeps improving, even though there's no guarantee. In my book, things can and will go wrong. Anyway, how are you, D?"

"I'm great. Haven't even aged a day, let alone three weeks, since you've been away. Tell me about your trip and conferences."

"Well to begin, the ride was very rough for a while. In my many years of air travel it was my first time feeling scared in the air. The smog was thick, creating multiple air pockets. Everyone was glad when we finally touched ground."

"That sounds very scary and frightening. I'm glad you made it safely. So, tell me about your meetings."

"Well D, the Japanese are hard bargainers. I must tell you that they do their homework before entering the board room."

"Interesting," interrupted Deandra.

"Interesting indeed they are. They consider all the issues you can think of before committing themselves to any business deal."

"But I'm sure you were prepared to play hard ball too, Jeff."

"Yes, I am prepared, but I hope that Nufumans on the whole will analyze many international deals more thoroughly to avoid unfavorable results. Over here the New World Order and the concept of the global village are seriously examined before papers are signed. Folks over hear want to know what the ramifications are in these changes and what's in store for them."

"I give them credit. I think they are smart. We shouldn't expect anyone to put another interest first."

"Agreed, but report to me. How are you?"

"I told you I was fine, and that's a fact, Jeff."

"Tell you what, the way things are moving along, if there are no unforeseen developments, I might even surprise you."

"Are you suggesting that you might return earlier?"

"That's highly possible. I miss you very much indeed," declared Jeff before he hung up.

Deandra murmured to herself, "This guy never fails in trying to keep me guessing." She then closed her eyes for a few minutes.

Deandra suddenly recalled Sister Katinga's prediction that there would be three men in her life. There was, without a doubt, Jeffrey Boles, who would soon be returning home; and there was Paul, who was determined not to exit very easily. But who was the third powerful man, she wondered. Finally it occurred to her that Cliff Riggs had also declared his love for her, months ago when she had just arrived in Nufuma. She smiled and silently wished Cliff well. He was a very decent man who believed in family values and deserved the best, she mused.

The sprained ankle somewhat reduced Deandra's activities. On the other hand, she settle down to putting the finishing touches on and proofreading the manuscript. But as Deandra thought of Jeff, Paul, and Cliff she wrote:

Love is connecting, revealing, and exciting.
Love is healthy, natural, and essential.
Love makes you warm and forgiving; it makes you glow.
Love is not just an exclusive act; it is giving and receiving.
Love is to be cherished, not abused.
It is beautiful and peculiar, but always a treasure.

CHAPTER THIRTEEN

Deandra's confinement to her apartment was not as terrible as she had imagined, for although she was not able to visit more places, she had time to catch up with answering letters. Many of the letters were long overdue and some of her friends were beginning to believe that she was deliberately trying to end their friendship by not replying to their letters.

If there was one friend that she did not want to lose, it was Sara at Gray's Newspaper. Sara was a nice person and Deandra had maintained contact with her after quitting her job with Mr. Gray. Sara had a terrific sense of humor. As a matter of fact, she was good for Deandra, even though they often disagreed about certain personal issues.

In her letter to Sara, Deandra wrote:

Dear Sara:

You'd love it down here. There are many possibilities for meeting interesting people, especially the type of men you always joked about. Don't jump to any conclusion about me now. I'm enjoying being here, but I'm not ready to pack up my career and stay put.

I've been working feverishly, but it's paid off. I'm now in the process of tidying up my manuscript. You'll forgive my tardiness, I hope, and I will be in touch with you as soon as I return to New York. Stay clear of mischief!

Your friend,
Deandra

Later in the day, she called her mother, who had been anxiously waiting to hear from her daughter.

"Hi, my baby. I was just this minute thinking about you. Our spirits are communicating. I think this is what folks call telepathy. Anyway, tell me all the good news that's happening down there."

Deandra listened as her mother talked. She would definitely spare her the bad news about robberies and break-ins, she thought before she replied to her mother's question. "On the whole, Mother, things are quite tame down here. It's not totally the Garden of Eden, but all things considered, it's a quiet place."

"So Deandra, have you been reading my letters carefully?"

"Sure Mother, I always do."

"I'm glad to hear that. By the way, in your last letter you said something about the Outdoor Church. In my time there were quite a few of them, but with all the new cities you've been describing to me, I'm surprised to hear that a few of them are still around. Some of the old-time leaders used to be great healers too."

"I think there are still healers and advisers in the present Outdoor Church. As a matter of fact, I went and saw one."

"It's okay to get a reading. Did this person tell you about your future? I mean like marriage and having children?"

"Heaven's sake, Mother, stop pressuring me!"

"I'm sorry you feel that way, Deandra, but I'm not going to be around forever and I'd like to see my only child with a family of her own," she remonstrated in a low voice.

"Mother, I want you to know that I'm all for a family, but that shouldn't force me into getting married. Marriage should be more than having children. Did you ever hear of miserable married couples with unhappy children?"

"There you go again, giving me all that college new age talk. Furthermore, as I told you, I'm not going to run your life, but there's a man whose name is Paul who could make you happy and give you beautiful children too."

Deandra changed the subject and inquired, "So, tell me about your health. You've cleverly avoided answering this question that I've asked in all of my letters."

"My health is fine. Last time I went for a checkup, Doctor Leward said my pressure was on the high side, but I'm taking my tablets and following my diet. Right now I'm feeling fine."

"Okay Mother, please do not worry about me. Believe me, I can take care of myself, but I also listen to your advice. I must reassure you that I still believe in stability."

"I would hope that you just don't listen, but you will also use them. I love you, Deandra."

"Bye Mom, I love you too."

After she replaced the receiver on the telephone hook, Deandra had ample time to reflect. She had tried not to be too harsh with her mother. Being an only child had its advantages and disadvantages, especially in her case, as her mother had given up so much for her. And even though she was such a terrific mother, there were certain expectations she had for her only child.

In her involvement with her work, it wasn't until Deandra finally consulted the calendar that she realized that the following day would be exactly one month since Jeff had waved good-bye to her. He was expected back in three days time. She suddenly felt the urge to be near him.

That night, before Deandra retired, she removed the bandage from her ankle, but discovered the following morning that there was still some pain when she tried to walk. She was forced to reapply the bandage. She wasn't about to allow a mild pain to delay her work, however, and by mid-afternoon she had all the chapters of the manuscript nicely arranged and laid out on the dining table, ready to be put together.

She had just made herself comfortable on the large sofa and was wiggling the toes of her right foot when the doorbell rang. Deandra walked slowly toward the door.

"I had a premonition it was you, Jeff," she shouted in delight as she opened the door.

With a rakish look on his face, Jeff stepped inside. He stared from her head to her bare feet without speaking.

What was he thinking, Deandra wondered, as the warm blood rushed through her veins. She eyed him saucily and remarked, "You don't seem happy to see me, Jeff."

"Not happy?" replied Jeff rebukingly.

He led her by the hand, walking slowly to the sofa, and waited as she seated herself before speaking.

"You almost gave me a heart attack, lady. Here you are with a limping leg and you hadn't mentioned a word about it to me. Then you threw out a silly question—I'm sorry to say—about my not being happy to see you. I'm deliriously happy, but I'm anxious to know what happened to your foot."

He leaned over and kissed her lips that looked more seductive than ever. They kissed and neither wanted to stop. When they finally separated, Jeff lifted her leg and placed the bandaged ankle in his lap, touching it gently. "Does it hurt, D?"

"Not now, Jeff."

"Should I believe you, seeing that you've kept this problem a secret from me? Had I not returned unexpectedly, you'd not have told me. Am I correct?"

"Oh Jeff, it's only a sprain. Daniel looked after me. In another two days I will be able to return to my normal activities. Further more, why should you've been bothered with a minor incident, all the way in Tokyo?"

"Do me a favor in the future, please. Let me decide what's a bother. I'm annoyed with you. It all boils down to trust, D."

Deandra could sense that Jeff was upset and kept silent. When she finally told him how the accident had occurred, he calmed down.

Jeff gently stroked her leg from the knee down, then pressed his fingers at the point of the sprain and asked, "Does it hurt here, my dear?"

"Hardly, Jeff."

"I'd like to take you out to dinner, but can you a bear few steps?"

"I've been moving around here, so going out for dinner shouldn't pose any difficulty."

"Good. I'll wait until you're ready. We'll go to a very informal place, that way you can be as comfortable as you like."

"Great idea. Shorts will be acceptable then," she answered, then left Jeff sitting as she went to get dressed.

They drove for about thirty minutes, then Jeff turned off the main road and drove for another five minutes to reach the thatch-roofed Hutch. The Hutch provided a natural setting of clean scrubbed tables under a large, spreading, mahogany tree. They both ordered boiled lobster, baked potatoes, salad, and Deandra's favorite local wine.

They talked as they ate. In his usual mischievous manner, Jeff teasingly remarked, "You've not been taking care of yourself since I left the island, Miss Boggs."

"What on earth made you say that, Mr. Boles?"

"One of my senses, Miss Boggs. But seriously, you haven't been denying yourself because of the accident, I hope?"

"Not really. Lucreta and Daniel have been good to me. But, come to think of it, a little self-denial might be quite good at times."

"Self-denial? Like what?" asked Jeff.

Deandra winked her eyes flirtatiously, "Like not sinning anymore."

"You're too moral to be a wicked sinner."

"How can you know that I'm not a sinner?"

"Because I've tried tempting you, and hard at that." Jeff had suddenly stopped eating and looked at Deandra. He was delighted by the gusto with which she was enjoying her meal. Deandra slowly sucked the succulent meat of the lobster from the shell, savoring each mouthful. There was a definite difference between eating and enjoying one's food, Jeff thought. Maybe the way folks enjoy a great meal is an indication of how they approach love.

Deandra looked up from her plate inquiringly. "Is something the matter, dear?"

"Yes, but it's wonderful, sweetheart."

"Please don't keep me in the dark, you've made me curious."

"I had no idea you like lobster this much. Looking at you enjoying it evokes a warm feeling inside me. Not many of us know how to really sit, relax, and enjoy a meal."

Deandra swallowed a mouthful of lobster, wiped her lips, and replied, "I must confess that lobster is one of my favorites. As a matter of fact, I always enjoy it more in an informal place like this, where I can use my fingers to help me out."

"Now that I know, we'll do this more often. But you know something, my dear, because eating and love-making are so individualistic, folks get satisfaction from both, in the way they approach them."

"That's an interesting description. Maybe the French people have something going for them. They say they have mastered the art of dining and of making love."

"I agree, but not anymore than you and I, sweetheart."

When they had finished their meal, Jeff helped Deandra to the car, and drove back to her place. Before he left for Embers Glade, he shared some of his successful business deals with her.

"So Jeff, do the Canadians and the Japanese behave similarly about investing in Nufuma?" inquired Deandra.

"Let me try and answer your question. The ultimate goal in all business deals is making a profit, regardless of who you are or where you're from. However, people approach business somewhat based on what you and your peers might refer to as social and political constraints. But it would seem that culture and old traditions also play an important part. These were evident in the way the Canadians approach business compared to the Japanese, who have a much older culture."

"In a lighter vein, Jeff, tell me about social life in Japan. The women are described as elegant, gracious, and beautiful. How did you find them?"

"My limited observation confirms your description of Japanese women. From the airplane to the dining room, they were all of what you've said, very elegant indeed."

"What about the food?"

"Food was good. Don't forget, you can get a variety of international cuisines. I needed more time to acquire the taste for sushi, but that was balanced by my liking for the hot saki. Come to think of it, I almost forgot about a package in the trunk of the car. Let me go and get it."

He returned to the apartment carrying a beautifully wrapped package which he handed to her. "I picked up something in Japan for you. Hope you like it."

Deandra took the package and remarked, "The package itself is beautiful enough for me to like it," and proceeded to open it, trying not to tear the beautiful wrapping paper.

Jeff watched her. When she had finally opened it and taken out the gift, she exclaimed with delight, "This is absolutely gorgeous, Jeff! Let me take a guess, is this the very precious and rare pink jade?" she asked as she held up the beautiful one-strand necklace.

"Yes. It's the pink jade. Let me see how it looks on you." He reached up and clasped the necklace around her neck.

"There," he said. "But there's something else that goes with this."

"Let's see," replied Deandra, and picked up the small velvet box. In it she found a matching pair of earrings. By then she was beaming with delight. She turned and kissed Jeff, then thanked him.

"I'm glad you like them," he said.

"I love them, Jeff. Your taste is exquisite."

"Enjoy them in good health. Listen D, I will have to leave for the north coast tomorrow. It will take at least four days to get everything done from my last trip. I want you to bear with me, and to help me out as you've done before. I'm tired and need to get away for a few days, but I don't feel like flying or sailing. Do you have a suggestion on how best to achieve that kind of vacation?"

"How about Hide Away Villa?"

"Are you sure you could put up with me for a week or ten days in that corner of the world?"

"You haven't asked me to join you, Jeff," she replied as she remembered the scene with Sandra on the phone and what Lucreta had said about women chasing after him.

"Well, in your style, Miss Boggs, may I entreat you to go with me?"

"I'll think about it, Jeff. I love Hide Away."

"I'm not totally selfish, D. I'm giving you sufficient notice so that you can even finish putting away your papers, so neatly organized on your dining table."

"You've pleaded your case exceedingly well, in the true style of a lawyer. Without any interference I should be able to finish with my piles of paper in another week."

"So we have a date, Miss Boggs?"

"So we have," she replied.

Jeff left her late that night and promised to call her from the north coast. In another couple of days, Deandra was able to walk normally without a bandage.

She went to lunch at the Healthy Eating Restaurant, mainly to see her friend Claire. When she entered the restaurant, Claire was busy waiting on customers. She waved as Deandra found an empty table and waited to be served.

"Hello Deandra," Claire greeted her animatedly. "Long time I haven't seen you. I was beginning to think that maybe you were sick."

"I had to stay off my feet until my sprained ankle healed."

"So I wasn't over-concerned about that slip you had. Sorry I didn't know so that I could have visited you. I'm glad that you didn't suffer broken bones."

"Me too. They say broken ankles take a long time to heal. I'm quite well now. So how about you, Claire?"

"I'm beginning to feel a little closer to going back to school to finish the computer course I interrupted a few months ago."

"Tell me more about it, Claire."

"There isn't too much to tell yet, but I'm determined that by next year this time, I'll have more to say when I finish my course and land me a nice job."

"With your personality, drive, and motivation, Claire, I feel confident that you'll succeed."

"Thank you, Deandra."

Deandra finished her lunch and drove back home, determined to get as much work done as possible. By the end of the week, she had finally put the finishing touches on the chapters, leaving an opening for an added chapter or two, just in case she should discover something new that would be worth writing about.

When Lucreta stopped by to chitchat with Deandra that Saturday afternoon, each friend had a lot to tell the other. Lucreta looked more beautiful than ever. She was wearing a red sun-back dress with her hair pulled back and tied with a piece of black satin ribbon.

"Hi D. Can you stand some company?" Lucreta called out from the door.

"What kind of question is that to ask a friend?" scolded Deandra. "Come in . . . but wait a minute, where's your car?"

"That's what I've brought to show you. You're looking at the owner of a black BMW, my dear. Would you like to step out and touch it?"

"Sure Lucreta." Deandra would have liked to say, Lukie, but stopped herself, remembering the emotional and personal connections of that special name.

The two women examined the car while Lucreta explained the hi-tech features.

"Lucreta, it's gorgeous."

"Well, my dear, Daniel gave me this as a surprise for fulfilling another desire of ours, but mostly his. Let's go inside so we can talk."

"You've got me excited and curious, Lucreta."

When they had entered the apartment, Deandra couldn't help saying, "Lucreta, I can't recall seeing you looking like this before."

"What's this 'looking like this' business, Deandra?"

"You're glowing. You're extra pretty today."

Deandra poured two glasses of orange juice and they made themselves comfortable as they talked. Tell me about this surprise, Lucreta."

"Except for my raving beauty, Deandra," asked Lucreta tantalizing, "what else is physically different about me?"

"All that my visual sense reveals to me, Mrs. Clarke, is that . . . let's see how best to describe it. To me, your face is like a big yellow rose whose petals have burst open with the rays of the morning sun."

"Oh Deandra, you make me feel so good my dear friend. I must try my best to relay your poetic description of me to Daniel. He would enjoy hearing you say that himself, but he'll have to do with second best."

"So, relieve me of my anxiety. Tell me about this news," implored Deandra.

"I'm pregnant, Deandra."

"Lucreta! How can that be? Your body looks the same."

"I know. Except for my hips, even Daniel has difficulty detecting any change in my shape. I'm lucky that way, as a rule I don't have a big belly until around the fifth month."

"Your face conveys happiness, Lucreta. So how many months are you?"

"I'm three months pregnant with a boy quietly making his demands on me, the obstetrician informed us."

"Was that what both of you wanted?"

"Most definitely. Daniel wished for a boy. I wished for a girl, so a girl would have been equally welcome. But enough about me, tell me about you and lover boy, even though he is so much on the go."

"As a matter of fact, Jeff should be returning from the north coast tomorrow. He has asked me to go away with him for a short vacation . . . Let me show you what he brought me from Japan."

When Lucreta saw the jewelry, she too exclaimed. "That's what I consider class and taste! Would that be the rare pink jade?"

"Yes. It is."

"I'm happy for you. It is a beautiful gift. I'll repeat, Jeff is in love with you and from what I've managed to squeeze out of Daniel, Jeff is worried that you still have your mind set on returning to New

York."

Lucreta paused, looked at Deandra, and continued to talk. "Oh D, I wish things will work out the best possible way for you and Jeff. I can just imagine seeing you and Jeff with a baby . . ."

She stopped talking abruptly.

Deandra crossed and uncrossed her legs before answering Lucreta. "Lucreta! Don't you put any goat-mouth on me, I beg of you."

"I didn't think you still remembered about goat-mouth."

"Why not?" retorted Deandra. "You're not the only Nufuman who still believes in obeah, spiritual readers, and goat-mouthing. Remember I spent my childhood here too."

"How did you guess that I believe in spiritual readers? Anyway, if ever you want a reading, I can take you to see someone. She'll only see you by recommendation. Sister Katinga is very gifted. It was only six months ago that she did a reading for me and told me that she saw me feeding a baby."

Deandra's mind wondered off. She remembered Sister Katinga's place and the gold ring hitting the sides of the glass although her hand was held steadily. Truth is stranger than fiction, she mused when she discovered that both Lucreta and herself had gone to Sister Katinga for readings. Anyway, she wasn't about to reveal that she too had consulted the reader, but based on Claire's, and now Lucreta's, story of Sister Katinga, it seemed she was a force to be reckoned with.

Deandra finally looked at her friend with searching eyes and remarked "You know something, Lucreta, I believe in keeping an open mind. Who am I to say that Sister Katinga does not possess some special gift. But returning to your pregnancy, I hope everything will turn out well for you and the baby."

The friends embraced each other as Deandra saw Lucreta to the door.

Before falling asleep that night, Deandra couldn't help thinking about cultural beliefs. In Nufuma's culture, it was very important to have babies. As for the male, this was a sign of his virility.

As soon as Jeff arrived home from the north coast the following day, he emptied his mail box. He looked through the pile of letters and discarded the unimportant ones. He opened a large envelope. Enclosed was a lovers card sent by Sandra. At the bottom she had

written:
> P.S. You and I have shared a lot of good times together, and I hope we can get back together and stop the hurt. I still love you—Sandra.

If only Sandra had not been so abrasive and demanding, Jeff might have settled for her. After all, she was a young, intelligent, and attractive professional, but the more she revealed her insecurities, the further away she pushed Jeff. After reading the card and her postscript, he toyed with the idea of calling her to say good-bye. She was good company when she wasn't too demanding. But, finally, he decided against doing so.

CHAPTER FOURTEEN

The sisterly bonding had grown very strong between the two friends. They confided more and more in each other. Lucreta shared some of her intimate feelings with Deandra, and before Deandra left for the trip with Jeff, Lucreta invited her to accompany her to select some fashionable maternity clothes.

Deandra couldn't get over the change in her friend. She was bubbly and excited as she talked about her pregnancy. As they shopped, Deandra asked, "Say, Lucreta, were you this excited with your other pregnancies?"

"I'll have to give you two answers, Deandra. I always felt good being pregnant, and to be honest, I enjoyed Daniel's doting on me, but this time is even more special."

"May I ask why this time is more special?"

"Because soon we'll have two teenagers who may request to be sent away to boarding schools just to get away from us. But, more importantly, Daniel and I have always had the desire for another child, which we postponed in order to fulfil some of our personal and professional goals. But now we are ready for a new baby. And, don't forget, on my next birthday I'll be that critical age of thirty-five."

"It sounds both romantic and logical. It must be a great feeling to have things work out the way you had planned. Now I can better appreciate your happiness. What kind of family planning did you use?"

"I used the pill. The question you asked is a very serious matter these days, especially with AIDS and the other sexually transmitted diseases around. Daniel and I have been quite frank in discussing such issues and, although I trust my husband, we discussed the importance of all men having condoms at their disposal, including him."

Deandra bit her lip before responding. "But some might see that as giving the man consent and freedom to fool around."

"To me that's only one side, and myopic, in my opinion. I try to approach life from a realistic point of view when dealing with us imperfect human beings. The condom protects the man, just in case he makes that one mistake. Furthermore, it allowed Daniel to make love to me without any barrier so that I could get pregnant when we were ready."

"I don't want to pry into your business, but what about you or other wives? What I mean is, what about infidelity among women?"

"That's a good point. All women should demand safe sex from their partners. I've been faithful to Daniel and he trusts me. With this approach to safe sex, just in case he should stray, he avoids infecting himself and giving it to me."

Deandra had a befuddled look on her face. She finally remarked, "You and Daniel seem to love and trust each other very much. I admire your approach to keeping a good relationship going."

Thank you for that, Deandra, but that's life and the sooner we face it intelligently, the safer it will be for the family. Let me add to that, if I were you, I wouldn't worry about Jeff not being careful. Daniel is not only his best friend, but his doctor and we have discussed these issues openly."

Lucreta stopped and stared into space then continued. "I've just said a prayer, dear friend."

"A prayer?" repeated Deandra.

"Yes. A prayer that was for my two best friends, Jeffrey Boles and Deandra Boggs," she said with a serious look on her face.

When they had finished shopping and returned home, before Deandra exited from Lucreta's brand new BMW, she turned and said, "You know something, Lucreta, you've taught me so much today. Thank you. We'll talk some more when I get back."

"That's what friends are for—to communicate honestly with each other. Take care, and be nice to Jeff."

Deandra entered her apartment feeling somewhat bewildered. Listening to Lucreta had given her a new perspective on life. "It's absolutely true," she mused, "every moment, every day provides opportunities for new knowledge. I really learned a lot from Lukie today, although I might not agree totally with all she said."

The afternoon was a little sticky. Deandra opened the French door that lead to the small patio and took a deep breath. The air was fresh and clean and she felt invigorated. She ran a bath, poured in some scented bath oil, and prepared herself for a leisurely soak in the tub. She had just stepped into the tub when the doorbell rang. What a time to be interrupted, she thought as she grabbed a bath sheet and went to answer the bell. She could see it was Jeff through the peep hole, so she let him in.

"Caught you off guard again, D," whispered Jeff as he held her tightly and kissed her. She clung to him in response. By then the bath sheet had fallen.

Deandra drew a pose quite similar to the much talked about "September Morn."

"Where's your fig leaf," he teased.

"You've destroyed it."

"It was unintentional, my dear."

"I feel very vulnerable."

"Why, may I ask?"

"Jeffrey, stop hiding the towel behind you."

"Let me help you."

Before Deandra knew what was happening, Jeff had carried her and deposited her in the bath and closed the door behind him, calling out, "You need to be more careful with your privacy. Now enjoy yourself. Call me if you need a back washer."

When she emerged from her bath, Jeff was stretched out on the sofa—a sight she'd grown accustomed to.

"I've been calling you all morning and afternoon, D, but of course you were out."

"Correct Jeff, I was out."

"Well, what were you up to this time?"

"Shopping with a friend."

"Do I know this friend?" he asked, indicating a spot for her to sit beside him.

"Yes you do. She's a special friend who needed my assistance in selecting some special clothes."

"The cat was out of the bag long ago, so you and Lucreta don't need to erect any wall of secrecy."

"Who ever made that mistake about men being secretive, I'll never know," she said with a haughty laugh.

Jeff started to reply, but decided to keep quiet for a while as he silently wished that Deandra was the one pregnant with their child. However, he didn't want to voice the thought and scare her off "Well, D, do you think you'll be ready to leave for Hide Away the day after tomorrow?"

"Definitely Jeff. But how long will we be there?"

"I'd say anywhere between seven and ten days. Anything else you'd like to know, my dear?"

"You've answered my question and I'll be ready and prepared for that vacation, if that pleases you, sir."

"I like it when you tease. How about something cool to drink? Not fruit juice though."

"Think I can manage that, but it won't be anything stronger than wine since you'll be driving."

"So you're deciding what I do for the evening. For your information, I'm not going to be driving."

"That's fine with me."

Deandra fixed a drink using the rum he liked and poured herself a glass of wine. They sat close to each other and slowly sipped their drinks. Jeff lifted her legs and placed them in his lap then asked, "Which was the injured one, D?"

She wiggled her right foot and replied, "This was my problem child."

Jeff stroked her leg, then kissed her ankle and remarked, "I'm so glad you're fine, my dear. You always smell so darn good, D." He continued to stoke her leg.

He looked at her seriously. "I want you to realize that being a father is very important to me. But I need a woman with warmth and maturity to be the mother, and that woman is you."

She shifted herself, not saying a word.

Jeff broke the brief silence by saying, "Sleep on it, sweetheart," and lowered her legs.

The following morning Jeff drove away from Lucky Pond at about eight o'clock and headed straight for his house. Later that evening he packed his bag and put some magazines and a couple of light novels in an old brief case for Deandra. When he had finished packing, he placed his luggage near the dining room door.

When he turned around, Mrs. Cato, his housekeeper was standing holding a yellow laminated plastic bag. "You musn't forget your package, Mr. Boles. I'll keep it until you are ready to leave."

"What goodies have you put together this time, Mrs. C?"

"Your favorite banana rolls and a special surprise."

Deandra was ready when Jeff arrived at her place the following day. She was wearing black slacks and a blue striped shirt, with the sleeves rolled up. She had packed a small bag and her cosmetic kit with her toilet articles, some magazines and her diary into her straw carryall bag.

"Hello there," Jeff called out as he walked toward Deandra's door. "Where's your luggage, sweetheart?"

"Right there Jeff," she said, pointing to them.

"I can see that you're travelling rather light."

"Yes. But I think I've packed everything that I'll need down at Hide Away."

They drove off for Hide Away early in the afternoon. Jeff turned on the cassette he had bought in Japan. It was an unusual mix of European classics, Jamaican reggae, and traditional American jazz.

Deandra closed her eyes and murmured, "What a combination! Such talents."

"You love the music, D."

"And how! It's peaceful and soothing."

"Good. I thought you'd appreciate it."

When they arrived at Hide Away, the sun had just started to set, casting its golden glow on the quiet surface of the sea.

Jeff stepped out onto the patio facing the sea and commented, "How about us getting a dip before the sun disappears, D? Come to think of it, last time we were here, the rain had competed with our swimming."

"I'd love that," answered Deandra, and she quickly changed into a white bikini bathing suit.

Jeff carried the two large towels and his camera. They walked hand in hand to the beach. They were alone. Jeff waded into the warm water and shouted for Deandra who stood surveying the sea before entering.

"Come and join me," continued Jeff. "You look the perfect picture of a lost mermaid, darling."

Deandra decided to surprise him. She dove and swam to where Jeff was standing and moved her fingers against his legs.

Suddenly she stood facing him.

"Let's do a few laps, D."

"Sure. Come to think of it, this is only my second dip since I've been here."

"Well, look around, my dear, and tell me who and what you see."

"You, me, and the quiet sea," she replied and splashed him with the salt water.

"So we can do whatever our hearts desire, darling," replied Jeff with mischief sparkling in his eyes."

They waded in the water. Jeff turned and asked as he hugged her closely, "How about skinny dipping?"

Deandra made a funny face and asked, "Have you ever done it before?"

"Of course, my dear. With all this privacy, why should I be afraid of my own body? It's like being in a giant private bath."

"You're right, Jeff. Some of us are afraid because of the way we were brought up."

"So, are you going to join me?"

"Give me a minute to make up my mind."

"One, two, three . . . " Jeff counted.

When he got to twenty he shouted, "Time's up!" He walked to Deandra who had been standing looking down at her belly.

"Let me help you, sweetheart," he said as he tried to undo the hook of her white bikini top.

"I feel naked," Deandra said softly.

"You look beautiful. You are the perfect subject for an artist, but I wouldn't allow any other to see such beauty, but me. I won't force you to do anything you don't want to. Half is better than nothing. Relax and enjoy."

Jeff lifted her and carried her further out into the sea. By then the sun had started to disappear. He swam quickly back to the beach, waved to Deandra and shouted, "Walk back to me, D."

Without suspicion she walked toward him. Jeff clicked the camera.

"Jeff!" she shouted. "You've tricked me."

"I've done nothing of the sort. Why do you try to deny your

beauty? You've got the most beautiful bosom my dear, and it is one of your beauty spots, I must tell you."

"So you are saying that my physical attributes are the most important to you?"

"You know that's not true. Nufuma stands tall when it comes to beautiful women, but you stand head and shoulders above all, and it's because of the person you are. I'm sure you don't see your body as being ugly. I'll show you some beautifully adorned bare-breasted people in the latest edition of the *National Geographic* magazine. It arrived only yesterday and I've brought it along."

Jeff put away the camera and rejoined Deandra. They swam until the sun had completely disappeared, then walked on the deserted beach. Jeff covered her shoulders with the large beach towel. She smiled at him as they walked back to the villa.

While Jeff showered, Deandra unpacked the goodies that Mrs. Cato had packed for him. In the package was a large Pyrex dish, filled with Jeff's favorite escovitched snapper fish. Blossom, the housekeeper at Hide Away, had left everything in order and a note explaining to Mr. Boles that she would be there in the morning.

After Deandra had showered and put on a robe, Jeff commented, "I'm going to call the dining room to send us over dinner. What shall I order for you, dear?"

"Surprise me," Deandra said, then laughed and continued, "You're a master of that anyway."

"Now that you've mentioned surprises, what did Mrs. Cato put in the package that's supposed to surprise me, D?"

"Well, there's a large roll of delicious-looking banana bread, a jar of pickles with large scotch bonnet peppers, a jar of homemade seville orange marmalade and, listen to this, a huge container of escovitched snapper fish that looks mouth-watering."

"Only you could describe food so temptingly. That's also another special endowment of yours and not just your body, D. Shall we play it safe and order curried chicken?"

"That sounds excellent. I also like curry."

After dinner, they relaxed to the sound of Beethoven's "Symphony Number Five." They lay quietly side by side, without an utterance until the music stopped. They gently touched each other.

Jeff spoke softly, "Eh D, are you back to Hide Away yet?"

"Sort of."

"I always played Mr. B to get in that frame of mind, when I want to forget work and get in touch with more of Jeffrey Boles."

"You've said that so nicely, Jeff. But I must confess, had I been listening alone, my eyes would have been watery. That guy sure knows how to reach your soul."

"I understand. The man evokes all kinds of emotions inside you."

"When I listen to certain Nina Simone, Billy Holiday, and Bob Marley pieces they also make my eyes watery," remarked Deandra.

"Now that you've so ably described your reaction to these artists, why don't we call it a day and turn in for the night."

"Good idea." Jeff finally turned off the lights. They both slept like logs and were awakened the next morning when Blossom turned the key in the front door.

Blossom had been taking care of the villa for almost two years. She had started working there a few months before Jeff's marriage had fallen apart. She knew how to conduct herself when a woman was at the villa. She had to admit, however, that since Mr. Boles and his wife had parted, only once did he bring a lady down for a weekend. But how interesting, Blossom thought, that in such a short span of time, he has brought this lady a second time.

Blossom stopped speculating about her employer and began her duties. She plugged in the coffee pot, picked up the empty glasses, and waited to find out what they wanted for breakfast.

Jeff pulled up the blinds to let in some sunshine.

"What time is it, darling?" asked Deandra.

"Have you forgotten why we're here, my dear?"

"Remind me, Jeff."

"Then listen. It is strictly to be with you, not to be disturbed by, or concerned with, time or anyone."

"I'll hold you to that."

"You know what, D?"

"What?"

"I've not been around another woman who looks as beautiful, and even more beautiful first thing in the morning."

"Stop your flattery."

"Flattery? I've known you for a long time now and I also know a lot about you, and we've passed that stage."

Deandra pulled in her bottom lip and changed the subject. "Who is going into the shower first?" she asked.

Jeff reached and pulled her out of bed saying, "Come let's see."

They showered together then put on their robes and went to the dining room.

"Morning Mr. Boles."

"Morning Blossom. Have you been here long?"

"No sir. Just a few minutes."

"You met Miss Boggs before, didn't you?"

"I remember her from when yu brought her down the las' time."

"Well Blossom, we're going to be here for a few days. You won't have to change your schedule. I mean, you know what to do when two people are here."

"Yes, Mr. Boles. I know what to do."

In the meantime, Deandra had been enjoying the view from the patio and mused silently, "I could easily get used to this way of life—a gorgeous home in the exclusive neighborhood of Embers Glade, a private villa, a yacht, and plenty of money—tempting, but I must keep my priorities straight. There's nothing in the world that should make me submerge my being. The good life must be more than things . . . Of course, I'm terribly fond of Jeff. He's a great guy, but we'll see."

She walked slowly to the dining room.

"Good morning, Blossom."

"Good morning Miss Boggs, you were enjoying the view, I notice."

"Yes Blossom. It's beautiful and quiet here."

"Yes miss. I'm glad you like it down here."

Blossom had finished setting the dining table for two and asked, "Is there anything special you want for breakfast Mr. Boles and Miss Boggs?"

"D, why don't you select breakfast," suggested Jeff.

"How about omelets?"

"Great. Matter of fact, the last time I had it was at your place."

They had breakfast then Jeff called the main office to send them the newspaper. They could hear the splashing of the waves bouncing against the barrier of the beach as they sat reading on the spacious patio.

Jeff quietly reflected about the dreadful scene with his second wife, Angelica, two years ago. He had bought her a Toyota Cressida for her twenty-sixth birthday. Instead of showing appreciation, Angelica had chided, "How much more ordinary can anyone get."

"Excuse me," Jeff had retorted. "Are you talking out loud to yourself again?"

"No, I'm talking to you, Jeffrey," Angelica had snapped at him.

"I'm aware of the fact that most times you're in another world, but right now you've taken me totally by surprise. Tell me what's so ordinary about me, Angelica."

"Why should I have to settle for a Toyota when all my friends have Benzes? For all I know, you might have already given a Saab to your woman."

"For God's sake, woman, shut up or leave. If our relationship is based on a Benz and competing with your friends, there's no redeeming grace for us!"

Jeff's flashback took him to when he had first met Angelica. She had just received a degree in business accounting and applied for, and got, a job at Boles Export Company. Jeff was twenty-nine and not so long divorced from his first wife. Angelica was twenty-two, but struck him as a mature goal-oriented young woman. For the first two years of their marriage she had worked part-time and took courses in interior decorating.

They had agreed about raising a family, before their marriage, but when he suggested that they begin the family, Angelica's reaction was far from what they had agreed on. As a matter of fact, it was down right juvenile when she said, "So, you've got it all planned, how to keep me at home."

Her behavior was very much out of character. He realized that something might have gone wrong during his business trips. And what a shock he got when he discovered that his wife had become involved with the wrong type of party-loving people who also used drugs that affected people's moods. Although Angelica denied any drug use, her behavior became more and more unpredictable. He had wanted to help his young wife even though it was difficult for him to accept addiction as an illness. They discussed the problem and finally Angelica decided to go into treatment for her illness. After a few sessions with the therapist, she stopped and continued to party with the crowd.

Having a family was no longer on her agenda. Furthermore,

what kind of children would she produce? It was a very painful situation, but they had to go their separate ways.

Deandra had finished reading the papers, she looked up at Jeff and said, "Hi there."

"Hi D. What's on your mind?"

"I was about to ask you that question too, but since you've asked, not much. What about you?"

"Well, to be honest, I've been reminiscing about things that will never get written about."

"It's difficult for me to agree with 'never.' Furthermore, coming from someone like you, I'll be hard put to believe that."

"Some things that seem so simple become problematic when you get down to the eleventh hour, D."

"Things such as?"

"Like having a family."

Deandra remained silent for a while before answering. "I agree. Having a family is a very important and serious part of life."

"What role do you see yourself playing in the family life."

"That's a heavy one. Let's see how best to respond. I imagine myself as being actively and directly involved, and if that's not accomplished, I'll settle for vicarious involvement."

"That sounds complicated. Explain those terms please."

"Well, if and when I get pregnant, I'll be directly and actively involved. On the other hand, if I can't get pregnant, I'll adopt a child; that way I'll be actively involved with this child even though I'd not experienced pregnancy directly. And if those don't work, I suppose I'll have to be a vicarious mother."

Jeff passed his hand through his hair and, in deep concentration, spoke. "There's a great deal in what you've said. Men and women seem to differ slightly with the active and vicarious roles. Being still relatively young and healthy, I'm hoping for a biological offspring resulting from the union with . . ."

He stopped abruptly, walked about the patio, kissed Deandra and asked, "Are you happy, darling?"

"Being with you makes me happy, Jeff." Deandra could detect something mysterious about Jeff and wondered why he had ended his explanation about biological union in the middle of a sentence. But she wasn't going to intrude into what was a very serious subject with him. She recalled how profoundly he'd talked about the death of his son.

Blossom was busy fixing lunch. She walked to the patio and inquired, "Would you like to take lunch out here, Mr. Boles?"

"Is it that time already?" remarked Jeff. Turning to Deandra he asked, "Do you feel like eating, D?"

"Not really, if you don't mind, Jeff."

"Blossom," said Jeff, "we're going to pass for lunch, but we'll have an early dinner, about five o'clock."

"Okay sir. I'll have dinner ready."

Jeff led the way to the beach carrying a pillow, while Deandra carried her straw basket with a couple of magazines. He selected one of the large lover's hammocks, helped her in, then climbed in after her. They made themselves comfortable with the pillow tucked under their shoulders. They had a complete view of the sea, disturbed only be a few fishing canoes that bobbed up and down with the movement of the water.

Deandra closed her eyes. Her lips parted as she smiled a smile of happiness.

Jeff lifted his head and kissed her, whispering softly in her ear, "My darling, you're delicious, beautiful, and tormenting."

With her chest heaving, Deandra tried to speak, but was prevented from doing so by another lingering kiss. When Jeff had released her, she opened her eyes and murmured, "Oh, Jeff."

"Yes D."

"Something special is in the air at Hide Away."

"I know darling. Do you like it?"

"Mmm," she sighed. "Can't you tell, my dear?"

"Yes D. Shall we have a dip before having dinner?"

"Sure."

They got out of the hammock and swam for half an hour before returning to the villa. It was already five-thirty when they got back.

Blossom was waiting to serve them. Deandra suggested to Jeff that he let Blossom go. She would take care of the necessaries when they were ready to eat. Jeff welcomed the suggestion, serving dinner would be no big deal.

After dinner they watched the television news before perusing the *National Geographic* magazines. Jeff called Deandra's attention to the article he had mentioned in reference to male and female partial nudity. Among the women, some had no covering just below the breast to the waist, some wore scanty bikinis with see-through brassieres, and there was a group ranging from pubescent girls to grandmothers without coverings from their heads to their waists.

When Deandra had finished scanning the photograph, Jeff asked, "Well, what do you think?"

"I find them more revealing and interesting than I did before."

"In what way?" questioned Jeff.

"For one thing, the social and cultural attitudes about the human body are quite evident."

"So, are you suggesting that people's perceptions and even their imaginations are clouded—for want of a better word—by such conditions?"

"Yes."

"I'm glad you've said that, it leads into my own thinking."

"Which is?"

"I've grown to develop an interest in beauty that transcends cultural barriers. In my way of thinking, even people's postures reveal a lot about them."

"How is that?" asked Deandra. "It sounds as though you're a frustrated sculptor."

"Maybe I am. As a freshman in college, I toyed with the idea of becoming one. But try and imagine, if you've not seen one before, an old man walking with a cane. He stops for a moment, straightens himself and stands erect without the cane."

"Help my clouded imagination, please."

"Imagination . . . imagination," muttered Jeff.

Then he said, "The old man might have been reasserting his dignity through simply standing tall. Another person's perception might imagine him as simply resting his tired hand from carrying the cane."

"I hadn't thought of perception and imagination in that light before. But now you've given them a new twist."

"Is that bad or good, D?"

"Very interesting and perceptive," she answered. "But tell me, D? What did you feel from looking at the women in the magazine?"

Deandra scratched her head and raised her eyebrows before answering. "I felt a sense of dignity without any trace of shame among them. It also points out the changes that women, especially, undergo."

"Such as what, D?"

"Well, women in our culture view sagging breasts as ugly, when in reality it's the natural order of being a woman. That is if we are lucky to experience it."

"I'm glad you saw it that way . . . the natural order. That's one of the reasons I like photography as a hobby, whenever I get the chance. It allows me to capture beauty in its natural way. No props, no pose. And, my dear, when I look at you, you're that to my imagination, perception and senses. Totally natural and all woman."

Deandra could feel the hot blood rushing through her veins as Jeff looked at her. Finally, she composed herself and inquired, "Are you saying Jeff, that you're discovering and recording time sequence through the human body?"

Her question evoked a new feeling in his mind. Discovering and recording, D?" he repeated. "Yes, I am," he said finally, after careful thought. He sensed there was more than he had imagined to this woman, and he felt as if he could go on discovering more and more about her.

"So, are you succeeding, Jeff?"

"Now you've put me on the spot, darling. But I am desperately trying to discover more with and about you."

Was he subtly using his legal and business techniques with her, or was he really sincere, she wondered. "Have you had the chance to photograph many female subjects with uncovered tops?"

"I had that chance with my first wife, in three stages."

"That sounds interesting. How did you manage that?"

"Quite simply and naturally. Before Gwen became pregnant, during her pregnancy, and also during breast-feeding. In none of those photos did I see lewdness as in pornographic pictures. For example, Gwen and I examined the photos and . . ." He stopped briefly, remembering his son.

"We agreed then, that our child at her breast exalted one of the mysteries of life—the sexual, personal, and nurturing qualities of the female's body."

"You've described it so beautifully, Jeff. We are indeed slaves to our cultures. Quite similar to the ethics versus morality situation."

"Yes. Similar to the two interpretations of the old man with the cane. By the way, if you want me to, I'll destroy those shots I took of you down by the beach."

"I'd be morally and ethically wounded if you did," answered Deandra laughing.

Jeff looked at her languidly. He got up and mixed two rum drinks and put them on the bedside table. They sipped the drinks as they listened to a love duet sung by Sara Vaughn and Billy Erkstein.

Jeff reached over for Deandra. And as he kissed her from head to toe, he whispered, "You're driving me crazy, your love has seeped into my blood. I can't get enough of you, my dearest."

Deandra was a little groggy as she responded, "I want you too, Jeff. What have you done to me?"

"Deandra, I want us to have a baby. Stop putting me off, sweetheart," whispered Jeff as he explored her body.

"Not now darling, please. Let's wait and see."

They enjoyed each other as usual that night, with Deandra being alert to Jeff's effort to get her pregnant.

With the swimming, walking, reading, discussions, and musical interludes, the time went too quickly for Jeff. The day before they left Hide Away Villa, he raised the old serious question to Deandra, but more pointedly. "Deandra," said Jeff "I want you to listen carefully to what I'm about to say. Would you have our baby before my divorce?"

Deandra was taken by surprise. She hadn't thought of Jeff being so frank, even though he'd tried every trick to avoid using the protection she'd insisted on.

"I have not been faced with this choice before." She bit her lip, stuttered slightly, then continued. "My child must be the first person in his or her parents' lives when I decide to have one, Jeff."

"What does that mean?"

"I mean, who knows whether or not you'll ever get a divorce. It seems to me that your wife, Angelica, still has some legal rights and for us to have a child before that's resolved would be putting the child at a disadvantage. Maybe you are looking at it too simplistically, Jeff."

"It's you D. I love you, that's why I want you to mother my child. Is it just the damn divorce or is it that your mind is still set on returning to New York?"

"It's all that and more. I need to think about a great many things. I need time."

"It's been almost eight months since we met, and with your intelligence and insight, you've long discovered that I'm in love with you. But I'm also at the stage where I need to be a father with . . ." He stopped then said, "Anyway, I'm not ready to throw in the towel. I want you to try and stop living in the nineteenth century. I'm not living with Angelica and except for the divorce procedure, she has no role in my personal life."

Jeff paused, then continued, "For us to allow an impending divorce to come between us is tantamount to reaching back for chastity."

"Jeff, I don't think it's fair to feel that way. I'm as much in love with you as you are with me, and you've known that to be a fact. But, I'll still say, in my way of seeing things, being great lovers alone shouldn't be the only criterion for having a baby at this time. You did say that you'll get your divorce next year, so why don't you hold off and see. If not, there are other avenues."

Jeff didn't reply, instead he toyed with Deandra's last words. *Hold off . . . other avenues.* Time doesn't stand still. As a matter of fact, it's moving very rapidly. Was she also implying that I look for another woman, he pondered.

In the meantime, Deandra was somewhat perturbed. She felt she was being pressured into something she wasn't ready for. She recalled Sister Katinga's advice and resolved that no matter what, she would not allow herself to be pressured into anything, regardless of her feelings for Jeff.

Blossom had prepared a delicious pumpkin soup. When she announced that lunch was ready, both Jeff and Deandra could hardly believe that they had spent all morning on the patio.

Jeff walked over to where she was sitting in one of the lounging chairs. He held her by the hand and helped her up. They stood and faced each other. Jeff hugged her and spoke softly. "Try hard not to give me anymore double messages, sweetheart."

"I'm sorry if I did. But I'm sure you want honesty."

"Without a doubt. Let's not keep Blossom waiting." They proceeded to the dining room.

After lunch, they walked through some of the property of Hide Away Villas, which was about four acres. Then they went to take a last swim in the warm salt water.

That night, before they turned in for bed, they sat on the sofa and listened to the soothing music of a flute player. Jeff shifted his position, stretched out on his back and put his head in Deandra's lap. As he looked up into her face, he reached for Deandra's hands and kissed each finger slowly and carefully. Deandra smiled.

Jeff spoke softly and deliberately. "I need to tell you, darling, how wonderful these ten days have been for me. The kind of world I operate in doesn't allow one to relax. This holiday has been calming, revealing, and educational."

"Educational?" repeated Deandra.

"Yes, educational. I've learned a lot from you and about you."

"To begin with, you've destroyed the myth that a professional and intellectual woman lacks warmth, feelings, and the need for good wholesome love-making. You've allowed us to enjoy sex without any ulterior motives."

"I hadn't thought of love and ulterior motives as going hand in hand. The way I perceive it, when we mix love with ulterior motives, it is no longer love. I call that control, domination, and deceit. My late friend, Aunt Clem, helped me to differentiate between love and control."

Jeff smiled, then remarked, "So you and the old lady also talked about sex and love?"

"Why not? She had lived and had many interesting stories to tell. Furthermore, they say there are many young minds living in some old bodies. Isn't love intergenerational?"

"See what I mean by education," said Jeff, then picked up the conversation where they had left off. "But going back to what I said, I'm very serious. Not even once did you show any sign of restlessness, being in a quiet place like this. I didn't feel pressured into changing with you being here. And even though the Boles' sperms were trapped, you are the greatest," he said, ending with his penetrating look.

"Jeff, with your creative and romantic approach, how could anyone be bored? But tell me, do you feel very rested?"

"I've just told you so, sweetheart. More than I've ever felt before."

The music had long since stopped playing. Jeff grudgingly lifted his head from Deandra's lap and, easing himself on to his feet, pulled her up from the sofa and into the bedroom.

The following day, Jeff and Deandra drove away from Hide Away, feeling relaxed and comfortable with themselves.

CHAPTER FIFTEEN

As Deandra lay awake that night, she tried to analyze some of the words so often used to define and describe people's feelings and lifestyles. The words, love, sex, values, rules, and morals kept pounding in her brain as she debated with herself.

Rules, she mused. Rules defined by many, observed by whom? Rules to be broken or not to be? But if a rule was not broken, how would the rule makers defend morality and ethical behavior. Come to think of it, she continued her monologue, to some, making love as Jeff and I did for those ten glorious days, might be seen as far less than moral. But with the value we place on love, our intimacies might support our actions as both moral and ethical. But had I denied the fact that I wanted Jeff as much as he wanted me, that could probably be considered unethical. And as I think back now, becoming pregnant only to satisfy Jeff's pressing desire would possibly end up with a child of diluted love, and that would be unfair.

Suddenly Deandra switched her thoughts. "Damn it girl, stop being such a bore, say it like it is. You and Jeffrey Boles enjoyed each other and it's nobody's business."

She finally fell asleep and woke up to the sounds of the birds that nested near to her apartment.

When Deandra called Lucreta the following evening, she was eager to hear all about her exclusive Hide Away vacation. "It's great to hear your voice, Deandra. I hope you and Jeff had a wonderful time at Hide Away."

"I sure did. And from what Jeff said, he had a great time too and was very rested, at that."

"I knew you would be good for him. He really needs a levelheaded and secure woman around. Anyway, I'm glad that you got something out of it too."

"Well you know, Lucreta, it would have been idiotic to agree to be involved in a situation where it would be totally one-sided. So, tell me about you."

"I'm fine, except for a little tiredness at times. But I'm going to delegate more responsibility to my assistant. I must report to you that I wore my first maternity dress to work today. You remember that royal blue, two-piece dress? Well, even my boss complemented me for my good taste. But I had to explain that it was my friend who had selected that outfit for me. When are we going to get together again?"

"We'll make a date soon. I'll check with you before. Bye now."

Around ten o'clock the next morning, Deandra picked up her mail at the post office. She said good-day to the few people who had been waiting in line.

She didn't recognize one of the old ladies she had met the first time she went to the post office. "Hello miss," came the voice of the woman. "I haven't seen you since that first day when we had that little chat."

"That's right, ma'am. How are you and the other ladies who were with you that day?"

"We are doing the best we can. I'm really here to buy a couple of air-letters to write to foreign."

"Is your daughter, the pharmacist, still living at Lucky Pond apartments?"

"How nice of you to ask. So you really remember us, that's good. She still lives there and she is getting married soon. That's why I'm going to write and tell a few friends in foreign."

It was Deandra's turn to get her mail. She moved to the window and smiled at Miss Benka, the postal clerk.

"Hi, Miss Boggs. There's a pile of letters and magazines here for you. I was just beginning to wonder why you hadn't picked up your mail for two weeks."

"Thanks for your concern and for keeping my mail, Miss Benka."

Deandra smiled to herself and thought about the intimacy and camaraderie of this small community. Almost everybody knew one another, and if they didn't know what was happening in each other's lives, they used their imaginations.

When she returned home, she first opened the letter from the publishing house. In that letter, her boss reminded her that they were looking forward to her presenting her manuscript in a few weeks.

"So what else is new," murmured Deandra. She always intended to fulfill her contract, and with that, she pledged to put the final touches on the manuscript.

By the following week she had completed her last paragraph. She then wrapped it in a piece of thick brown paper, tied it with a big red bow, and placed it in the center of the coffee table, then said, "Yes-s! . . . I've got you babe, now it's my time."

No sooner had she said that, when Jeff knocked on her door. When Deandra opened the door, he remarked, "Didn't know your neighbors were still peeping through their blinds?"

"I suspect they do it less now. I can't recall seeing them lately. We do say hello, though, whenever we bump into each other. They're a little strange."

Jeff stood by the coffee table, looked at the brown paper package and exclaimed, "What a beautiful package! May I ask what's in it?"

"My manuscript."

"May I hold it please, Miss Boggs?"

"Most certainly, Mr. Boles."

He lifted the package and held it close to his chest, then said, "You know something sweetheart? You're special. I'm really holding a lot of you and parts I'm sure couldn't be experienced through the spoken words or even holding you."

"What a nice thing to say, Jeff. I hope you won't be disappointed when you read the finished product, which I'm assuming you will."

"Stop assuming anything. You must know that I've been curious about your writing all along. Rest assured that I'll read it as soon as possible."

"By the way, Jeff, there's a play opening at one of the small theaters, about AIDS. I'd love to see it. What about you?"

"I'll say yes to that. The public needs to be educated about this killer. We only get one shot at life, yet you'd be surprised to hear the myths that many of us have about the disease."

"So, we'll go and see the play?"

"Yes. But why don't you handle the arrangements? You are

better at such things than I am." He sighed, then continued. "I wish you'd give up this place and stay at Embers Glade. That way I would always have you there when I got home."

"Now that you've mentioned moving, I got a letter from my publisher reminding me to be in the States very soon."

"But you've completed the manuscript, so delivering it shouldn't be any problem, even though it would be better if it could be delivered by express mail. But to make up for the time you'll be away, you should stay at my place. Furthermore, by that time, I'll have only a few more months to get Angelica out of the picture . . . Freedom."

"Things have a way of working out, Jeff. It's quite possible that I could return to Nufuma. Then we could take it from there."

"I've decided not to get into a fight with you. When last were we together since Hide Away?"

"Close to a week, I'd say."

"And yet you're intent on tormenting me by leaving me alone in that house. At least you can't tell me you're unable to stay longer at Embers Glade, now that you have a beautiful brown paper package sitting in front of us."

"So what are you suggesting?"

"I'm suggesting you come and stay at least two days with me. I'll need that time with you before I leave for the north shore next week."

Deandra sat quietly thinking, then concluded silently that Jeff was determined to have her spend more time at Embers Glade. Truth was, she was quite excited about his proposition. She finally responded to Jeff's request by asking, "Since you've stripped me of any excuse, at least I need to know when."

"Now sweetheart," he said. He loosened his tie, took off his jacked then asked, "So?"

"Okay. You win."

As they walked out of the apartment, Jeff asked, "Would you like us to revisit the Hutch, D?"

"Most definitely, Jeff."

They were lucky to get the last two boiled lobsters. Jeff was extremely happy. He hoped Deandra would enjoy the lobster as she did the first time they had eaten there. And she didn't disappoint him.

He had called and told Mrs. Cato not to wait to serve him dinner.

When they got home, the house was deserted. "You're in charge, D. I'm your humble servant and at your command."

"If ever there was a slight twist of the facts, it's your statement Jeff. Who's always in charge around here?"

"Stop making up tales, you know that you could tell me to jump and I would," said Jeff with his devastating laugh.

After they had settled down, Jeff changed into his bath trunks and asked Deandra to join in for a short swim in the pool.

"You've tricked me again. I didn't bring a bathing suit."

"Shame on you," teased Jeff, then went into the bedroom and brought out a yellow bikini. He waved it playfully in front of Deandra, then dropped it into her lap. It was a brand new bikini that he'd bought at one of the plazas.

Jeffrey completed two laps before Deandra joined him. In a few minutes they were showering together. He drew Deandra to him and kissed her with all the force of his pent up passion. Deandra had to remind him of their plans for the evening before he would release her.

The two main characters in the AIDS show were played by two promising young actors. The theme centered on two young people. The girl was eighteen and had been sexually active, or more correctly, promiscuous, from age fourteen. The young man was twenty-two. He also admitted to being promiscuous for five years. Both young people were convinced that they could not become infected even though they had practiced unsafe sex.

There was an intermission during the play. Jeff and Deandra went outside. They couldn't help overhearing the discussion of two older women. "I'm glad you dragged me to see this play, Mary," said one of the women.

"You couldn't be more pleased than I," answered her friend. "But I must admit that for a long time I believed that this AIDS thing affected only certain people."

"Me too, Mary. But now we know it's not so. It's a serious thing. Too many of our young people are dying. How are we going to stop this epidemic?"

"Well, my dear, I must confess that we'll have to be more honest with our children."

"How, Mary?"

"You know, like unveiling the mystery and taboos surrounding sex. In my day—and even today—many parents misinformed their children. They told them we reproduce ourselves through some form outside the act of sex. You know, the immaculate conception thing. Meanwhile everybody is doing it."

"Doing what, Mary?"

"Having sex. We lie about sex because there's a silly notion that it's dirty and sinful. And so we don't talk with our young people about the beauty of sex when people are mature enough to handle it. This kind of teaching should include self protection. Too many of our children go about endangering themselves and others."

"Who should teach this sex education then?"

"Parents, schools, and all informed persons."

The play ended dramatically with two young emaciated bodies waiting for death in a hospice. Jeff and Deandra drove back to Embers Glade, touching each other frequently. When they got out of the car, they moved toward each other and entered the house with an arm around each other.

The two days had gone by much too fast for Jeff's liking. He didn't want Deandra to leave, admitting that he was a little selfish when it concerned the two of them.

When Deandra returned to her apartment, there were some letters which she had not yet read. Her mother's letter was among them. The tone of Mrs. Boggs' letter wasn't the usual style of expressing herself. She focused more on herself and less on Deandra. It was obvious that her mother was displeased about something. She phoned her immediately. "

"Hello Mother," called Deandra.

"Is that you, Deandra? Are you okay, baby?"

"Yes Mom, it's your only daughter. "

"Thank God yu okay. I been calling yu for the las' two days an' couldn't get yu."

Deandra knew that her mother was upset. She spoke Patois whenever she was.

"Mom, are you all right?"

"Now that I'm talking with you, I'm okay, but when I couldn't get you on the phone I was scared out of my wits. With all the crime around, you never know."

"I'm one of the luckiest women around, Mom. I have a mother who worries, and sometimes too much, about her daughter."

Mrs. Boggs remained silent for a while, then replied petulantly, "About that pressuring business, Deandra, I won't do that anymore. I just want you to be happy, my dear. But just the same, I'm longing to see you. So when you hang up the phone, I want you to remember I am not pressuring you."

When she had finished talking with her mother, Deandra smiled and felt relieved that she had called. She admitted to herself that she had been neglecting her occasionally.

Later, she called Lucreta and they made a date for the following day. She was dressed and ready to leave for the luncheon date when the doorbell rang. She opened the door. There was a man holding a beautiful bouquet of flowers.

He asked, "Are you Miss Deandra Boggs?"

"Yes I am," she replied.

"These flowers are for you ma'am. Please sign for them."

She was running late and had time only to select a spot away from the sun to put the flowers, then she put the card in her bag and drove away. She arrived just as Lucreta was getting out of her BMW.

"Hi!" she called out to her friend, as Lucreta waved to her.

Lucreta's pregnancy was beginning to show. Her belly was pushing out just under her belly button.

"You look like a high fashion model, my dear, instead of a pregnant woman."

"Thank you, Deandra. But why shouldn't a pregnant woman look gorgeous?"

"Can't think of any good reason. But I don't remember helping you to select this dress?"

"You did though. Remember holding up the dress against my face, then saying the red looked great with my copper color?"

"Now I remember. You do look good. I can understand why Daniel dotes on you."

They laughed.

"He does so now, more than ever."

"Enough of that mushy talk. I'm still a single girl."

"And maybe not for too much longer, from what I've heard."

They went into the restaurant laughing. Lucreta had reserved the same table she got when she had first taken Deandra to the Water Front Restaurant.

As they waited to be served, Deandra remembered the card that came with the flowers. Her eyes widened in surprise when she saw that it was from Paul.

"Excuse me while I glance at this note, Lucreta."

"Stop being so formal, read your love card."

The Female and the Universe in Motion

She is the mother of the universe
The universe long since changed,
She is the mother of the beginning
The beginning of life force . . .
That force which fosters community and commonality
She is the succor and hope of our survival,
Yes. The mother whose love embraces us all

To my dearest princess,
From the guy you can't run away from,
Paul

Deandra looked up at Lucreta as the waiter greeted her and took their order. When the waiter had left, she said to Lucreta, "I've just read a poem that was meant for me, but it has a universal appeal. As a matter of fact, in your very pregnant state, it's rather appro-pro for you."

"Now that you've teased my curiosity, are you going to serve me an intellectual appetizer, before we eat?"

"Since you insist I'll share it with you," retorted Deandra before she read the poem to Lucreta.

Lucreta slowly absorbed each word and remarked, "How profound, Deandra. It conveys a feeling of concern for the world, placing the woman in a very pivotal role . . . It's deep."

"You've described it so well, Lucreta. I must agree that a lot of thought was put into it."

By then, the waiter had arrived with their lunch. They talked as they ate. From the look on Deandra's face, Lucreta guessed that the note might have been from Paul. Deandra had once mentioned how cerebral he could get.

"Well, Lucreta, tell me about the commonly talked about food preferences during this phase of a woman's life."

"Except for ice cream, my appetite remains normal."

"But ice cream is fattening."

"Yes. I know, but Daniel and Aunt May try very hard to keep me in check. But as I sit across from you, Deandra, I can't help remembering when we came here many months ago."

"Yes. I remember that so well. A lot of water has gone under the bridge since."

"And how, my dear! You've helped me a lot, Deandra."

"I don't know about that. You were brought up in a different world, so you had to be exposed to another. That's all. I must admit though, that unlike our first time here, you are a picture of calmness and contentment."

Lucreta smiled. Her eyes flashed a look of agreement. "Yes, indeed, my dear. Things are better than ever with Daniel and me. Do you know he has threatened to sabotage my job if I don't cut down on my work load. Now I'm able to lunch with you without rushing."

After lunch, Deandra drove straight home, avoiding the rundown areas she had explored before. At last she was able to relax and do all the things she wanted to.

The flowers greeted her as she entered the apartment. She sat, looked at them, then realized that the bouquet was made up only of delicate purple and red flowers. Yes, of course, she recalled Paul had always reminded her about the role of the color red in their relationship, and he had always called her his princess. She moved the flowers and placed them in the center of the dining table, away from the glare of the sun. She read the poem again and locked it away in her drawer.

The day before Jeff left for the north coast, he dropped in to say good-bye.

"Hello sweetheart. Anything exciting to share since I saw you?"

They chatted for a while. In the meantime Jeff had been eyeing the flowers.

"I haven't sent you flowers lately, D, but you seem to be pretty well supplied anyway."

"I wouldn't put it quite that way, Jeff. I don't need flowers everyday. Your presence means more than flowers. Don't get me wrong, I love flowers."

"Again, I'm thrilled to hear that my presence means more than flowers, sweetheart," Jeff said with a tinge of sarcasm.

Deandra's heart was beginning to beat fast. "What can I get

you, Jeff?"

"A glass of water will do."

He clenched his teeth as she went to get the water, trying desperately to conceal his feelings.

"So, who sent you that special basket of flowers?"

"Oh, those?"

"Yes. Those D."

Actually, they were a surprise . . . Transatlantic."

Jeff was beginning to be irritated, or just plain jealous.

"Stop playing games. Are those flowers from your old flame in New York?"

"I don't know the meaning of your connotation for old flame, but they are from an old friend whom I've not seen for over a year."

"So how the hell did he get your address to wire you flowers, Deandra?"

"Don't push things to the extreme, Jeff. I hope you haven't forgotten that I still have a mother living in New York, who just happens to have my address."

She realized that Jeff was upset and that this was due to jealousy. He rarely called her Deandra, except when he was angry. Deandra nestled up to him and rested her head on his shoulder.

Jeff ruffled her hair and whispered, "I don't like that guy from New York sending you flowers." He then held her face between his hands and kissed her with a burning fervor.

Before he left, they had mended their lover's tiff. Deandra was left alone to ponder her private thoughts. They were similar in many ways, but still each was different from the other, she thought. For a while Paul wanted her to settle down, he tried to allow her more time to make up her mind. On the other hand, Jeff was more aggressive and rather in a hurry. Sometimes she felt he had already made up her mind for her.

It was about twelve o'clock on the same night when she was awakened from a deep sleep by the ringing of the phone.

"Hello," answered Deandra sleepily.

"Hello sweetheart, I love you."

"Jeff darling, I love you too."

"Go back to sleep. Good night."

It took her a little while to fall asleep. She dreamed of Jeff sailing on his big yacht.

It had been some time since Deandra had spoken with Esme Nwanga. There was something about Esme that interested her. Esme was a very bright woman, yet so unassuming. Deandra got a lot of insight from her as she talked about Emanuel's frequent trips to Africa. That sounded similar to Jeff's frequent and extensive trips. She decided to speak to her later in the day.

She had just poured herself a glass of fruit juice and was returning the bottle to the fridge when the phone rang. As a rule, no one ever called so early in the day. She suddenly thought of her mother and hoped that she was okay. When she picked up the receiver, Jeff was on the line.

"Jeff!" She called. "Is everything all right?"

"No sweetheart."

"What is it, please?"

"I just got a call that Emanuel and Esme Nwanga were in an accident. Emanuel was killed on the spot. Esme received minor injuries."

"Oh my God . . . Oh no! Jeff, believe it or not, I had planned to call Esme today. I'm numbed."

"I'm in shock too, but life goes on. Esme and her child will need their friends to rally around them now. I'll be home tomorrow. We'll get more details then and we'll visit Esme, all right D?"

"All right Jeff. I'll be here."

Deandra sat on the sofa with her head in her hands. Tears came to her eyes as she recalled how proud Emanuel had been of his wife, and she wrote:

Fragile Life
Boundaries separating life from death
Boundaries so fragile, they are hard to define.
Boundaries as fragile as a butterfly,
A butterfly that flutters in your hand then dies
Life is that much fragile too . . .
And will take a lifetime to be defined!

Later that day, Lucreta called to talk with Deandra about the accident. Ten days after the accident, Jeff, Deandra, Lucreta, and Daniel witnessed the burial of their young friend, Emanuel Nwanga. They tried their best to comfort Esme who broke down in tears. As they left the funeral, Deandra was more convinced than ever that each person is mirrored in the other, for regardless of values or philosophy, when that selfish veil of death lays its claim, no one can escape it.

CHAPTER SIXTEEN

The death of Emanuel Nwanga affected not only his immediate family, but many of his friends likewise. To Deandra, Jeff, Lucreta, and Daniel, his passing ran deeper than just the loss of a friend. It had brought home to them their own mortality, and the fragility of life in general. They were in the same age range, give or take two to four years; they had had may things in common. They were hardworking, family-oriented and were in the prime of their lives. Everything had seemed so well-organized; they were enjoying the good life. But suddenly, one of their own had been snatched away by that impartial villain.

Jeff was very supportive of Esme. As a matter of fact, he was called upon quite often to advise her about her late husband's business. In the meantime, Deandra and Lucreta supported Esme and her two-year-old son by just being there. They visited in person and by phone as often as they could.

One Sunday afternoon, after Deandra and Jeff had returned from sailing, with Emanuel on both of their minds, they talked about life in general.

"Tell me, D," asked Jeff, "do you believe that life treats us fairly?"

Deandra looked off into the distance. A brief silence followed before she answered, "It's a difficult question and I don't have an answer. But it might well be that it's not how life treats us, but rather how we go about seeing and living life."

"You've made an interesting point, but Emanuel put a hell of a lot in his life and, mind you, not just for the present, but for the future as well. Then came that crazy crack-head to take his life. That was nothing less than a wanton and immoral act. How are we going to get these people from behind the wheel of a moving vehicle?"

Deandra listened carefully and thought about life defined from infancy to old age. But in reality, it didn't necessarily follow that path, as she remembered Aunt Clem and now Emanuel who had not even completed the young adult stage.

"I couldn't agree with you more, Jeff. Curiously, I've been thinking about morals and morality for the last couple of weeks. And the more I try to analyze them, the more difficult it has become to find them in an undiluted or, better yet, unpolluted state."

"Is that what you would describe as searching for a needle in a haystack?" asked Jeff.

"I suppose you could put it that way."

They had stopped talking. Jeff got up and moved toward the phone, remarking, "Let me give Esme a ring to see how she is doing with that lawyer I recommended."

They spent the rest of the afternoon in a reflective, but not morbid, mood. Jeff stayed over and left early the following morning.

Lucreta's belly was really showing. At four months, she had gained too much weight and looked about five months pregnant. Daniel suggested that she quit working in her seventh month. She had even started to plan the nursery for the baby, sometimes asking Deandra for suggestions.

On one such occasion, Deandra laughed and said, "You mustn't forget that you're seeking the advice of a novice. I'm sure Daniel can do better than I can."

"Are you joking, my friend? My dear husband is color blind. He has excellent vision, but not when it comes to decorating."

"What about yellow paint and some interesting wall paper with animals, Lucreta?"

"That's a good idea," she replied, and made a note of it in her baby-book. She turned and continued, "We're planning to have an outdoor family party next week. It will coincide with Daniel's birthday. I trust you and Jeff will be around."

"Thanks for the invitation, but I can only speak for myself. You know the kind of schedule your friend has. Check with him."

"I'll do that, but I want you to know so that he won't sneak you out of town."

The barbecue would take place on a Saturday afternoon. Jeff would meet Deandra at the Clarke's. As Deandra drove the little Volkswagen to Embers Glade, she had mixed emotions. She was excited, yet sad because in a matter of weeks she would be leaving Nufuma and hadn't fully decided on a possible return trip.

She had not paid sufficient attention to the Embers Glade community before today. She drove slowly up the long avenue, looking at each house in turn. She couldn't get over the huge, palatial houses, surrounded by enormous grounds. This place was home of the rich and powerful in Nufuma, a class which included a fair number of expatriates. The roads were wide and beautifully kept. Both sides of the roads were lined with croton and bougainvillea plants, with low stone walls around them. The place was beautiful but almost too sterile to be real. She was happy to see two teenage boys in walking shorts and sneakers racing each other on bicycles.

When she rang the Clarke's doorbell, it was one o'clock in the afternoon. As Lucreta let her in, she could hear the voices of the children in the background. "Jennifer, if you don't leave that alone, I'm going to hit you," came the voice of Raymond.

"Glad you got here early, hope you can tolerate my two bundles of energy who you heard yelling in the back," remarked Lucreta.

"Will you please stop explaining to me about the kids. I might not be a mother yet, dear heart," Deandra teased, "but I adore children. As a matter of fact, on my way up, the neighborhood seemed so quiet, had it not been for two boys who were out biking, I would have thought that Embers Glade residents didn't have children."

"You're not too far off base, Deandra. This is a community where people have between two to three kids. Suppose it's close to the two point five children per family that we've been hearing about."

Suddenly the two children were running toward their mother. Raymond, the older one, was chasing his sister, Jennifer, who held onto a part of his new train set, a gift from their grandfather. They stopped abruptly as soon as they saw Deandra, calling out, "Hello Aunty D."

"Come here you two. Now your Aunty D will believe me when I tell her that you are no angels," reprimanded Lucreta.

Deandra smiled and chatted with the kids, saying as an aside to Lucreta, "Each time I see the kids the more I'm certain that their photos don't do them justice. They are gorgeous."

"Thank you, Deandra," said Lucreta as she ushered them out of the room. "Do you want to freshen up before we go out to the back? You know where to find the dressing room," called Lucreta. "By the way, my in-laws are joining us today."

Deandra went into the dressing room, adjusted her hair, applied a little lip gloss, and smoothed her cheeks. She examined the narrow strapped white jumpsuit that she was wearing, making sure there were no soiled spots, then dabbed her neck and arms with Elizabeth Arden Blue Grass before going out to meet the rest of the family.

Lucreta introduced her to Mr. and Mrs. Clarke, Daniel's parents. They looked more like brother and sister than wife and husband. Maybe it was true, Deandra thought, that couples grow to look and even behave like each other.

Daniel was busy at the barbecue pit and called out, "Hi, Deandra, how was your ride up?"

"It couldn't be any better, Daniel. It's a perfect day for driving."

The back veranda was huge and overlooked the swimming pool. The air was sweet with the perfume of the white gardenias that were planted close to the side of the house. The atmosphere was very relaxed; it was a day for family interactions. Everything was laid out for no-fuss dining. Aunt May had interrupted her day off and, as a member of the family, insisted on helping Daniel at the barbecue pit.

Lucreta looked happy and extra pretty in her green maternity shorts and orange top. She wore her hair in a pony tail and looked more like a teenager than a very pregnant woman. She was heading toward the table with the refreshments when she spotted Deandra sitting on the veranda.

"Deandra, come over here, you're family now whether you know it or not. Select what you want."

Deandra decided to start with fruit punch and filled a glass before going outside to investigate how Daniel and Aunt May were coping with the cooking.

"Daniel," Deandra called out, "I didn't realize you were a pro at the pit."

"Maybe it's better if you play it safe and don't say too much, until you've tasted the outcome."

"Don't let him fool you, Deandra," interjected Lucreta. "Daniel is a good chef. He specializes in gourmet foods. I want you to know that he has a special barbecue sauce that he refuses to share with me or Aunt May."

Deandra went and sat by the rose garden. She felt lucky to have such wonderful friends. She felt a tinge of jealousy of the warmth and closeness of their family life. As she soaked up the beauty of the place, she thought about the idea and possibility of settling down and starting a family of her own.

As soon as she was about to get up, a voice shouted, "Please don't move." It was Raymond who had been assigned photographer for the day. She resumed her sitting position and touched a fully bloomed rose, as Raymond snapped his camera.

As she looked at Raymond and Jennifer walking by the pool, she decided that they inherited equal parts of their parents. The two had a kind of yellow-brown complexion with curly black hair.

Lucreta had forewarned Deandra about her father-in-law's flirtatiousness, especially with young women. But even with the warning, Deandra was surprised when she returned to the veranda and old man Clarke blurted, "I've heard a lot about you from my daughter-in-law. She told me how pretty you are, but seeing you for myself, I must say you are indeed a beauty."

It was a little more than Deandra had expected. She felt self-conscious and blushed. "Thank you for the compliments, Mr. Clarke."

"You're not married yet, Deandra?"

"No, Mr. Clarke."

"What's the matter with our men today? A woman like you should have been Mrs. Somebody long ago," said the old man.

His wife came to the rescue and remarked reproachfully, "Jerry, things are not like they were when we were young, you know. Nowadays, you'll find women don't want to get married, or they get married later."

Lucreta joined in and said, "Thank you Mom, please let Dad know that women have more choices today than in your day."

Mr. Clarke again spoke, "I don't care what they say, it's good to settle down early. That's why we were happy when you and Daniel tied the knot as early as you did. By the way, Deandra, are you from a big family?"

"I'm an only child."

Lucreta again intervened. "She's an only child just like your Daniel."

Deandra was saved by the sound of the doorbell. "Oh, it's you, Jeff," said Lucreta as she opened the door. "We were beginning to wonder whether or not you were off to some other place."

"Nonsense, Lucreta," he said, hugging her. "You look mighty beautiful. Pregnancy becomes you sweetheart."

"Thank you, Jeff," answered Lucreta as she led the way to the party. Jeff was no stranger to the clan. They greeted each other with light pleasantries before Jeff walked over to Deandra, kissed her on the forehead, and asked, "Have you been here long, D?"

"Not really, but when you're having fun, time isn't important."

Old man Clarke winked and smiled at Deandra.

Jeff then proceeded to find Daniel at the pit. "Hi, old boy. So they got you cooking your own birthday dinner again."

"You know how it goes fellow. The boss gives the orders and I obey. Anyway, this time it's my decision."

"I know that Lucreta didn't lasso you into this one. You never miss a chance to show off your cooking skills. You make the best barbecue that I know of, though."

The two men chatted as Daniel cooked the last piece of chicken. It was just around four o'clock when Lucreta announced that everything was ready. It was quite a spread of chicken, spareribs, hamburgers, and fish. Aunt May had prepared boiled breadfruit and green pea salad, yellow rice and a huge vegetable salad. The spread could feed at least forty people, but it was a picnic and no one was going to be counting calories. If anything was expected, it was to fill up your plate at least twice.

When everyone had finally settled down with a plate of food, they all agreed that Doctor Clarke was indeed hiding his talents. The food was delicious. As soon as they had finished the main course, Aunt May rolled out the dessert wagon with the birthday cake.

Lucreta stood by the wagon in the center of the veranda and announced, "Well, as you all know, today just happens to be Daniel's birthday and, even though he would prefer to throw away the calendar, we just wouldn't let him get away with it."

"That's right, Lucreta," joined in old man Clarke. "My son is as good as new. The man hasn't even started to live yet. Look, he has got two people standing there in one."

Daniel knew his dad very well, and intervened before he became a little too explicit. They proceeded with a champagne toast and sang, "For he's a jolly good fellow . . . so say all of us."

As they started to cut the cake, the doorbell rang. It was their friends the Lees, who had been delayed by an unexpected visit from an old friend. The Clarke's could understand the delay. Dropping in unannounced was a Nufuman custom.

Before Deandra and Jeff left the Clarke's that evening, Lucreta chatted with her friend then inquired, "Did you have fun, Deandra?"

"And how! Plenty, plenty," said Deandra laughing.

"I warned you about Dad, didn't I?"

"You sure did. But what a guy!"

She thanked Lucreta and Daniel for a delightful and fun party. She and Jeff finally said good-bye to all and drove away to Lucky Pond.

As soon as they entered the apartment, Deandra declared, "I need to get out of this jumpsuit. I feel like I'm bursting at the seams after all that food."

She disappeared into the bedroom, and emerged moments later in her dressing gown. Jeff made himself comfortable in his usual position on the sofa.

"You seem to have had fun today, sweetheart," remarked Jeff.

"The Clarke's are a great family, including Daddy Clarke," he said smiling at her.

"You can say that again. What an old man! He put me through . . . Anyway, he spoke his mind."

"D, you haven't been around men very much. You lost your father early in life, you told me."

"That's true."

"Well, men are a peculiar type of animal, especially from the old school. Most times their bark is more than their bite."

"I see. That may be one good reason for growing up with two parents—I mean good parents—to expose you to both the male and female world. The two sexes tend to see and approach some things differently."

"I must admit that you're right."

Jeff changed the subject. He remembered Deandra's reaction to his proposal of having a child before his divorce. "I need to bring you up-to-date about Esme and Emanuel's estate. Emanuel had asked me to be his executor for the estate—just in case . . . Anyway, knowing the time involved and my frequent trips abroad, I declined, but consented to guide and recommend reputable legal advice. There's quite a lot of work involved, but Esme seems satisfied with the lawyer I recómmended. She wants to continue the business on a reduced scale."

"I'm glad that you're able to assist her, Jeff. I can only imagine. But she must be hurting very much, what with a young child to rear. It sounds as though she's taking the right approach in scaling down the business."

"Yes. She's quite a bright and astute business woman—a side of her I wasn't aware of until this tragedy."

As they sat silently ruminating, Deandra felt pleased about Jeff's assessment of Esme. Women have always played the supportive roles while too often their creative and other skills go unnoticed, she felt. She wished Esme good luck and hoped that she would do as good a job with her son as Marion Boggs had done with her.

"Hi D. What's buzzing in that brain of yours?" asked Jeff as he reached for her and untied the satin dressing gown she was wearing.

Deandra attempted to rewrap the gown around her waist, but Jeff had already taken possession of the belt. She pulled away from him and moved to the kitchen where she got some drinks. And as she walked back to the living room carrying the two glasses, she was aware that Jeff watched her every move. With each step she made, the open gown revealed her firm and shapely legs.

Jeff wanted to conceal his desire for her at that moment, but the passion she aroused in him was overpowering. He took the two filled glasses, put them on the floor, and kissed Deandra, whispering, "You've done something to me. I can't get enough of you. I won't give up."

He continued to kiss her entire body until she was completely disrobed. Deandra's body had become limp as he led her to the bedroom. Deandra attempted to speak, but her lips were by then completely possessed by Jeff. It was like drinking wine, the way he kissed her while touching her smooth skin all over. Neither of them wanted the love-making to end. It was total ecstasy all the way.

* * *

Lucreta and Deandra visited Esme together on the following day. It was a very cloudy and dull day. As soon as they entered the house, the weather suddenly changed to thunder and lightening.

"It's so good to see you two," Esme said, smiling as she greeted them.

In the background they could hear Odeki yelling, "I wan' my daddy. Where's Daddy, he's not coming home, mummy?"

Esme lifted her child and held him fondly to her chest, then accompanied Lucreta and Deandra to the living room.

"It's so nice of you to come out here in this dreadful weather. Odeki always screamed for his dad whenever there was thunder and lightening. And I've always wondered why he felt a special need for his father at such times. Maybe when he is a little older, he'll let me in on his secret, if he remembers."

"Children are sweethearts, even when they pull and tear everything apart and scream when there's lightening," remarked Lucreta.

"I'm sure you and Esme could write a guide on child rearing for novices like me," observed Deandra.

By then the thunder and lightening had stopped. The toddler had become engrossed with a wooden toy wagon that Deandra had brought him.

"But my goodness, Lucreta, you're simply gorgeous, my friend. When is the great event, may I ask?" inquired Esme.

"Another four months or so. And I'm trying to keep Deandra around to be the midwife," answered Lucreta with a tease in her voice.

"I'm really happy for you, Lucreta . . . By the way, how's the book coming, Deandra?"

"I've finally completed the manuscript and within the next three months I should be handing it over to the people who are paying me to be here."

"That's great news. I hope I'll have the honor of getting an autographed copy."

"Most definitely, Esme."

"Wouldn't it be great if we could keep her here and send the manuscript by air express."

"Indeed that would be great, but I think it's important to make that presentation in person."

"Maybe with Jeff's help, we will get her back here, especially for an exciting and well-organized book party."

"I'm relying on you to help me work on that, Esme," remarked Lucreta. "So, how are things working out for you, Esme?"

"Well, let me begin by saying that without friends like you, it would have been very rough. But especially Jeff, he's been my guide. He's been very helpful with steering me in the right direction concerning the business, not to mention that whenever he drops in, Junior tries to take him over. He follows his Uncle Jeff around and makes demands to be lifted."

"That's nice to hear," interjected Deandra. "But I understand that you're quite an astute and capable business woman, Esme."

"Esme suddenly became sad, lowered her head, and replied, "Thank you for boosting my morale, but in times like these, someone has got to take charge and it falls on me."

They said good-bye to Esme and her son, and left for home. Deandra decided to spend the rest of the evening perusing some of the magazines she had stacked in one corner of the living room. Just when she had turned off the light and started to ready herself for bed, the phone rang.

"Hello," spoke Deandra into the receiver.

"Hello there. How are you?"

"Is that you, Paul?"

"Yes. It's Persevering Paul."

"Before we say anymore, Paul, it was my honest intention to call and thank you for the beautiful flowers, but you've sabotaged it."

"Me, a saboteur? And with you! Never in your wildest dreams. Anyway, I'm pleased to hear that the flowers were delivered."

"They took me by complete surprise and . . . the colors were so evocative."

The word evocative lifted his optimism. He had long hoped that there would be some lingering remnant of their past that would rekindle their love. "I'm glad to hear you say that the colors brought back memories. I'm hoping that such memories are pleasant ones."

She evaded answering any pointed question and remarked, "By the way, Paul, that poem was profound and with a universal connotation."

"So you like it?"

"Very much."

"Well, my dearest, although your universal interpretation of the poem may be applicable and appropriate, it was written with only you in mind."

Deandra mused about the poem, recalling Lucreta's reaction when she had read it to her. Finally returning to the telephone conversation, she replied, "Anyway, I'm flattered to be the inspiration for a simple yet profound poem."

"Before I forget, Deandra, I was in Canada last month. My folks asked about you, and hope that you will visit them soon."

There was no doubt in her mind that Paul was aiming for a trump card by mentioning his family with whom she had always had a good relationship. She decided to end the conversation.

"Well, Paul, it was nice of your family to remember me. Who knows, we might bump into each other. Please return my regards to them when you talk with them again. It's good of you to call."

"As I was saying, you possess that special something that forever lingers with whomever you come in contact. Stay well, and I will be talking with you soon . . . could even surprise you, my dear."

With that he hung up.

Deandra lay on top of the sheets and stared at the ceiling as Paul's voice lingered with her. The memory of meeting his family was as vivid in her mind as though it had just occurred.

It was a cold New Year's Eve when Paul took me to meet his family in Canada. When we arrived in Toronto, it had been snowing so heavily that we could hardly see where we were going. The taxi driver drove slowly. Even with the artificial fur-lined coat I was wearing, I was shivering when we entered Violet Wisdom's home. Mrs. Wisdom opened the door and, with a broad smile on her face, greeted us jubilantly.

"Come in, you two," she said. "It's too cold for even a polar bear to be out there."

Paul hugged his mother and grinned at her. "Hi Mom! You feel so nice and warm, meet my friend Deandra.

"Hi Deandra, sorry we couldn't have kinder weather to welcome you to Toronto. We'll make sure you're warmed up soon," she said as she escorted us to the living room where there was a glowing, crackling fire.

When Paul returned from hanging up our coats, Violet turned to me commenting, "I heard a lot about you, Deandra. I'm so glad to meet you in person."

"I too heard a lot about you, through Paul. I must tell you, he's very proud of you."

"Trust that son of mine to inflate my ego with his praise. But I must tell you, the feeling is mutual, for my son, he's a swell guy."

Paul left us talking and went to find something to warm us up. He returned with a scotch for himself and some wine for me, then remarked, "I'm sure Mom will make us some hot tea or coffee soon."

"As I was saying before we were rudely interrupted," said Violet smiling, "I don't know if Paul told you, but we're a very informal family. I want you to feel comfortable. You may call me Violet or whatever you're comfortable with. We want you to feel at home, my dear."

Violet Wisdom made fresh coffee and sandwiches for us. Over coffee she described to me her family. Her description was indeed correct. That New Years day, Paul's two sisters, their husbands and children assembled at their mother's home to celebrate. They made me feel as though I was a member of the family clan.

Before meeting the Wisdom's family, I wondered how Violet Wisdom would react to me, the other woman who would probably share her son, but to my surprise, I discovered that she was pushing her son to marry me, based on his description of me.

The following day, Deandra returned to her routine in preparation for delivering the manuscript that she had devoted so much of herself to.

CHAPTER SEVENTEEN

Deandra walked around the apartment the following morning, half dressed, as she tried to clean up all the accumulated newspapers that had piled up around her. She paused when she saw a photo of Jeff in one of the papers. She read the full-page display and write-up about Jeffrey Boles, with interest. He was a dominant player in both the banking and export business sectors. Just looking at Jeff standing between his two business associates, Deandra realized why women pursued him. He stood out among the crowd. She reflected on his urgent need to have a child and the reason he was in such a hurry, having so tragically lost his son. She sat on the floor with the papers spread out in front of her. She had time to reason with herself and turned to her trusted diary. She wrote:

> At this time in my life, I must not allow my emotions to rule my heart. Jeff loves me and I love him, but I cannot allow myself to be rushed or pressured into something so precarious, especially when it will involve another life. Jeff isn't trying to understand my side. He's rich, powerful, handsome and persuasive. I need to give myself time. I'll test myself when I return to New York. Who knows, I might decide to catch the next plane back to Nufuma. But, at least, I'd have given myself time and space to assess my own feelings.

She pinched herself, got up, showered, and made breakfast. She was discovering more villages on her own as she travelled in the small car. She had become a familiar face in the community and whenever she drove through Lucky Pond, she always ended up giving rides to folks who usually waved her down. The local people expected such favors; they saw that as neighborly and friendly behavior.

On one such trip, Deandra stopped to buy fresh fruit at a roadside stall. She ended up buying four large pineapples. That same day she stopped by the Healthy Eating Place for lunch and took one of the pineapples for Claire. Claire saw her as she entered the restaurant and walked towards her.

"Long time no see."

"It didn't seem that long since I was here, Claire. Maybe it's because I've been a little busy."

"So I heard! I even heard that you are running a local taxi these days."

"Taxi?"

"Yes man. I mean you help out the folks with rides and all that. They talk about it, and think you are a nice lady."

"How could I pass people waving me down while I'm occupying only the driver's seat? So how's business, Claire?"

"Well, as you can see, today we are not too busy, but some days we're really rushed."

Deandra ordered her lunch and thought about Claire's broken love affair, a love affair ended mainly because of her best friend. But then, she thought, the man was no better than the friend. Maybe he didn't deserve someone like Claire.

"Well, I hope you like this lunch. It's our special stewed peas with all the goodies," remarked Claire as she served Deandra.

"I brought you a pineapple I picked up on the road."

"Thanks, Deandra. These are the sweet ones. It smells sweet already. So what's happening with you?"

"Well, it's not too long now before I'll be saying so long to you."

"You mean you'll be leaving us soon?"

"Yes, Claire."

"We'll miss you, but that's the way life is."

"So, tell me about Sister Katinga and Brother Solomon."

"They are fine. As a matter of fact, they are gearing up to start a series of revival meetings soon. If you are still here, maybe we can attend one together. Oh, I almost forgot to tell you, Deandra, I'm dating a nice guy by the name of Eric, and listen to this . . . who should call me two nights ago, but that old deceiver of mine!"

"Claire, you've got me thinking fast, but to begin, I'd love to go with you to the meetings, if I'm around. Now, about this new romance of yours, I'm really happy for you. But did I hear you correctly that your former boyfriend is trying to get back into the picture?"

"Yes, Deandra. But as far as I'm concerned, the closest that deceiver will get to me is hello and good-bye."

"Well, my friend, I wish you the very best of everything."

"Thank you, Deandra. I'll need all the luck," said Claire.

Deandra finished the meal. She paid Claire and left for home, driving slowly, savoring the unhurried pace of Nufumans, while comparing the different and varied lifestyles that she had been fortunate to experience. She remembered the naturalness of the women at the river bank, the friendly bantering among the people of the first shanty town Pablo had shown her, and the contrast of the affluent society of large homes and luxurious lifestyles.

* * *

Jeffrey Boles' export company was caught up in a union dispute. The radio and television carried the news. Coffee workers were asking for an increase of one hundred percent. They claimed that the export price for coffee had quadrupled in three years, compared to their fifty percent increase in salary. The negotiations continued for four consecutive days, keeping Jeff at the table until three and four o'clock in the morning. It was about eight o'clock that Friday evening when Jeff called.

"Is that you, Jeff?"

"Yes. I'm sure you're aware of the labor negotiations we've been involved in for most of the week."

"Yes, I imagine you've all settled or, more correctly, resolved the problem."

"Yes, we have. Even though some of the demands were hardly less than horrific. Anyway, that's past and I should not drag you into such a discussion."

Was Jeff implying that a woman couldn't handle tough negotiations at a bargaining table, Deandra wondered. She finally told herself that she was pushing things a little too far and returned to the conversation.

"I'm glad to hear that things are back to normal, Jeff. I suppose the saying still holds—'weary is the head which wears the crown.'"

"Thanks for your concern and support. Anyway, tomorrow I'll have to conclude a contract, and I hope that we can get together for a peaceful day on Sunday?"

"Okay. Any specific plans?"

"Not really. We could relax at Lucky Pond or Embers Glade, but preferably the latter since there's a swimming pool, and by now you must realize that I like water. Furthermore, Mrs. Cato will have everything in order just in case we should decide against eating out."

It didn't require any deep insight to detect that Jeff had had a rough week and wanted to be at his home where he could unwind.

"That sounds fair enough to me, Jeff. I'll drive out to Embers Glade about ten o'clock on Sunday morning."

"You make me happy, darling. I'll have Mrs. Cato prepare breakfast for two. Is there anything special that you'd like for dinner or breakfast?"

"I'll allow Mrs. Cato to surprise us. See you Sunday, darling."

As Deandra continued to get rid of her unwanted papers and old magazines, she was reminded of some of the activities she used to enjoy, especially as she read an old New York newspaper. She suddenly felt a need for the stimulation she usually got from the lectures and book parties in Harlem, especially at the Schomburg Center for Research. It was there that she often immersed herself in books about Africa, its history and people, and learned of aspects of black people's history and culture she had not heard of before.

Yes, she mused, it wouldn't be too long before she could return to the city that could wear you out, torment you, and even consume you, yet, at the same time, could excite you like no other place could. Yes, dear old New York was where she had experienced the variations in human interactions, where the invisible and sometimes visible boundaries between people were played out in different ways.

She thought fondly of the exotic and unique African market in the center of Brooklyn. This market was a mingling place for Caribbean, American, and African peoples, once each year. The memory of the exotic colors and spicy creole foods made her feel warm and comfortable.

She finally got the papers out of the way and relaxed for the rest of the day. She wanted to be calm for her day with Jeff.

When Deandra arrived in Embers Glade, Jeff was waiting to greet her. She drove into the expansive driveway, parked, and walked to meet him. He seemed a little tired, but still maintained a sense of humor.

"Hello there!" Jeff called out to her. "Thought you'd arrive in a helicopter. See all the wide open space I saved just for you, my dear?"

"I thought I'd heard it all, Jeff. But a helicopter? That's rather extreme, wouldn't you say?"

"Not at all, my dearest. After all, you do have transatlantic and Caribbean connections . . . Have I ever told you that I love to see your beautiful lips quiver when I tease you. Let me stop them from exploding," he said and kissed her tenderly.

Mrs. Cato served them breakfast, which was actually a large lunch, at the poolside. They ate, wearing their bathing suits. Deandra had covered her bikini with one of Jeff's shirts, which she wore as a beach coat. They had fun. It was her intention to return home the same evening, but with Jeff beseeching her to stay, she finally decided to spend the night.

Jeff left early for work on Monday morning. Deandra had her usual juice and black coffee, chatted briefly with Mrs. Cato, and left Embers Glade around ten o'clock.

The days were getting longer and quite warm. As soon as she entered the apartment, Deandra changed into shorts and a halter top. She'd just stepped out onto the small balcony with a tall glass of iced water when the phone rang.

"Deandra," came the familiar and friendly voice of her friend Lucreta, "why don't you stay home. I tried calling you all of last week, but you were always out."

"I've been travelling a lot these last few days. Now that I've fulfilled my obligations, I have greater freedom to do more for my personal pleasure. I must also tell you that I returned to Cedar Grove . . ."

"You went to Cedar Grove alone?" questioned Lucreta.

"Is there any good reason why I shouldn't visit Cedar Grove alone?"

"Not really. But there are hardly any remnants of the old place, which should make it almost impossible for you to recognize it."

"I see what you mean. The truth is, I didn't rediscover it independently. I was taken there by Pablo, the taxi driver who drove me from the airport the very first day I arrived. I would not have recognized the place without the tour I took with Pablo."

"I wanted to tell you that your suggestion for decorating the nursery has been implemented. Daniel and I selected a beautiful wallpaper with a blue background. It has a tropical landscape with farm animals. We'll paint the ceiling white and one of the walls in yellow. So your input will be around for a while."

"The color scheme sounds perfect. The blue is not only traditional, gender-wise, but it is soft and will blend in nicely with the sunny yellow color. Are you planning to decorate soon?"

"We'll have it finished before you leave, and when you return there will be laughter coming from the voice of another Clarke. Before I forget, Esme asked for you when I called her a couple of days ago. She is really an unusual woman. I'm learning more about her since the tragedy. She reinforces the adage that 'beside every great man there's a woman.'"

"I couldn't agree with you more. I like Esme. I hope that the future will treat her fairly."

"We are going to rally around her, you can be assured, Deandra."

When she had finished talking with Lucreta, Deandra walked to the bedroom and murmured to herself, "When I listen to my friend Lucreta talk about her pregnancy, it evokes a feeling of mystery that's probably shared only by women who have been there."

She looked at her image in the mirror to see her physical self in a different light. "Let me see how well I'm keeping up with time. There's no obvious change since the last birthday, but soon there will be another, and whether or not my face shows it, woman, your biological clock is moving forward. Maybe," she continued, "it's time I take that giant step and change my life . . . settling down as my mother likes to call it."

She walked back to the patio, stood and stared in the distance, realizing that in a few weeks she would be leaving Nufuma. That evening, she collected her thoughts and wrote:

Waiting, planning, waiting,
Waiting for the right time.
Sixty seconds, sixty minutes
All add up to a whole day,
Then the days move quickly into years
While we wait, and wait, and wait,

For the right day, and right time

The following day Deandra continued to prepare for her return to New York with the manuscript. She decided to stay up late that night; she wanted to be awake when her birthday came around. It was one o'clock in the morning when she finally settled into bed, feeling somewhat alone.

The ringing of the phone jarred her from a deep sleep. It was exactly eight o'clock, and Deandra rolled over sleepily, picked up the receiver, and answered, "Hello."

"Happy birthday, my baby."

"Oh Mom! What a way to be awakened. It feels so good to hear your voice."

"Today is a big day for you, my darling. I wish you everything that's good and much more than I wish for myself. So, it won't be long now before I can look into your face again. I'm checking out the apartment situation as you asked me to do. I'm hoping I'll find something on the upper West Side, knowing how much you like that area."

"You're so thoughtful, Mom. So tell me about you."

"There isn't that much to tell—few more gray hairs. Otherwise I'm behaving myself, taking my blood pressure pills and listening to the doctor. So, Deandra, do you feel any different today than you did yesterday?"

Deandra recalled her self-analysis the day before and answered, "I don't feel any different, Mom, but I'm fully aware of the fact that time moves on and it's up to me to move with it."

"I know you will, my dear. I know that you'll do what's right when you're ready. Anyway, have a nice birthday, even if you spend it alone . . . Bye."

There was no doubt that Mrs. Boggs had restrained herself from meddling too much in her daughter's private life.

There was no need to stay in bed any longer, sleep had gone from her eyes. The day moved along rather uneventfully until later in the afternoon when her doorbell rang. When Deandra answered the bell, there was a package brought by Federal Express. She signed for the package, which was marked from Paul Wisdom. She sat on the sofa and opened it. Paul had sent her a box of her favorite bittersweet chocolates. She removed the sealed envelope that had been attached to the box, opened it, and read:

You Brought My Senses to New Heights

Was it the eyes that helped us to find each other
The touch of your soft face that rekindled
warmth in my finger tips,
The clarity of your voice that brought music
to my ears,
The nectar from your kiss that was unlike
anything I had every tasted,
Or the words you spoke, the extension
of your intellect? It was all of these and more . . .
You are you; you are special;
And you are the only one . . .

Happy birthday, and celebrate life my dearest,
Always,
Paul

Paul knew one of the secrets to Deandra's heart and soul that many might have missed, and he knew how to use it. She liked and enjoyed intellectual stimulation and, despite their disagreements, he was not threatened by her intelligence. After reading Paul's words, she ate two of the chocolates, put the box in the refrigerator, and ruminated.

It's the sixth year after our meeting, yet not once did he forget my birthday. Even when we fought, he always managed to reconcile the differences. The memories of their past flooded her mind as she moved about quietly in the apartment.

It was late in the evening when Jeff called.

"Hello D, what's happening in Lucky Pond?"

"I only know what's been on the radio because I didn't get any newspaper today. The happenings aren't much different than yesterday or the day before, and before."

"You sound as though you've been saturated by the news?"

"Not exactly, but we do get a lot of redundant news, much of which could be omitted."

"How right you are, my dear, but what about you?"

"Well, I've entered a new threshold in my life."

"New threshold?" Jeff repeated.

"Yes I'm a year older, my dear."

Jeff suddenly remembered that it was her birthday and hated himself for being caught off-guard. He recovered and said, "Darling, will you forgive my tardiness in wishing you a happy birthday? I'll make it up to you for my gross mishandling of a very significant event."

"Jeff, there's no need for you to feel that you've mishandled anything. Soon I'll stop counting birthdays; not to mention that whenever we are together it's significant."

"We haven't been to the Blue Hole for some time. How about us dining there tomorrow?"

"Jeff, you've been very gracious to me, but please don't feel pressured into this birthday thing. I only mentioned it casually. After all, it's a fact that none of us can escape, we are all growing older. But I'll accept the invitation for tomorrow evening."

"That's my D. I must go now. I'm meeting some fellows at the club tonight. So long darling, until tomorrow."

Deandra wished she hadn't mentioned her birthday to Jeff. After all, she pondered, Jeff is a high-power, international businessman. His business is the most important thing in his life at this point in time, and rightfully so. He is still a single man without the strong home support as that of Daniel and his late friend, Emanuel.

Later she pampered herself, starting with a leisurely bath. She set the table with two yellow candles and a red rose she had bought the day before. She ended dinner of the special curried shrimp she had made herself, turned to an FM station, moved to the sofa with a glass of wine, then listened to the soft music. She went to bed feeling relaxed and happy to have experienced another milestone in her life.

The next day, she decided to thank Paul for his gift. Deandra's hands shook as she reached for the phone. Strangely her heart started racing. She went to the bathroom, brushed her teeth, and returned to the bedroom and dialed New York.

"Hello," came Paul's deep baritone voice.

Deandra hesitated, then answered, "Hello Paul."

"Is this Miss Deandra Boggs calling?"

"Yes. This is she, Paul." She could hear the tease in his voice.

"Give me a minute babe, to pull on my robe."

She waited nervously until he returned to the phone.

"Well, babe, what's up?"

"Not much Paul, except that I got the gift you sent me for my birthday."

"I'm glad it arrived on time. These days even Federal Express can mess up. So, how was the birthday?"

"Nice and quiet. But I think you out did yourself with that poem. It's rather mind boggling."

"You're very extravagant with your compliments, sweetheart. A little more and I'll need another body to carry around a swollen head."

"I really mean it. You can switch to poetry when and if you ever get bored with engineering."

Paul chuckled then said, "Would you be willing to lend me rent money when the poems aren't sold? So how does it feel to be a year older?"

"Right now I feel the same as I felt last week. They say you're as old as you feel, and I still feel young, although I know that we age by the minute."

Paul wiped the soap from his half-shaven face and listened to Deandra talk. He remembered their telephone conversation about making up and beginning a family before she was thirty-five. He knew how independent she was, and wasn't about to push her anymore.

"Well now Miss Boggs, what about your assignment, if I'm not prying too much?"

"Nonsense Paul, you're not prying. Whatever I write will eventually be for the public. I'm delighted to know that you're interested in my work."

"You know that I've always been a member of your fan club."

"That's true, Paul. That's something quite special about you."

"Thank you for good memories, Deandra."

"You're welcome, Paul. I think I caught you in the midst of your toiletry," said Deandra laughing teasingly, "and I'm going to say good-bye."

"You'll be hearing from me soon real soon, Deandra," answered Paul, and they both rang off.

Later in the day when Deandra let Jeff into her apartment, he had one of those mischievous looks on his face that had captivated her on their first meeting.

"Hello birthday beauty."

Deandra smiled and replied, "Nice to see you."

"Glad you feel that way, darling," said Jeff as he handed her the designer shopping bag he was holding.

"What have you done now, Jeff?"

Before they moved from the door, Jeff kissed her and wished her a happy belated birthday. She reached into the bag and withdrew the flowers he'd brought. There was a note that read, "Special Delivery!"

Deandra put the dozen long-stemmed roses in the vase and placed it on the coffee table, then turned to Jeff and commented, "These are just absolutely gorgeous, Jeff. Thank you, darling." She kissed his forehead.

It wasn't long before they left for the Blue Hole Restaurant. The place was busy, but not crowded. Their table was in a secluded area of the restaurant, adding an extra touch of romance. The five-course dinner was superb, living up to the reputation of Blue Hole's elegance. As they sipped the wine, Jeff looked at Deandra and remarked, "You get prettier each day, D, and you don't look a day more than twenty-five."

"Thank you for the compliment. I've long passed that number, but am quite comfortable with where I'm at."

"I love to hear that and, if you recall, I told you I'd love you even if you were seventy."

There was still a lot of spark in their relationship, but Deandra could sense that Jeff had something pressing on his mind. He looked tired as well. They finished dinner and drove back to Lucky Pond.

After they had made love that night, Jeff sat up, put her feet on his lap, and talked. "D, these last few weeks have been everything but smooth sailing. With the free market system, extra demands are made for continued evaluation and reshuffling. At the club meeting last night, we decided that it is imperative to attend a conference that will take place next week in Atlanta. From there, we'll proceed to Canada and, hopefully get things going the way they should. So I'm going to be away for at least three weeks."

"To be a business person entails not just brains, but brawn as well, I'm told," responded Deandra. "This is your life, Jeff, and if you expect to remain at the top, that's what it takes. So I wish you continued success, but try and get as much rest as possible."

"You're so understanding. Thanks for your concern."

"So when will you be leaving for North America?"

"In five days. I'll miss you very much, my darling."

It was way past midnight when Jeff left her for his house.

CHAPTER EIGHTEEN

Jeff called to say good-bye to Deandra before leaving for Atlanta. She hadn't been aware of the large Caribbean population living in that city until Jeff informed her about the ongoing friendly and business relationships between Nufuma and Atlanta.

Slowly, the following day, Deandra retraced her steps to where she had encountered the scene of the incident with Corrine and Jewel. The scene was quiet. Surrounding the spot where she had seen the couple was a healthy growth of plants. Among them were flowering gungo (pigeon) peas plants that would probably result in a bumper-crop of peas.

An elderly man passing bowed to her and remarked, "Yu seem interested in farming, miss."

"I suppose to a certain degree I am. A few weeks ago when I passed this very spot, there were no gungo peas plants, but now there are many, soon to produce a crop."

"Dats interesting coming from a foreign lady like yu. Dat little farm yu looking at belongs to Mass Jewel. He's from the next village. He's a hardworking man who mek sure his woman an' pickney don't need nuttin'. But excuse me miss, aren't yu the lady who use to visit the old lady under the tree?"

Deandra smiled then replied, "Yes, I used to visit Aunt Clem. But how did you come to know me?"

The man knitted his brow, then retorted, "Well you know, miss, we have a saying like this—'Bushes have eyes and ears.' So we know plenty of what's happening 'round us." Then he went on his way.

As she ambled home, Deandra wondered about Jewel and Corrine, whether or not Corrine still felt that Jewel loved her and his love justified or made it necessary for him to give her a few licks.

A couple of days later, Jeff called to say he had arrived safely in Atlanta and was busy attending business meetings. He ended the conversation by reminding her of his love.

Early in the following week, Deandra got the shock of her life when Paul called and said he was in New City, Nufuma!

"You're where, Paul?"

"In Nufuma, Deandra. You sound so surprised, my dear."

"But, of course I'm surprised."

"I said I'd surprise you, remember? And even if you'd forgotten, I hope Nufumans welcome Canadians, especially me."

This was an occasion when Deandra was lost for words. She was totally unsuspecting when Paul had said he would surprise her soon. She couldn't have imagined that he would be talking to her from New City.

"When did you arrive in the island?" she asked in bewilderment.

"Forty-eight hours ago, to be exact, and loving every minute of it."

Deandra clenched her teeth, carefully selected her words, and said, "Well, let me be among those to welcome you to Nufuma, Paul."

She sounded almost exactly the same as when he had first rang her doorbell in the southern United States, Paul thought.

"Now that you've welcomed me to your island, how far away is your place from New City?"

"It's about two and a half hour ride in light traffic. Where are you staying in New City?"

"I'm at the Palace, but it won't be long, since my plan is to visit a couple of islands. So, my dear, what's up since we chatted on your birthday?" he inquired earnestly.

"Well, it's been interesting, quiet, and enlightening. Everything's been fine so far."

"Your mother gave me a package for you. I'd like to come over to your place soon to deliver it."

Suddenly she felt a slight flutter when Paul said he wanted to come over soon. She was determined not to lose control of her emotions. After all, it had been more than a year since she had seen him. So much had happened since then, yet she wondered whether or not he had changed in his appearance.

"Tomorrow looks like a full day, Paul. How about Thursday?"

"That sounds divine, my dear. Now that you've welcomed me, and I, in turn, have been so polite and restrained, Princess Deandra, I can hardly wait to see you. I've been thinking maybe you could suggest something exciting and interesting that we could do on Thursday. Of course, the selection would be left to you, the popular and sophisticated Nufuman woman. I'm sure you'll be able to figure out something. Deandra, I love you and I'm longing to see you."

Surprise. Solitude, mused Deandra, for to be so taken by surprise requires solitude to think things through.

A sudden rush of blood passed through her veins, creating a peculiar sensation. "Hell no!" Deandra told herself. "Breaking up, making up, running away, and suddenly again Paul appears, soon to be at my doorstep. It's almost uncanny that he should show up when Jeff is away. Could it really be that Sister Katinga's predictions are much more than intelligent guesses? After all, Lucreta and Claire swore by her clairvoyance, so who am I to be the skeptic? There may be more to it than meets the eye."

She walked slowly around the garden of the complex, ignoring the raindrops that had started to fall. She continued walking, then looked up in the sky and saw two bright rainbows. It was an unusual sight. She stood and looked at the perfect and colorful spectrum for a long while, until she had her fill. Her hair was dripping wet, but her head was much clearer. She returned to the apartment, shrugged her shoulders and decided that she was a part of the rainbow and would fit into the spectrum.

Deandra felt calm, cool, and collected that Thursday morning, until the doorbell rang. The sight of Paul Wisdom through the peep hole, triggered the same sensation he had created in her over the phone. Her palm was sweaty as she turned the doorknob to let Paul in. He looked awesome as he stood looking at her. He was wearing white linen slacks with a sky-blue silk shirt, opened to the middle of his chest. His ebony jaws seemed more squared than ever.

With his tantalizing smile, he inquired, "Are you going to ask the stranger in, my dear?"

"What on earth are we waiting for?" Deandra replied. "Please come in, Paul."

Paul closed the door, then greeted her. "Hi babe," he muttered softly and kissed her on her forehead.

They walked to the living room and sat on the sofa.

"So, how was the drive over?"

"Not bad at all. As a matter of fact, I made the trip in two hours and had the chance to see some of the new developments that are occurring in the island."

"They are developing rapidly. From your vantage point, what do you think, Paul?"

"Well, I know so little about the topography of the island that it's difficult for me to give my opinion, but based on what I've seen, those in charge seem to know what they are doing. I'm sure your mother will be surprised when she makes that much talked about trip. By the way, here's the package she asked me to deliver."

"Trust my mother for fussing," Deandra remarked as she opened the package exclaiming, "She knew just what to get! You can't have too many blouses. It's beautiful." She fingered the pale blue, long sleeve, silk blouse.

"She'll be happy to hear you say that. Each of you knows what the other likes, anyway," commented Paul. He'd been eyeing Deandra as they talked.

He suddenly burst out, "But Deandra, you look marvelous. The tropical climate seems to bring out some more of your physical beauty."

"You've not done too badly either, Paul." She moistened her lips with the tip of her tongue and continued, "You seem slightly slimmer, I mean, not too much."

Paul smiled. "Thank you for noticing, my dear. I've been doing a lot of walking these days, that might account for my trimming down."

"I've been running my mouth so much that I neglected to offer you a cool drink. What shall I get you?"

"Water, juice, soda, anything from you will be more than sufficient."

Deandra got some of the fruit juice she had made.

"So, have you covered most of the island as yet, Deandra?"

"I've seen a fair amount, but not all. You mustn't forget that I've been working."

"Of course not, just curious."

"You'd mentioned something about island hopping. May I ask which of the islands you plan to visit?"

"Jamaica."

"Jamaica!" she exclaimed animatedly, then stopped herself from exhibiting too much exuberance.

"Jamaica is the place where my granddad came from, remember?"

"Of course I do. How could I forget that you also have roots in Canada and the United States?"

"Well, I might just resurrect some Jamaican relatives. But they are having a reggae sunsplash and since I'm so near, I wouldn't miss it. By the way, I have a full itinerary for five to six days down there. I also picked up some good information at the Nufuman tourist board, which includes a few restaurants I passed driving down this morning."

"Now that you've mentioned restaurants, I'd thought that we might decide on eating out and we could look through the yellow pages together, but you seem to have an idea where to find eating places."

"I'd love to take you to dinner. If you have a preferred restaurant, that's great with me, babe."

"Not really, Paul. You're always resourceful in discovering places."

"I was about to show you the itinerary for Jamaica. Here it is."

"Wow! This is a packed and rather interesting schedule."

"Glad you think so, darling. Life is too darn short to delay doing interesting and exciting things."

Deandra remembered Emanuel. She remained silent for a moment, then responded, "You're right, Paul. One never knows what the future holds."

Later Paul drove south of Lucky Pond for about forty minutes, then stopped at the Talk of the Town Restaurant. It had lived up to the four star ratings.

During dinner, Paul remarked teasingly, "You wouldn't hold it against me if this place didn't live up to the ratings, would you Deandra?"

"Hold it against a tourist? You know what they say about being a tourist—you take a chance and hope it works out. It's an elegant place and it's my first time here."

On their drive back to Lucky Pond, Paul cautiously mentioned, "You know, Deandra, I have an open reservation for two to Jamaica. It would be great if you could go down for a few days. Please don't feel pressured. No strings attached. But I know that you've always wished to visit the land of reggae, rum and coconut water."

"You sure know how to spring surprises, Paul. A week ago I talked with you and you were in New York. Today here you are, taking me totally by surprise, and suddenly you have two open reservations to Jamaica."

"All right. You're right to be reacting this way. But please, babe, sleep on it tonight, think about it the day after, then make a decision. What do you say?"

"I don't know if I can go. I'll have to think about it."

"Good. But I'll keep my word, no strings attached. We'll have separate rooms. I can even get separate hotels or villas if you would prefer that arrangement."

"I said I didn't know if I could go, remember?"

"Of course I remember, sweetheart."

It was about ten o'clock when she walked Paul to the door and before she opened it he held onto her hands. She felt tense.

He bent and whispered, "If only you knew how much I love you, babe." He kissed her gently and left.

The thought of reggae sunsplash ignited curiosity and excitement in Deandra. After a long deliberation with herself, she shrugged her shoulders, commenting, "What do I have to lose? I'm free, single, not engaged, and just passed another milestone in my life. This opportunity might not present itself again."

"So, what's your decision?" inquired Paul when he called.

"I accept the invitation."

"Excellent. This is great news, Deandra. We leave tomorrow about noon. Will that give you sufficient time to take care of your business?"

"I believe I can manage. I'll meet you at the airport."

"That sounds perfect. See you tomorrow, Deandra."

She had promised to have dinner with the Clarkes that evening and decided to pack her bag before driving to Embers Glade. She packed four pairs of linen walking shorts, four sundresses, two bathing suits, two jumpsuits, one pair of walking shoes, one pair of black sandals and her gold sandals, leaving only her toilet articles to be packed in the morning. Deandra smiled as she locked the packed suitcase and put it into the living room before driving off to her friends'.

When Deandra saw Lucreta, her belly seemed so much larger to her, that she had to resist the urge to make comments about it. The whole family was present and, as usual, made her feel like a legitimate member of the clan.

Just as Aunt May started to serve the dessert, Deandra remarked, "Well guys, I have some news to share with you."

In the meantime, Jennifer was making a face at Raymond.

"If you don't stop your teasing, Jennifer, I'm gonna ask Mother to remove you from the table," said Raymond.

Lucreta gave Jennifer a stern and warning look and she stopped pulling Raymond's shirt and settled down.

"You were about to share some news with us before those two acted up," remarked Lucreta.

"I've decided to splurge and attend the reggae sunsplash in Jamaica."

"That sounds exciting, but when did you decide to go?" asked Lucreta.

"Since we were together the last time, and since I'm so near, I've decided to expand my world before saying good-bye to the tropics."

"That should be an interesting trip," remarked Daniel. "But in the meantime, I hope we're not hearing a finality in that good-bye you mentioned."

"Sorry it came out sounding that way. How could I ever entertain the idea of not returning to visit you all and to enjoy some more fabulous and leisurely lifestyle. I'll return."

"Aunty D, can we go with you to the sunsplash?" asked Jennifer seriously.

"We who, Jennifer?" inquired Raymond.

"You and I, of course."

"Speak for yourself. Who would ever take you to sunsplash? Not me."

Once outside the dining room the two children forgot about the sunsplash and turned their attention to something else. Lucreta, Daniel, and Deandra talked about the good times they had had.

Lucreta wished her friend would be around for the birth of their son while showing her the wallpaper she and Daniel had selected for the nursery.

It wasn't too long before Deandra looked at her watch and announced, "I always have a hard time getting away from this place. You've been so great to me, but I must say good night."

"Have fun in Jamaica!" they all said at once, sounding almost like a chorus, as Deandra set out for Lucky Pond.

She was preparing herself for bed when the phone rang. Deandra picked up the receiver.

"Deandra! At last I got you."

"You make it sound as though you'd been calling all day, Jeff."

"Only three times, sweetheart. Anyway, how are things in that region?"

"Great Jeff. Just great. What's with you?"

"Well, we've been working very hard. The Caribbean community in Atlanta can play a big role in our banking business. We're working towards getting as many of them as possible to do business with us. The fact is, we offer them high interest rates on their dollars, and the bottom line is getting as much for your dollar as you can."

"I don't see anything wrong with that. If there's an opportunity, why not use it?"

"You're beginning to sound like a business woman."

"I thought I was. Even though not many writers become rich from writing, it is a business."

"You're correct, Deandra. So, is everything okay with you?"

"Yes. Matter of fact, I've decided to fly over to Jamaica for the reggae sunsplash."

"Oh. When did that come about?"

"Since you've been gone."

"I see. Does that mean out of sight, out of mind?"

"I don't understand."

"Well, it would seem as though I'm the last to know. Had I not called, I'd not have known."

"That's unfair. There was no way to reach you and while I have told you, I've only decided on going a few days ago."

"I don't want you to get the idea that I'm not happy for you, but I feel a little left out. So when do you leave for Jamaica?"

"Tomorrow around noon."

"Is there a number where I can reach you?"

"I don't have one, but I'll be back in six days. If you will still be in Atlanta, you could give me your number."

Deandra got the feeling that Jeff was becoming possessive.

* * *

Paul arrived early at the airport. After half an hour had passed and Deandra had not arrived, he became anxious, walking up and down the check-in area. I hope she has not changed her mind, he thought. But she's not that type of person; Deandra is usually straightforward. He finally phoned her house. The phone rang for a long time. He replaced the receiver, comforting himself with the thought that she was on her way.

As he walked to the entrance, Deandra had just alighted from the taxi. He composed himself to conceal his anxiety and greeted her warmly.

"Hi sweetheart."

"Hi Paul. Thought we would never get through the traffic jam. A trailer and pickup collided and backed up the traffic for miles."

"Are you okay, Deandra?"

"I'm fine."

"That's what's important, dearest."

He helped her with her bag to the check-in counter. Soon after that they were proceeding to the plane, and within ninety minutes they had landed in Montego Bay, Jamaica.

The taxi drove slowly as they enjoyed the scenery on the way to Castles by the Sea Villas in Rose Hall. The balcony of the shared villa overlooked the sea. To the west of the villas were large, rolling hills with houses scattered about. Both Paul and Deandra were captivated by the beauty of the place. They stood on the balcony and looked at the expansiveness of the sea.

"What do you think of the place, Deandra?" asked Paul.

"Beautiful, refreshing, charming, and maybe more."

"Glad you feel that way. I must confess that when the travel agent described the place to me, it sounded too beautiful to be real, but here we are, standing on the balcony of the Castles, which reminds me of the gingerbread houses described in the Hans Christian Anderson fairytale."

"I can't add anymore to that. That's exactly what this place looks like."

Paul transferred the suitcases from where the bellhop had put them to the separate bedrooms. They sat on the balcony and overhauled the packed itinerary.

"So, dear lady, I need your assistance to plan this tight program."

"If I might suggest, why don't we do the Castles today, then we can sit by the pool, or by the beach, and figure out the rest."

"Marvelous idea."

Heads turned to look at them as they strolled serenely through the grounds and gardens of the villas, ending at the beach. There they had lunch at the Castle Hut. Paul ordered rum to mix with his coconut water. Deandra couldn't resist mixing hers to experience the Jamaican thing and ended up having rum and coconut water too. They ate, swam, chatted lightheartedly, basked in the warm sun at the beach, and planned their six days. Before returning to the apartment, they walked to the taxi stand. Paul arranged with a taxi driver named Willard, to take them around to the different places on their schedule.

That evening a buffet supper was served at the pool side. Deandra wore a green halter back dress, her black sandals, and white earrings. Paul had dressed early and was quietly enjoying the view from the balcony, when Deandra walked out to join him.

He stood, looked at her admiringly, and commented, "How lovely you are, princess. Where did you appear from?" Then he kissed her on her forehead.

Deandra's heartbeat quickened. Paul looked every inch a prince. He was wearing brown slacks, a white shirt, and tan shoes. There was no denying, the guy commanded attention. She stood still, then smiled at him.

"Have you had your fill of the view as yet?" she inquired.

"Not really, but by the end of the trip, I hope we'll both have sufficient memories to take home. Gramp always bragged about Jamaica, but I had no idea that it was this beautiful, Deandra."

"From what I've seen so far, I must say it is indeed more than I'd imagined."

"Shall we go, dear?" said Paul.

They stepped out to the walkway that led to the pool. Paul reached for her hand and locked his fingers around hers while they walked slowly to the pool side and selected a table for two.

It's been too long since I sat with the only woman I've ever loved by my side, Paul reflected. As they sat and waited for the waiter to bring the cocktails they had ordered, he leaned over, patted Deandra's hands, then remarked, "It's been lonely without you, Deandra. There were times when I felt almost abandoned by the only woman I've ever loved, the woman who allowed me into her private world, that no one else was privileged to, the woman with a mind of her own—a mind that probes and challenges. The woman who exudes beauty wherever she goes."

Deandra batted her eyelashes playfully as Paul played with her fingers and continued to talk. The waiter finally brought their drinks. Paul watched her as she swallowed the first sip of wine and felt an urge to kiss her. It had been too long since he'd really kissed her.

"Well?" asked Deandra.

"I was thinking about the special way you sip your wine and the fact that you still love chocolates."

Sitting across the table from Paul brought back memories of their first date that created a feeling of excitement. Deandra tried to conceal her feelings and inquired, "So, what's so significant about those?"

"Precisely those qualities that you've maintained. Considering how many women are substituting coke for chocolates makes you even more beautiful and unique."

"But men also get caught up in snorting that white stuff. As a matter of fact, it's believed that men are usually the initiators of the stuff where the women are concerned."

"That's true, but with a mind like yours, I doubt strongly that any man could confuse you, my dear."

After dinner, they stayed for entertainment by local musicians who were as good as any. On their way back to the villa, there was a sudden, swift moving light.

"Look babe, it's a shooting star!"

"How marvelous, Paul! It went so fast that I almost missed it."

"Meteorites, or celestial bodies, visit us from time to time, but in large cities where we're locked up indoors for one reason or another, we miss them. This one should be a special memory for us to take back," he said, then held her around the waist.

"If I'm not mistaken, I thought I heard that a shooting star has some significance."

"I've heard that too. They say you must make a wish and I made mine the moment I saw it."

"Yes, of course. There's a song which says, 'When you wish upon a star.'"

"That's correct sweetheart," responded Paul as he felt a surge of happiness.

The following day, Willard took them to the exotic and famous Dunna River Falls. Deandra climbed the huge rocks at the falls cautiously to avoid another sprain. Paul helped her as they climbed to the top with the cool clear water beating against their bodies. Going down the falls was just as challenging, as they made sure not to slip. They finally ended their climb and sat in the garden.

Paul watched the young lovers strolling leisurely in the garden and couldn't help remarking, "I wonder if these young people practice safe sex when they make love."

"What made you say that, Paul?" inquired Deandra.

"Because of the HIV/AIDS virus, my dear. It is a fact that young people are sexually active and it is a fact that too many are dying from AIDS."

Deandra sighed and said, " It's a dreadful or rather deadly disease. Do you have any advice for young people, Paul?"

"I strongly suggest that all sexually active persons get themselves tested for the virus and get a card with their HIV status and practice safe sex."

"I didn't know there was such a card. It sounds like you're carrying around your blood type."

"You're right. It's like carrying around your blood type card. As a matter of fact, I have one in my wallet," he said and showed it to Deandra.

"Thank you for such an important piece of information, Paul."

The conversation shifted. Deandra turned to Paul and said, "Paul, I must tell you, I am delighted that you invited me. Just to experience the falls is worth the trip. It's nature at its best. I wonder if the locals really know how blessed they are to have such a piece of the planet? For even with the fear of unsavory and sick minds, these things will pass, and even with geological changes, the island will be here for some time yet."

"How well you describe the falls, and if we only allow ourselves to relax and enjoy the Creator's handywork, we'd soon discover that there's no greater beauty than what nature provides. Right now, darling, I'm the happiest guy in the world."

"How can you be so sure of that?"

"With this setting and the most beautiful woman I know sitting next to me, I know I'm the happiest guy around. Even though my destiny lies in your power, my dear."

"That's a lot of power to attribute to me, and one that I do not crave or relish."

"Well, let's say that the power lies in both of us, but I've surrendered mine to you, a fact you know only too well."

Deandra reflected on the heated conversation they had had months ago over the telephone, when Paul had said that she was allowing the feminist thing to interfere with their lives. Then she changed the subject saying, "I don't know about you, Paul, but I'm starving."

"There's supposed to be a place here where we can get jerk or roast fish. Should we try that?"

"Sounds delicious already."

They had both kinds of fish, plus jerk pork and rice and peas under the lignum vitae tree. Willard drove them back to the Castles at about eight o'clock that evening. Deandra dragged herself out of the car. She was sore from the exercise at the falls.

Paul teasingly told her that she'd been sitting at the desk too long and suggested room service for dinner. He ordered champagne with room service.

Later in the evening, they moved out to the balcony where Paul toasted her with the champagne. The place was enchanting, with a sense of romance lingering around them. Paul reached for Deandra's hand and pulled her to him. He could feel her heart pounding against his chest. Her eyes seemed extra large and her parted lips more alluring. He kissed her face, then her lips. He kissed her as he'd never done before, then rested her head on his shoulder.

He wanted her more than ever, but she would have to want him too. He believed in reciprocal and equal yielding in love. They went inside. Paul reminded her that his destiny was in her hands and bid her good night.

Their next trip took them to one of the new shopping centers. The plazas were as splendid, but much larger than those in Nufuma. They visited the craft markets as vendors called out to get their attention. Paul bought Deandra a beautiful coffee set that was made in Jamaica, while she got him a couple of paper weights.

They then proceeded to one of the book shops. There was an interesting display of books from the United States, Europe, Jamaica and other Caribbean islands. Paul had almost missed the display from which he selected a book for himself entitled *On a New Philosophy and Approach to Rituals*. He then bought a copy of *Local Heroes* for Deandra and a creole cookbook for Marion Boggs.

From the bookshop, they headed for the popular vegetarian restaurant that was owned by a Rastafarian couple. Paul quickly made friends with the couple and got an introduction to the Rastas' philosophy of helping each other.

Paul consulted the tourist guide map before they left the plaza. He examined the guide and found a place that was supposed to be perfect for picnics as well as eco-tourism.

"How about a very quiet day tomorrow, Deandra?" Paul asked.

"How quiet?"

"Like seeing more of nature, smelling some green grass, flying a kite, and climbing a tree."

"Who will climb the tree?"

"You, of course, my dear," he said laughing. "But seriously, how about a picnic in a fresh clean meadow, then later we can do a night club."

"I won't say no to that. One can't have too much of the good life."

"So I take it we have a date?"

"Yes Paul."

The place they selected for the picnic was idyllic. The air was filled with unfamiliar perfume that had been given off by the mixture of flowering plants.

How beautiful and lush the island was, thought Paul as he watched a swarm of bees settling in a flowering logwood tree. Those bees would not sting anyone unless they were disturbed. He thought of the important place of the queen bee in the hive as he looked at Deandra. He felt lucky to be with the only woman he had ever loved. To him her beauty was matched only by that of Jamaica, and her place should be like that of the queen bee, except he wanted her to live longer.

From where he sat, he could see the rolling hills with their towering peaks. To him, the mountains formed a perfect backdrop for the island. There was a thick fog over the mountains. It looked like smoke belched up from the belly of some great hidden giants, while behind them the orange colored sun was rapidly sinking in the distance. His thoughts were interrupted when Deandra yawned and stretched as she rolled on the large picnic blanket that was hidden by the flowering trees, then closed her eyes.

Paul looked at her with a smile on his face. In the meantime, Deandra was thoughtful. Her thoughts had taken her back to that special place in the United States where she had surrendered to Paul, realizing that the setting was like recreating the past.

The poinsettias and birds of paradise were in their crimson radiance, while the branches of tall trees were bending from the weight of their berries as chirping black birds flew from tree to tree to find food. Those were obviously the unspoiled blackbirds, unlike those that lingered around the island's hotels, hopping from table to table to pick up crumbs left by guests. Even birds could fall prey to ready-made and easy-to-get things, rejecting their habitat. The truth was, their habitat was disturbed, leaving them no other choice but to take what they could find for food to survive.

Scattered in the nearby pasture where cattle grazed were large, commanding, flamboyant trees, flaunting their beauty as far as their branches would allow. Standing under one of the trees was a cow that had started to give birth to her calf.

"Look sweetheart, there's going to be a birth," said Paul.

It was an event and experience that neither one would forget. The birthing cow, with her legs extended, pushed as the calf started to egress from her body. One half of the calf was born and there was a cessation of expulsion. As the mother cow maneuvered and pushed, Deandra broke into a cold sweat, holding onto Paul's arm so tightly that she dug her fingernails into his flesh. They both sighed and looked at each other in relief as the calf was completely expelled from its mother's body. They watched in silence as the cow, though tired-looking and drained, turned around and cleaned the newborn, licking the sticky substance from its tender skin—just as a mother would bathe her infant.

Paul patted Deandra's hand and asked, "Are you okay, my darling?"

"Yes Paul, I'm fine," she said, releasing his hand.

Deandra sat quietly for a while, then turned and said, "I was thinking about the difference between human kind and lower forms of animals, Paul."

"Such as, may I ask?"

"Well, similar to a woman, the cow carries its calf for nine months. Even though humans have superior cognitive abilities to think and create, on the other hand, the cow seems superior. The human infant is incapable of physical independence."

"Now that you've said it, Deandra, the human infant is indeed held a prisoner, flat on the back, totally dependent on someone else to meet the basic needs. The calf, on the other hand, soon after birth is able to stand and suck its mother's milk. It is something to think about."

"Do you think that test tube culture will make a difference, Paul?"

"That will be the day, my dear."

Most of the remaining afternoon was focused on the mystery of life. Both decided that those were some of the imponderables that added to the mystery of human kind, and as they saw it then, would not be resolved by any one theory or personal belief.

They dined and danced at one of the elegant night spots that night, and returned home early. Paul ordered a bottle of the best wine to he brought to their villa. They sat on the balcony and sipped the aged wine.

Paul turned his chair around to look at Deandra's face, then spoke. "Deandra, this has been a truly wonderful day, in many respects. But in case you don't realize it, our relationship is no synthetic affair. It's love predicated on friendship and respect. It's similar to the wine. The older it gets, the better it is, for the longer I know you, the more certain I am that we're good for each other. There's been no demise in our relationship, despite your ambivalence about settling down. Not that I'm without feet of clay, but I can only offer you the best of me. My life's been on hold and I don't intend to continue this way. I mean, I need you, my dear."

Deandra was short of words. She mused about what Paul had said and what he'd been to her before and felt a resurgence of her suppressed feelings for him. She felt that after all was said and done, whatever fate had in store for you, would be yours in the end and she responded with a question.

"Do you think there's anyone without feet of clay, Paul?"

"I doubt it. Maybe you," he replied smiling. "But even you're entitled to a toe of clay."

She thought of Jeff when Paul had said toe of clay, then refocused her attention on him.

They talked late into the night. Paul told her about his new business ventures, often referring to it as our investment for the future. Deandra felt good when he asked her opinion about certain aspects of his business, saying, "Sweetheart, this will be ours, not just mine."

They went indoors and finished the bottle of wine. They had left the radio station on and Gladys Knight was singing, "We belong together." Paul held Deandra tightly. Her body went limp as her eyes revealed her desire for him. He carried her to the bedroom.

Paul knew then that she was ready to renew their love. As they made love that night, Paul remembered her inexperience in lovemaking when he had initiated her into another phase of womanhood. He talked, he kissed, and he touched her. He took his time to make sure that she would enjoy the experience as much as he would. He had studied her physical reaction to him and knew how to excite her. Probing every corner of her being, he whispered in her ears, "My darling, I've been dreaming of this night for too long. You're the single flower that blooms in the desert of my soul."

That night, Deandra gave herself to Paul as she'd never done before. Her ecstasy was evident as the tears rolled down her cheeks. Paul licked away the salty tears and filled her with love. They slept soundly, having exhausted each other, wrapped in each other's arms.

It was about six o'clock the following morning when Paul quietly got out of bed and decided to glance at his new book, *On a New Philosophy and Approach to Rituals*. He turned the pages and stopped when he noticed a poem written in bold letters, "Teach Us a New Way Lord." It caught his interest and he read:

> There must be a place between brutes and man;
> A place for a new philosophy and approach
> One hundred million doctrines
> Not far removed from one another,
> One hundred million doctrines
> Touching only a few.
> A new philosophy is due

> Between what we have and what we don't,
> About the passing of time
> And speaks to the long silence
> That muffles a new approach,
> That wrenches the hearts of those
> Searching and waiting . . .
> For spiritual wisdom, truth, and love,
> For the awakening from slumber
> To answer the call for a change
> And a new philosophy . . .

"A new philosophy . . . yes, but will it work," said Paul to himself as he thought about his college days in Canada, where in a political science class he had raised the topic of change predicated on philosophical thought, with some practical implications. The professor had totally ignored his idea, simply because it proposed change. Not even slight recognition was given for the ability to think, analyze, and question issues of substance; that was one of the difficulties of trying to inject anything outside the boundaries of some of the redundancies.

He read the last line of the poem again, "To answer the call for a change and new philosophy."

"Good morning," said a familiar voice.

He turned to see Deandra standing over him. "If you think hard and long enough about truth and beauty, they'll appear," he said as he kissed her and pointed to the poem in the book.

Deandra glanced at it and replied, "How profound. I see you're still in a philosophical mood."

"I'm no philosopher, but this poem is saying something. It has substance."

She read the entire poem and nodded in agreement.

"You are right on the money. The title of the poem is perfect, it sort of makes a statement by itself."

"I was thinking about the old saying, 'Nothing changes. The more they change, the more they remain the same.' Things just get moved around in a circle, only to return to their original places."

"That's as good an observation as any about the condition of man and the order of things."

"I was just trying to place my old Professor Myles' class into the middle of this poem. There was an abundance of rhetoric and a dearth of tangible outcomes," remarked Paul.

"How and where do we then find a platform for solid ground to demonstrate the new philosophy for change?"

"I would suspect that we begin from where we are."

"Explain how we can actually do that, Paul."

"Well, my queen, right at this very time and place we are reordering our lives for change, a change that is positive and one that can be understood by all, including literates and illiterates."

"So then, Paul, you are saying that the new philosophy is best demonstrated through the way we plan and live our lives?"

"Yes, babe," answered Paul. "Just as we'll do at reggae sunsplash today."

Deandra drifted into a pensive mood. She thought about the discussion she had with Paul on the new philosophy and the implication of his interpretation. She sighed and directed her thoughts to Jeff. There was no maybe about her feelings for Jeff, she still loved him. She tried to justify her actions by harping on the past.

"If only Paul had stayed out of my life, I wouldn't be in this predicament. Now I'm befuddled and pulled in two directions," she told herself.

Paul deliberately tried to change her trend of thought.

"Hi sweetheart, don't think too much. Would you like us to have breakfast courtesy of room service?"

"That sounds good," replied Deandra and turned her attention to Paul.

They had breakfast on the balcony. It was a favorite spot of hers. She loved to sit and watch the splashes of the sea on the shore, and did just that after breakfast.

Deandra was in one of those lazy moods, as she described it. She felt totally relaxed and had no inclination to do anything of great significance at that point. As Paul got on with his morning toilet, she stood on the balcony, leaned against the railings, and breathed in the clean, fresh air. For a while she felt as though she was in a dream state, but realized that it was all part of her relaxed state. She looked at a piece of paper lying next to her on the table. She reached for it and wrote:

> Sometimes it looks like millions of objects
> Competing for time and space,
> Foaming, frothing, bouncing,

Twisting and interlocking
Into knots of white diamonds on top of an emerald bed:
Sometimes it looks like no more than one
Expansive in its stillness, like a quiet, docile, and peaceful creature:
But at times it is like a mixture of many,
Carrying within its bowels
Billions of living organisms:
And what is this untameable creature?
It is the sea—the deep, deep sea
Of Turquoise, sky blue and navy blue
All blending as one . . .

She didn't know how long Paul had been standing there, but she could feel his presence. She raised her head and saw him watching her. He was his usual self, unintrusive, allowing her space when she needed it—and she needed the space that morning.

"Hi honey, you beat me to the punch. I feel lazy and laid back this morning."

"Who asked for any explanation," answered Paul. "It makes me feel good to see you so relaxed, but did I see you working?"

"Not exactly. I had one of those sudden impulses to jot down a feeling I was experiencing. She turned and handed him the piece of paper on which she had written her thoughts about the sea.

Paul read it, then leaned over the chair on which she sat and whispered, "It's beautiful and you are as deep and sweetly complicated as the sea."

"So you like it eh?"

"Just like I said, sweetheart, it's good."

Paul sensed delight coming from her as well as the need for his reassurance. He couldn't help remembering their first verbal fight, when he had wanted to help her fix a bookshelf in her new apartment and she'd seen his offer as smothering. But now it was apparent that both of them had matured to the point of including each other in a logical relationship.

* * *

As they drove to Negril where the sunsplash was being held, both Deandra and Paul were excited and anxious to experience the show, and as they listened to Willard, the taxi driver, raving about it, their expectations heightened.

"Well Mr. Wisdom, how's your holiday going so far?" Willard inquired.

"Very nice, man. With your watchful eyes looking out for us and your knowledge of the island, there's no other way for us but to enjoy ourselves. So what's in store for us in Negril, Willard?"

"You will hear all different versions of reggae performed by people from all over the world. Don't know if you and the lady know, but this little island of ours has exported reggae all over the world. Plenty people meking big bucks, I tell you. Anyway, I think both of you will have a good time. You really select the right time to attend sunsplash. This year they are staging it a little different. As I said, they are having a big mix of different acts. You will have a good time. Try and catch the sunset too."

To their surprise, when they arrived thousands of people were already there. It was like a huge park. People camped out under large umbrellas and some very creative sunshades made from cardboard and other materials. Paul and Deandra finally found themselves a spot to spread their blanket, with a good view of the stage.

The show was everything it had promised to be. The artists included Jamaicans, Canadians, Americans, Europeans, and Japanese. The show was a mixture of soca, jazz, calypso, rock, rhythm and blues and, of course, reggae. The dancers did their routines, bringing the crowd to its feet when they performed the famous dancehall butterfly dip.

Deandra realized that the Nufuman dances were only imitations of the Jamaicans' creation. The dancehall queen defied description when she wiggled and dipped to the floor. It was then that she got the chance to closely observe the correct movement of the original doctor bird dance as the dancers kept everyone spellbound and shouting for more. They were caught up in the excitement and joined the crowd in calling for more. Paul kissed Deandra, then they went to watch the sunset.

They watched the stupendous sunset, standing at the famous Lovers' Corner and were completely awed by it. Later, they had dinner and waited for the midnight blast out with the leading reggae performers.

They returned to Rose Hall near three a.m. They had both enjoyed the sunsplash jam-down to its fullest and decided that they needed a warm bath to induce sleep. They finally climbed into bed around three-thirty in the morning.

They had decided to visit the Maroon Town in the south of the island and had asked Willard to pick them up at eleven a.m. The place was located in a hilly area where the runaway Africans had found safe haven. It was lush and green, surrounded by farms of a wide variety of local agricultural products.

Before they entered the courtyard, Paul turned to Deandra and remarked, "Guess what I've been thinking?"

"I haven't the slightest clue, Paul."

"Do you see that gigantic mountain looking down at us?"

"Yes."

"Well, I'm naming it Survival Mountain."

"That's rather interesting. Is that some sort of psychological identification, may I ask?"

"You're so right, sweetheart. This will be our special name for a very special place we've visited together."

They entered a yard that reminded Deandra of the extended family compounds found in some African villages. They were greeted by a fine-looking and commanding man. His name was Major Obierika. They were later introduced to other members of the community. The houses were modest and nicely kept, and there was a small school situated on the compound. An adolescent boy was supervising the younger children in their weekend assignments. The children all waved to Paul and Deandra, then welcomed them in Creole. Paul was fascinated by the children's chatter and laughter, even though he needed Deandra to translate Creole to standard English. The Jamaican Creole was very similar to that spoken in Nufuma.

"Welcome to our village," said Major Obierika. "I get the feeling that you are visitors to our beautiful land of wood and water."

"Yes, we are visitors," explained Paul.

"Where are you from?"

"We're from New York, but I have roots here from my granddad's side and my friend has connections in Nufuma, where the Creole sounds very much like yours."

Following the formal introductions, Major Obierika asked, "So what can we do for you two handsome young people?"

"Well, we would like to know how far back you can trace your ancestry, and if you speak any other languages besides English," inquired Deandra.

"Let's start with languages. I speak another language of the people of Ghana. We are Akan people from West Africa. Now, let's think, I can trace back to my tenth generation, and we always try to include an Akan name when naming our children."

"Genealogy is very much in the forefront these days. People are trying to make reconnections," remarked Paul.

In the meantime, some women had passed by carrying baskets of fresh fruits and vegetables. They stopped and spoke briefly with Paul and Deandra. Deandra smiled with the women. She felt good to have been the proud owner of a gold bangle from Ghana.

"If it is not too intrusive, Major, could you tell us something about today's Maroon family structure?" asked Paul.

"Well Paul, my friend, the twentieth century has caught up with all of us. We still have very strong family values, where parents take care of their children, and children listen to their parents. But I must be honest, outside influences are creeping in. For example, when the youngsters go to the big cities for an education, they don't want to return, and when they do return, they behave quite differently. They dress very differently, fix their hair differently, and communicate strangely. On the whole, though, we are trying our best to hold on to some of the Akan culture, although it's becoming more and more diluted. But there's a lot of richness in the multi-ethnic and cultural mix in this land of ours."

Major Obierika invited them out to the vegetable garden. Soon a young man climbed a coconut tree and picked some nuts. He then opened a couple of the freshly picked nuts, from which Paul and Deandra drank the refreshing coconut water. They then proceeded to the craft shop, which was a part of the technical school. They bought a couple of wooden carvings that were created by children.

Before they left, Major Obierika laid his hands on their shoulders and said, "This has been a special day for us. I'm pleased to have met you two. I don't know what's your individual plans, but from where I stand, I see a beautiful couple who can, and will, make a great difference in the world. I wish you both a long and beautiful life."

On their way back to Castles by the Sea, both Deandra and Paul spoke very little. They reflected on the interesting stories that the

Major had shared with them. They felt that maybe, after all the years of breaking up and making up, it was time to acknowledge the fact that their relationship had reached the point for them to share their lives.

As they packed their suitcases that night in order to catch the ten o'clock Air Jamaica flight, Paul pulled Deandra to her feet and held her hands as they stood facing each other and said to her, "The six days have gone much too quickly, my darling. But this is just the beginning of a brand new chapter in our lives. I love you dearly, Deandra."

He kissed her, and with his kiss, Deandra felt they had sealed their relationship.

The plane took off on time and landed in Nufuma around twelve noon. Paul remained on board. He would take off within an hour for New York. Deandra kissed him good-bye and walked outside to catch a taxi for Lucky Pond.

CHAPTER NINETEEN

Deandra reflected on the exciting time she had had with Paul in Jamaica as she taxied back to her apartment in Lucky Pond. The place seemed somewhat strange, although she'd only been away for six days. As soon as she got inside the apartment, she flung open the windows and French door that opened onto the balcony, kicked off her shoes, and rang her mother.

"Is that you, now Deandra?" inquired Marion Boggs.

"Yes Mom, it's your daughter."

"I might as well not have one, if I must always guess when it's proper to call you. I won't worry about anyone else but me. From now on . . . I won't have to get any heart attack worrying about you. But just the same, you could say when you're going to be away."

"Mother, could you just listen to me for once. I was in Jamaica for six days and I tried calling you twice, but you were out. Furthermore, when you're travelling, it's not always easy to get to a telephone. The system there is quite different than in New York."

"All right then, so you went alone to Jamaica?"

"No, Mom. This may surprise you, but I was with Paul."

"With Paul? Did I hear you right?"

"Yes, you did. He took me by surprise and finally convinced me to go to the reggae festival."

Deandra could hear the excitement in Marion's voice at the mention of Paul's name. "So tell me, Deandra, did you have a good time?"

"It was fabulous, Mother. I'm going to get you a ticket for a trip to Nufuma and Jamaica as soon as I get back, which won't be long now."

"I'll think about a trip later. But I'm so happy to hear that you and Paul had a fabulous time together." Marion sounded great to Deandra, and a little giddy with pleasure at the idea of her daughter and Paul spending time together.

"So Mother, how's your health? You haven't said much about yourself."

"There's nothing much to say. Your mother is getting old, and old age has its own problems."

"Problems, Mother?"

"Yes child, like chronic illness."

"Are you hiding something from me that I should know?"

"Please stop worrying your pretty head about me. Right now, I just want you to enjoy your life. Good-bye by darling," ended Marion and rang off.

Deandra unpacked her bag, walked about the apartment, then made herself a salad.

Later that evening she called Lucreta.

"So, you're back Deandra. I missed you, but I'd better get used to you not being around. So, tell me about your exciting trip."

"It was great. A packed six days of fun. Rather laid back as we say in New York."

"Your voice sounds as though you're still floating with excitement, my dear."

"Is my voice that revealing?"

"Maybe not always, but right now you sound great and carefree, to which you're entitled."

""So what's with the Clarkes?"

"Well, I'm in the process of taking my maternity leave, and your niece had an accident and wants her mother home."

"Is something wrong with Jennifer?"

"Yes, she broke her left arm, but the doctor says she'll be okay soon. Young bones heal fast."

"Poor darling. I'll be over tomorrow to see her. What about you, Lucreta?"

"I'm great, only ten more weeks before the arrival of the new Clarke. Daniel made plans to be with me this time, if only to see the birth of his son, since I'll be delivering at his hospital."

"That sounds wonderful, Lucreta. I'm happy for you, my dear

friend. Give my regards to all, and I'll see you tomorrow."

She had just gotten to the last chapter of *Tar Baby* when the phone rang.

"Hi, how are you doing?"

"Doing fine, Paul. And what about you?"

"Marvelous. Divine. Stupendous, my darling. But it would have been even better if you were right here by my side."

"Is that Gladys Knight I'm hearing in the background?"

"It is the one and only Gladys, to be followed by Lady Aretha."

"I recall how partial you are to those two women. I like them too. How was your flight over?"

"Rather uneventful, and calm. But even if there was a circus on board, my mind was completely occupied with a woman named Deandra."

"Do you seriously mean all of that?"

"Absolutely."

"It sounds as though you were in a stupor then."

"You've got it right. Anyway, I've never before had such an exciting six days. I just hope that soon we'll be able to do it again. So how are things with you, Deandra?"

"Quiet and peaceful. I was just trying to finish *Tar Baby* when you interrupted."

"Toni Morrison is another sister I admire. She's quite a woman and I respect her."

"Agreed. The sister is special. By the way, have you spoken to my mother?"

"Not yet, why?"

"When I spoke with her this afternoon, I picked up something in her voice. Sounds like she's little under the weather."

"I'll check her out and if there's anything the matter, I'll get back to you."

"Thanks Paul. And to answer your question, I'm fine."

After they had said good-bye, Deandra lay a while on the sofa and reminisced about the different twists and turns the relationship between herself and Paul had gone through. The more she thought about it, the clearer it seemed that there was a strong force that had kept bringing them together. She decided that this time, no matter what, she was going to see it through to the end. There was, of course, Jeff. Her mind shied away from Jeff and she returned to her reading with thoughts of Paul and Jeff running through her mind.

When next Deandra saw Lucreta, she couldn't help asking, "Lucreta, are you sure you're not carrying twins?"

Lucreta laughed and replied, "From what I know it is one baby. Daniel thinks it's going to be our biggest baby yet. But you, my dear, look radiant and happy. Jamaica certainly did something special to you."

"You really think so, Lucreta?"

"Yes, and if I may take the liberty, you need to do more of whatever you did," she replied teasingly.

It was not difficult for Deandra to figure out that Lucreta was trying to get some special news from her. She felt that Lucreta may have suspected that she had a rendezvous with Paul. But Deandra wasn't about to relieve her friend's curiosity.

"Aunty D, you're back!" shouted Jennifer.

"Yes, darling. And how did you manage to break your arm?"

"I was trying to catch a netball and I fell down, my arm buckled underneath my body. Anyway, Daddy and Doctor Lee say it's going to be all right."

"Can you bend your fingers?"

"Yes, let me show you," Jennifer said as she bent each finger.

"So, Aunty D, will you come back from America next year to visit us again?"

Jennifer asked, as she tried clumsily to unwrap the jewelry box made of sea shells that Deandra had brought her from Jamaica. When she saw it, she exclaimed, "How pretty, Aunty! Thank you so much. Let me show it to Mother."

Deandra had grown quite fond of the Clarkes' two children, and sometimes felt that she might have missed out on certain aspects of life having been an only child. She recalled that she had been only a year older than Jennifer when she left for New York City.

Back in her apartment, Deandra felt pleased about her enjoyable afternoon with the Clarkes.

It had already been four days since her return to Nufuma, and Jeff had not called. She thought a lot about the relationship between herself and Jeff for the months they had been lovers, and she became increasingly aware of the complexities of life. She had been so certain that Paul would not move her again that she had begun to wonder about a future for herself and Jeff. The problem was that Jeff wanted to put the cart before the horse, to use a famous quote of Nufuman saying. Perhaps his desire for a child was smothering her. She didn't like being pressured. And, then there was his marriage. She knew that he was separated and hoping for a divorce and, while that was a good basis on which to start a relationship, it didn't seem the right situation in which to have a child. She wondered what he was doing and why he hadn't called. She wasn't sure what to say to him when he did call.

When Jeff finally called, Deandra was just about to clear the table after a late supper.

"Oh, you're home, Deandra."

"But of course, Jeff. Where are you calling from?"

"From Atlanta. We've just about completed our business down here."

"Oh! Thought you might have left for Canada."

"We should have, but there were some rough edges that required more attention. As a consequence, we'll be away for at least another week. So, what have you been doing? How was that exciting trip to Jamaica?"

Deandra picked up something different in Jeff's voice. Was she too analytic, she asked herself, or was he really a possessive man? She finally refocused her thoughts and returned to him. "You make it sound as though I'd been away for weeks instead of six short days. And, by the way, I've been back for four whole days, Jeff."

"Okay sweetheart, you don't have to account to me. I'm desperately longing to see you though. So, tell me what's happening in Lucky Pond and Embers Glade?"

"Things aren't much different. Now that I have more time, I tune in to various talk shows. You can get a cross-section of ideas. Lucreta is now on maternity leave and Jennifer broke her arm, but it is healing nicely."

"So Lucreta really has her hands full. Give them all my regards and tell Jennifer I love her. By the way, have you talked with Esme lately?"

"Not since I got back from Jamaica. But I'll give her a call soon."

That night, Deandra stayed up late. She racked her brain about the love triangle that she was caught up in, and wondered how it could have happened to her after all these years. The more she thought about her predicament, the more distressed she became. She poured herself a glass of wine and walked out to the balcony. She sipped the wine and finally accepted the fact that neither she nor Jeff had signed a contract, nor had they made any vows to each other. They were, after all, grown and mature adults who had enjoyed what each had brought to the relationship. They had both taken a risk because, as she now knew, nothing lasts forever. With that thought uppermost in her mind, she fell asleep.

Sara sprung a surprise on Deandra. She replied to Deandra's brief letter of excuses and wrote:

> Dear Girlfriend,
>
> Your letter was rather exciting and refreshing. As a matter of fact, it has infused new vigor in me. But let me congratulate you on completing your manuscript. I'm looking forward to reading the finished product . The tone of the letter tells me that your concept of man-woman relationships has changed, and I like it. I almost took the next flight down to the island after reading about those fantastic eligible men.
>
> Well my dear, your girlfriend was celibate for over two years because of the fear of the HIV virus. It was okay being celibate, but I hope I won't have to return to it. I like to be loved by a man who respects me and who is health conscious. By this, you might be wondering about what it is that I'm leading up to. Well, I've met a fine man at the most unlikely place. He'd been repairing my car for years, but there was no indication that the guy had been carrying around a flame for me, until one day we got to talking about healthy lifestyles. I was surprised to discover that he was well read and knew a lot about health. Well, we ended up going for a drink and that was the beginning of a love-fest between us. By the way, the in-thing now is getting into love instead of falling in love. But which ever way I entered it, I'm now in love with a wonderful guy named Lex, who makes me feel loved and warm. We're trying out living together before we enter into anything else.
>
> I almost forgot to tell you, I got a promotion. Mr. Gray's wife died, and he's dating a middle-aged widow. Well listen girlfriend, please call me as soon as you get back to New York. We have a lot of catching up to do.
>
> Bless you,
> Sara.

Deandra smiled as she read Sara's letter. It had been exactly twenty-four days since she'd returned from Jamaica. She was feeling out of sorts, but attributed it to the cold she'd caught. Sara's letter lifted her spirits and helped to put her in a better frame of mind. By the time Jeff returned to Nufuma, she was in bed suffering from a full-blown viral flu.

At the first ring of the phone, Deandra picked it up and asked, "Is that you, Jeff?"

Her voice was husky because of the flu.

"What's the matter, D? You don't sound like yourself at all?"

Suddenly she was seized by a spell of coughing. She caught her breath and replied, "I'm suffering from the flu."

"I'm sorry to hear that sweetheart. Something tells me that you don't take care of yourself when I'm not around. Anyway, I'll be over later this evening to see you. Shall I bring you anything special?"

"No thank you, Jeff. I'll be fine."

She had barely returned the telephone receiver to its place when the doorbell rang. She dragged herself out of bed to let Jeff in. For some unknown reason, she became teary.

She wiped away the tears before he could notice and remarked, "I'm glad to see you Jeff, but I'm also sorry to greet you in this condition."

"Nonsense, D. It's only the flu and we all get sick some time."

They embraced warmly before Deandra quickly pulled away saying, "Let's be careful, darling. I don't want to pass on this flu to you . . ."

Before she could finish the sentence, she bolted for the bathroom and closed the door. Jeff could hear her vomiting and decided that, whatever it was, Deandra had it badly. She came out of the bathroom and went back to bed. Jeff followed her, seating himself on the edge of the bed.

"Shall I get you some tea, D?"

"I just couldn't swallow anything now. I'll be okay. They say after a couple of days, I'll be fine."

Jeff felt out-of-place. He'd never developed the nurturing role and really didn't like to be around sick people. He spent an hour with Deandra, then kissed her on her forehead and left. On his way home he stopped at Esme's.

"Hello Uncle Jeff!" screamed Odeki, Esme's son, as he ran to greet him.

"Hi big fellow. You're growing faster than I can think."

"You can think, Uncle Jeff," repeated Odeki, tugging at Jeff's pants.

"Darling, don't pull on Uncle Jeff's clothes like that," scolded Esme.

"That's okay, Esme. A boy needs to have some fun," said Jeff and ruffled Odeki's hair.

He picked him up and threw him on the sofa.

"Mummy, look how Uncle Jeff lift me up!" screamed Odeki as he laughed.

Esme poured Jeff a glass of wine and one for herself. They talked about business and Jeff shared a few pleasantries about his recent trip. Esme was a good listener and it was past midnight when Jeff said good-bye to her.

Deandra had a horrible night. Her head and chest hurt, but the pain in her head was like someone had been pounding on top of it. She had to change her nightgown three times because of her profuse sweating. It was three a.m. when she finally fell asleep.

When Jeff called her the following day, she was no better. As a matter of fact, her coughing had become worse. She was worried. This must be what they call the killer flu. Anyway, I hope it will go away as quickly as it came, she told herself. For the rest of the week, except for tea and some soup, Deandra ate hardly anything. She had lost her appetite and, even if she hadn't, it was difficult to keep food down. Each time she tried, she'd vomit.

On Tuesday when Jeff arrived to take her out for a ride and possibly dinner, he could see that Deandra wasn't her usual self, although she was trying to be brave. He waited for her to get dressed; it seemed to take forever.

"Is anything the matter, D? It's unlike you to take so long to get dressed."

Deandra found tears welling up in her eyes again and answered, "I'm terribly sorry Jeff, but I'm not my usual self. I'm not feeling right since the flu."

When she entered the living room, Jeff took one look at her and remarked, "You do look out of sorts. I think whatever it is you've got, you picked it up in Jamaica."

"I don't care where I got whatever it is, I just hope it will go away soon."

"I take it, darling, that you'd prefer not to go out?"

"Yes, Jeff. I think I should stay in."

"I'm going to call the restaurant to send us dinner."

"That sounds good, Jeff. Thank you for your concern."

As Jeff watched her pick at the food, he knew that she was sicker than she admitted to.

"I take it you've been taking some medicine?"

"Only some cough syrup."

"Let me see if I can get a hold of Daniel," said Jeff, as he reached for the telephone and dialed.

"Jeff old boy, what's on your mind?" asked Daniel when he answered the phone.

"Listen, Daniel, do you know anything about this flu? Deandra seems to have it quite bad, it's been over a week and she's still not well."

"There's a new strain of flu going around . . . it can be very debilitating. Some people are bothered with a hacking cough and weakness for several weeks, Jeff."

"That sounds exactly like D."

"Why don't you bring her over. That way, I'll be better able to say what's going on. We didn't know she was that ill."

"She's trying to be brave and independent, but we'll be there in half an hour's time."

Daniel's assessment of Deandra confirmed that she was suffering from a new strain of the flu. He prescribed medicine for her cough and recommended vitamins.

Before they drove off for Lucky Pond, Lucreta scolded Deandra. "Don't you go trying to be Miss Independent, now, hiding things from us, Deandra. We need our friends, especially when we're sick. Don't forget to call us if you need anything at anytime. We love you."

The Clarkes' warmth had cheered her up. She was less depressed by the time Jeff took her home.

When she had settled down and was more composed, Jeff held her hands gently and said, "I hate to see you this way, D."

He leaned over on the sofa and kissed her. He kissed her tenderly, but she was unresponsive. In fact, Deandra's body language was like that of a stranger. She stiffened herself in his arms. Halting at the door as he said good night, Jeff felt somewhat helpless and troubled. Helpless because he was not adept in a sick room, and troubled because of Deandra's coolness towards him. Could it be the effect of the flu, he asked himself, or was there someone else competing for Deandra's affection? His mind turned to the flowers and he felt a pang of jealousy. Something was rather peculiar, it was not just the flu. The guy in New York, could he have moved back into Deandra's life during my last extended trip, Jeff wondered.

He wished Deandra a good night's sleep and left for his home.

She was startled by the loud ringing of the phone.

"Hi sweetheart. What's happening down at the Pond?" inquired Paul.

"Not much has happened since we talked, except that I'm left with something people call the blues."

"That sure doesn't sound like you. Can you think of anything that might be causing you to feel this way?"

"Not really. I don't know if Nufuman flu leaves its victims with this kind of hangover. Anyway, I'm hoping that it will go away soon."

"But sweetheart, don't you think it's wise to consult a doctor?"

"I saw one. He says that it's a new type of flu, so I'll have to wait and see."

"Please babe, don't wait too long. If you continue to feel the same, maybe you should see another doctor."

"We'll see, Paul."

"Promise me one thing," Paul insisted. "Please see another doctor if you're not getting better. I'll call you in the evening, okay?"

Deandra agreed and they rang off.

That night, she was having a dreadful nightmare when the ringing of the phone woke her. It was two a.m. The nightmare had been so real that she was drenched with sweat when she was awakened.

"Who is calling?" she queried in a muffled voice.

"It's Paul, sweetheart. I'm sorry if I scared you."

"It's just that I was in a deep sleep when the phone rang."

"Tell me, are you feeling any better?"

"A little," she replied.

"I'm relieved. I have some news for you, but I want you to listen carefully and not become nervous."

"What's going on, Paul? Is something wrong? Is my mother all right?"

"Hold on sweetheart. I'm calling from the hospital."

Deandra sat up straight in bed and interrupted him. "Hospital?" she repeated.

"Yes. I'm with your mother. She had a mild stroke."

"No. Oh no! I'm not hearing right. My mother had a stroke?"

"Okay sweetheart, I know it's hard to take, but it's a very mild stroke."

Deandra paced the floor anxiously as she talked. "A stroke is a stroke. I don't care how mild you say it is. Please explain to me exactly what happened."

"Well, Marion can sit up. Her speech is slightly slurred, but she's in control of herself otherwise. I just talked with one of the doctors who said they will keep her here for a few days for observation."

"Do they seriously believe that she'll be okay, Paul?"

"Based on what they said, they all have good reasons to believe that she'll recover fully."

"Oh Paul, what would I do without you? . . . Hold please," she requested and dashed to the bathroom.

She vomited as though she'd spit out her innards. In her anxiety, she'd left the bathroom door open. Paul could hear her moan each time she retched and was worried about her.

When she returned to the phone with an apology, Paul brushed it aside. "Sorry for what darling? Are you okay? That's all I want to know."

"Just a little upset stomach, that's all."

"That's not all. Anyway, you'll be here soon and we'll have you seen by a doctor."

"So, does Mother recognize you, Paul?"

"To begin, she gave the hospital staff my number, so that means that she's able to think. When I arrived here, she held my hands and with her slurred speech said, 'Paul. Please call my baby.'"

By then Deandra had become a little calmer. She sat on the bed and asked, "Are you calling from her room?"

"No, but I'll give you the desk number where you can call anytime."

"Tell Mom I'll be there as soon as I can get a flight out and I'll call you, Paul. Thanks again."

"Before you go, sweetheart, promise you'll take care of yourself. I'm getting more and more worried about you."

Sleep had gone from her eyes. Deandra felt spent as she pondered silently. What's happening to me . . . happening to me? That's just what Paul said before he hung up. Something is happening and I don't even know why.

When morning finally came, she pulled herself together, did some deep breathing, and wrote down her thoughts in her diary.

Reality and maturity . . .
Are they both intertwined, or does one precede the other?
Is reality what you make it to be,
Or maturity which directs the reality?
My reality, your reality, their reality.
For what may seem to be, is really not,
And that which is not, is really that.
Maturity evolving over time, over time!
Is the link that helps us to see, to feel, to explore
And to understand the different realities.

* * *

Outside in the street, there was a parade of revellers promoting the soon-to-open young talents' show. Deandra headed for the shower. She could hear the laughter of people in the street and turned on the water, drowning out the noises.

Her thoughts were crystal clear as she mused, "I've certainly passed through many states and phases of my life, which hopefully have helped me to mature. And the decisions I make will, without a doubt, be influenced by such growth . . . Strange though it may sound, the news about my mother today, though causing me discomfort, has helped me to come to grips with many things that I've been befuddled about. For at this state, I must reconcile the fact that joy and sorrow, love and hate, pain and pleasure, are all part of living. Therefore, the only logical and sensible approach to life, is to comprehend the realities of love, birth, and separation . . . For as I listened to Paul, I sense that he had been dealing with reality, based on facts . . . This new awakening is also helping me to look at things more objectively, especially regarding Paul and me. Now as I look back, I realize how foolish I've been all these years, to have pretended not to need any one to share my life with . . . Come to think of it, I'd been caught up in the new me-ism attitude, denying Paul the chance to penetrate some of my space . . . Mom is, after all, wise and insightful. She'd long felt that Paul was warm and sensitive and would be good for me."

As soon as the reservation office opened, Deandra booked a flight that would be leaving directly for New York in two days. She then called Jeff at his office.

"Hello D. What a pleasant surprise to get a call from you at the office, my dear," remarked Jeff when he heard her voice. "So my lady, tell me what's on your mind."

"Many things, to be honest, including you, of course, which is why I'm calling you at the office."

"Talk to me, sweetheart. The suspense is building up."

"I'm afraid the news is not very cheerful. I got a call from New York in the wee hours of the morning. My mother has been hospitalized. She had a stroke."

Jeff tapped his desk with his fingernails than replied, "Oh, my dear. I'm sorry to hear. Is there anything you'd like me to do?"

"The situation makes it difficult for me to think of anything special, except your support of course, and before we hang up, I've just booked my flight for New York."

"When will you be leaving, my dear?"

"Day after tomorrow, Jeff."

"Hold on just for a minute, Deandra."

She could hear him speaking to his secretary, "Check my schedule please and see what can be canceled within the next two days, Mrs. Singh."

"The schedule is rather tight, but there are a couple of appointments that can be pushed back to the day after tomorrow, Mr. Boles."

"Sorry to keep you holding so long, D, but I'm having my schedule checked. What time will your flight be leaving?"

"Three o'clock in the afternoon, Jeff."

"Tell you what, I'm completely booked for tomorrow, but this afternoon I'll be over to see you dear, and the day you leave, I'll be there most of the time . . . You sound as though you're holding up very well though, considering how close you are to your mother."

"I'm trying to think positively, although not being there for her gives me a funny feeling . . . It's like I've abandoned her."

"I understand, D, especially being an only child, with no other sibling to help out. Try not to be too upset, sweetheart. I'll see you later."

Deandra calmly broke the news of her mother's illness to Lucreta. She was quite upset and inquired, "What can we do to help you in the next two days, Deandra?"

"Just your usual friendship and warmth, Lucreta."

"You've got those and more, my dear. But I'll be praying for your mother's recovery. I imagine you want to be near the telephone, and won't be able to take a run out here."

"That's correct, Lucreta. I've planned to stick around the apartment. I've arranged everything for my departure, so it's just waiting for the day now. How's everybody, especially Jennifer?"

"Everybody's doing fine. Tell you what, if Daniel isn't delayed at the hospital, we'll come by this evening. How about that?"

"That would be great, Lucreta. See you later then."

That afternoon when Jeff visited her, they didn't talk about love and romance. They reflected on life and the unexpected events that were a part of it. And as Jeff drove back to his office, he recalled the good times he and Deandra had had. The way she excited him was beyond description.

Just as Lucreta and Daniel were about to leave for Lucky Pond, Aunt May said, "Mrs. C, please tell Miss Deandra that I'm going to say a special prayer for her mother. Tell her to hold on and to have faith in God."

Lucreta walked slowly and laboriously as she balanced her abdomen to enter Deandra's apartment.

"So glad to see you, my friends," Deandra greeted them warmly.

"So, how are you feeling, Deandra?" asked Daniel.

"I'm trying my best to be calm, but I must say that without friends like you, coping with this sudden illness of my mother would have been much more difficult."

They talked about the good times they had had and hoped that Marion would recover fully.

Lucreta handed her a package saying, "Here's some dinner sent by Aunt May for you. She never forgets details, Deandra."

"Bless her. Thank her plenty for me, Lucreta."

Deandra had just said good-bye to Lucreta and Daniel when Paul called. His voice was calm and reassuring as he talked with her.

I'm reporting to you about your mother, sweetheart," commented Paul. "She's holding her own. She's out of bed most of the time. Except for her speech, she's looking good."

"Thank God. She certainly sent the shock waves through my entire being. It's good that I have you to break things down in layman's terms. The nurse whom I spoke with said Mother was satisfactory and had had an uneventful day . . . Very medical and sterile, I thought, but then each profession has its own jargon. But tell me, Paul, is my mother aware of everything around her? Can she feed herself?"

"She's very alert. The only reason she's not allowed calls is because they want her to be as calm as possible. And about feeding herself, the answer is yes, even though it takes her longer to eat. You should have seen how her eyes lit up when I told her that you'd be coming on the earliest available flight."

"Now that you've mentioned flight, I shall be leaving at three o'clock in the afternoon on Air Jamaica, day after tomorrow."

"Great news, but why Air Jamaica?"

"Air Nufuma flies only twice a week."

"I'll be waiting for you at the airport and just in case you should need me, you know where to reach me . . . But sweetheart, you didn't tell me about you?"

"About me?"

"Yes, Deandra. You're not well, are you?"

"I don't want to get into that now, Paul."

"I'm not going to pressure you, but I can only help if I know what's making you so sick. Are you still vomiting?"

"No, Paul. My tummy seems calmer now."

"I'm glad to hear that. You scared me earlier when I heard you moaning, sweetheart. See you later," he said as he hung up.

The conversation with Paul greatly reduced Deandra's anxiety. That night, she slept well. The following day, she got everything in order and waited anxiously for the day of departure to arrive.

She had time to herself to reminisce about her almost fairytale-like romance with Jeff and smiled as she reflected. It is a fact, thought Deandra, that Jeff and I have had a marvelous and deep relationship, and one that has certainly added riches to my entire being. And even though it seems uncertain that we will be spending our lives together, what should have been did occur. We shared our love, not in a frivolous way, but rather with a lot of feelings, and for that we owe no one an apology. Jeff is a romantic and a great lover. He's a great human being, but the bottom line is marriage and settling down are more than romance and wealth. It's a family affair, and for years now, Paul has made it his business to be a part of my small family. Only time will tell.

Deandra was up early on the day of her departure. She put the last touches to her packing, then locked her bags. She had just finished dressing and had started to flip through an old *Essence* magazine, when Jeff arrived.

As they walked toward the sofa, Jeff paused, held her closely and kissed her, then sat down and remarked, "You're looking more cheerful today than two days ago."

"I suppose time has allowed me to better deal with reality, Jeff. It's interesting to note how many of us try to deny a painful situation when it occurs unexpectedly. For although I'm still upset about my mother's illness, I'm not as devastated as when I first heard the news."

Jeff thought about his late mother and son, then said, "I can empathize with you, D, but based on what you've told me there seems to be a good chance for your mother's recovery."

"Thanks for your support, Jeff."

"You're welcome my dear," he replied and continued to talk. "I realize this is a rough time for you, but we need to be more definitive about our relationship, seeing that you're returning to New York today. What I want to know is, where do we go from here?"

Deandra fidgeted with the cushion on the sofa before responding. "Jeff, I want you to know that you're one of the most sincere men I've known. I also know that your greatest desire is to have a child and rightfully so. But as I've tried showing you, I need to think this through."

"So what are you trying to say, Deandra?"

"Please don't make it any more difficult for me, Jeff. The situation with Angelica hasn't changed and that's why I've always said to wait and see how your divorce goes, and take it from there."

"You're not making too much sense, my dear. I'll have to be frank, though it might hurt. Could it be that you're using your mother's illness to run away from a relationship? I insist on hearing from you where we stand as of now."

"Darn, that term running away, again," mused Deandra quietly before answering Jeff's question.

"It's like I said before, Jeff. I need to return to New York and see how things evolve. And I'm not using my mother's illness to runaway from you. We both knew all along that I would eventually return to New York with the manuscript. I only wish that you'll try and understand that I don't want to hurt you. But right now there are many things going on in my head that I must resolve. And because of that I need time and space to sort things out. And to me, that's not running away. Without harping on it too much, the love that we shared will live with me for ever. Please try to understand my side, Jeff. I love you."

Jeff listened intently to Deandra as she talked, and realized that something was happening to her, that baffled him greatly. She was more evasive than he'd experienced before.

He finally looked at his watch and inquired, "What time is your flight again?"

"In two hours. I didn't realize the time had gone by so quickly."

"Well, it will take us half an hour to get to the airport, so that should give you sufficient time to check in."

They were both in a pensive mood. Deandra stood and held tightly to Jeff. Tears welled up behind her eyelids. Jeff patted her gently on the back and kissed her without saying a word; they left for the airport.

Jeff watched Deandra as she went through the turnstile to the passengers' lounge. She lingered on and waved good-bye before moving on.

Jeff watched her walk away slowly and waved as she turned around to get a last look at him before disappearing. He returned to his car, drove away, and with mixed feelings of hope and despair, increased his speed and headed backed to the office.

CHAPTER TWENTY

Paul was waiting to meet Deandra at Kennedy Airport. He was filled with excitement and concern as he waited for her to clear customs. Deandra walked quickly to join the short line for American citizens.

The custom's officer looked at her and asked, "Anything to declare, miss?"

"Nothing except five pounds of Jamaican Blue Mountain Coffee I bought while on a weekend down there."

"No fruits . . . no mangoes?"

"None at all."

The officer glanced at her passport and remarked, "Oh, you're a writer, I see."

"That's correct."

He merely looked inside her luggage, stamped her passport, and said, "Welcome home."

Deandra smiled then beckoned a porter to take her bags where Paul was waiting to greet her. He couldn't see her inside the customs area. Paul saw her approaching. He walked quickly towards her and, with a welcoming smile, kissed her then proceeded to tip the young man who had helped her with her bags.

"Oh babe, it's so good to see you again. How was the flight?"

"It was smooth and on time. How's my mother, Paul?"

"She seems to be holding her own."

"I'd like to go to the hospital."

Paul checked to make sure that the back of the car was properly closed after the man had finished packing Deandra's bags inside.

He returned to her and asked, "Do you want to go straight to the hospital, Deandra?"

"Yes, I can't wait to see my mother," she said, opening and closing her hands nervously as she talked.

"Okay sweetheart. I'll get you there very soon," said Paul as he leaned over from the driver's seat to kiss her on her cheek.

He drove quickly and carefully, noting that Deandra looked tired. They didn't talk a great deal during the drive. Deandra reflected on her mother; she was uncertain as to what to expect, although Paul had reassured her that Marion Boggs was improving. As soon as they turned off the East River Drive, Paul remarked, "Soon we'll be at the Roosevelt Hospital, sweetheart. Are you all right?"

"I think so, Paul, but I'm anxious to see Mom."

"I understand, and just in case we have difficulty finding a parking space, I'll drop you off first. How about that?"

"All right, Paul."

In another ten minutes, they were in front of the hospital, just in time to get a parking space. The brief elevator ride to the sixth floor seemed like hours to Deandra. Finally they arrived. Paul walked with her to the nursing station and introduced her as Mrs. Boggs' daughter.

"Your mother has been expecting you," said the nurse. "She's in six-fifteen."

"Thank you," said Deandra.

Paul gently touched her elbow as they walked to the hospital room he had visited quite often in the last three days. Marion Boggs was sitting in a chair by the side of her bed with her right hand on the bed squeezing what looked like a round ball. She looked away from her hand and saw Deandra.

"My baby! My baby!" she cried with tears rolling down her cheeks, and she stopped doing her hand exercise.

"Mom! My dear Mother," answered Deandra as she bent and hugged Marion Boggs.

The two women were crying as Marion tried to express her delight at seeing her daughter. Her words were still slightly slurred.

Deandra hugged her again and said, "It's all right, Mom. Take your time. I'm home to be with you. I love you."

"I love you too, my darling," answered Marion. Paul had left the room to allow Deandra and her mother time to themselves.

"So, Mom, how are you feeling now?" asked Deandra.

"Much much better, especially since you walked through that door. I can feel my twisted mouth straightening up, child." She smiled with pleasure at seeing Deandra.

"I was so scared when Paul called and said you had a stroke. I felt so isolated and helpless, not knowing the full details of your condition."

"Don't worry anymore, my baby. Your mother is doing real good. If you notice, my mouth is only slightly twisted now. It's quite different than a few days ago. In another day or two the doctor will be discharging me home. But that Paul, he's some man. He's been like a son to me. By the way, where's he?"

"I suppose he's in the waiting room."

"Waiting room? He doesn't have to be out there. He's part of the Boggs family. Go get him, Deandra."

"My mother wants you inside, Paul," said Deandra.

"Well babe, how do you feel now?" asked Paul.

"Much better Paul," she said and reached for his hand. They walked hand in hand back to room six-fifteen.

Marion Boggs' face lit up as they entered. Before they left the hospital, Marion stood, straightened her shoulders and said, "See, I'm almost my old self," as she walked slowly to the elevator that took Paul and Deandra to the main floor.

Night had fallen when Paul and Deandra returned to the car. The street lights had come on and the streets were less crowded.

"So, my dear, where's our next stop?" inquired Paul teasingly as they entered the car.

Deandra breathed a sigh of relief and replied, "To Marion Boggs' place for the time being. She had hoped to find an apartment for me, but that's on hold as things are now."

Paul listened without responding, then changed the subject. "What about you, Deandra? You're looking rather tired, and a little pale."

"I haven't been myself for the past few weeks, and my mother's illness created more stress."

"Well, don't you think you ought to see a physician real soon?"

"Yes, Paul. I will, but let's not push the panic button. Not yet. anyway," she said looking at him tenderly.

"Okay, sweetheart. I'll be right here whenever you need me."

They had barely entered Marion Boggs' apartment when Deandra fainted. Luckily Paul was close enough to catch her in his arms. He lifted her up and placed her gently on the bed. He got a cold, wet towel with which he wiped her face. He loosened her clothes, sat on the side of the bed, and held her hand.

Deandra opened her eyes and asked softly, "What happened, Paul?"

"You scared the hell out of me, babe . . . You fainted. How are you feeling now?"

"A little funny in my stomach. It was really strange. As soon as I stepped inside, the place became totally dark like the middle of the night and my head was as light as a feather. I only hope I won't have another blackout."

"I hope not, darling," said Paul while he reached for the phone. "I want you to call your doctor. If you're not up to it, give me the number and I'll call."

Deandra had recovered sufficiently to call and make an appointment with her long-standing physician for the following day. Paul refused to leave her alone in the apartment. Deandra packed a small bag and went with him to his large apartment on Columbus Avenue.

Later that night, as they made love, Paul was extra tender to his beloved princess. He whispered softly in her ears, "My darling, I want to love you tonight in a very special way."

He paused and imagined her becoming his wife soon. He encircled her firm belly with the small sunken navel where he always tickled her. He kissed her belly as though he was tasting honey and murmured, "Oh my darling, I love you so!"

Deandra remembered the first time Paul had made love to her. She felt safe and secure with him then as she did now. Her response was ecstatic. Paul made certain that she was enjoying him as he was enjoying her. After they had made love, Paul cuddled Deandra's body and they slept peacefully through the night.

Paul waited anxiously in Doctor Barnes' waiting room while Deandra was being examined. He flipped through a stack of magazines as he waited.

When finally Deandra appeared Paul stood, took one look at her, and asked, "What's wrong, sweetheart?"

Deandra hesitated and looked away as Paul continued to talk.

"I've never seen you looking like this before. You're dreadfully pale. All the blood seems to have left your face."

"Let me sit for a few minutes," said Deandra.

"Sure sweetheart."

He waited for her to settle down. Paul felt nervous as he waited for her to speak and inquired, "So what did the doctor say, Deandra?"

She looked at him and with confusion and disbelief in her voice said, "Paul, I'm pregnant."

Paul leaned over and took both her hands in his. He was almost beside himself with excitement, which he was not trying to conceal.

He asked tenderly, "Darling, you're not teasing me, are you really pregnant?"

"Yes Paul, Doctor Barnes just confirmed it."

Paul leaned over, kissed her, and said softly, "You've made me the happiest man in the world, Princess Deandra. Could we talk with the doctor for a minute or so, I wonder?"

"Doctor Barnes expected that. He promised to talk with us as soon as he's through with the next patient."

Paul felt like a totally new man. He was experiencing all kinds of emotions. He had hoped, even suspected, that Deandra may have been pregnant all along, but this confirmation knocked the breath out of him. The love of his life was carrying his child. He felt tenderness for her overwhelming him and vowed to himself never to do anything to upset her.

The conference with Doctor Barnes was very instructive and enlightening. The myths of do's and don'ts were discussed, especially surrounding love-making during pregnancy.

On their way back home, Paul eased carefully into the heavy traffic. As he drove, he thought about all the years he had been loving this woman, the moments of despair when he had felt that nothing would ever come out of their relationship, and now, here she was seated beside him, carrying his child.

Deandra reached for his hand.

Paul clasped it, saying, "This is the happiest day of my life, Deandra. I hope it is for you too, my dearest."

She smiled in acknowledgment without speaking and, even though bewildered, she reflected on what Paul had once said; too many women were delaying motherhood while teenagers who were neither physically nor psychologically mature enough were having babies.

Deandra looked at Paul and said, "Maybe you should drop me off at my mother's place. I need to get a few things sorted out for her before she returns home."

"Do you feel up to it, Deandra?" asked Paul.

"Yes, I think I can manage."

"Whatever I can help you with, just let me know. I'm not so sure you're up to doing too much at this point in time," Paul responded with concern in his voice.

"I'll let you know if I need help, darling."

"Tell you what then, I'll drop you off and pick you up later. We have a lot of planning to do, sweetheart."

Deandra plodded slowly into her mother's apartment. A feeling of confusion took hold of her as she mulled about the unplanned pregnancy.

"When did I get pregnant," she questioned herself. "It's been several months since Jeff and I were in a close relationship. Could he have tricked me and gotten me pregnant?"

She paced the floor, opened the window overlooking the courtyard, and returned to her thoughts.

"I need an answer. Was it that night of reunion with Paul in Jamaica?"

Finally she declared, "Yes! Now I know. It wasn't the flu that caused my delayed period. It's beginning to be clear in my mind. I've always been regular with my menses, just like there are twenty-four hours in a day. It was after I went with Paul to Jamaica that, for the first time in my life, I missed my period. It was at the Castles By the Sea."

Suddenly her confusion began to disappear. She looked at an old photograph taken of herself with her mother, when she was only six months old. Marion was kissing her with such love and tenderness that it came through clearly in the photo. Deandra sat down and felt at peace with herself. The doubts had gone from her mind.

"This is a child of undiluted love," she said, and went about preparing for her mother's return to the apartment.

Paul picked her up late and headed for his place on Columbus Avenue. He was beaming with excitement. As they entered the apartment, he turned and asked, "Are you feeling okay, darling?"

"Yes, Paul. I'm gradually trying to handle what you've done to me."

"Yes sweetheart, I imagine it's taken you completely by surprise, but you did it to me," he said then kissed her with a special kind of passion.

After all, a part of him was now inside her body. He was overcome by the reality of impending fatherhood.

"Isn't it strange, Paul," said Deandra, "to think that after all these years we've been on and off you impregnated me during an impromptu trip to Jamaica?"

"One never knows, princess, does one? How about us spending our honeymoon in Jamaica?" he asked with a mischievous smile on his face.

The mention of a honeymoon brought back memories of Jeff to Deandra. It was quite clear now that there was no turning back for her. She was carrying Paul's child, that was part of her. And even if she did one day return to Nufuma, she would be a mother and a wife. She needed more time to decide how best to end the relationship with Jeff. She remembered his demanding an answer about their future on the day she had left Nufuma for New York and hoped that he would not be angry with her for disappointing him. She decided to call him the following day.

Jeff had just entered his house when Deandra called.

"Jeff, this is Deandra," she said over the phone.

"Oh Deandra, it's good to hear your voice. How's your mother doing?"

"She's recovering nicely, Jeff. She should be home within a few days now."

"I'm delighted to hear that she is getting better. But what about you, Deandra?"

Jeff didn't really know what to expect from her. He had agonized over their relationship since her return to New York.

"Well, so far I'm doing well." The anxiety came through in Deandra's voice. The more she talked, the more rapid her speech became. "I've seen another doctor and I'm now under his care."

"So, did this doctor find anything other than the flu?" asked Jeff.

There was dead silence. Deandra opened and closed her sweaty sticky hand. Suddenly she was overcome with panic and wished she didn't have to answer Jeff's pointed questions.

She sighed and said, "I'll have to wait for the results of some tests. Anyway, I'm feeling much better."

Deandra had not totally misinformed Jeff, she rather elaborated on the explanation. Doctor Barnes was indeed doing tests for her general health status as a pregnant woman.

Jeffrey Boles was too sophisticated not to detect that Deandra was not telling him everything that was going on in her life. She was evading his questions. He listened to her talk and before they said good-bye, in a somewhat somber tone he asked, "When do you plan to return to Nufuma, Deandra?"

She'd hoped he wouldn't ask that question, and replied, "Right now, I'm in a kind of daze, Jeff. So much has happened and so fast. I hope you won't be angry with me, but I need to sit down and write you a letter of explanation."

Deandra felt as though she was going to faint when Jeff said curtly, "Thank you for calling, Deandra," and hung up.

Jeff's hope for her return had been dashed to pieces. He felt a sense of let down and some anger. He felt certain that his suspicion of Deandra's friend in New York was right. He had moved back into her life. He told himself that he and Deandra had just said goodbye. It wasn't that gorgeous, intelligent women had stopped showing interest in him, but his main interest had been with Deandra, the sophisticated, complex, yet unspoiled woman who could be equally comfortable with a peasant as with a Prime Minister, the woman he would always remember who had shared her love with him and given him a great deal of pleasure.

* * *

He walked to the back veranda, stood and gazed at the swimming pool. He returned to his bedroom, took off his tie, and listened to his recorded messages on the answering machine. He then showered, sat down to supper, and tried to get Deandra out of his mind.

Deandra's world had been drastically changed and very rapidly, after a six-day reunion in Jamaica with the first man she'd known intimately. Marion Boggs recovered fully to be involved in the planning of the wedding of her only child and Paul Wisdom, the man she'd loved as a son. Deandra and Lucreta's friendship remained intact. They talked about the sudden developments that had occurred in Deandra's life and, although Lucreta was disappointed for Jeff, she was happy that her best friend had finally decided to settle down, and wished her all the best.

Deandra and Paul were married on a warm Sunday morning in July, in the presence of a beaming Marion Boggs, the warmth and affection of the Wisdom family, and many friends.

She and Paul had decorated his large two-bedroom apartment. A lavender and pink nursery had been prepared for a beautiful baby girl who Deandra gave birth to six months later. The baby was named Paula Deadre.

The Wisdom family bragged that Paula had inherited most of her father's genes. She was the female image of Paul, they claimed. Marion Boggs declared that her granddaughter had eyes and a forehead like her late grandfather, Frederick Boggs.

Deandra exchanged photos of Paula Deadre with Lucreta for those of Lucreta's son, Daniel Jr., who was growing rapidly. Esme was five months pregnant with Jeff's child, and would be married to him within a few months when his divorce would be finalized. Lucreta suggested a reunion of the three couples in the future. She had written in her letter to Deandra:

> My Dearest Friend and Sister,
>
> Isn't it strange the way things and situations have turned out? Who would have imagined last year that you and I would be exchanging photos of a son and daughter, just like old times with you and I. Let's hope that they'll grow up to follow in our place of deep love for each other, Deandra. And I must tell you that Jeff couldn't have done any better, once you removed yourself, than selecting Esme. She's stable, intelligent, and family-oriented. Keep me abreast of all the excitement in your married life, my dear.
>
> Love you always,
> Lucreta

Deandra was moved by her friend's warm and reassuring letter. She too hoped that their children would keep the family friendship going, and replied to Lucreta:

My Dear Lucreta,

Your letter was like a special gift to me. I'm so glad to know that you and Daniel aren't upset with me. I too am happy for Jeff and Esme and, although things didn't work out for Jeff and me, I still believe he's one of the finest men around. I think Esme has the character and temperament to make him a beautiful and secure home. I've always admired her approach to life.

My life is quite full now, as you can imagine, and the way it seems, who knows what else may happen. We're hoping to have another baby in another year or so. An only child, though ideal in certain cases, faces some disadvantages too.

Let me not bore you with my plans. Kiss Jennifer and hug Raymond for me, and a big squeeze for the doctor. Paul and I will think about your suggestion for a friendship reunion. With all my love, I close.

Your friend,
Deandra

As Deandra pasted the airmail stamp on the envelope addressed to Lucreta, she thought of their friendship, the many things they had shared, and smiled.

Paula Deadre was screaming at the top of her voice. Deandra walked quickly to the nursery, stood and looked at her baby. She lifted her and hugged her lovingly, seated herself comfortably, and breast-fed her. Paula fell asleep at her mother's breast. Deandra kissed her and returned her to the crib and, as was her custom when her thoughts raced as they were doing now, she reached for her brand new diary and wrote:

To Paula Deadre

Who says there's no joy in life?
Who says there's nothing that's sacred?
Who says that the impossible cannot be made possible?
Who says that passion cannot result in love?
You, my darling, have nullified all of those
Who says . . .
You've brought two people together,
You're equal parts of both people.
You're the joy of our lives . . .
You're the continuum of our tree!
You're sacred.
You're human.
You're loved!

Paul came in just as she'd written the last line of the poem. He tiptoed quietly behind her.

"Hello Mother," said he to Deandra pleasingly.

She looked up at him and smiled.

Paul read the poem dedicated to their daughter, and pulled his wife to her feet. They walked slowly and quietly, hand-in-hand, to the nursery and stood by the crib.

Paul looked at his wife, smiled, and said, "I love you more each day, darling."

They embraced and kissed as passionately as the very first time they had met, then walked quietly from the nursery.

GLOSSARY OF JAMAICAN AND CREOLE USAGES

Jamaican		Standard English
A	as in "A don't know."	I don't know.
Ah	as in "Ah so it go?"	Is that how it goes?
Bammy		A flat bread-substitute made from cassava flour. Cassava is known by other names e.g. manioc.
Big people		Term used for senior citizens or other prominent persons.
Buil'		Build or built
Bradda		Brother
Bwoy	as in "Hey bwoy."	Friendly greeting for young males.
Breadfruit		Large round fruit, eaten, boiled, roasted, or baked.
Cyaan	as in "I cyaan make it."	I can't make it.
Calalloo		Popular spinach-like vegetable.
Dan & Dat	as in, "I need more dan dat."	I need more than that.

Jamaican		Standard English
De	as in "I like de soun'."	I like the sound.
Dem	as in "Dem cyann come."	They can't come.
Dese	as in "Dese tings."	These things
Doctor Bird		Hummingbirds of various species.
Duppy		Ghost
Ena	as in "Go ena de house."	Go into the house.
Fe me	as in "Is fe me money."	It's my money.
	as in "I have fe go."	I have to go.
Fe we	as in "A fe we money."	It's our money.
Fren		Friend
Goat Mout	as in "Don't put your goat mout pon me."	Don't bad mouth me. Bewitching, similar to the evil eye.
Grata cake		Sweet made with grated coconut and sugar
Coconut drops		Sweet made with small, cut pieces of coconut and sugar
Hoo dat?		Who's that?
Lawd		Lord
Madda		Mother

Jamaican		Standard English
Me	as in "Me head hurt."	My head hurts.
Mek	as in "Me cyann mek up me mind."	I can't make up my mind.
Mus'		Must
Nuttin'		Nothing
Nuf	as in "This is nuf."	This is plenty.
Ole	as in "ole people"	Old people
Pickney		Children
Run-down		A stew made from coconut milk and vegetables, chicken, or fish.
Set-up		Wake held days before the funeral of a deceased person.
Seh	as in "What yu seh?"	What do you say?
Soh	as in "Soh hoo will tek yu to de dance?"	So, who will take you to the dance?
Sour-Sop		Fruit with prickly appearance and thick, white, juicy flesh. Can be eaten as a fruit or made into an exotic drink or ice cream. Has a distinctive taste.

Jamaican		Standard English
Tek	as in "Tek yu time."	Take your time.
Tink	as in "I'll tink about it."	I'll think about it.
Ya	as in "Come ya."	Come here.
Wash belly		A woman's last child.